A GRAPHIC NOVEL

JACKY HA-HA

MY LIFE IS A JOKE

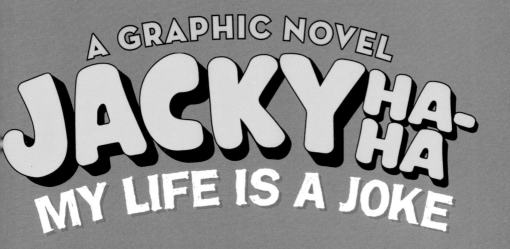

A GRAPHIC NOVEL
JACKY HA-HA
MY LIFE IS A JOKE

JAMES PATTERSON
AND CHRIS GRABENSTEIN

ADAPTED BY ADAM RAU
ILLUSTRATED BY BETTY C. TANG

COLORED BY KEVIN CZAP

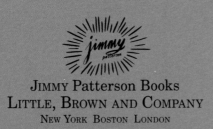

Jimmy Patterson Books
LITTLE, BROWN AND COMPANY
NEW YORK BOSTON LONDON

Copyright © 2021 by James Patterson

Hachette Book Group supports the right to free expression and the value of copyright. The purpose of copyright is to encourage writers and artists to produce the creative works that enrich our culture.

The scanning, uploading, and distribution of this book without permission is a theft of the author's intellectual property. If you would like permission to use material from the book (other than for review purposes), please contact permissions@hbgusa.com. Thank you for your support of the author's rights.

JIMMY Patterson Books / Little, Brown and Company
Hachette Book Group
1290 Avenue of the Americas, New York, NY 10104
JamesPatterson.com

First Graphic Novel Edition: August 2021

JIMMY Patterson Books is an imprint of Little, Brown and Company, a division of Hachette Book Group, Inc. The Little, Brown name and logo are trademarks of Hachette Book Group, Inc. The JIMMY Patterson Books® name and logo are trademarks of JBP Business, LLC.

The publisher is not responsible for websites (or their content) that are not owned by the publisher.

The Hachette Speakers Bureau provides a wide range of authors for speaking events. To find out more, go to hachettespeakersbureau.com or call (866) 376-6591.

Cataloging-in-publication data has been applied for at the Library of Congress.

ISBN 978-0-316-49789-3

Printing 1, 2021

Printed in the U.S.A.

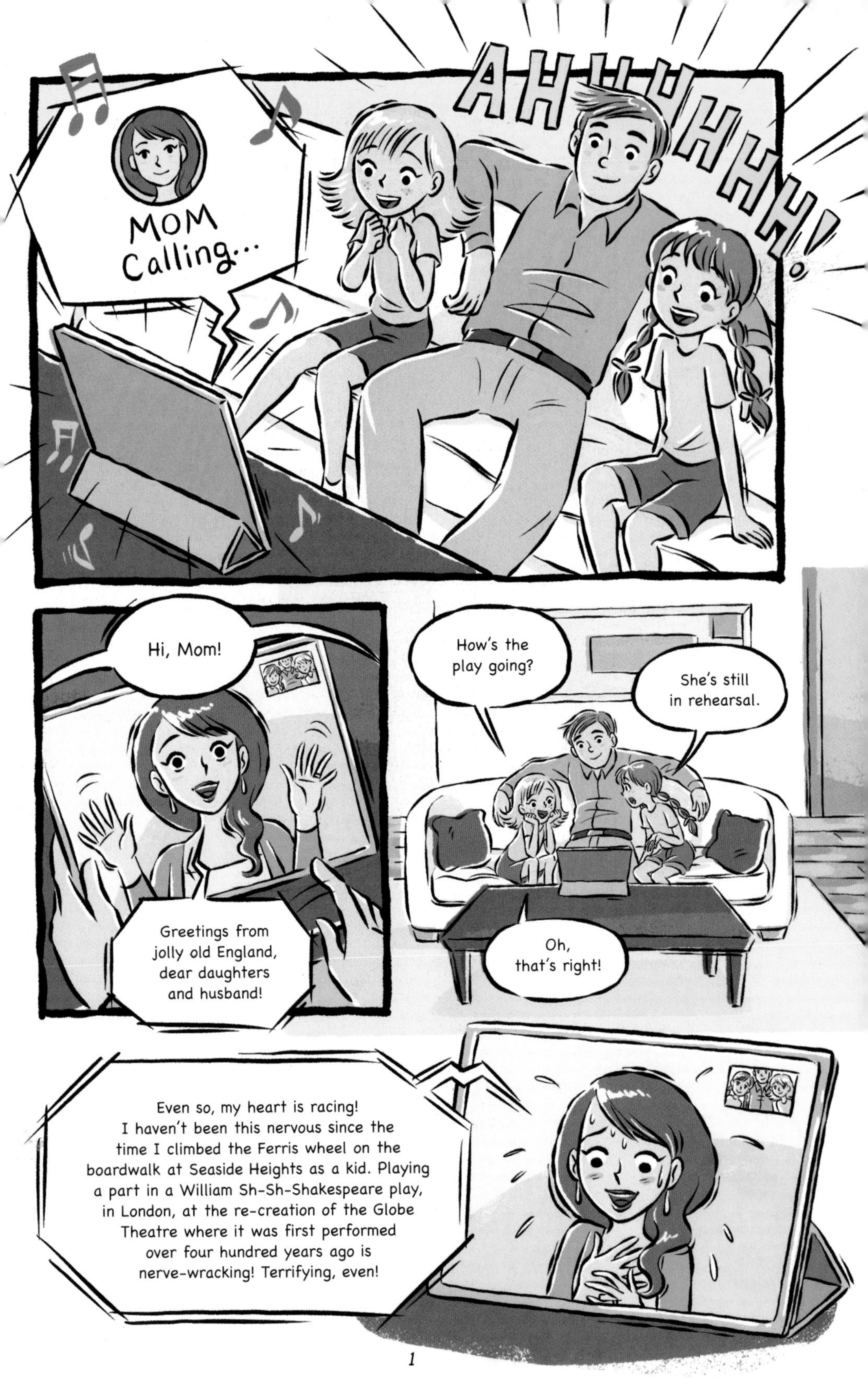
MOM
Calling...
AHHHHHH!
Hi, Mom!
Greetings from jolly old England, dear daughters and husband!
How's the play going?
She's still in rehearsal.
Oh, that's right!
Even so, my heart is racing! I haven't been this nervous since the time I climbed the Ferris wheel on the boardwalk at Seaside Heights as a kid. Playing a part in a William Sh-Sh-Shakespeare play, in London, at the re-creation of the Globe Theatre where it was first performed over four hundred years ago is nerve-wracking! Terrifying, even!

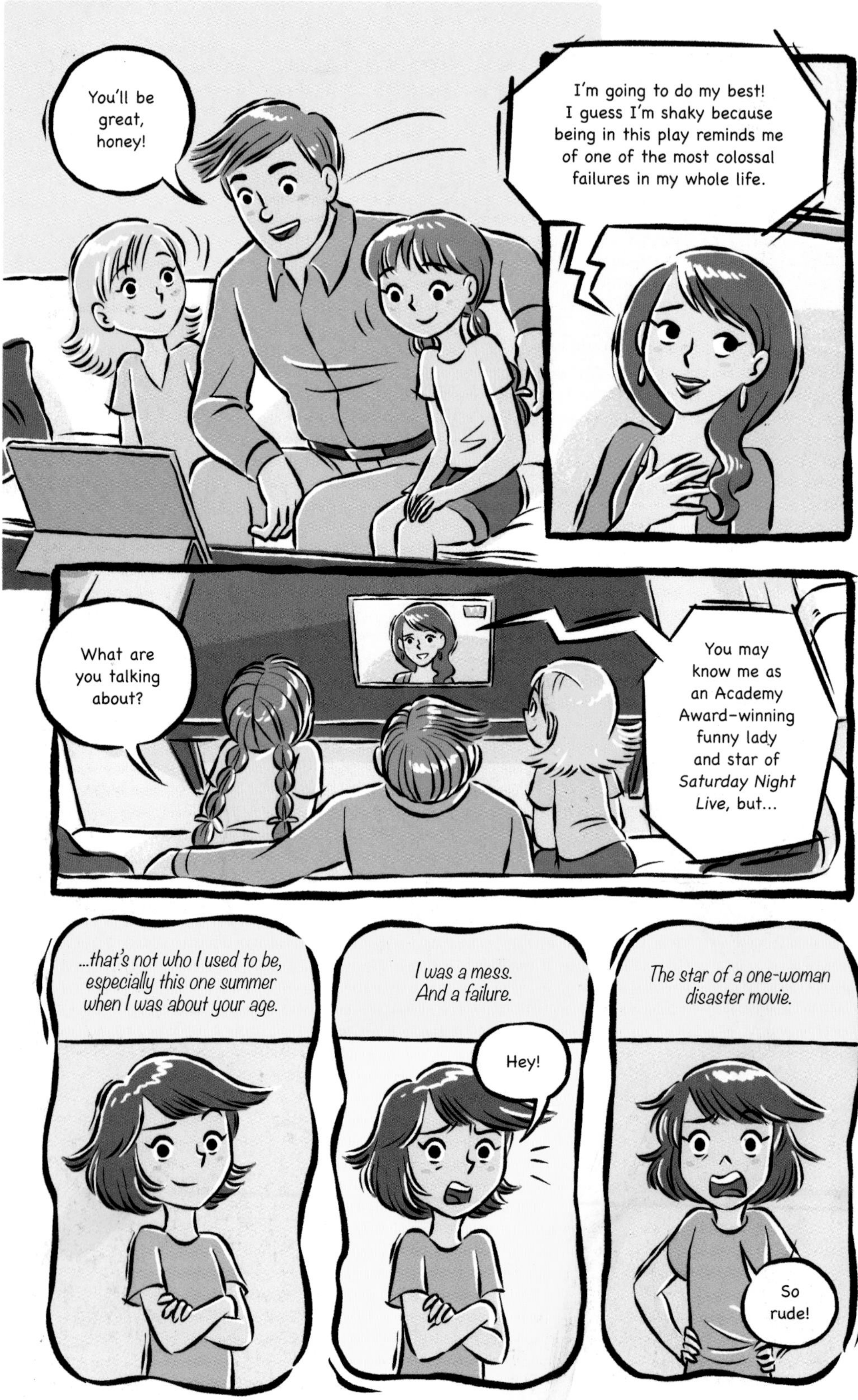
You'll be great, honey!
I'm going to do my best! I guess I'm shaky because being in this play reminds me of one of the most colossal failures in my whole life.
What are you talking about?
You may know me as an Academy Award-winning funny lady and star of *Saturday Night Live*, but...
...that's not who I used to be, especially this one summer when I was about your age.
I was a mess. And a failure.
Hey!
The star of a one-woman disaster movie.
So rude!

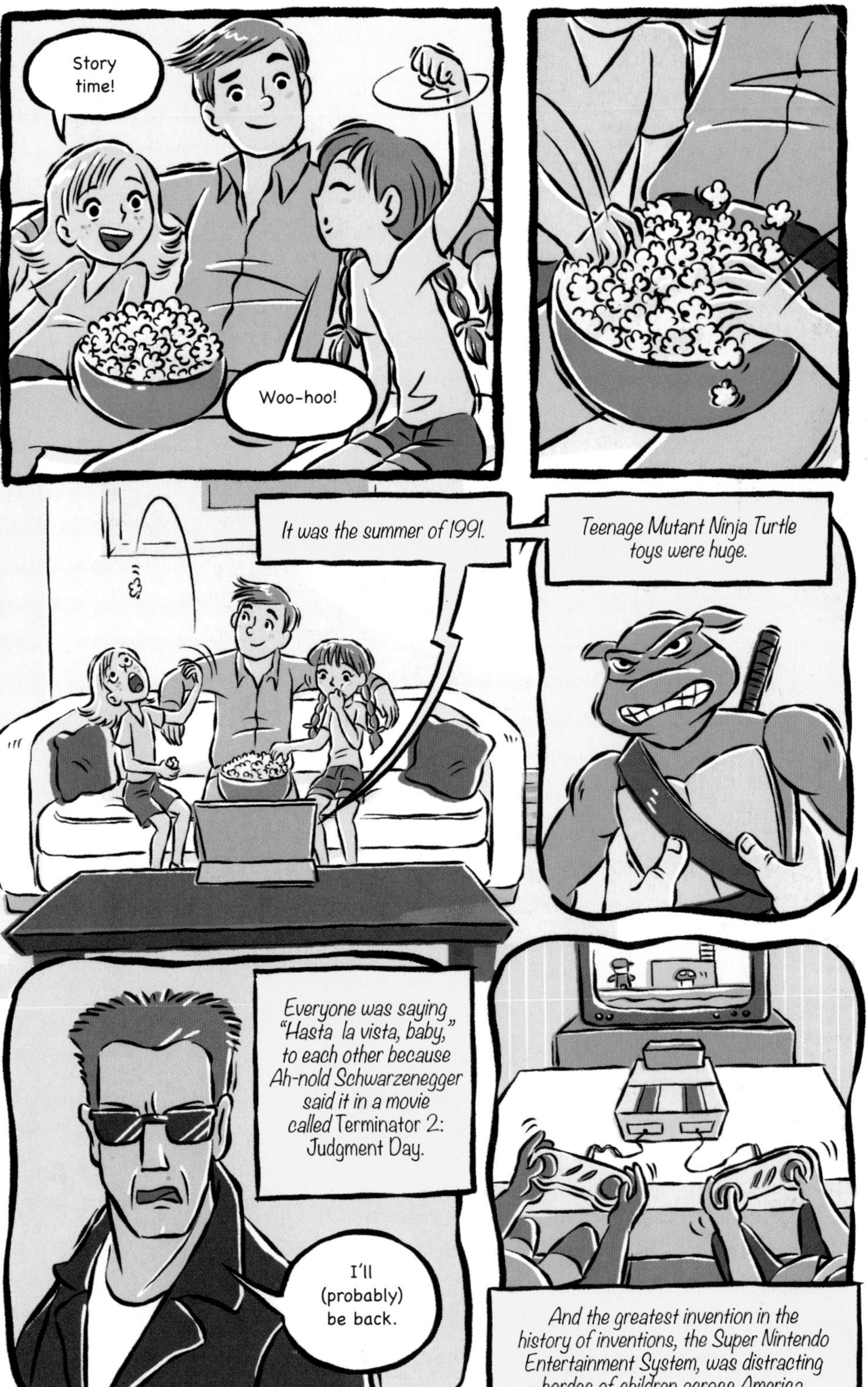
Story time!
Woo-hoo!
It was the summer of 1991.
Teenage Mutant Ninja Turtle toys were huge.
Everyone was saying "Hasta la vista, baby," to each other because Ah-nold Schwarzenegger said it in a movie called Terminator 2: Judgment Day.
I'll (probably) be back.
And the greatest invention in the history of inventions, the Super Nintendo Entertainment System, was distracting hordes of children across America.

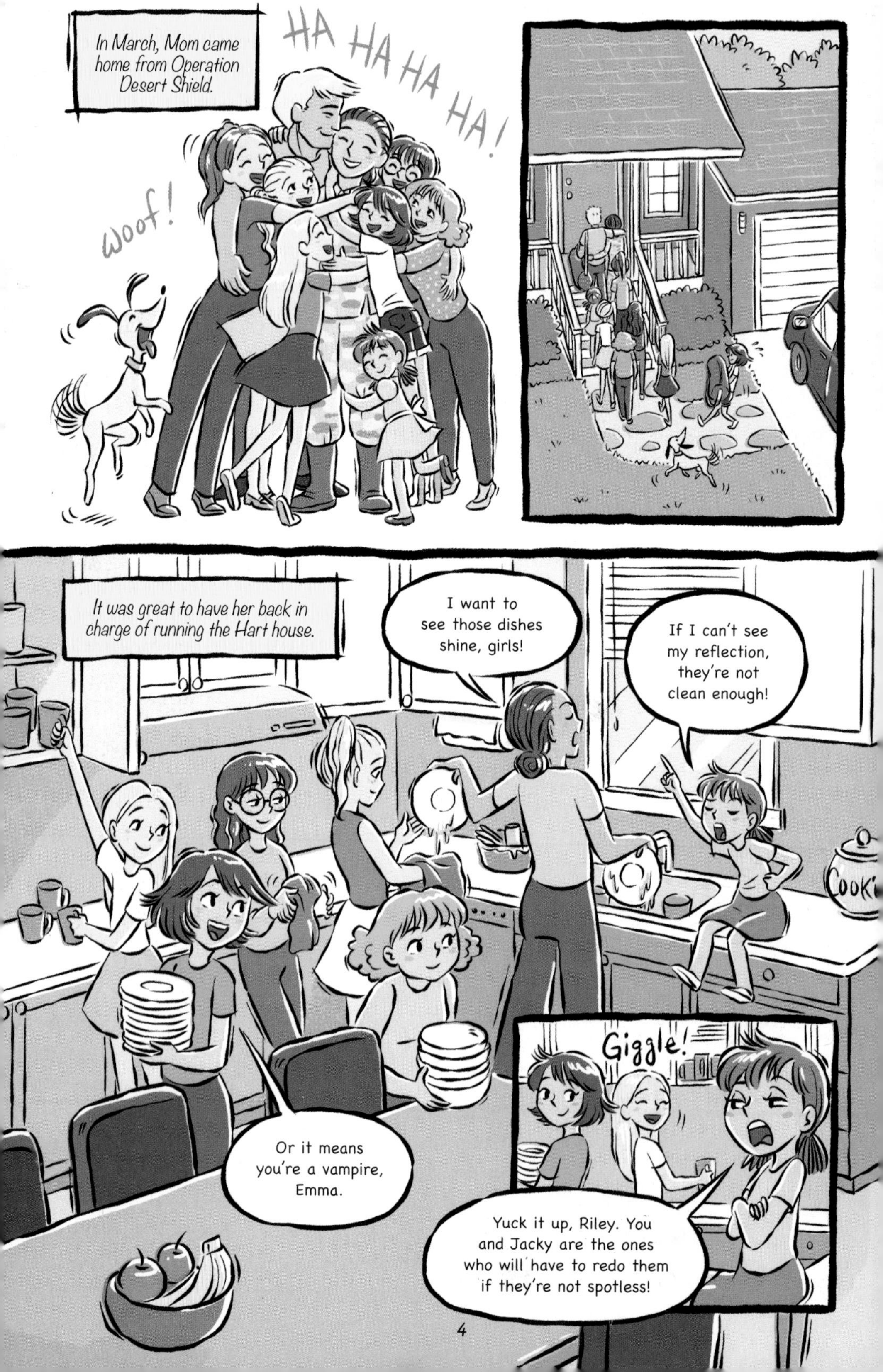
In March, Mom came home from Operation Desert Shield.
HA HA HA HA!
woof!
It was great to have her back in charge of running the Hart house.
I want to see those dishes shine, girls!
If I can't see my reflection, they're not clean enough!
Or it means you're a vampire, Emma.
Giggle!
Yuck it up, Riley. You and Jacky are the ones who will have to redo them if they're not spotless!

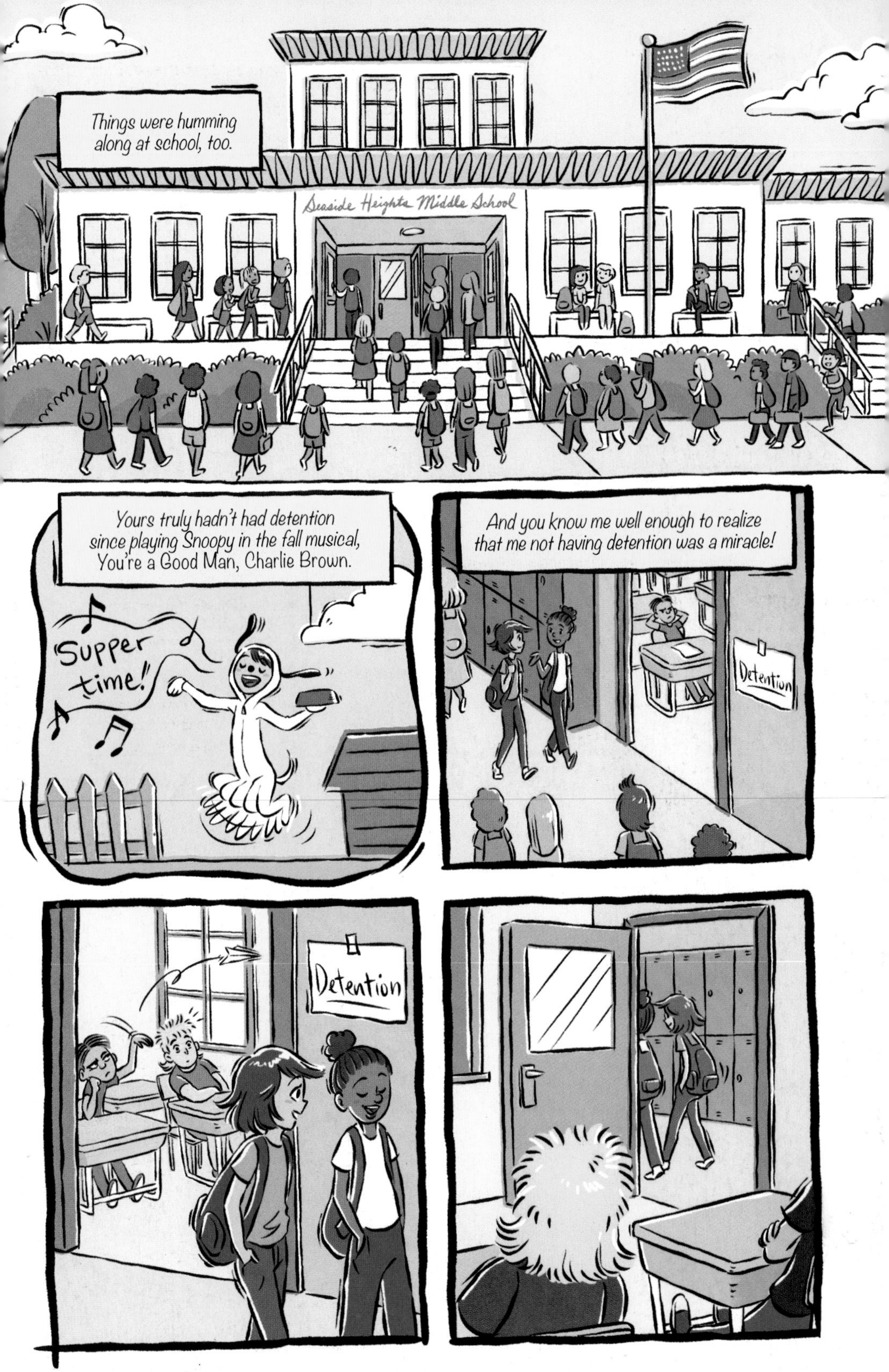
Things were humming along at school, too.
Seaside Heights Middle School
Yours truly hadn't had detention since playing Snoopy in the fall musical, You're a Good Man, Charlie Brown.
Supper time!
And you know me well enough to realize that me not having detention was a miracle!
Detention
Detention

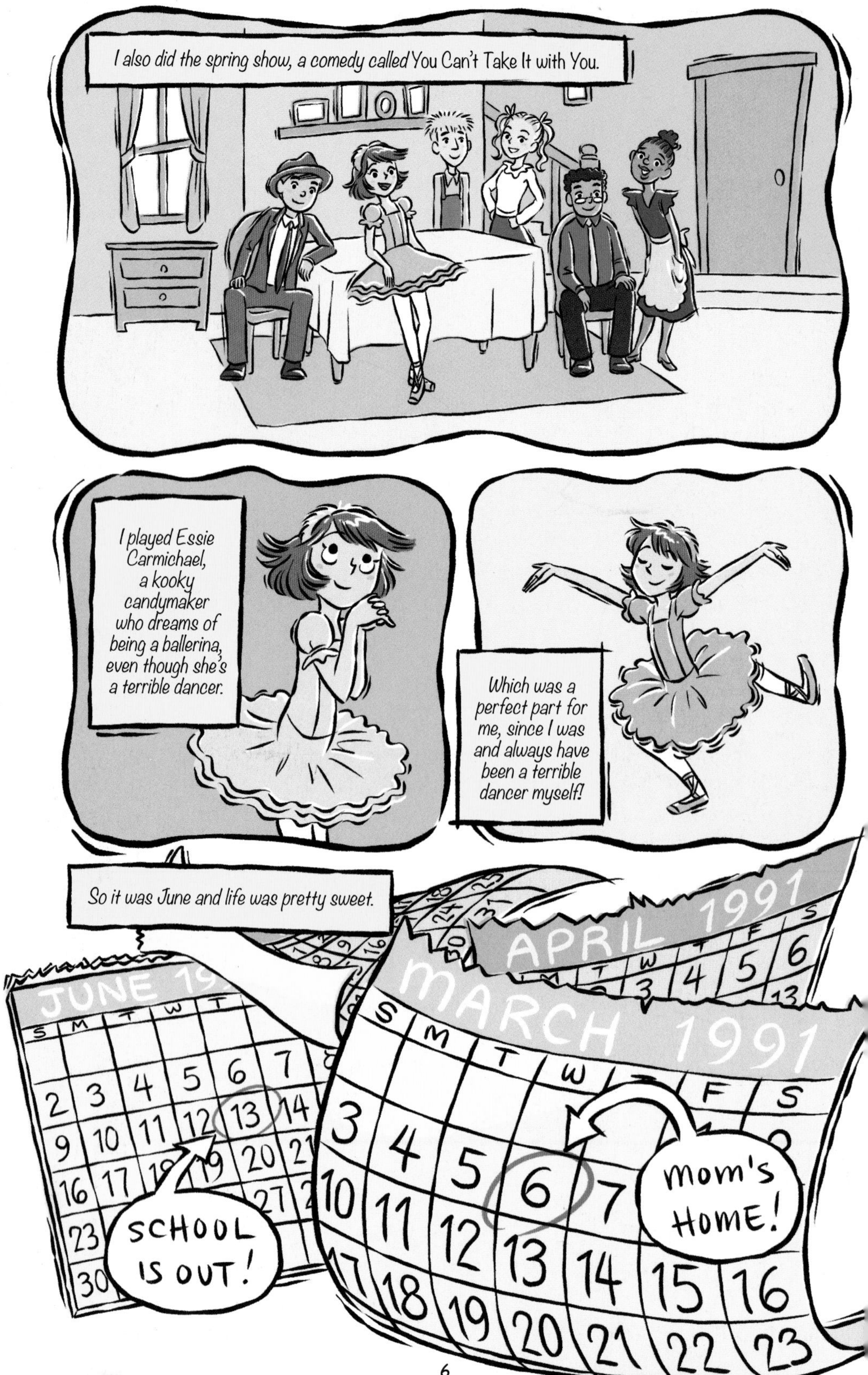
I also did the spring show, a comedy called You Can't Take It with You.
I played Essie Carmichael, a kooky candymaker who dreams of being a ballerina, even though she's a terrible dancer.
Which was a perfect part for me, since I was and always have been a terrible dancer myself!
So it was June and life was pretty sweet.
APRIL 1991
MARCH 1991
SCHOOL IS OUT!
mom's HOME!

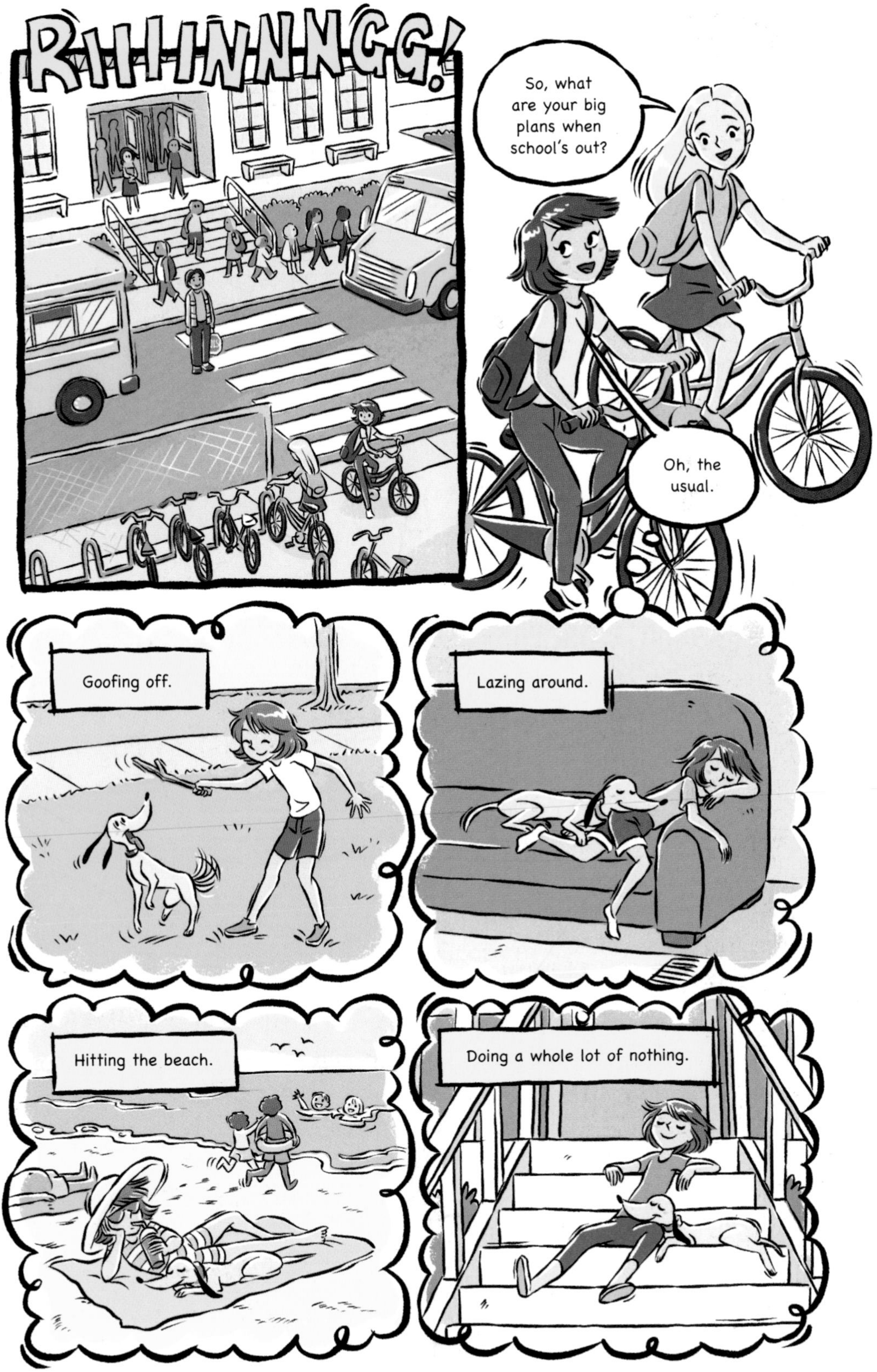
RIIIINNNGG!
So, what are your big plans when school's out?
Oh, the usual.
Goofing off.
Lazing around.
Hitting the beach.
Doing a whole lot of nothing.

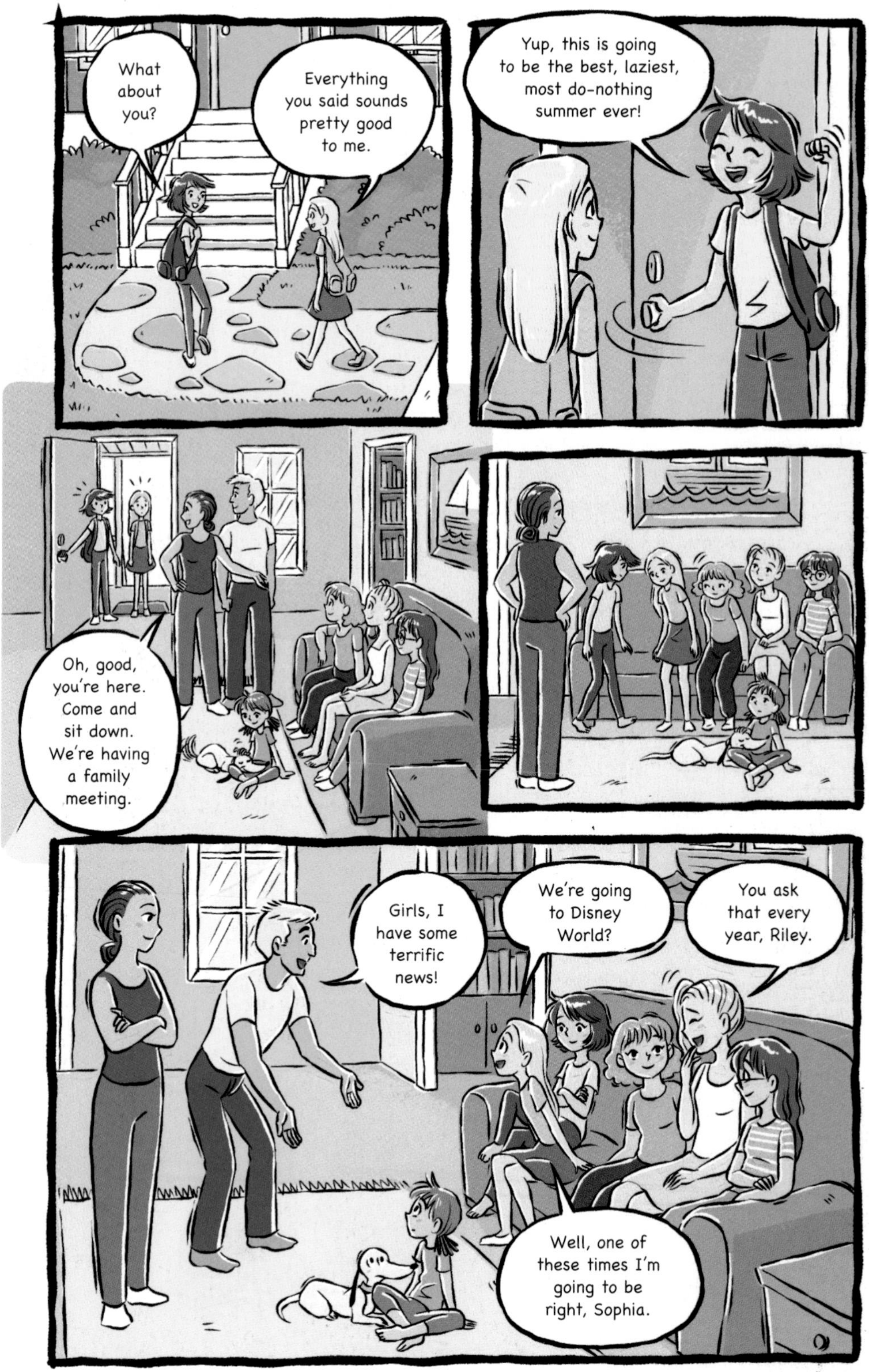
What about you?
Everything you said sounds pretty good to me.
Yup, this is going to be the best, laziest, most do-nothing summer ever!
Oh, good, you're here. Come and sit down. We're having a family meeting.
Girls, I have some terrific news!
We're going to Disney World?
You ask that every year, Riley.
Well, one of these times I'm going to be right, Sophia.

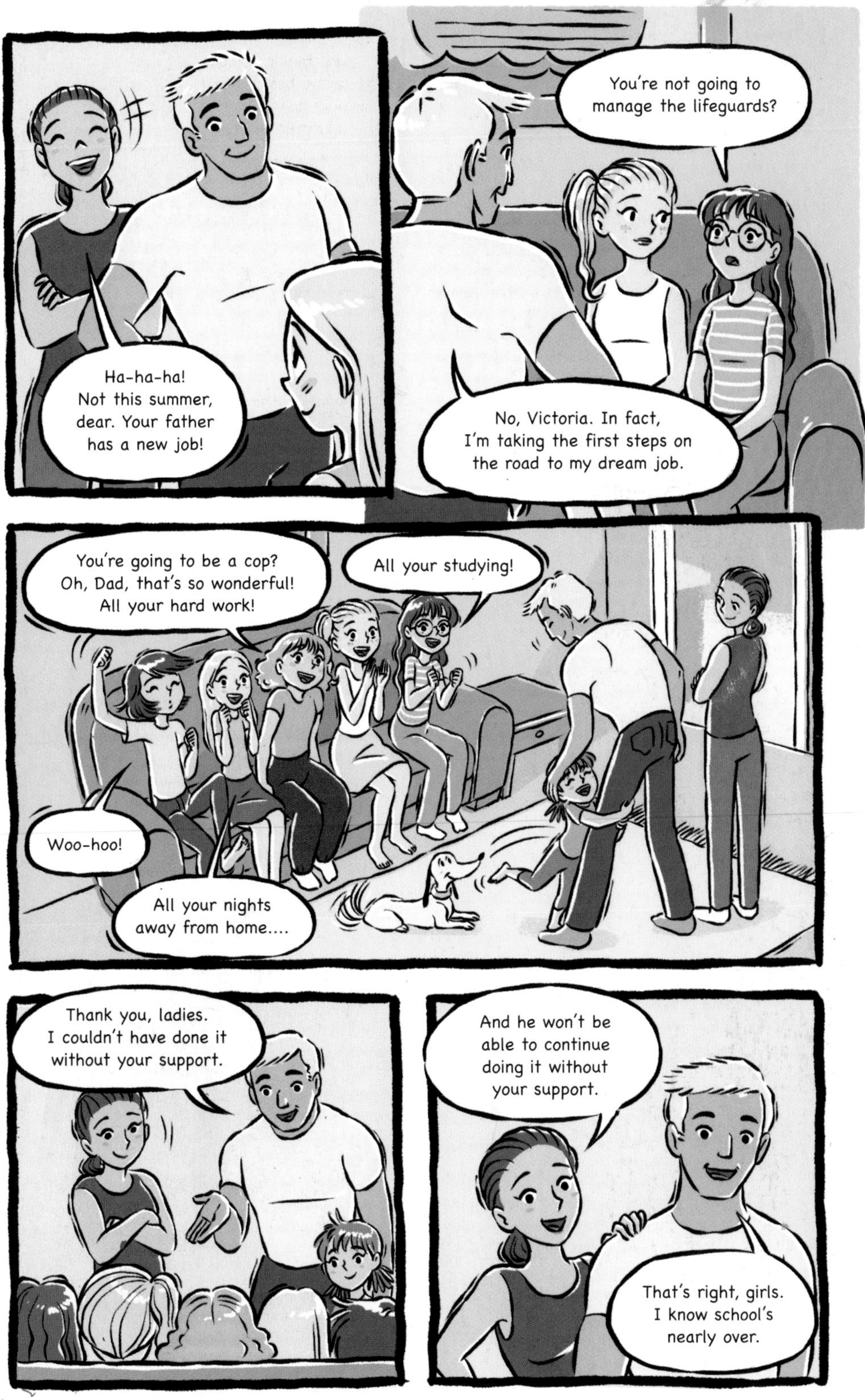
Ha-ha-ha! Not this summer, dear. Your father has a new job!
You're not going to manage the lifeguards?
No, Victoria. In fact, I'm taking the first steps on the road to my dream job.
You're going to be a cop? Oh, Dad, that's so wonderful! All your hard work!
All your studying!
Woo-hoo!
All your nights away from home....
Thank you, ladies. I couldn't have done it without your support.
And he won't be able to continue doing it without your support.
That's right, girls. I know school's nearly over.

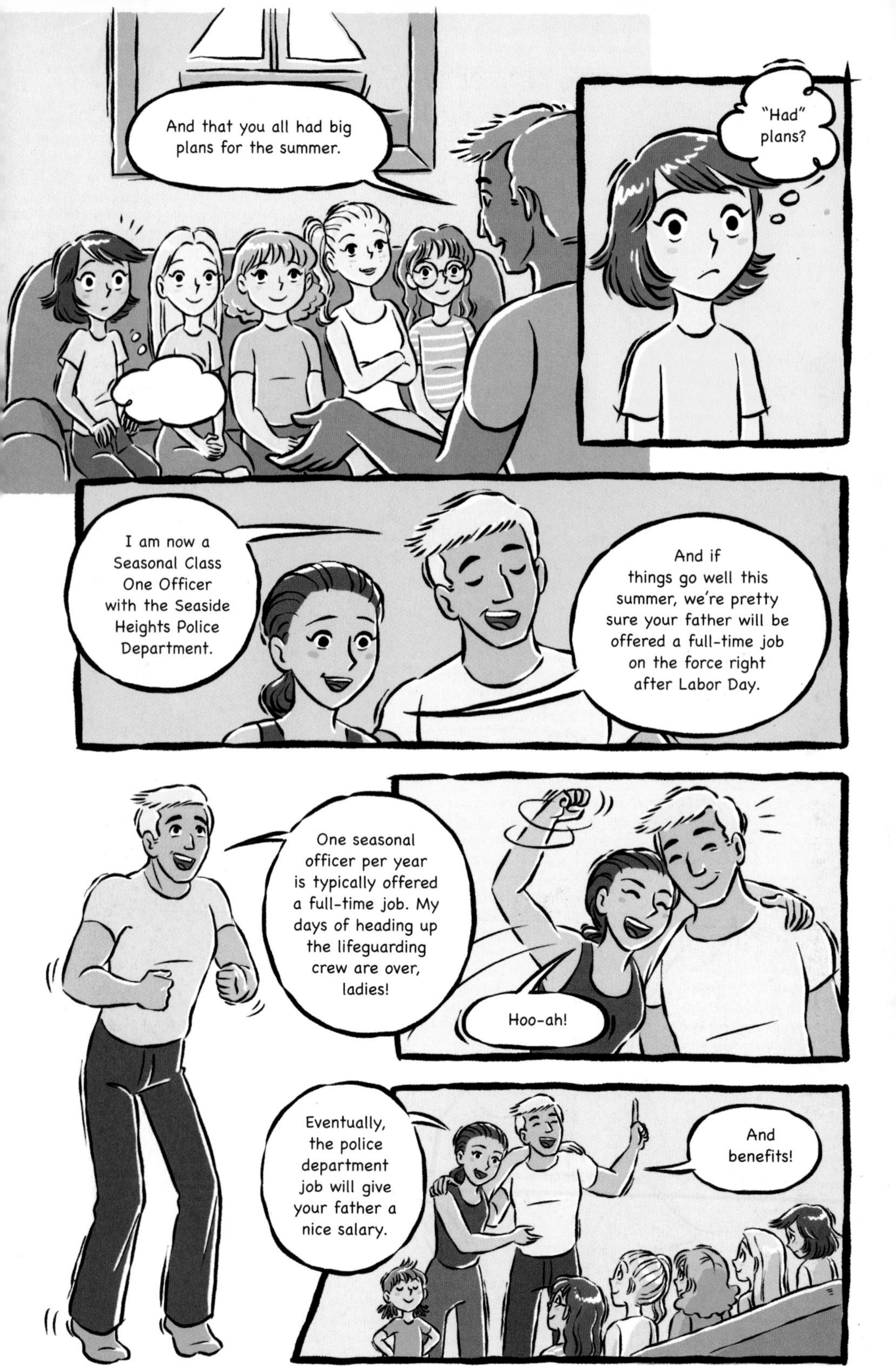
And that you all had big plans for the summer.
"Had" plans?
I am now a Seasonal Class One Officer with the Seaside Heights Police Department.
And if things go well this summer, we're pretty sure your father will be offered a full-time job on the force right after Labor Day.
One seasonal officer per year is typically offered a full-time job. My days of heading up the lifeguarding crew are over, ladies!
Hoo-ah!
Eventually, the police department job will give your father a nice salary.
And benefits!

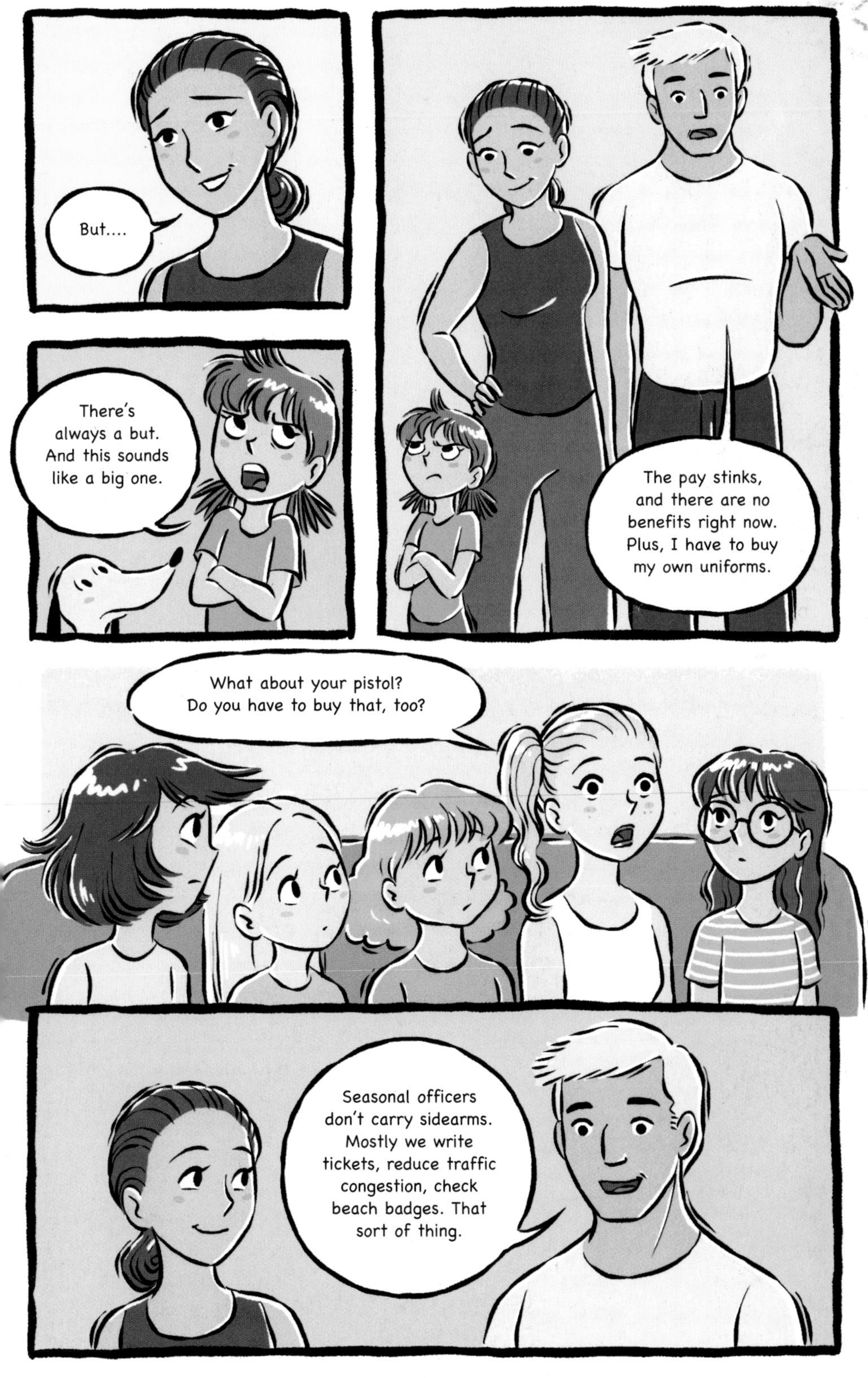
But....
There's always a but. And this sounds like a big one.
The pay stinks, and there are no benefits right now. Plus, I have to buy my own uniforms.
What about your pistol? Do you have to buy that, too?
Seasonal officers don't carry sidearms. Mostly we write tickets, reduce traffic congestion, check beach badges. That sort of thing.

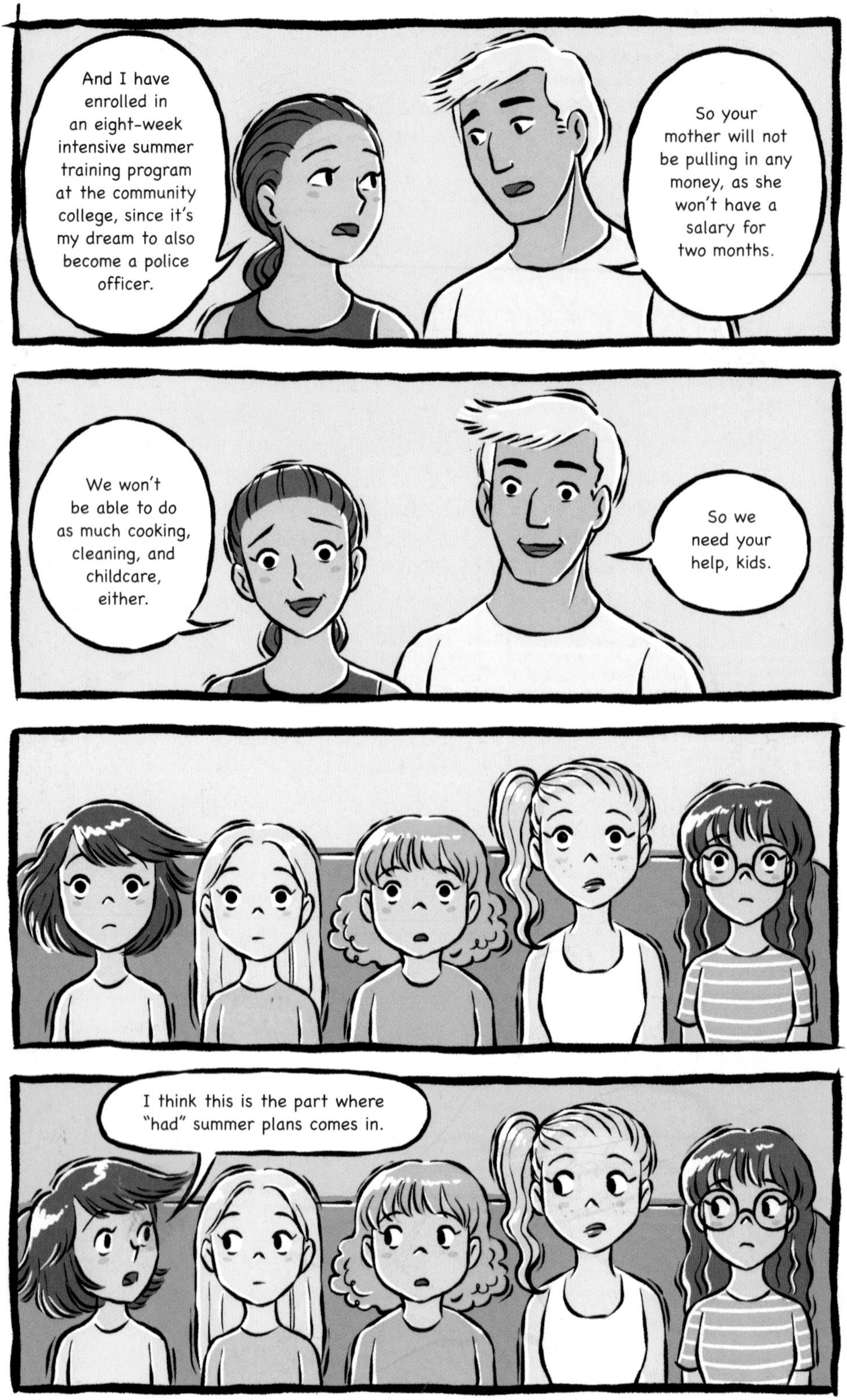
And I have enrolled in an eight-week intensive summer training program at the community college, since it's my dream to also become a police officer.
So your mother will not be pulling in any money, as she won't have a salary for two months.
We won't be able to do as much cooking, cleaning, and childcare, either.
So we need your help, kids.
I think this is the part where "had" summer plans comes in.

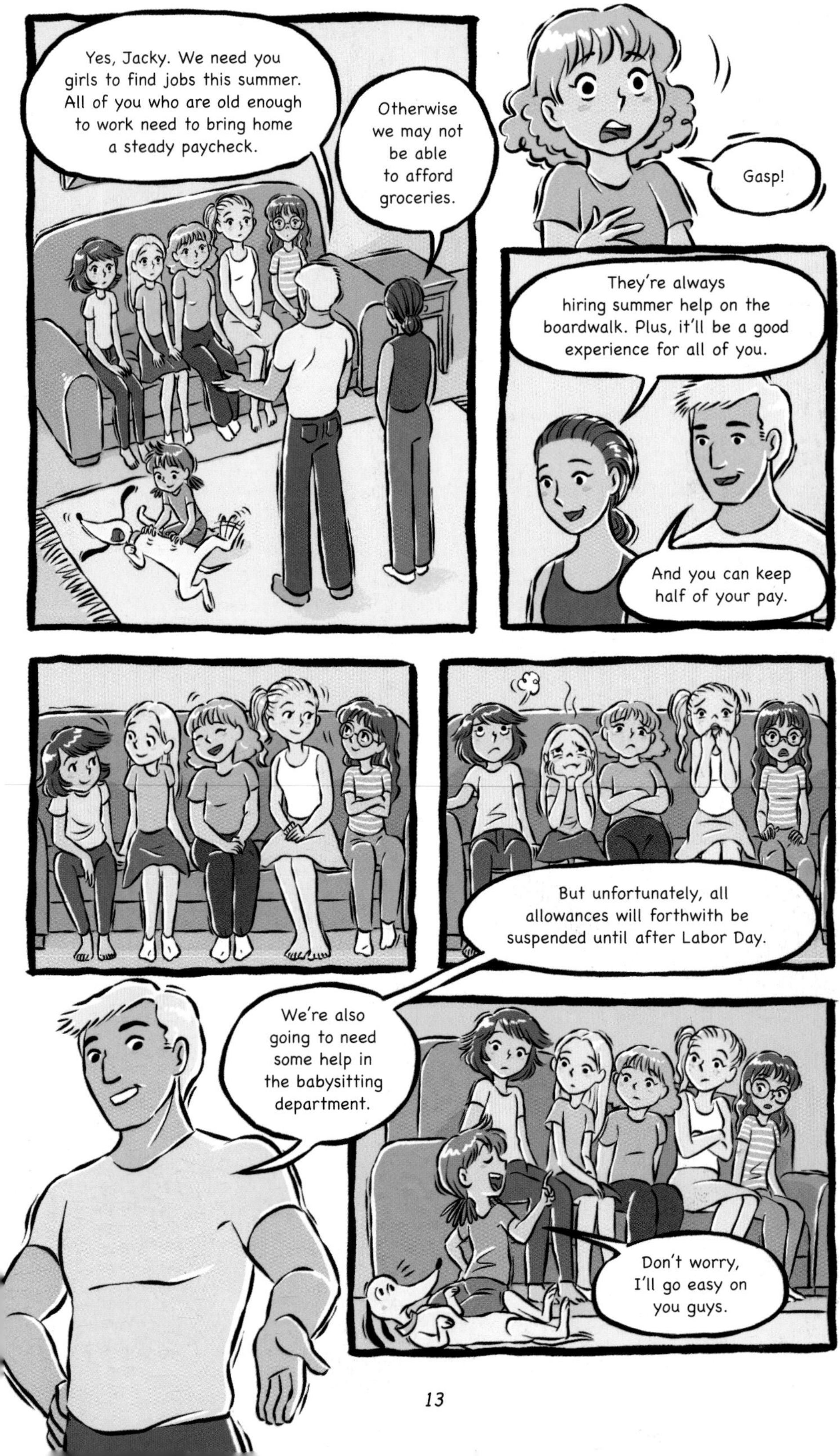
Yes, Jacky. We need you girls to find jobs this summer. All of you who are old enough to work need to bring home a steady paycheck.
Otherwise we may not be able to afford groceries.
Gasp!
They're always hiring summer help on the boardwalk. Plus, it'll be a good experience for all of you.
And you can keep half of your pay.
But unfortunately, all allowances will forthwith be suspended until after Labor Day.
We're also going to need some help in the babysitting department.
Don't worry, I'll go easy on you guys.

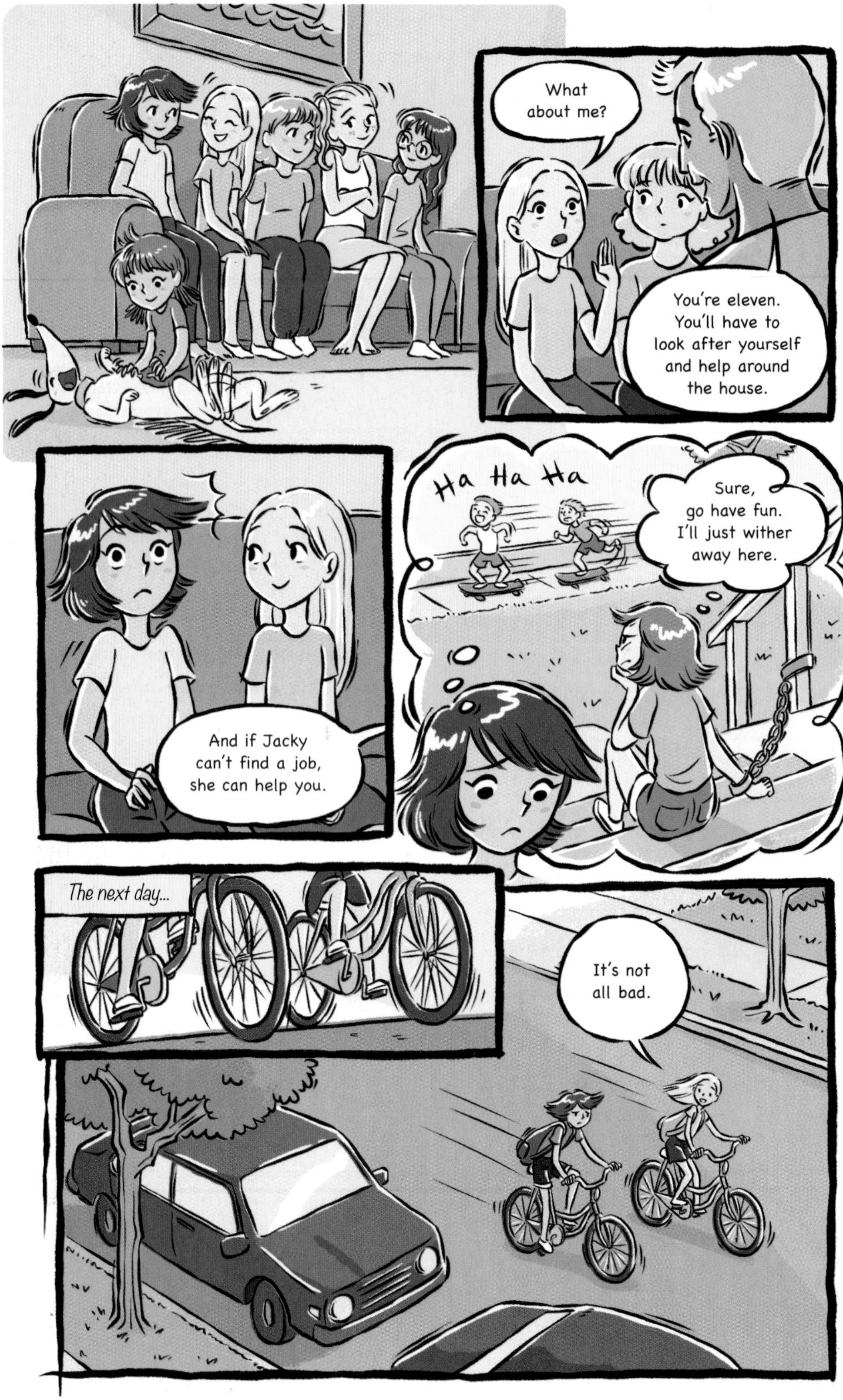
What about me?
You're eleven. You'll have to look after yourself and help around the house.
And if Jacky can't find a job, she can help you.
Ha Ha Ha
Sure, go have fun. I'll just wither away here.
The next day...
It's not all bad.

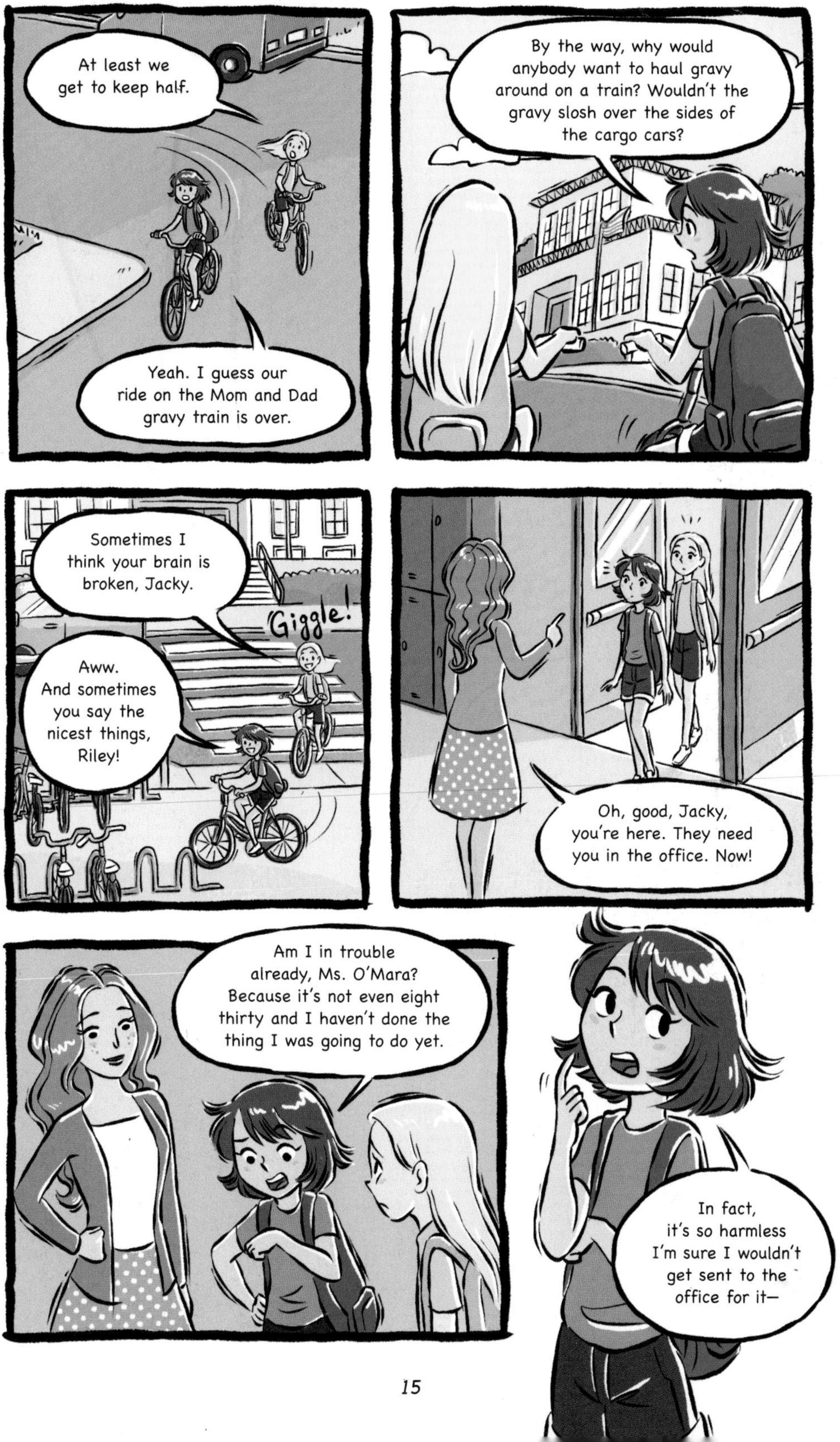
At least we get to keep half.
Yeah. I guess our ride on the Mom and Dad gravy train is over.
By the way, why would anybody want to haul gravy around on a train? Wouldn't the gravy slosh over the sides of the cargo cars?
Sometimes I think your brain is broken, Jacky.
Giggle!
Aww. And sometimes you say the nicest things, Riley!
Oh, good, Jacky, you're here. They need you in the office. Now!
Am I in trouble already, Ms. O'Mara? Because it's not even eight thirty and I haven't done the thing I was going to do yet.
In fact, it's so harmless I'm sure I wouldn't get sent to the office for it—

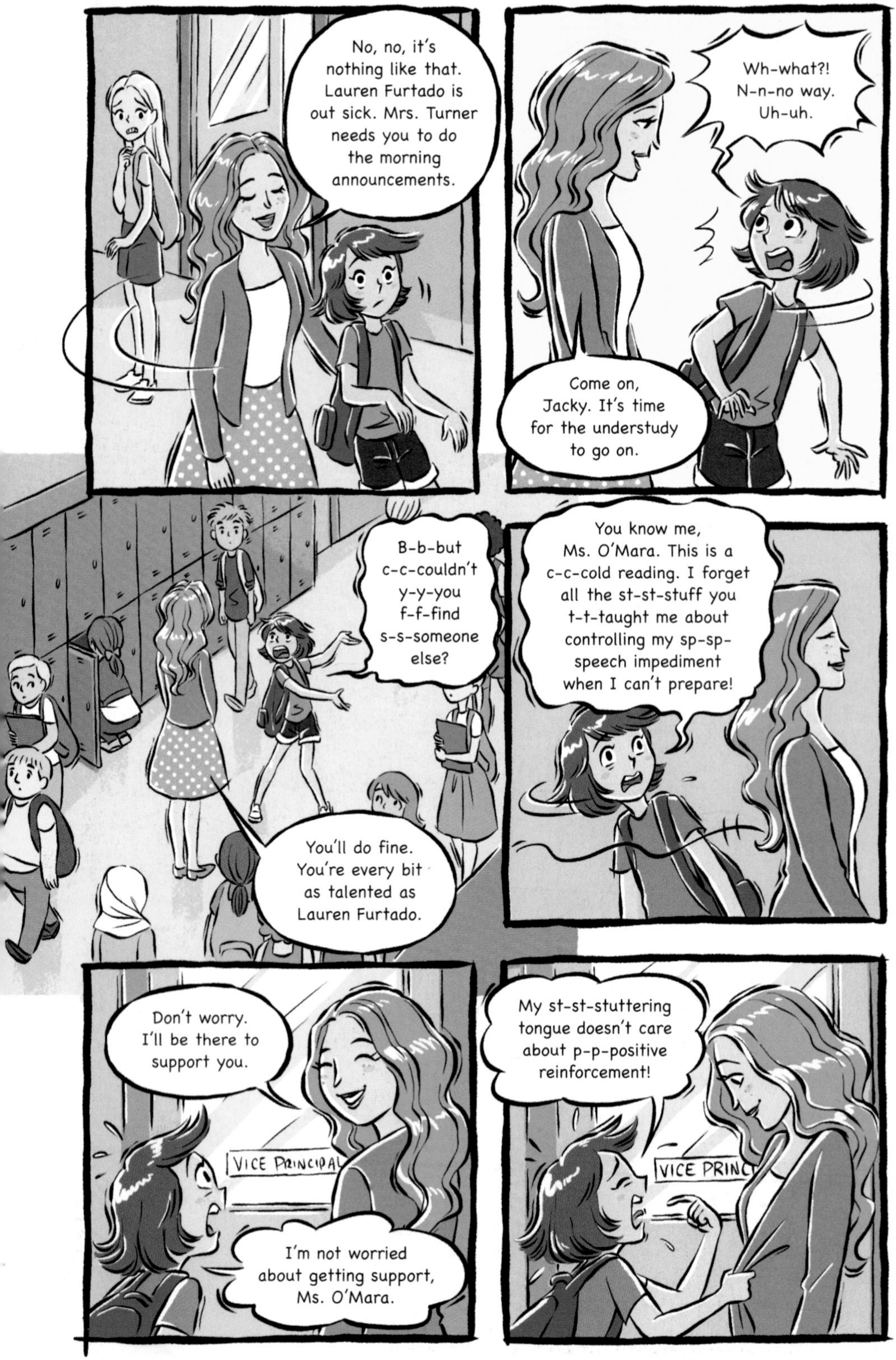
No, no, it's nothing like that. Lauren Furtado is out sick. Mrs. Turner needs you to do the morning announcements.
Wh-what?! N-n-no way. Uh-uh.
Come on, Jacky. It's time for the understudy to go on.
B-b-but c-c-couldn't y-y-you f-f-find s-s-someone else?
You'll do fine. You're every bit as talented as Lauren Furtado.
You know me, Ms. O'Mara. This is a c-c-cold reading. I forget all the st-st-stuff you t-t-taught me about controlling my sp-sp-speech impediment when I can't prepare!
Don't worry. I'll be there to support you.
VICE PRINCIPAL
I'm not worried about getting support, Ms. O'Mara.
My st-st-stuttering tongue doesn't care about p-p-positive reinforcement!
VICE PRINC

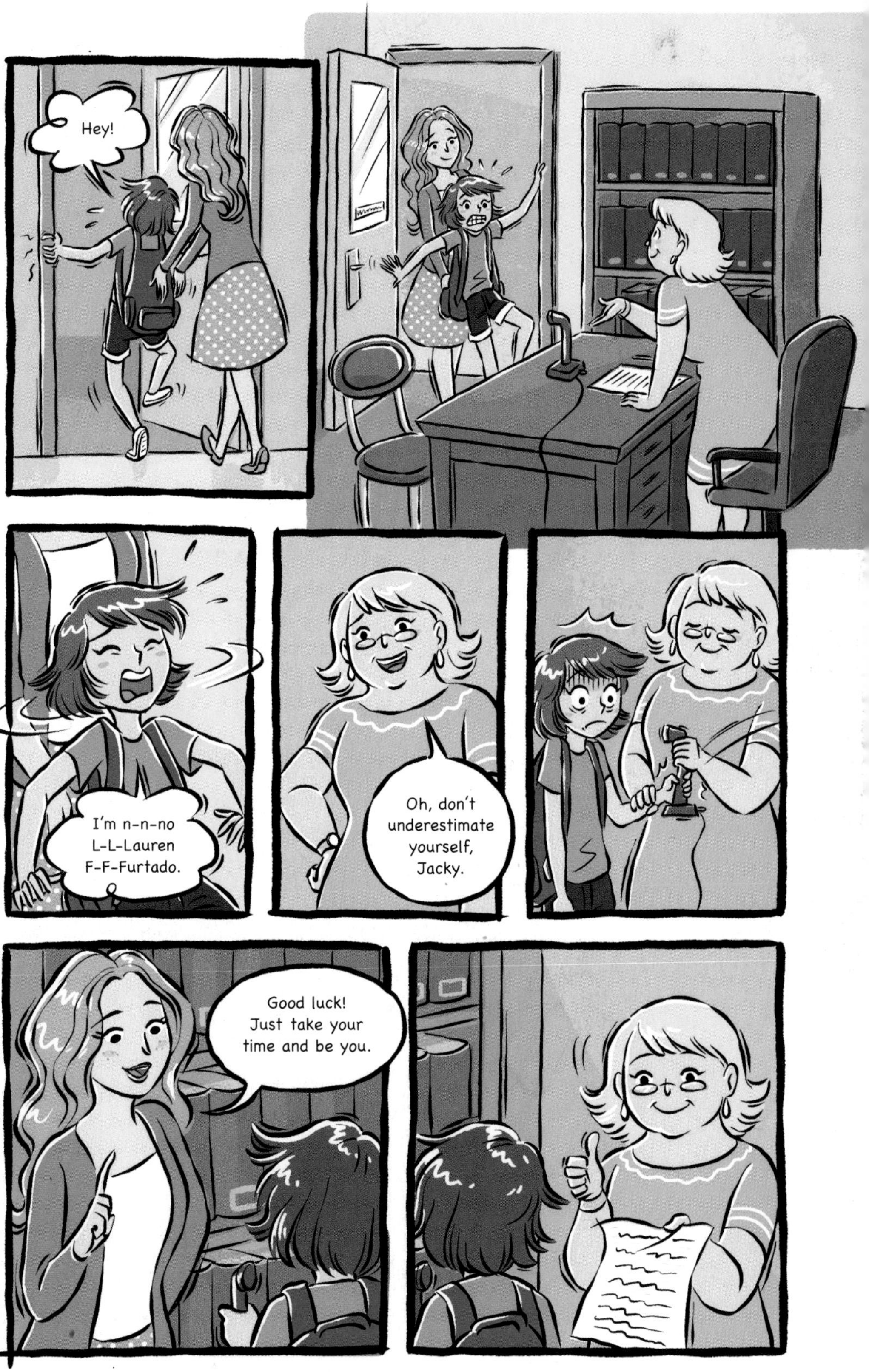
Hey!
I'm n-n-no L-L-Lauren F-F-Furtado.
Oh, don't underestimate yourself, Jacky.
Good luck! Just take your time and be you.

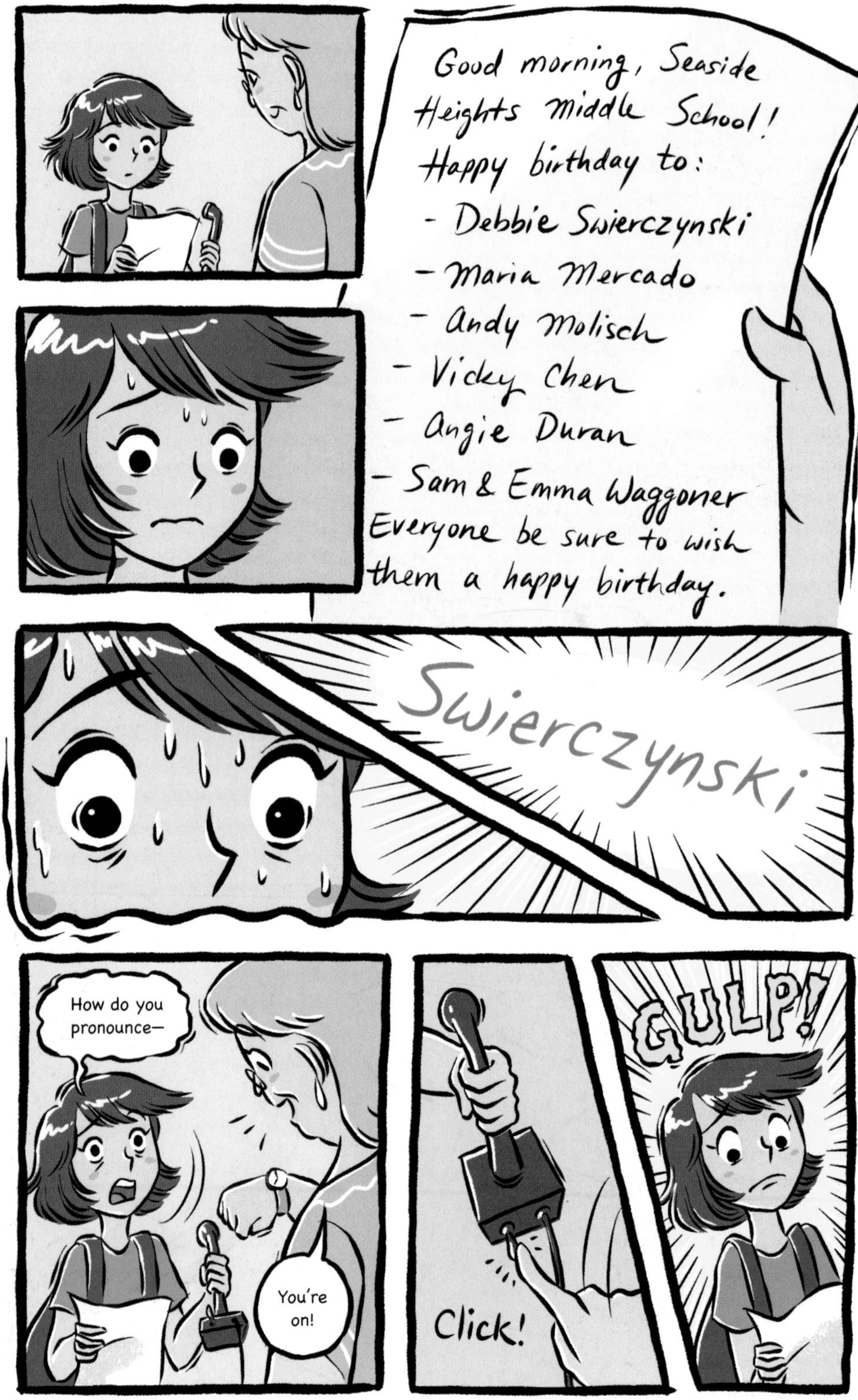

Good morning, Seaside Heights Middle School!
Happy birthday to:
- Debbie Swierczynski
- Maria Mercado
- Andy Molisch
- Vicky Chen
- Angie Duran
- Sam & Emma Waggoner
Everyone be sure to wish them a happy birthday.
Swierczynski
How do you pronounce—
You're on!
Click!
GULP!

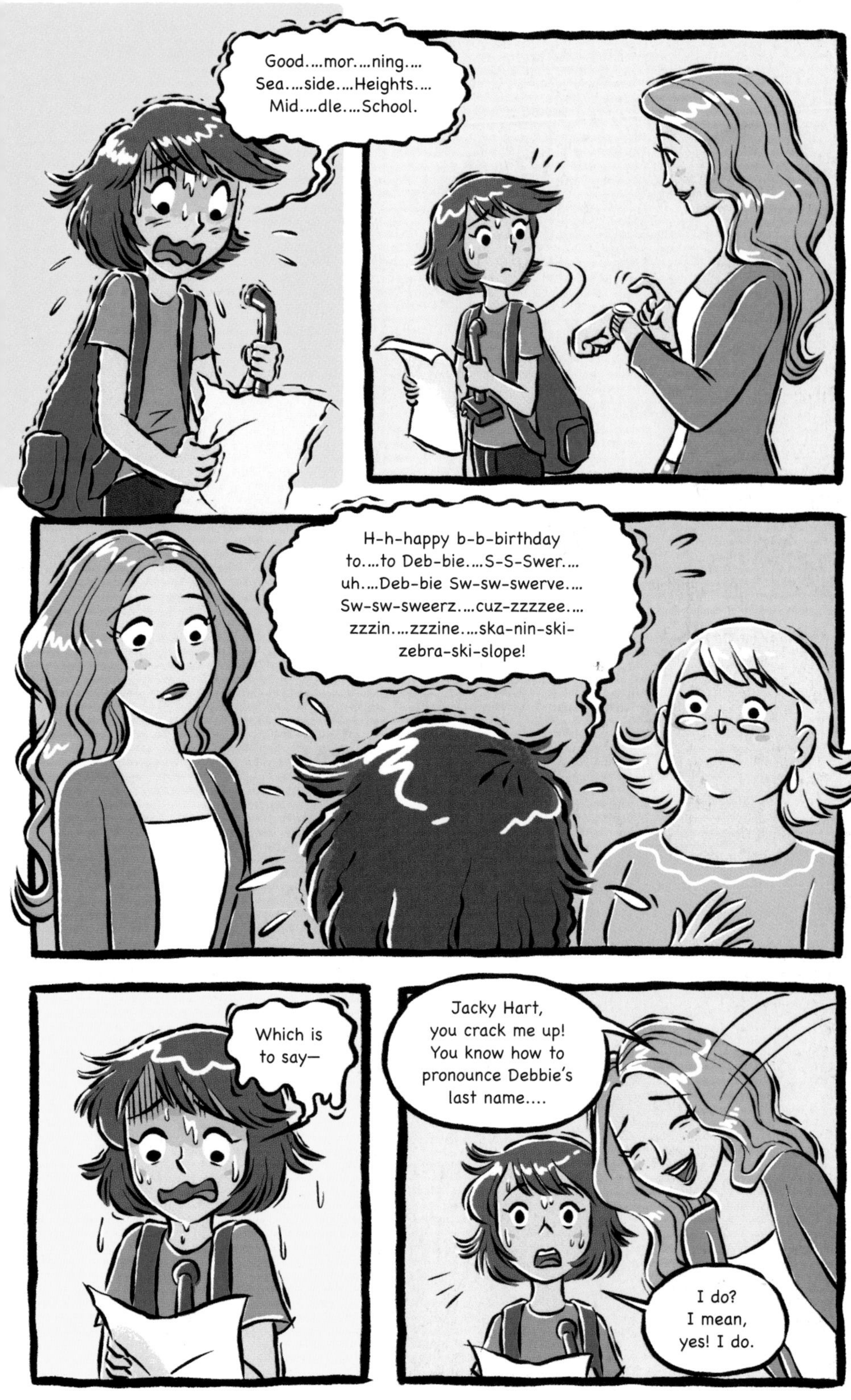
Good....mor....ning....
Sea....side....Heights....
Mid....dle....School.
H-h-happy b-b-birthday to....to Deb-bie....S-S-Swer.... uh....Deb-bie Sw-sw-swerve.... Sw-sw-sweerz....cuz-zzzzee.... zzzin....zzzine....ska-nin-ski-zebra-ski-slope!
Which is to say—
Jacky Hart, you crack me up! You know how to pronounce Debbie's last name....
I do? I mean, yes! I do.

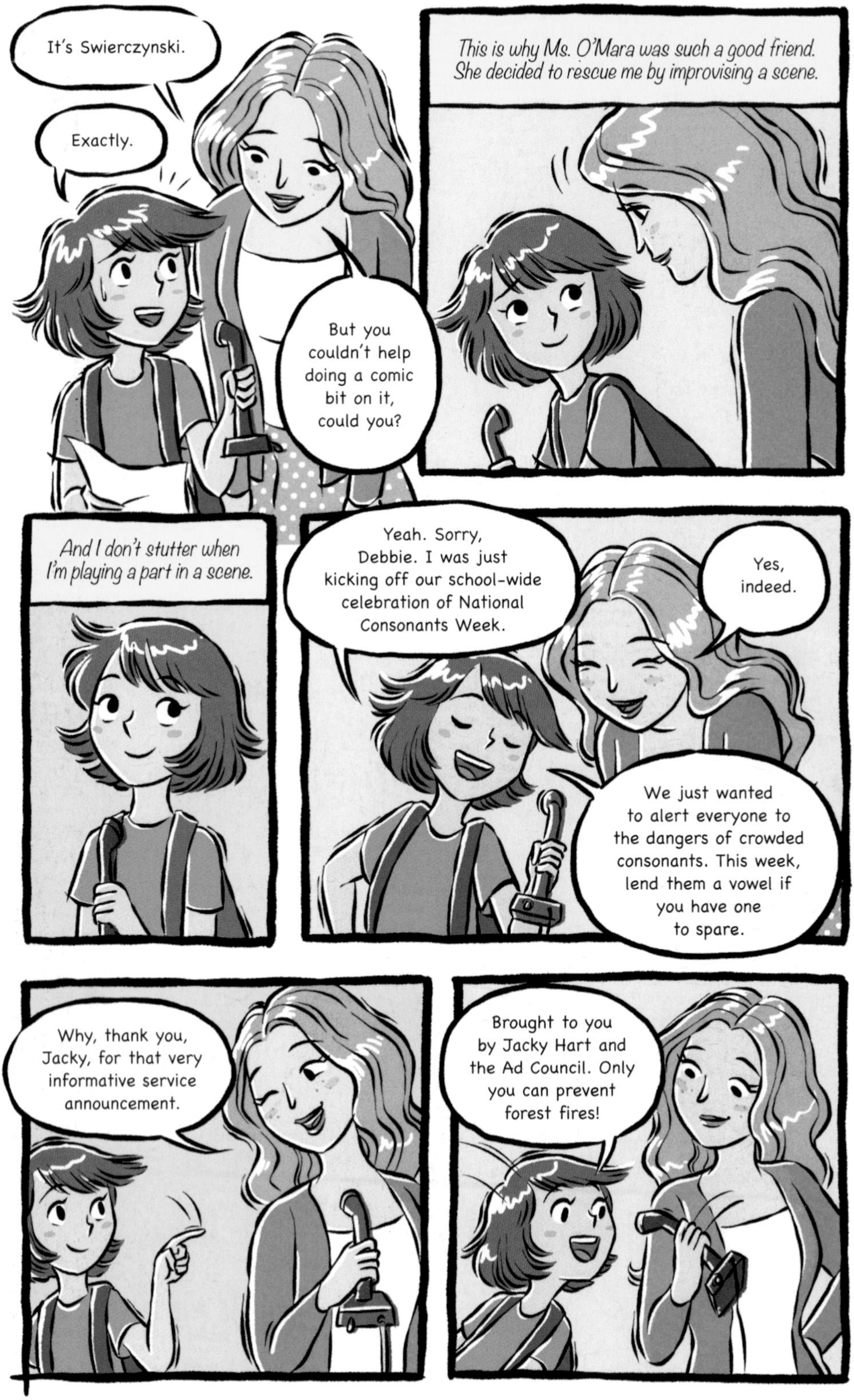
It's Swierczynski.
Exactly.
This is why Ms. O'Mara was such a good friend. She decided to rescue me by improvising a scene.
But you couldn't help doing a comic bit on it, could you?
And I don't stutter when I'm playing a part in a scene.
Yeah. Sorry, Debbie. I was just kicking off our school-wide celebration of National Consonants Week.
Yes, indeed.
We just wanted to alert everyone to the dangers of crowded consonants. This week, lend them a vowel if you have one to spare.
Why, thank you, Jacky, for that very informative service announcement.
Brought to you by Jacky Hart and the Ad Council. Only you can prevent forest fires!

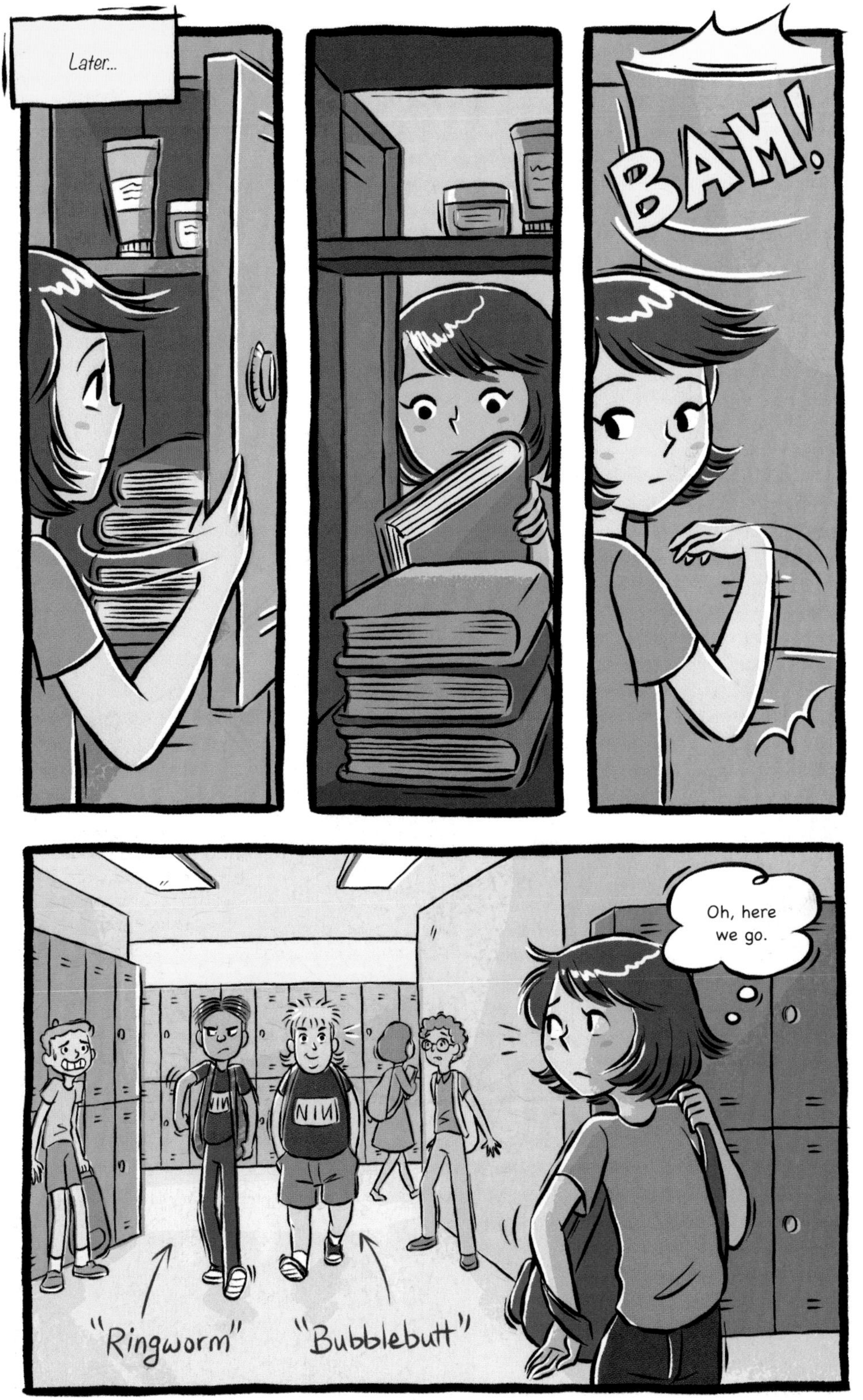
Later...
BAM!
Oh, here we go.
"Ringworm"
"Bubblebutt"

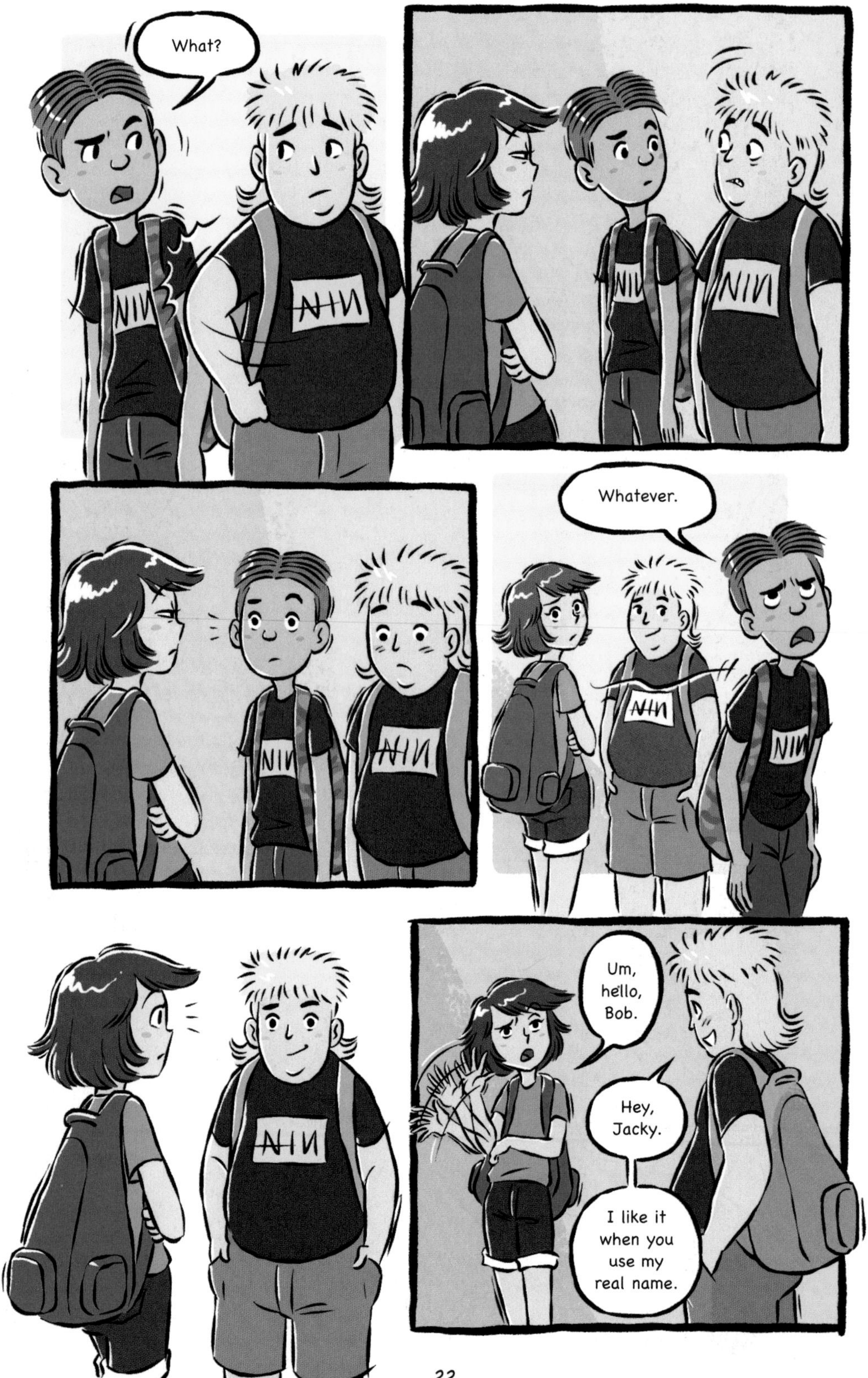
What?
Whatever.
Um, hello, Bob.
Hey, Jacky.
I like it when you use my real name.

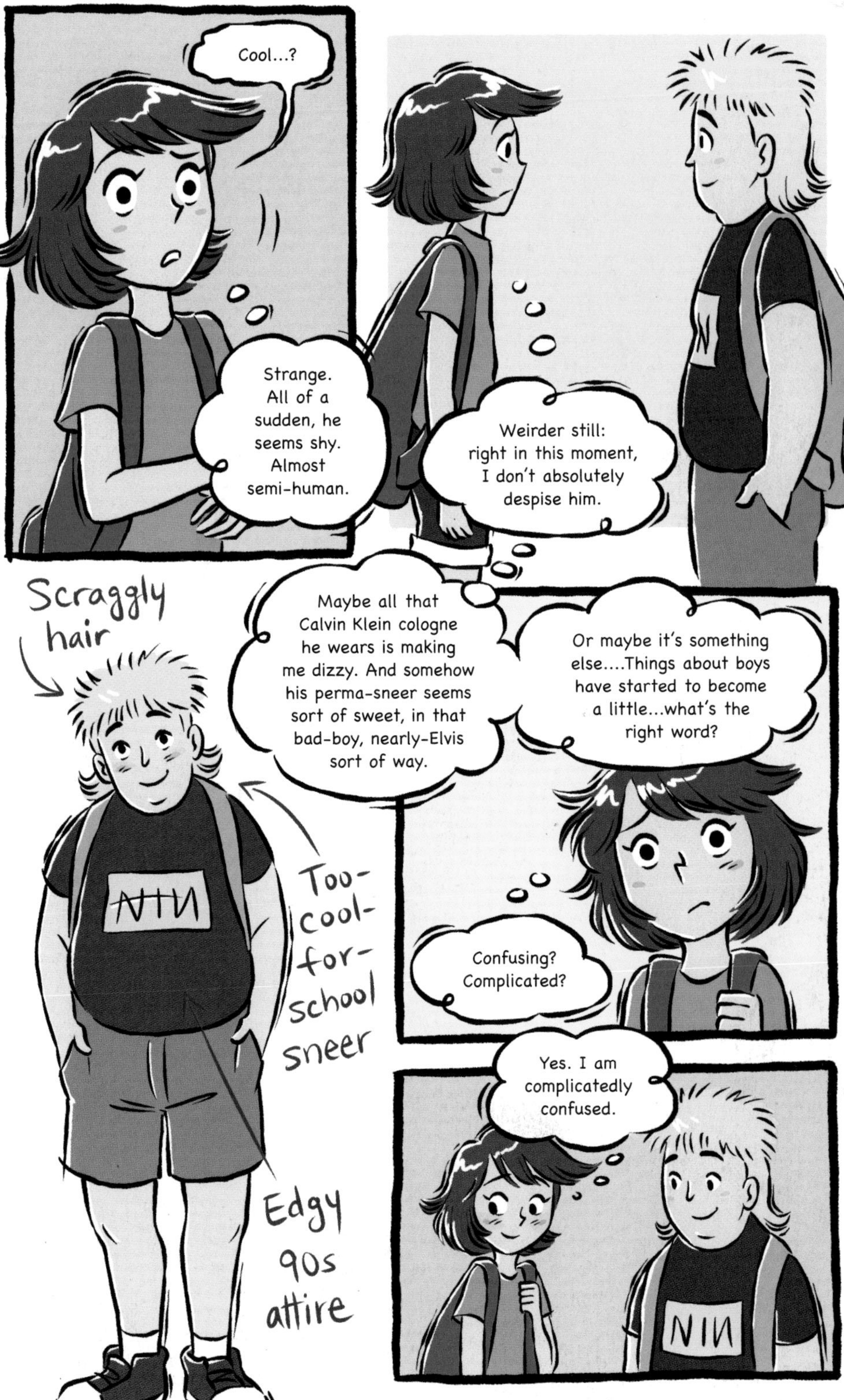

Cool...?
Strange. All of a sudden, he seems shy. Almost semi-human.
Weirder still: right in this moment, I don't absolutely despise him.
Scraggly hair
Maybe all that Calvin Klein cologne he wears is making me dizzy. And somehow his perma-sneer seems sort of sweet, in that bad-boy, nearly-Elvis sort of way.
Or maybe it's something else....Things about boys have started to become a little...what's the right word?
Too-cool-for-school sneer
NIN
Confusing? Complicated?
Edgy 90s attire
Yes. I am complicatedly confused.
NIN

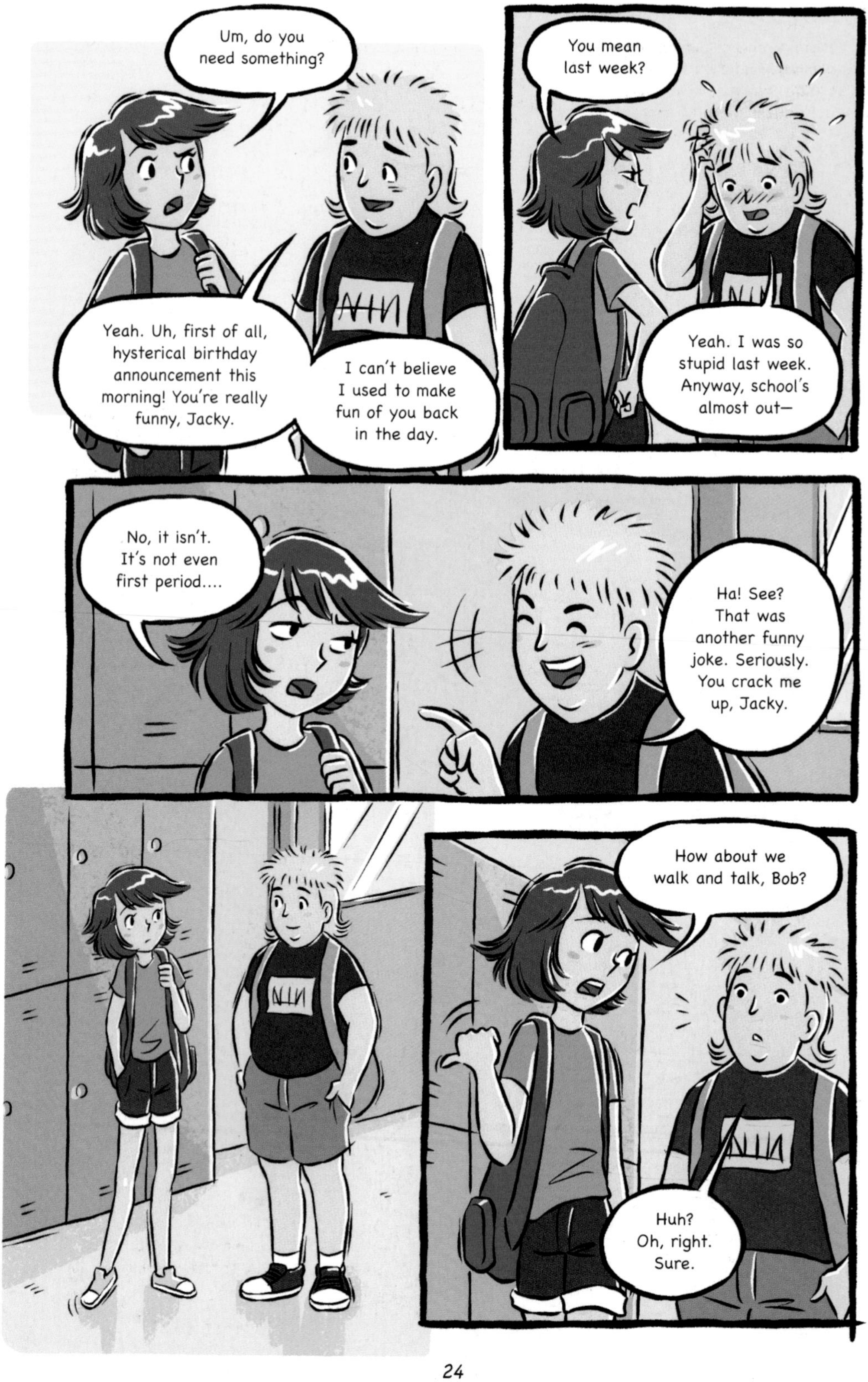
Um, do you need something?
Yeah. Uh, first of all, hysterical birthday announcement this morning! You're really funny, Jacky.
I can't believe I used to make fun of you back in the day.
NIN
You mean last week?
Yeah. I was so stupid last week. Anyway, school's almost out—
No, it isn't. It's not even first period....
Ha! See? That was another funny joke. Seriously. You crack me up, Jacky.
How about we walk and talk, Bob?
Huh? Oh, right. Sure.

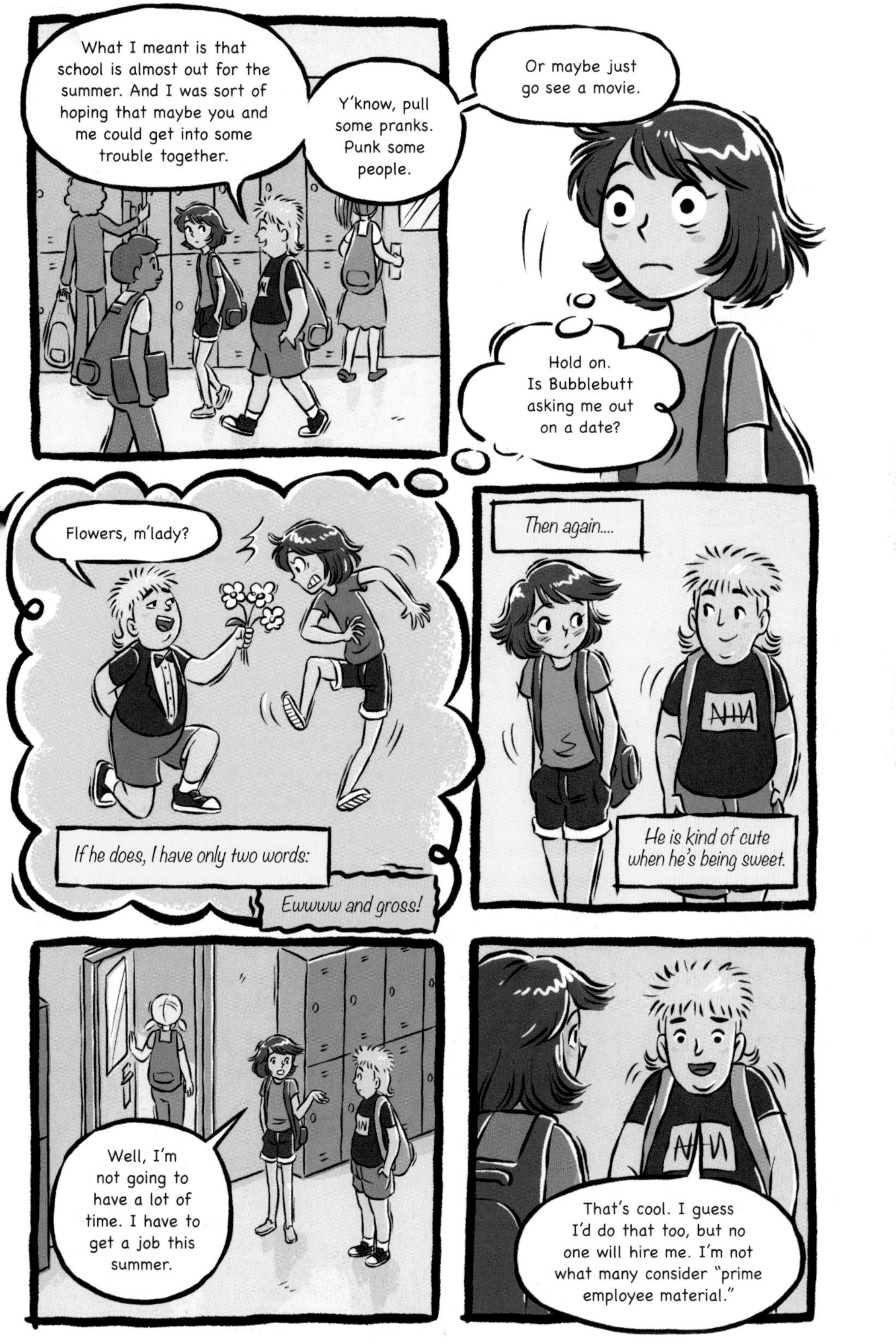
What I meant is that school is almost out for the summer. And I was sort of hoping that maybe you and me could get into some trouble together.
Y'know, pull some pranks. Punk some people.
Or maybe just go see a movie.
Hold on. Is Bubblebutt asking me out on a date?
Flowers, m'lady?
If he does, I have only two words:
Ewwww and gross!
Then again....
He is kind of cute when he's being sweet.
Well, I'm not going to have a lot of time. I have to get a job this summer.
That's cool. I guess I'd do that too, but no one will hire me. I'm not what many consider "prime employee material."

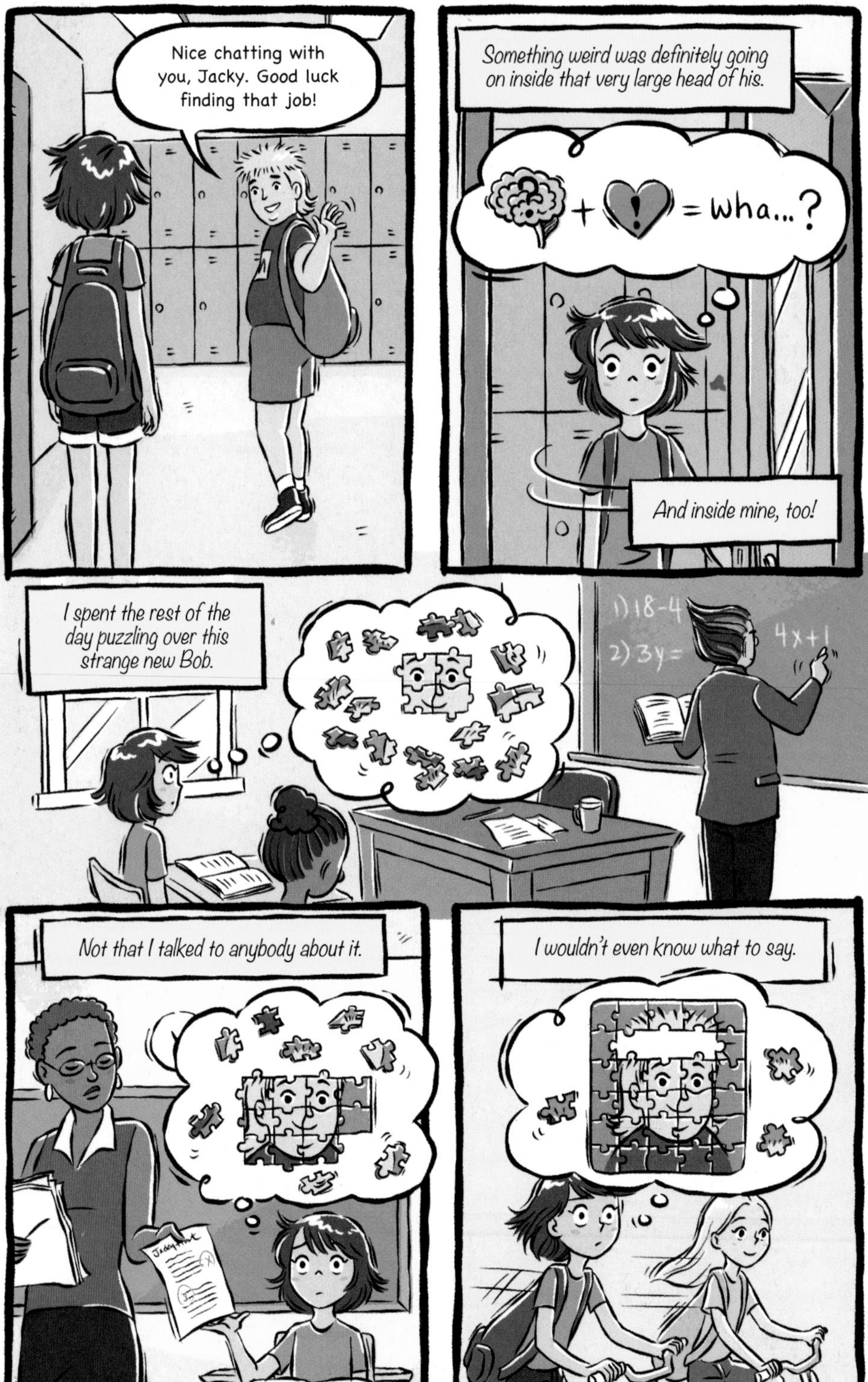
Nice chatting with you, Jacky. Good luck finding that job!
Something weird was definitely going on inside that very large head of his.
= wha...?
And inside mine, too!
I spent the rest of the day puzzling over this strange new Bob.
1) 18-4
2) 3y =
4x+1
Not that I talked to anybody about it.
I wouldn't even know what to say.

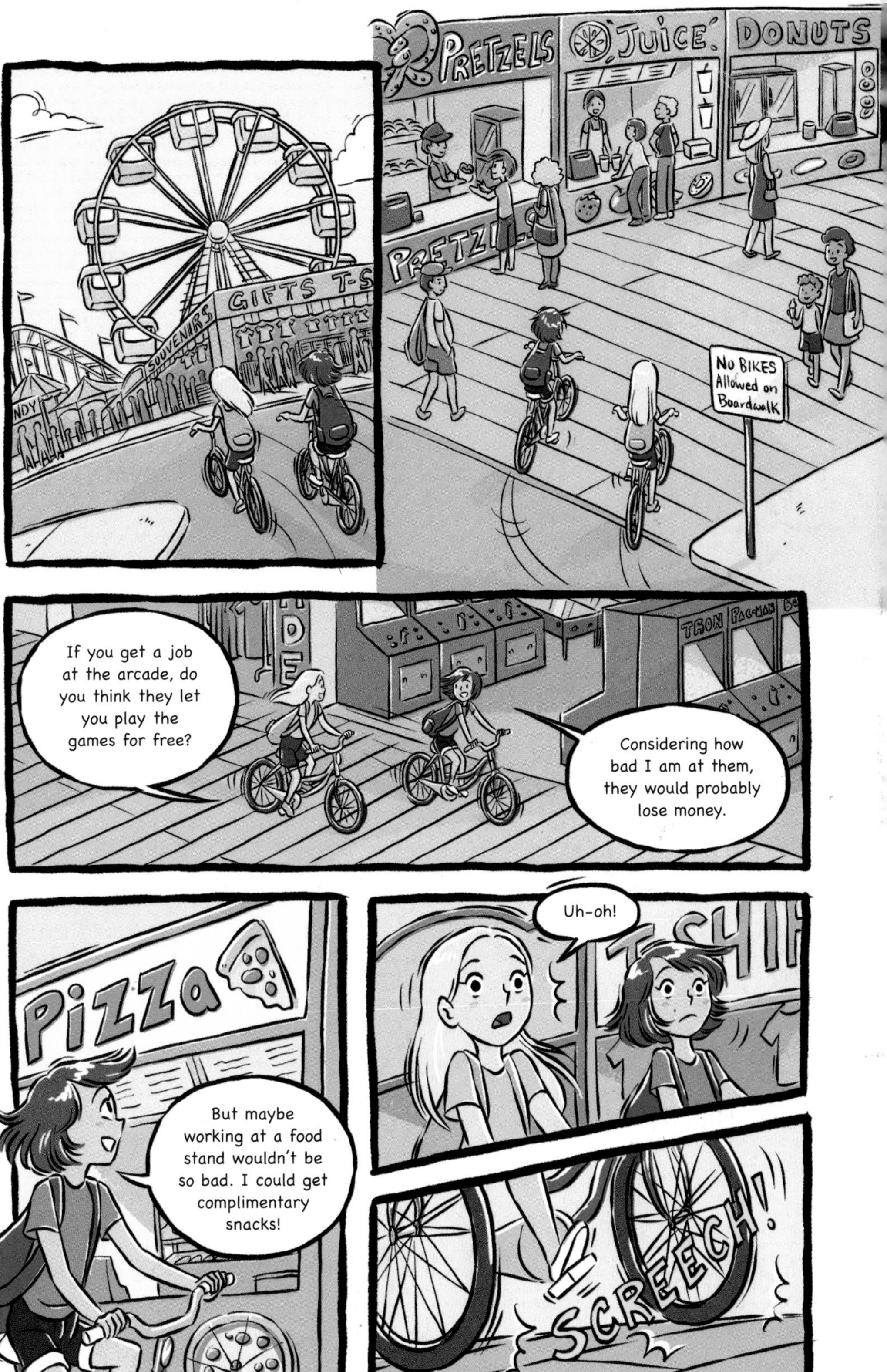
GIFTS T-S
SOUVENIRS
PRETZELS
JUICE
DONUTS
PRETZELS
No BIKES Allowed on Boardwalk
TRON
PAC-MAN
If you get a job at the arcade, do you think they let you play the games for free?
Considering how bad I am at them, they would probably lose money.
PIZZA
But maybe working at a food stand wouldn't be so bad. I could get complimentary snacks!
Uh-oh!
SCREECH!

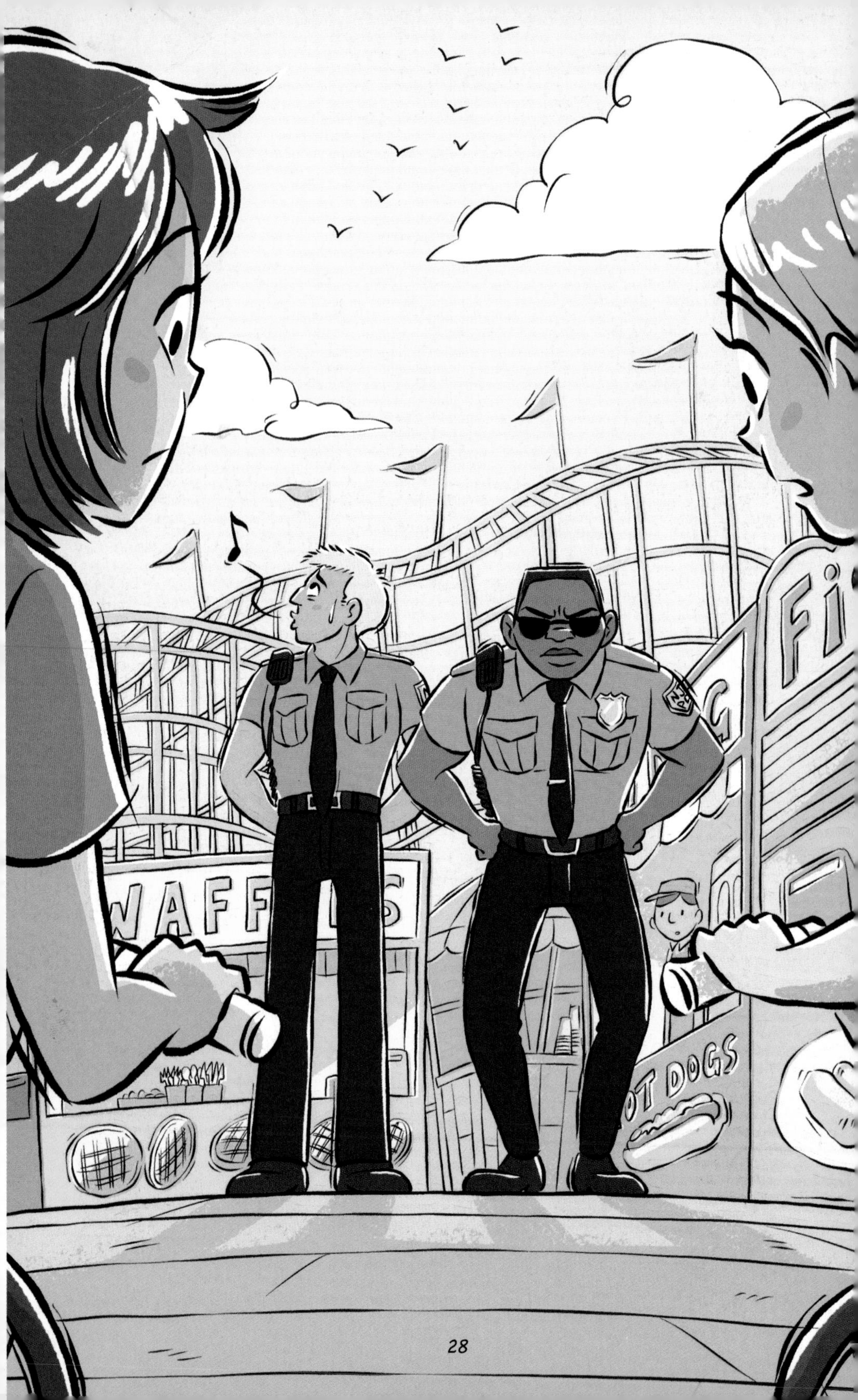
WAFF
OT DOGS

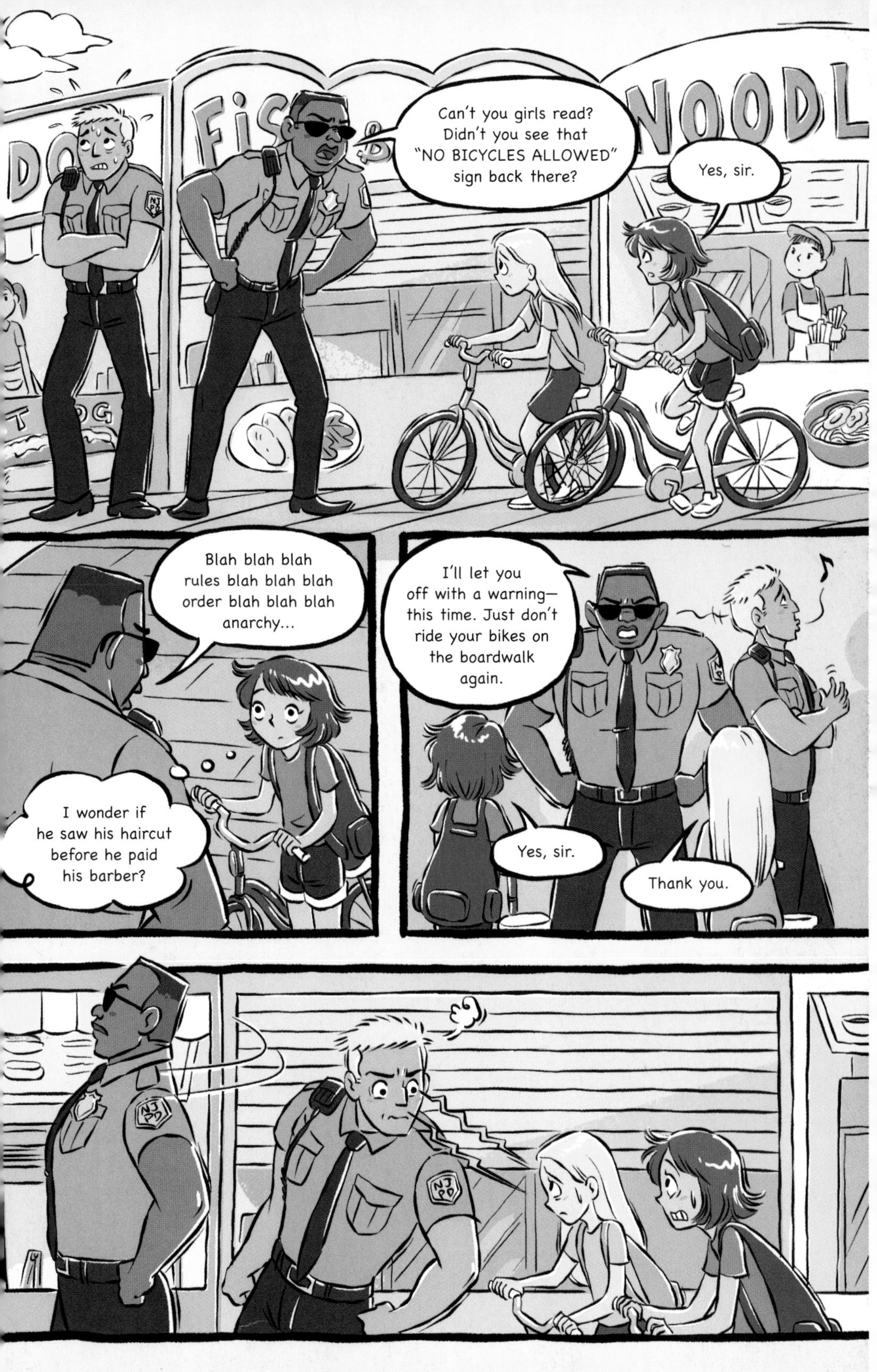
NOODL
Can't you girls read? Didn't you see that "NO BICYCLES ALLOWED" sign back there?
Yes, sir.
Blah blah blah rules blah blah blah order blah blah blah anarchy...
I wonder if he saw his haircut before he paid his barber?
I'll let you off with a warning— this time. Just don't ride your bikes on the boardwalk again.
Yes, sir.
Thank you.

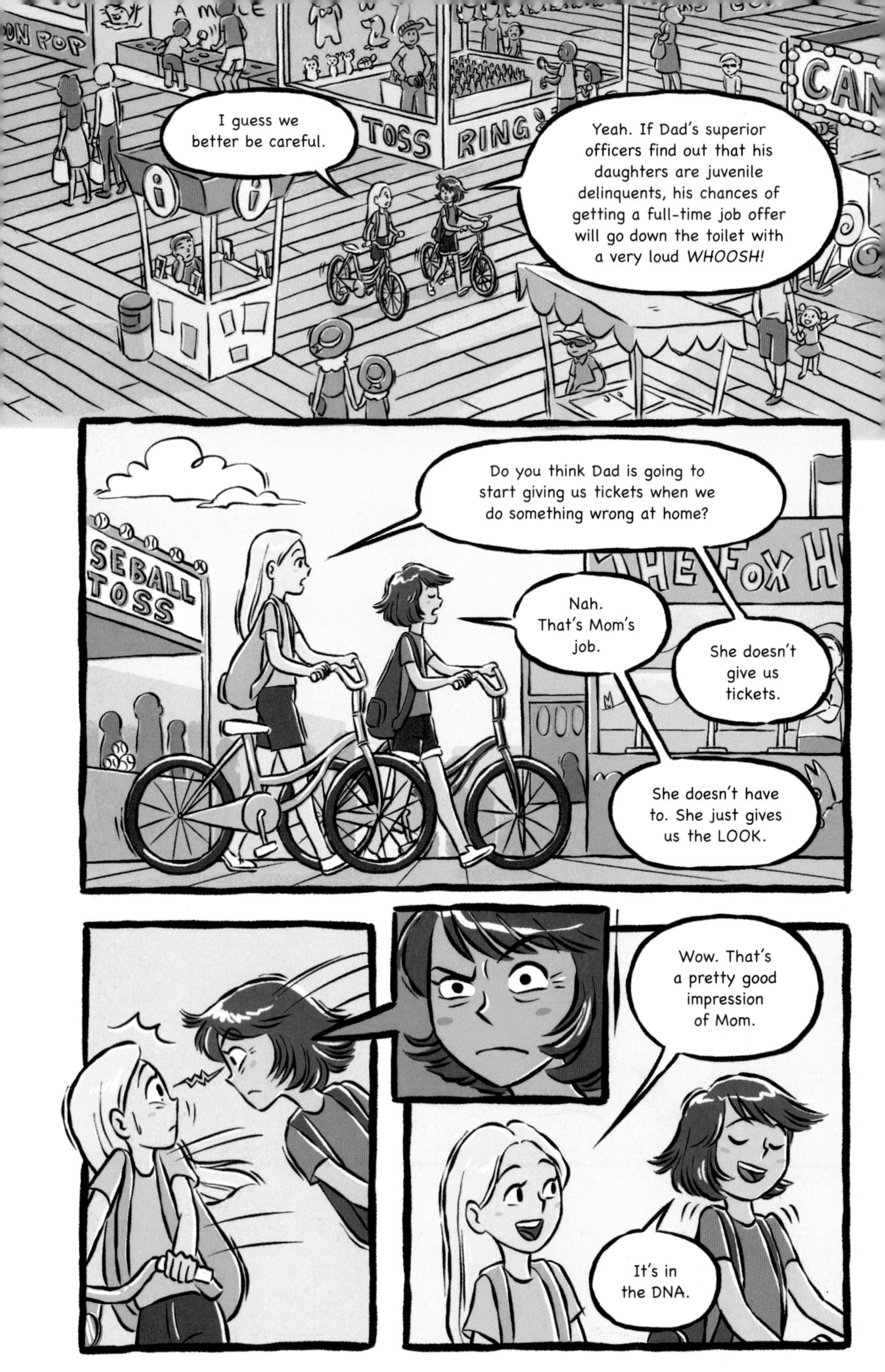
TOSS
RING
I guess we better be careful.
Yeah. If Dad's superior officers find out that his daughters are juvenile delinquents, his chances of getting a full-time job offer will go down the toilet with a very loud *WHOOSH!*
Do you think Dad is going to start giving us tickets when we do something wrong at home?
Nah. That's Mom's job.
She doesn't give us tickets.
She doesn't have to. She just gives us the LOOK.
Wow. That's a pretty good impression of Mom.
It's in the DNA.

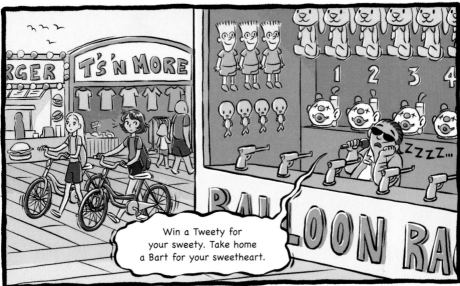

Win a Tweety for your sweety. Take home a Bart for your sweetheart.

Nothing says "I love you" like Winnie the Pooh.

Or something.

You coming? I need to get home. It's my turn to babysit Emma.

I'll be right behind you. I've got an idea.

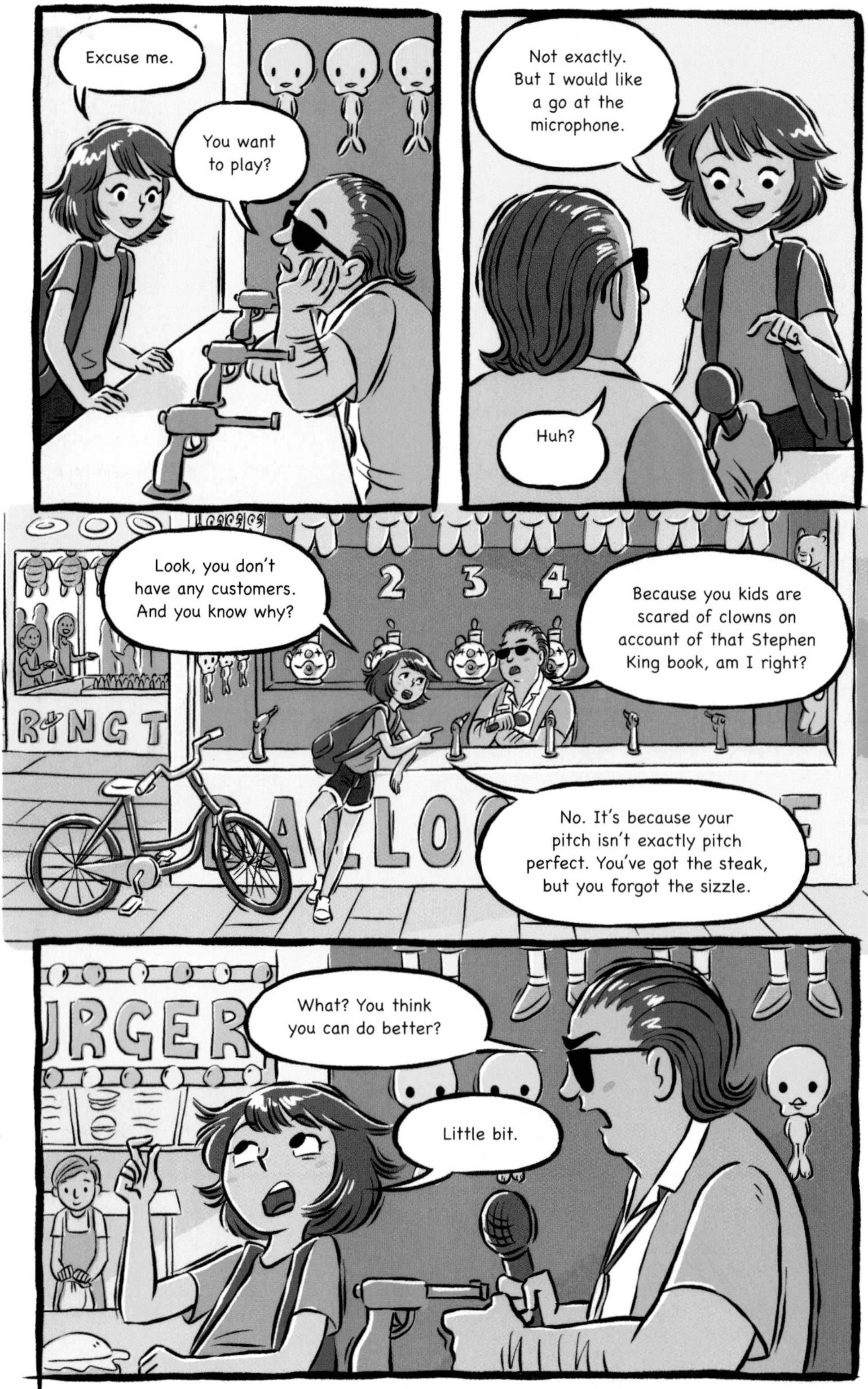
Excuse me.
You want to play?
Not exactly. But I would like a go at the microphone.
Huh?
RING T
Look, you don't have any customers. And you know why?
2 3 4
Because you kids are scared of clowns on account of that Stephen King book, am I right?
No. It's because your pitch isn't exactly pitch perfect. You've got the steak, but you forgot the sizzle.
URGER
What? You think you can do better?
Little bit.

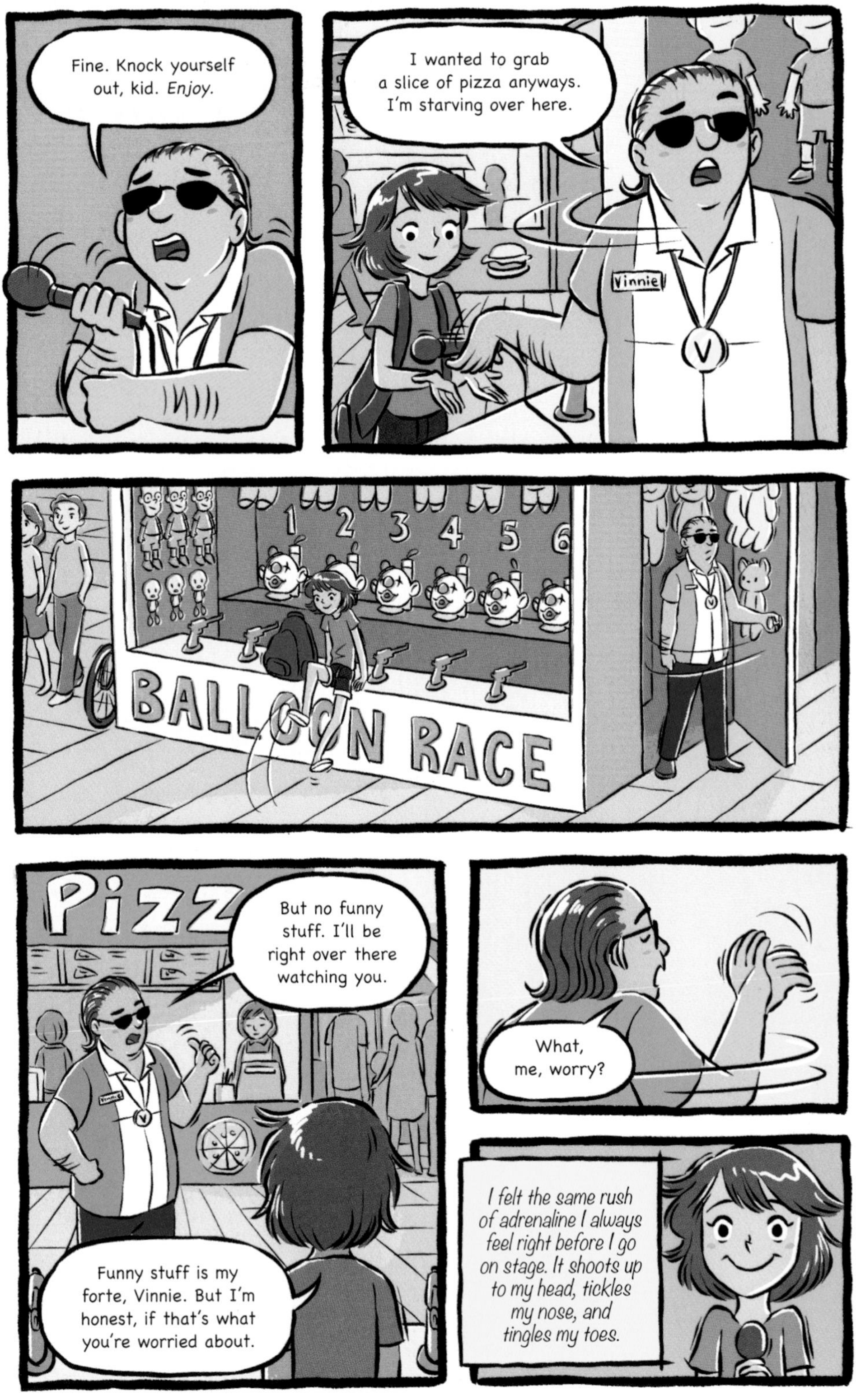

Fine. Knock yourself out, kid. *Enjoy.*
I wanted to grab a slice of pizza anyways. I'm starving over here.
Vinnie
BALLOON RACE
Pizz
But no funny stuff. I'll be right over there watching you.
Funny stuff is my forte, Vinnie. But I'm honest, if that's what you're worried about.
What, me, worry?
I felt the same rush of adrenaline I always feel right before I go on stage. It shoots up to my head, tickles my nose, and tingles my toes.

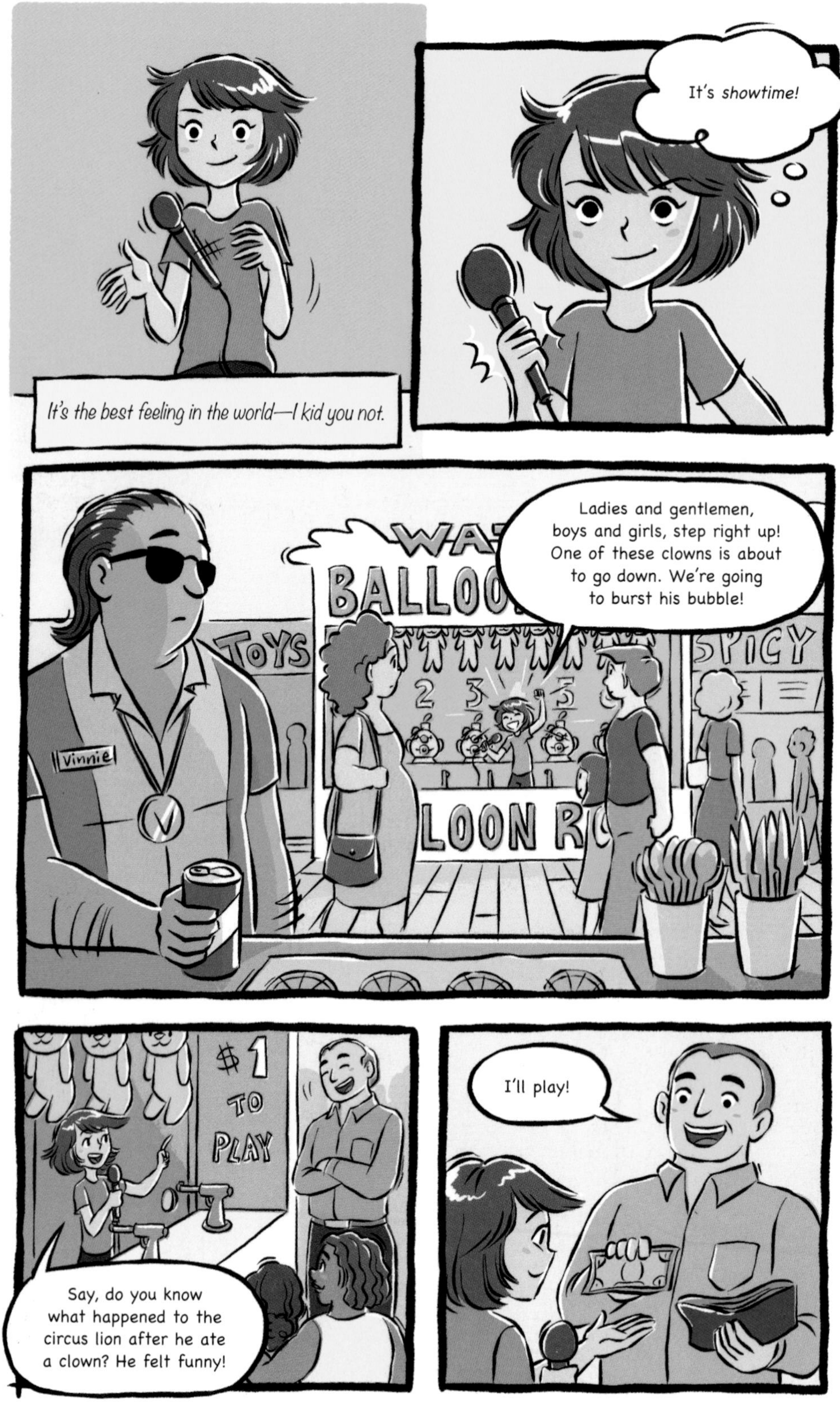
It's the best feeling in the world—I kid you not.
It's showtime!
Ladies and gentlemen, boys and girls, step right up! One of these clowns is about to go down. We're going to burst his bubble!
WA
BALLOO
TOYS
SPICY
LOON R
Vinnie
$1 TO PLAY
Say, do you know what happened to the circus lion after he ate a clown? He felt funny!
I'll play!

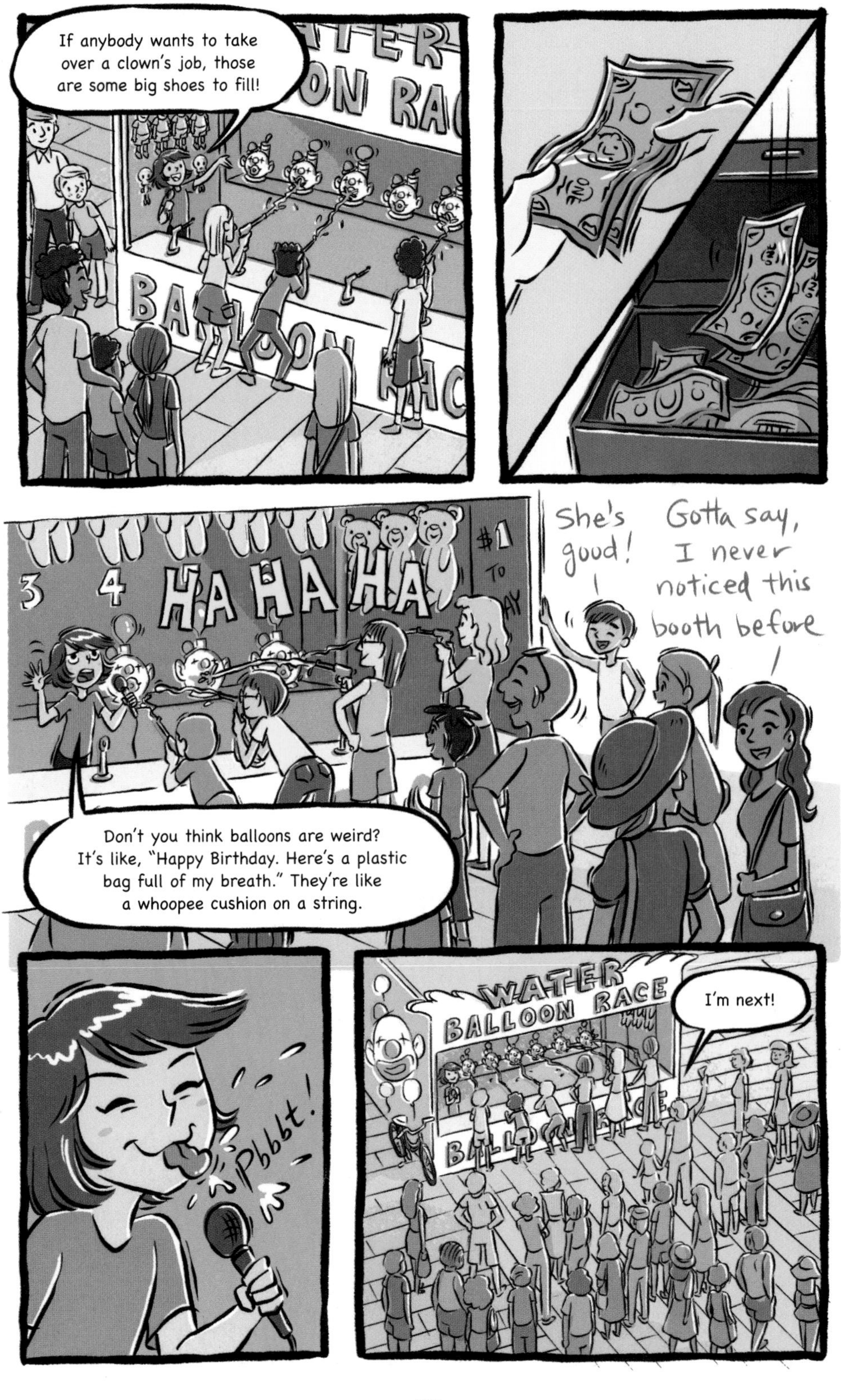
If anybody wants to take over a clown's job, those are some big shoes to fill!
WATER BALLOON RACE
BALLOON RACE
HAHAHA
$1
She's good!
Gotta say, I never noticed this booth before
Don't you think balloons are weird? It's like, "Happy Birthday. Here's a plastic bag full of my breath." They're like a whoopee cushion on a string.
Phbbt!
WATER BALLOON RACE
I'm next!

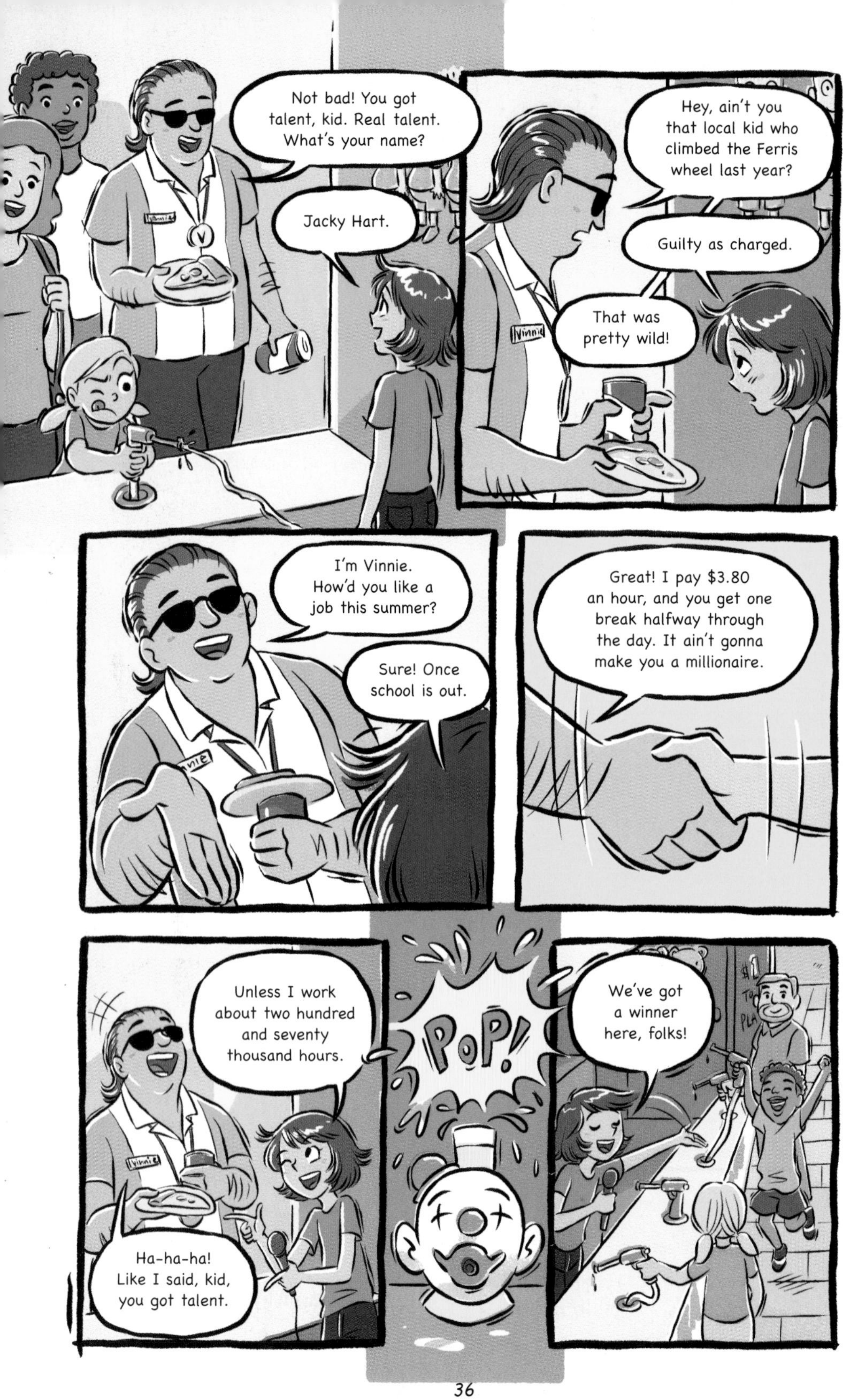
Not bad! You got talent, kid. Real talent. What's your name?
Jacky Hart.
Vinnie
Hey, ain't you that local kid who climbed the Ferris wheel last year?
Guilty as charged.
That was pretty wild!
Vinnie
I'm Vinnie. How'd you like a job this summer?
Sure! Once school is out.
Great! I pay $3.80 an hour, and you get one break halfway through the day. It ain't gonna make you a millionaire.
Unless I work about two hundred and seventy thousand hours.
Ha-ha-ha! Like I said, kid, you got talent.
Vinnie
POP!
We've got a winner here, folks!

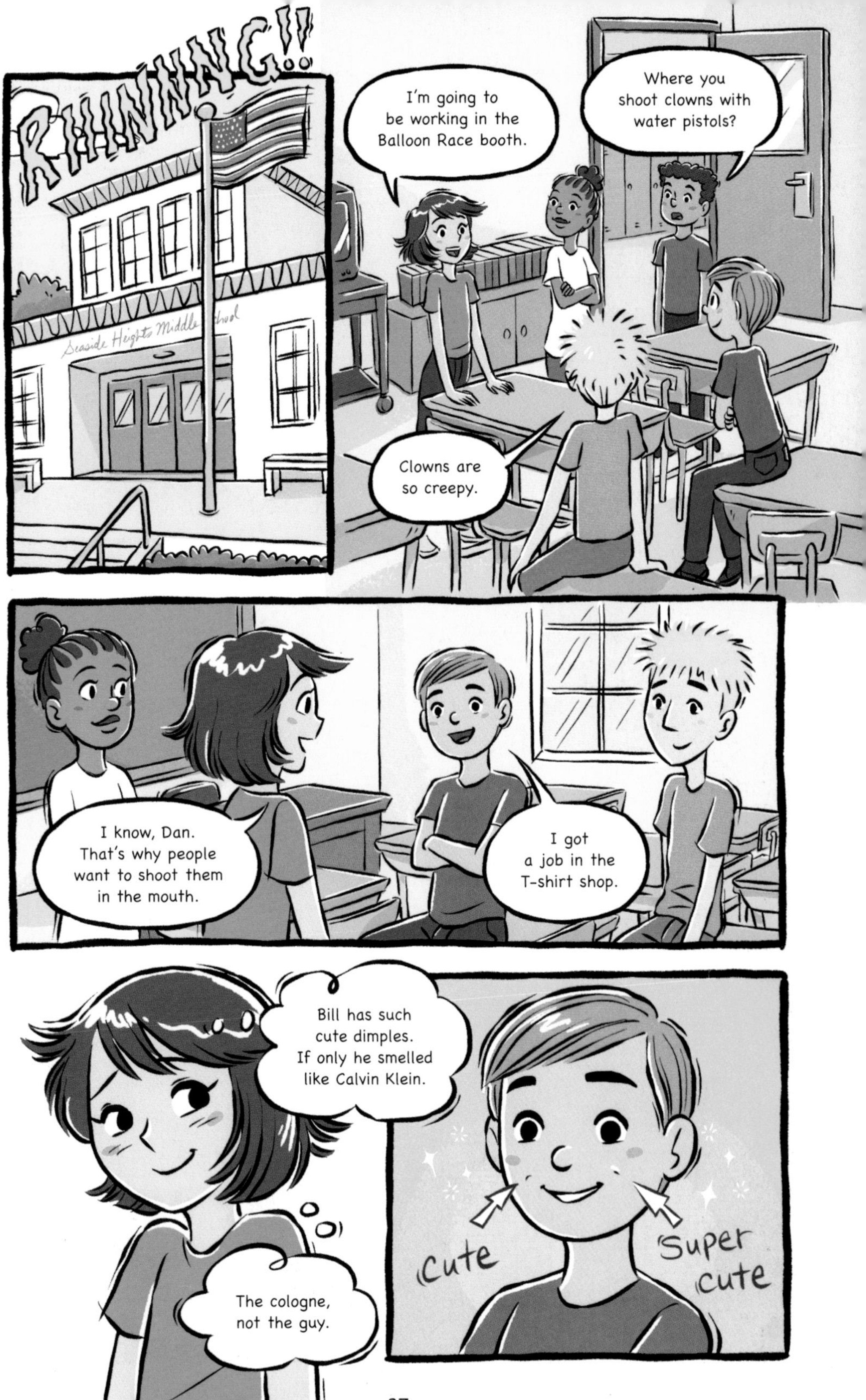
RHHNNNG!!
Seaside Heights Middle School
I'm going to be working in the Balloon Race booth.
Where you shoot clowns with water pistols?
Clowns are so creepy.
I know, Dan. That's why people want to shoot them in the mouth.
I got a job in the T-shirt shop.
Bill has such cute dimples. If only he smelled like Calvin Klein.
The cologne, not the guy.
Cute
Super cute

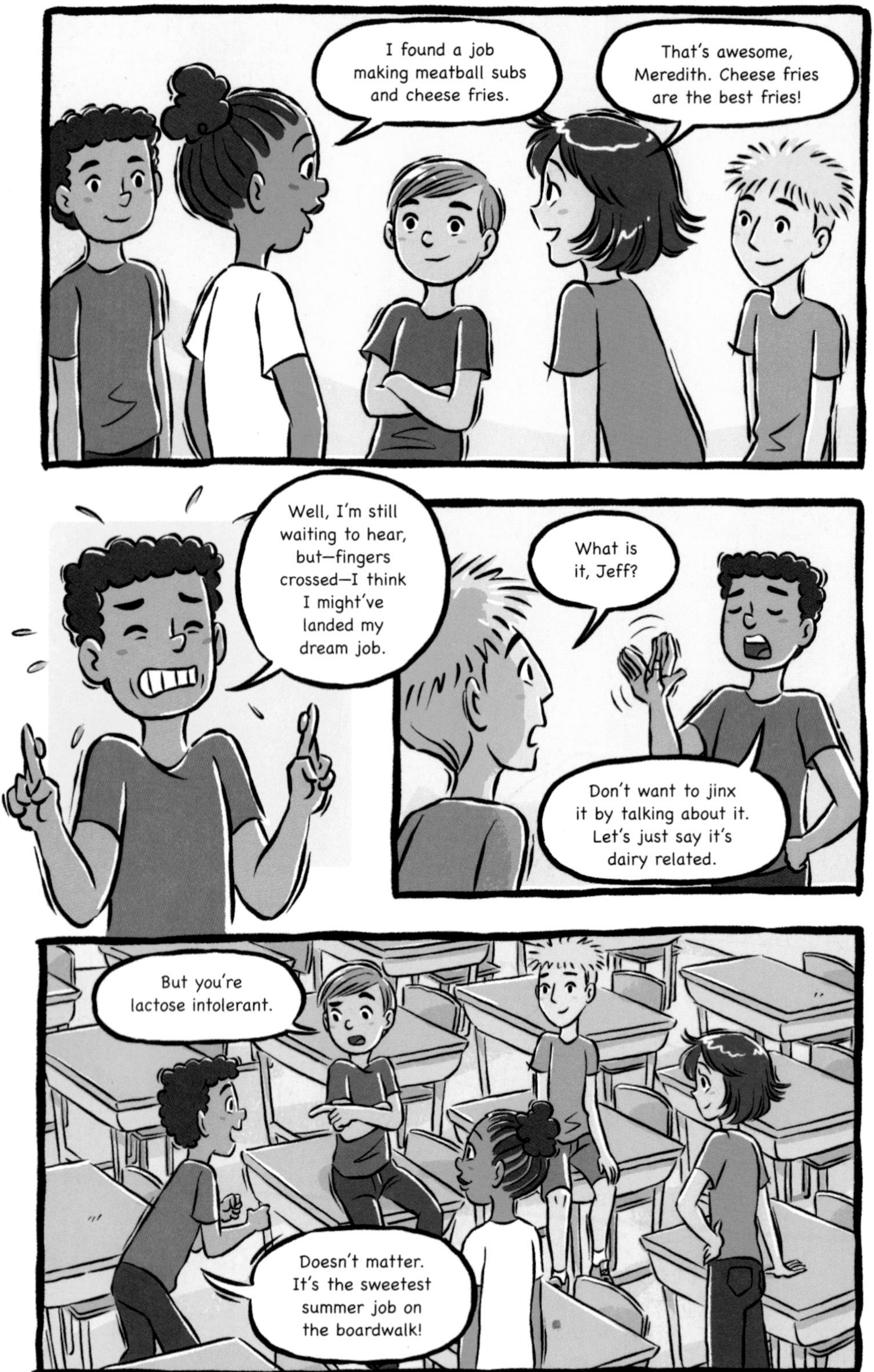
I found a job making meatball subs and cheese fries.
That's awesome, Meredith. Cheese fries are the best fries!
Well, I'm still waiting to hear, but—fingers crossed—I think I might've landed my dream job.
What is it, Jeff?
Don't want to jinx it by talking about it. Let's just say it's dairy related.
But you're lactose intolerant.
Doesn't matter. It's the sweetest summer job on the boardwalk!

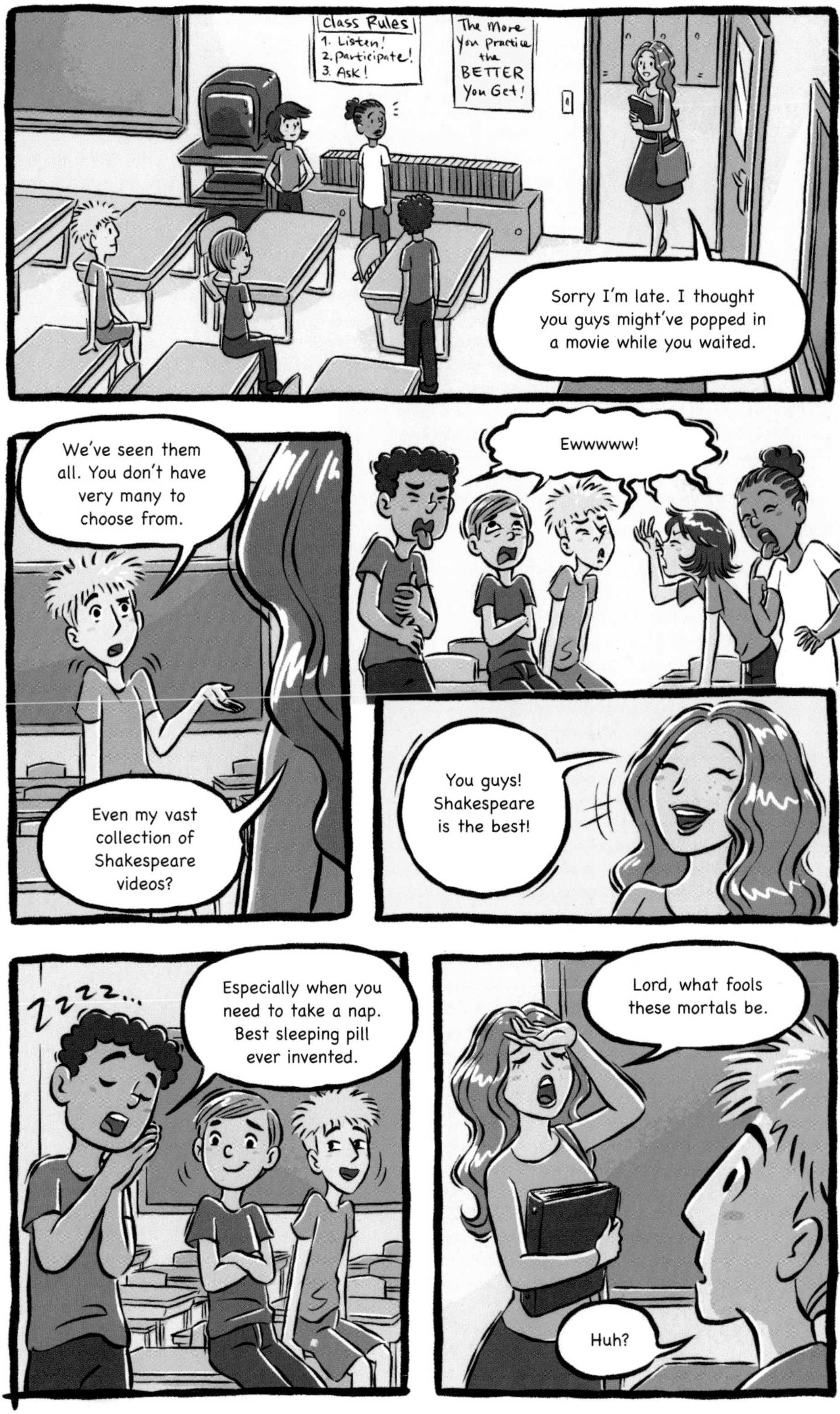
Class Rules
1. Listen!
2. Participate!
3. Ask!
The More You Practice the BETTER You Get!
Sorry I'm late. I thought you guys might've popped in a movie while you waited.
We've seen them all. You don't have very many to choose from.
Even my vast collection of Shakespeare videos?
Ewwwww!
You guys! Shakespeare is the best!
ZZZZ...
Especially when you need to take a nap. Best sleeping pill ever invented.
Lord, what fools these mortals be.
Huh?

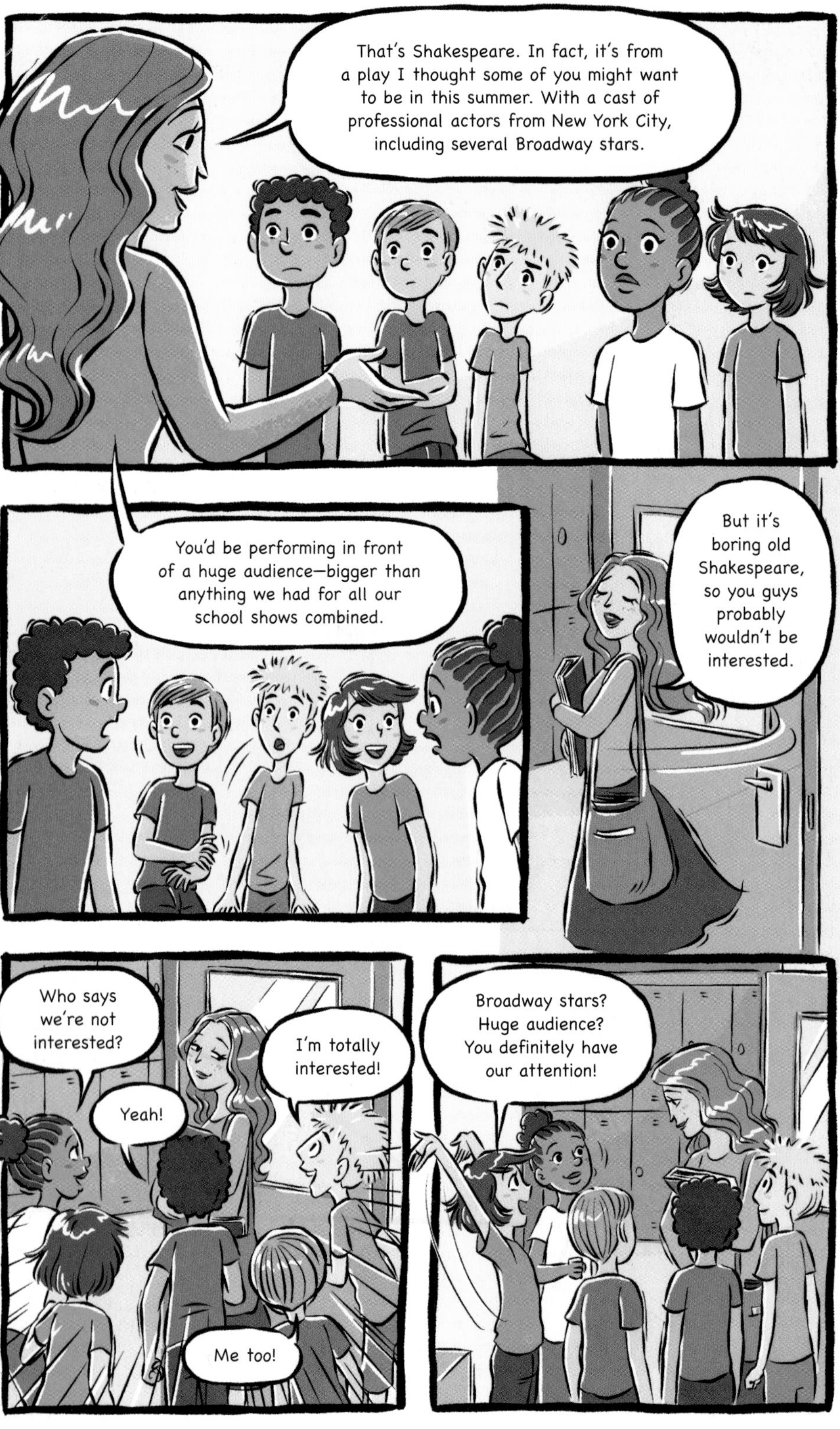
That's Shakespeare. In fact, it's from a play I thought some of you might want to be in this summer. With a cast of professional actors from New York City, including several Broadway stars.
You'd be performing in front of a huge audience—bigger than anything we had for all our school shows combined.
But it's boring old Shakespeare, so you guys probably wouldn't be interested.
Who says we're not interested?
Yeah!
I'm totally interested!
Me too!
Broadway stars? Huge audience? You definitely have our attention!

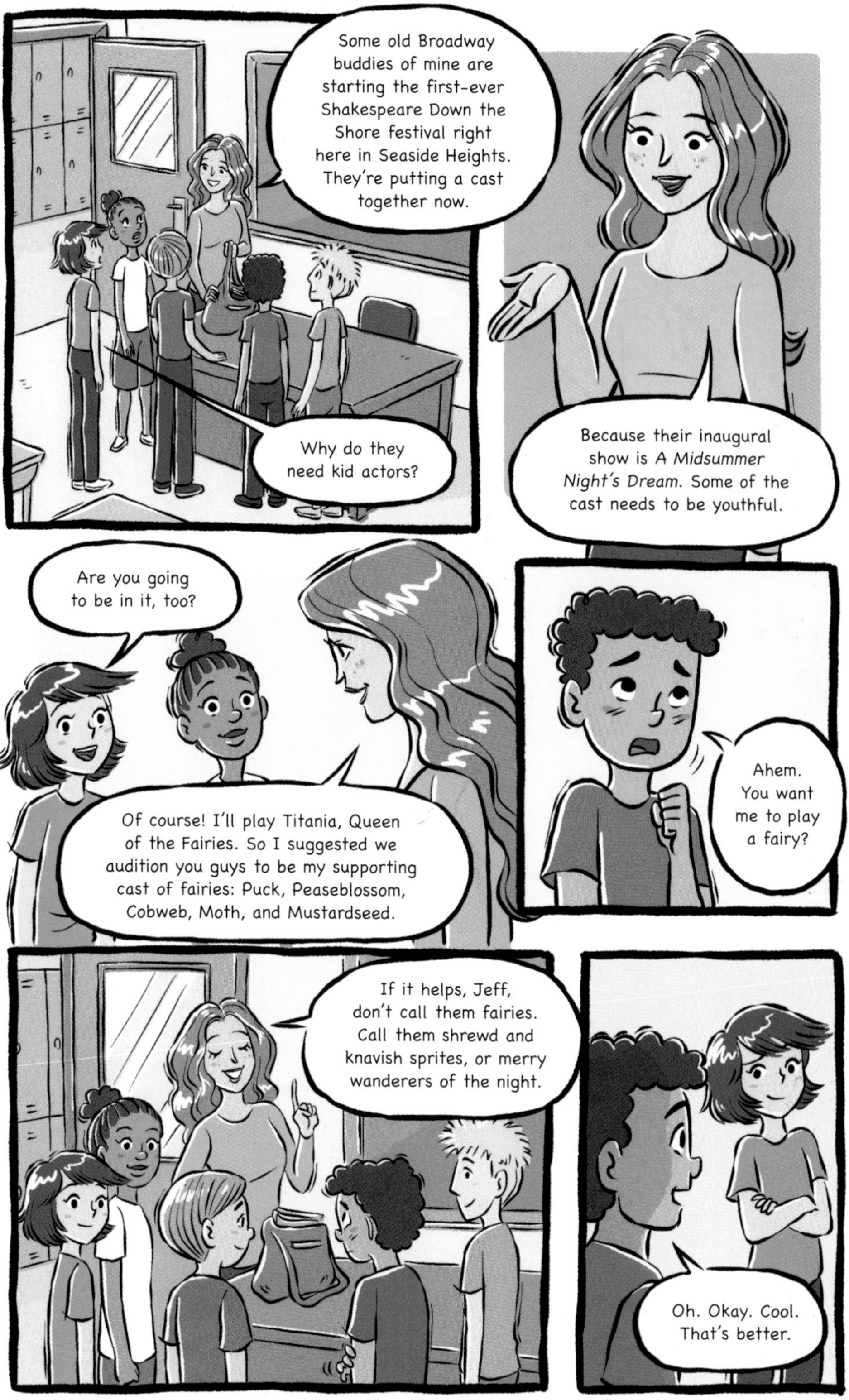
Some old Broadway buddies of mine are starting the first-ever Shakespeare Down the Shore festival right here in Seaside Heights. They're putting a cast together now.
Why do they need kid actors?
Because their inaugural show is *A Midsummer Night's Dream*. Some of the cast needs to be youthful.
Are you going to be in it, too?
Of course! I'll play Titania, Queen of the Fairies. So I suggested we audition you guys to be my supporting cast of fairies: Puck, Peaseblossom, Cobweb, Moth, and Mustardseed.
Ahem. You want me to play a fairy?
If it helps, Jeff, don't call them fairies. Call them shrewd and knavish sprites, or merry wanderers of the night.
Oh. Okay. Cool. That's better.

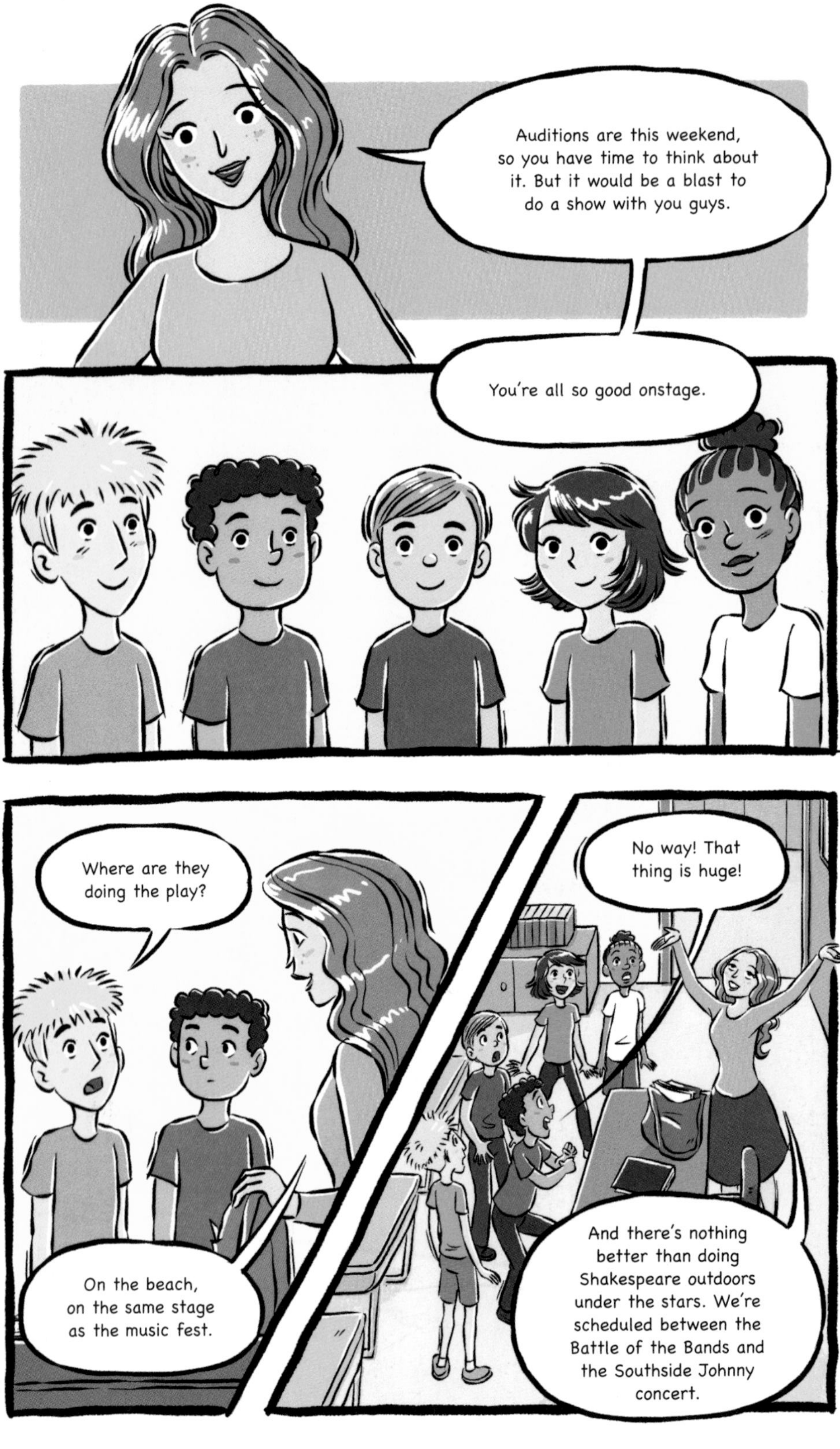
Auditions are this weekend, so you have time to think about it. But it would be a blast to do a show with you guys.
You're all so good onstage.
Where are they doing the play?
On the beach, on the same stage as the music fest.
No way! That thing is huge!
And there's nothing better than doing Shakespeare outdoors under the stars. We're scheduled between the Battle of the Bands and the Southside Johnny concert.

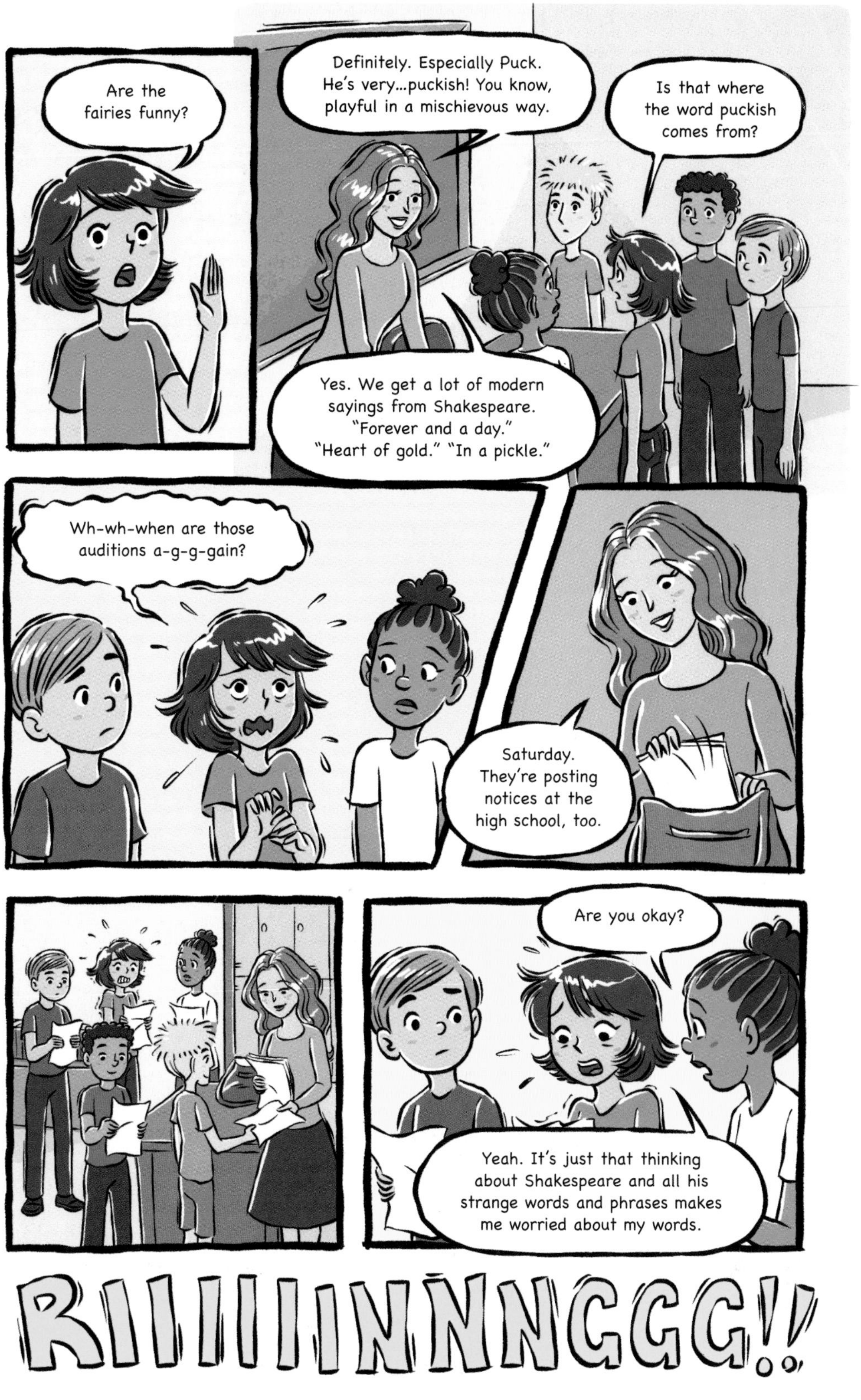
Are the fairies funny?
Definitely. Especially Puck. He's very…puckish! You know, playful in a mischievous way.
Is that where the word puckish comes from?
Yes. We get a lot of modern sayings from Shakespeare. "Forever and a day." "Heart of gold." "In a pickle."
Wh-wh-when are those auditions a-g-g-gain?
Saturday. They're posting notices at the high school, too.
Are you okay?
Yeah. It's just that thinking about Shakespeare and all his strange words and phrases makes me worried about my words.
RIIIIIINNNGGG!!

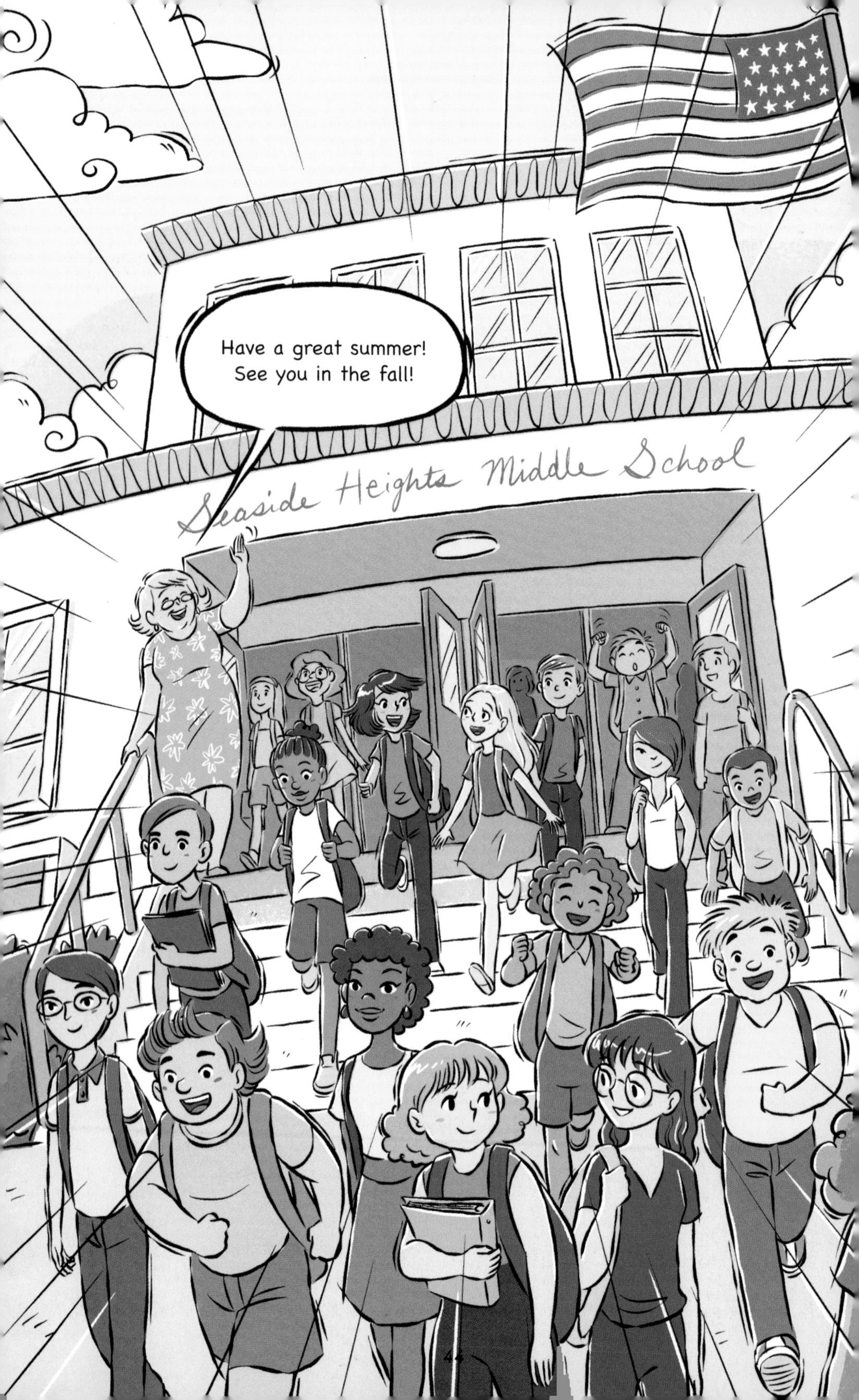
Have a great summer! See you in the fall!
Seaside Heights Middle School

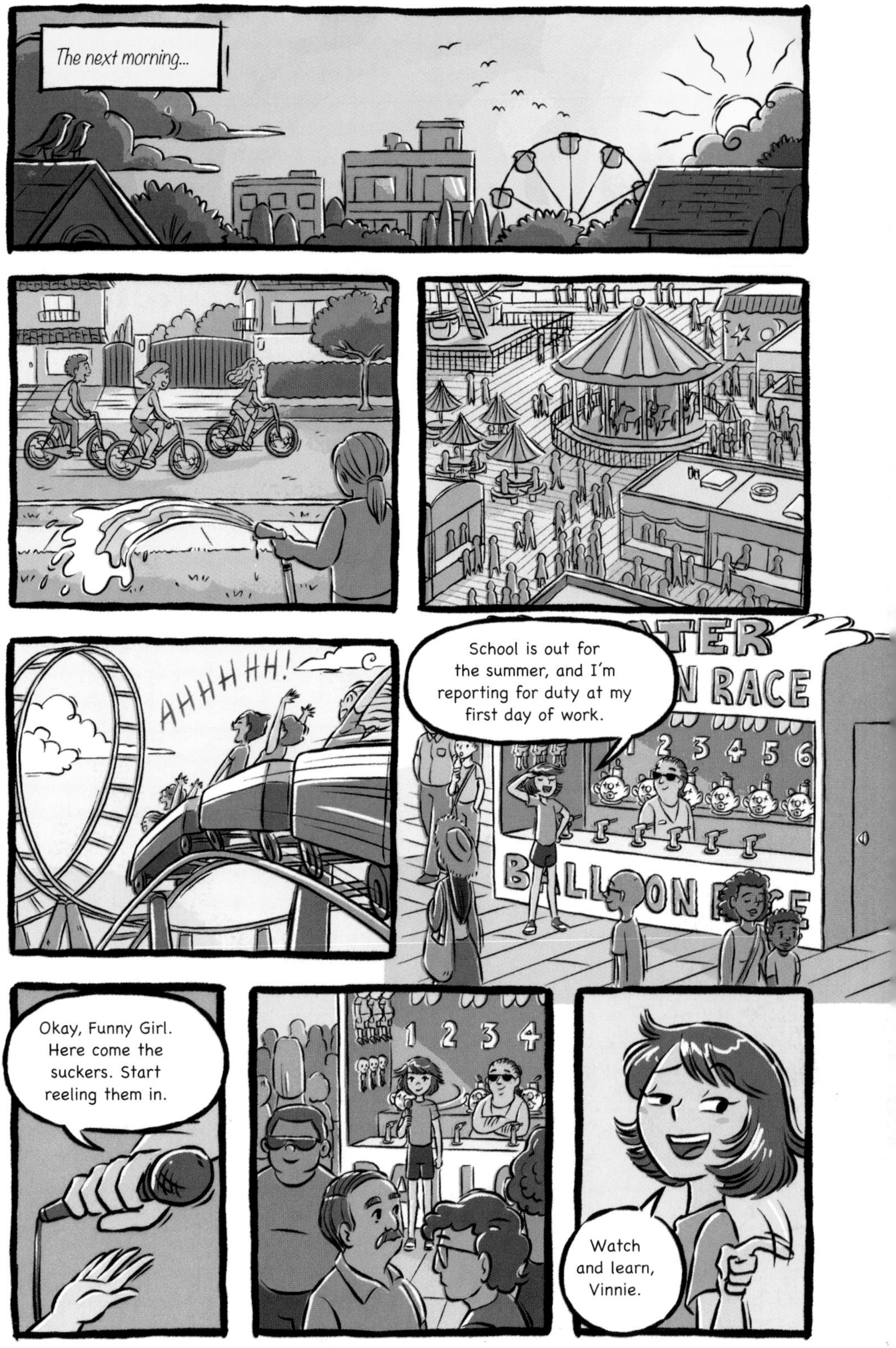
The next morning...
AHHHHHH!
School is out for the summer, and I'm reporting for duty at my first day of work.
BALLOON RACE
1 2 3 4 5 6
Okay, Funny Girl. Here come the suckers. Start reeling them in.
1 2 3 4
Watch and learn, Vinnie.

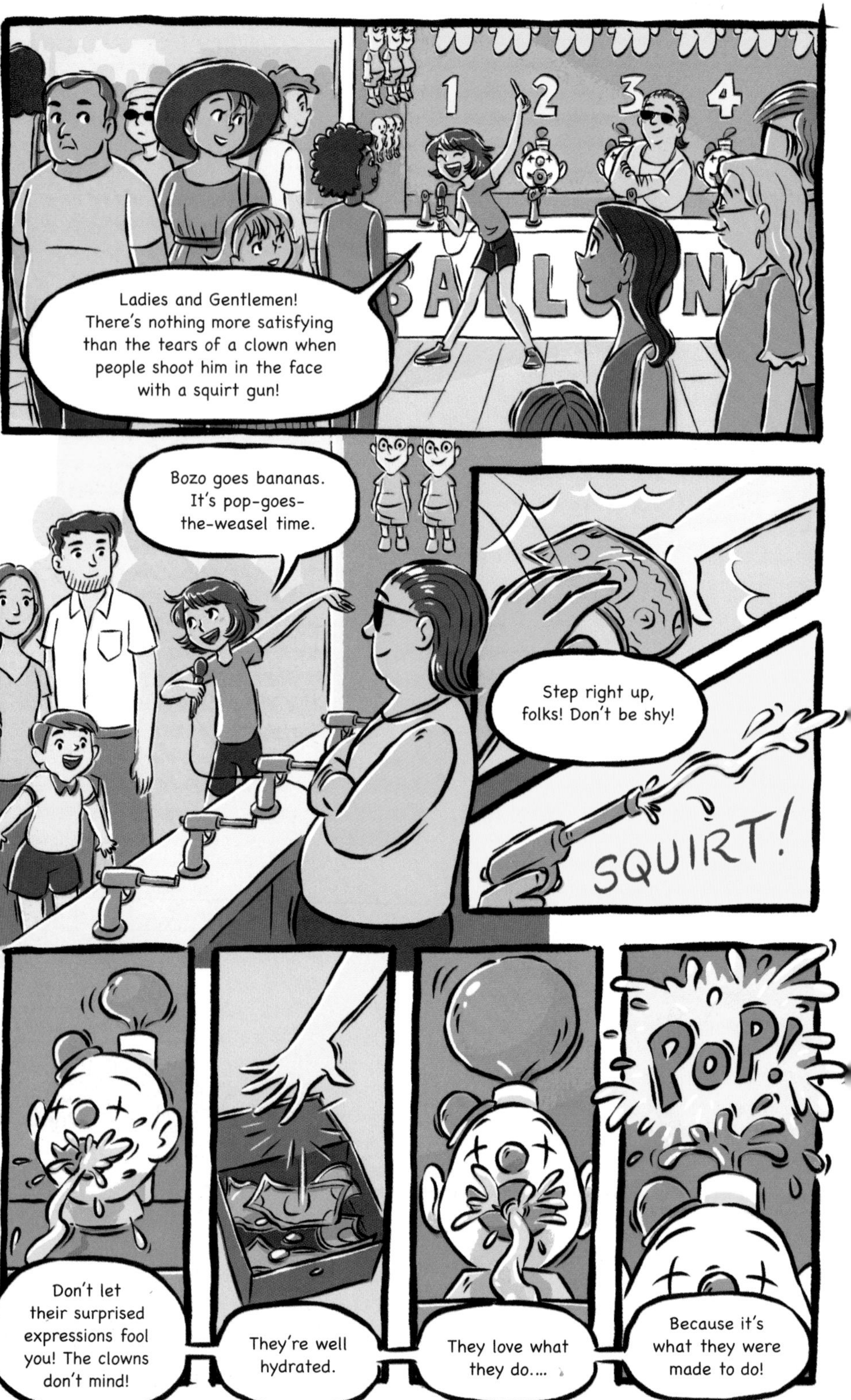

BALLOON
1
2
3
4
Ladies and Gentlemen! There's nothing more satisfying than the tears of a clown when people shoot him in the face with a squirt gun!
Bozo goes bananas. It's pop-goes-the-weasel time.
Step right up, folks! Don't be shy!
SQUIRT!
POP!
Don't let their surprised expressions fool you! The clowns don't mind!
They're well hydrated.
They love what they do....
Because it's what they were made to do!

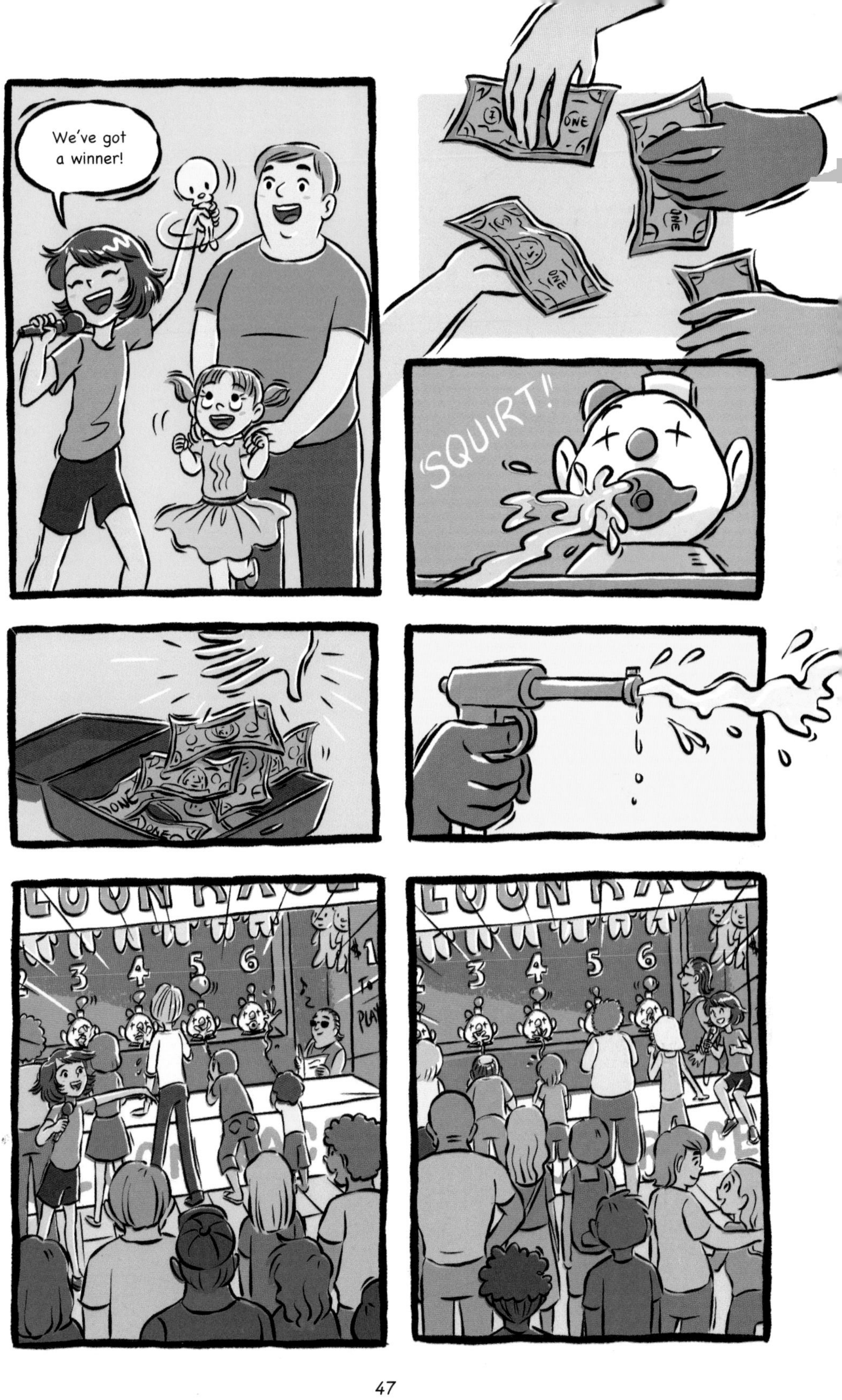
We've got a winner!
SQUIRT!

48

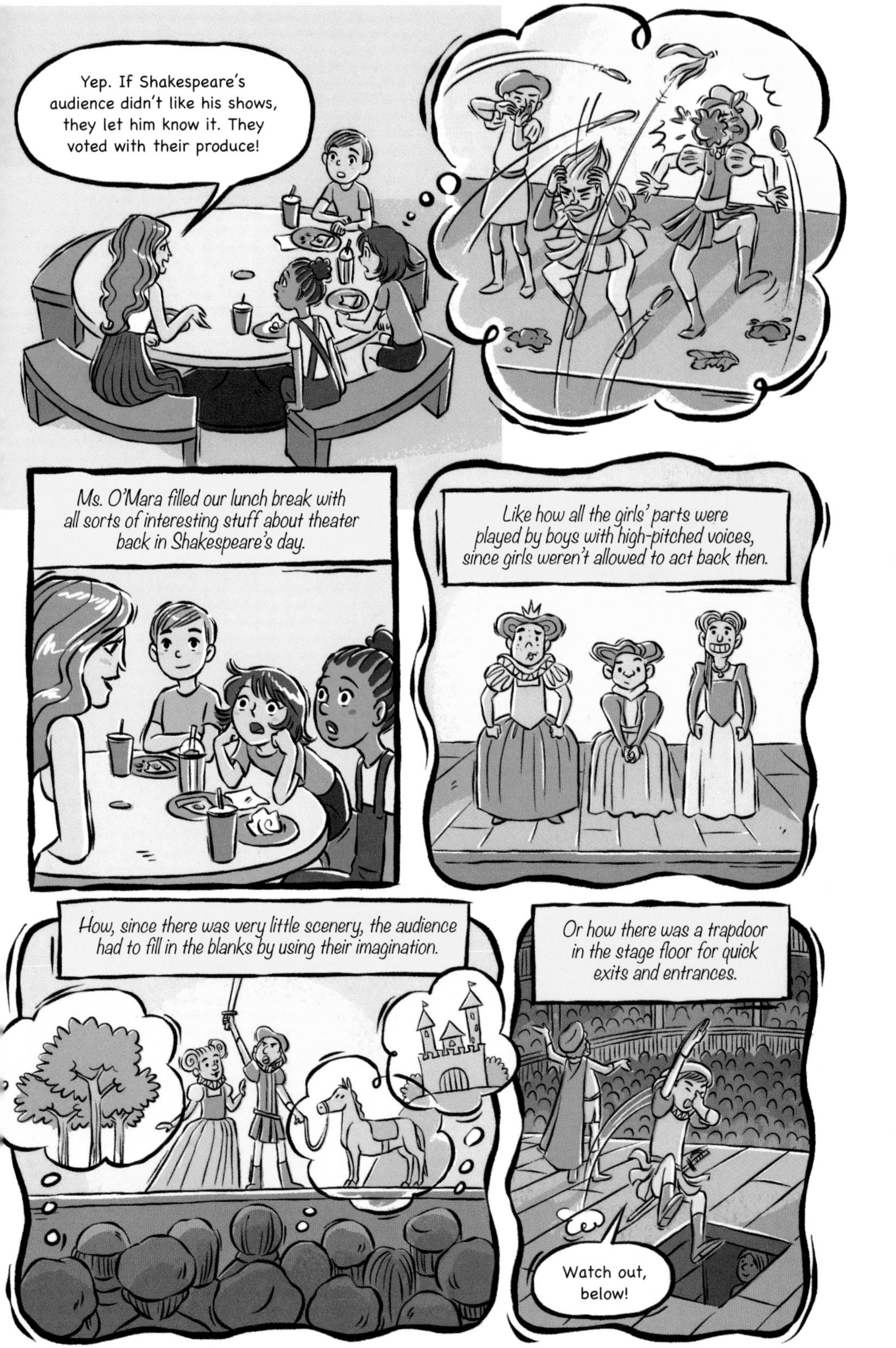

Yep. If Shakespeare's audience didn't like his shows, they let him know it. They voted with their produce!
Ms. O'Mara filled our lunch break with all sorts of interesting stuff about theater back in Shakespeare's day.
Like how all the girls' parts were played by boys with high-pitched voices, since girls weren't allowed to act back then.
How, since there was very little scenery, the audience had to fill in the blanks by using their imagination.
Or how there was a trapdoor in the stage floor for quick exits and entrances.
Watch out, below!

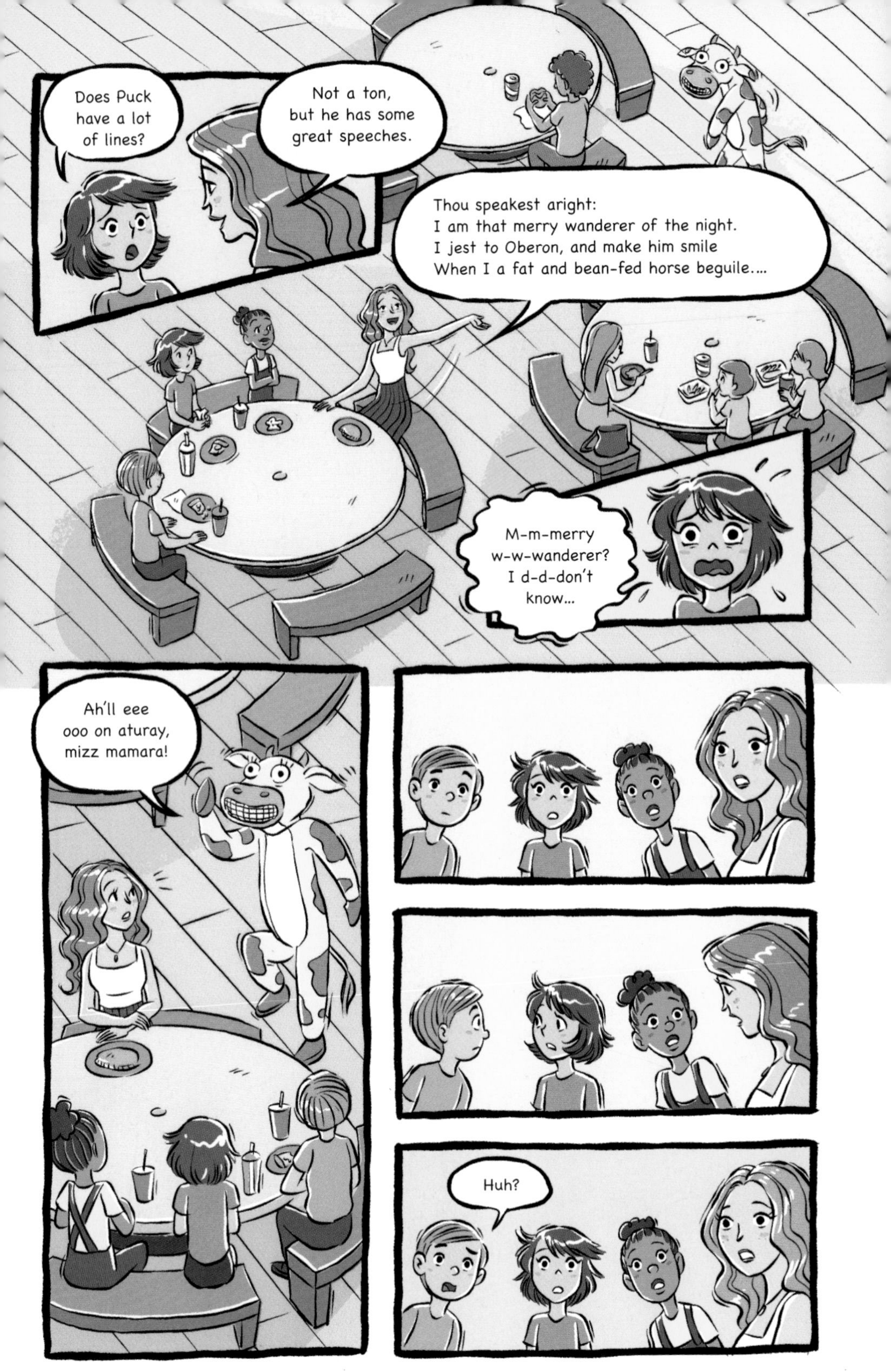
Does Puck have a lot of lines?
Not a ton, but he has some great speeches.
Thou speakest aright:
I am that merry wanderer of the night.
I jest to Oberon, and make him smile
When I a fat and bean-fed horse beguile....
M-m-merry w-w-wanderer? I d-d-don't know...
Ah'll eee ooo on aturay, mizz mamara!
Huh?

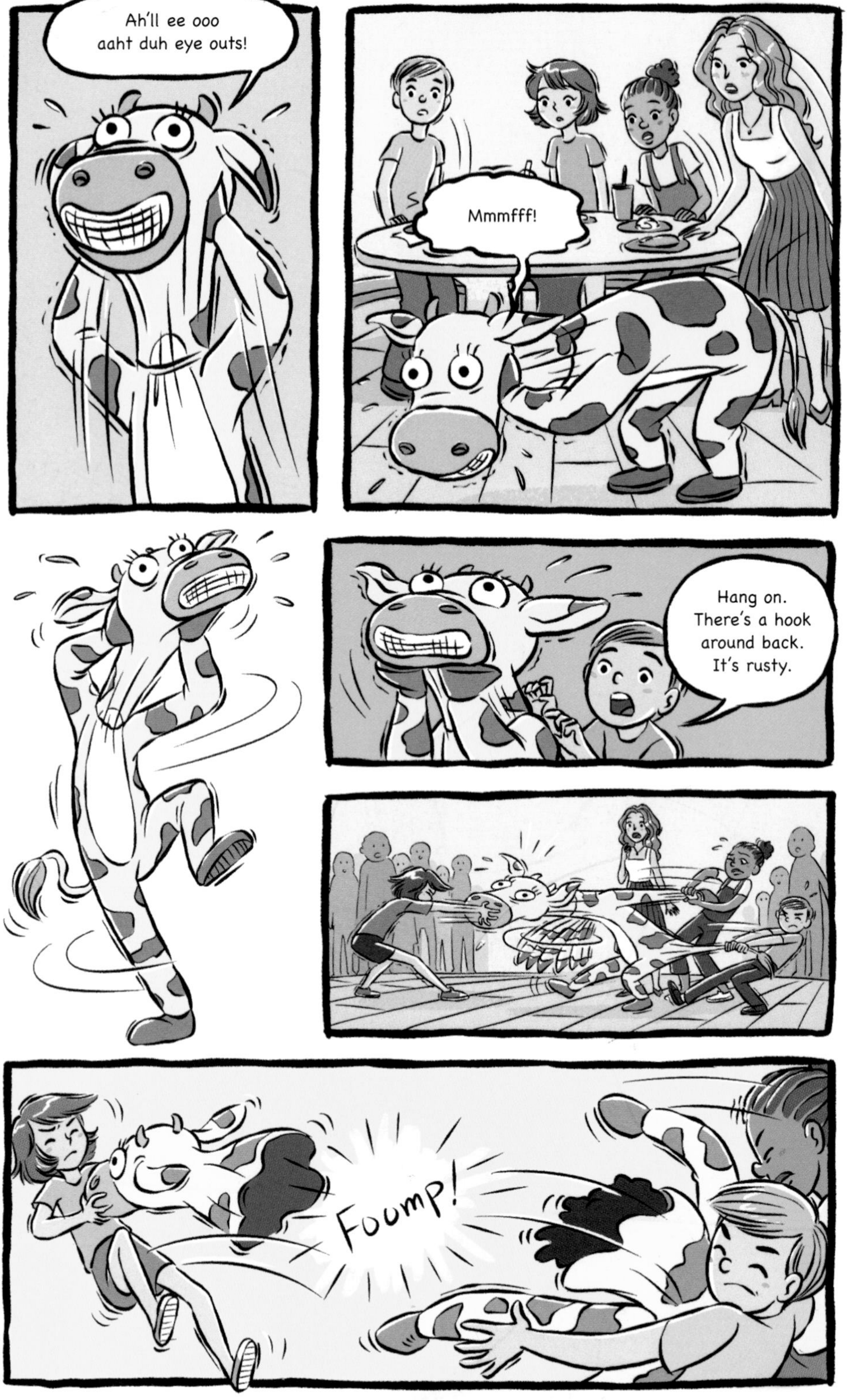
Ah'll ee ooo aaht duh eye outs!
Mmmfff!
Hang on. There's a hook around back. It's rusty.
Foomp!

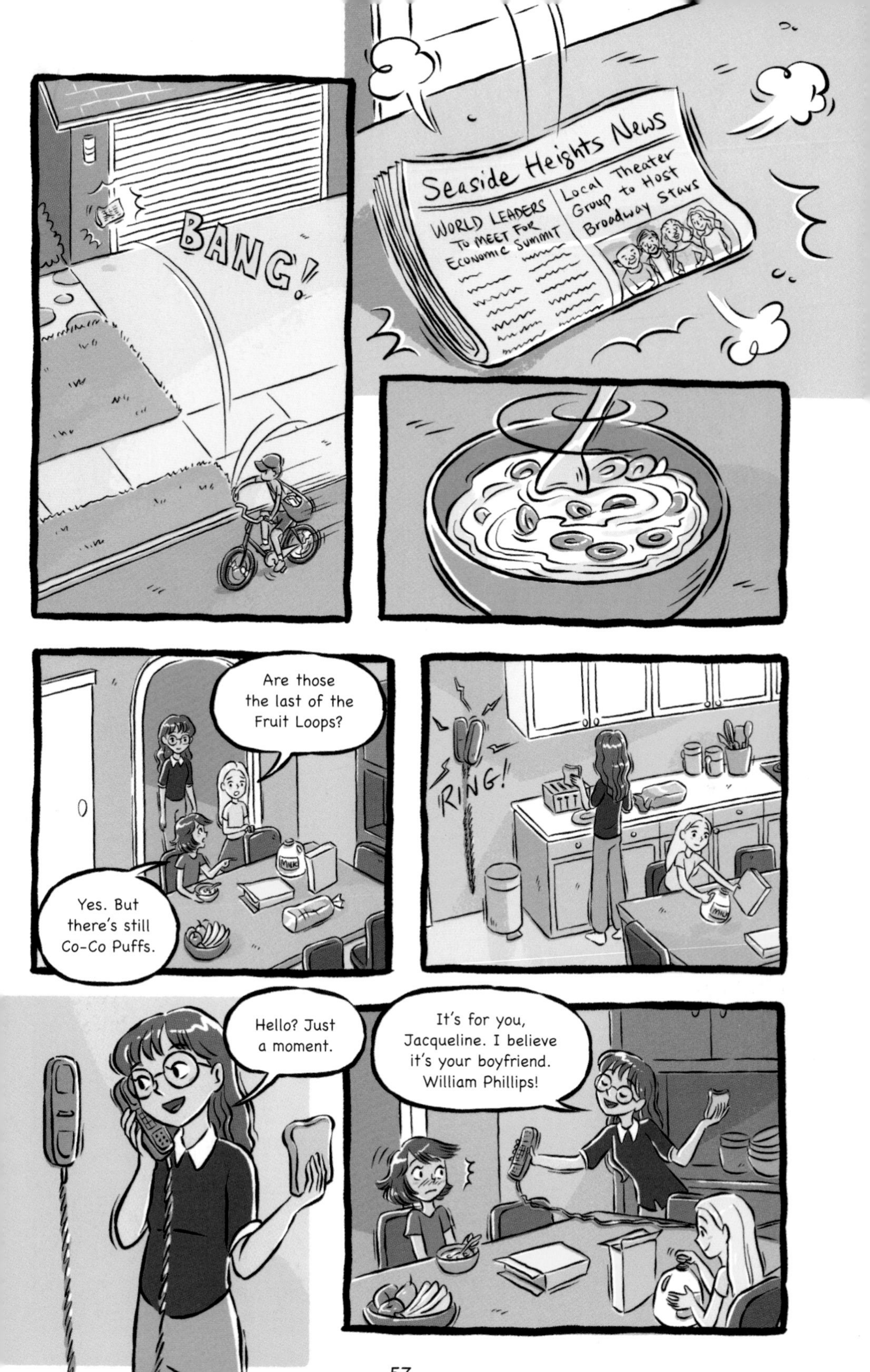
BANG!
Seaside Heights News
WORLD LEADERS TO MEET FOR ECONOMIC SUMMIT
Local Theater Group to Host Broadway Stars
Are those the last of the Fruit Loops?
Yes. But there's still Co-Co Puffs.
RING!
Hello? Just a moment.
It's for you, Jacqueline. I believe it's your boyfriend. William Phillips!

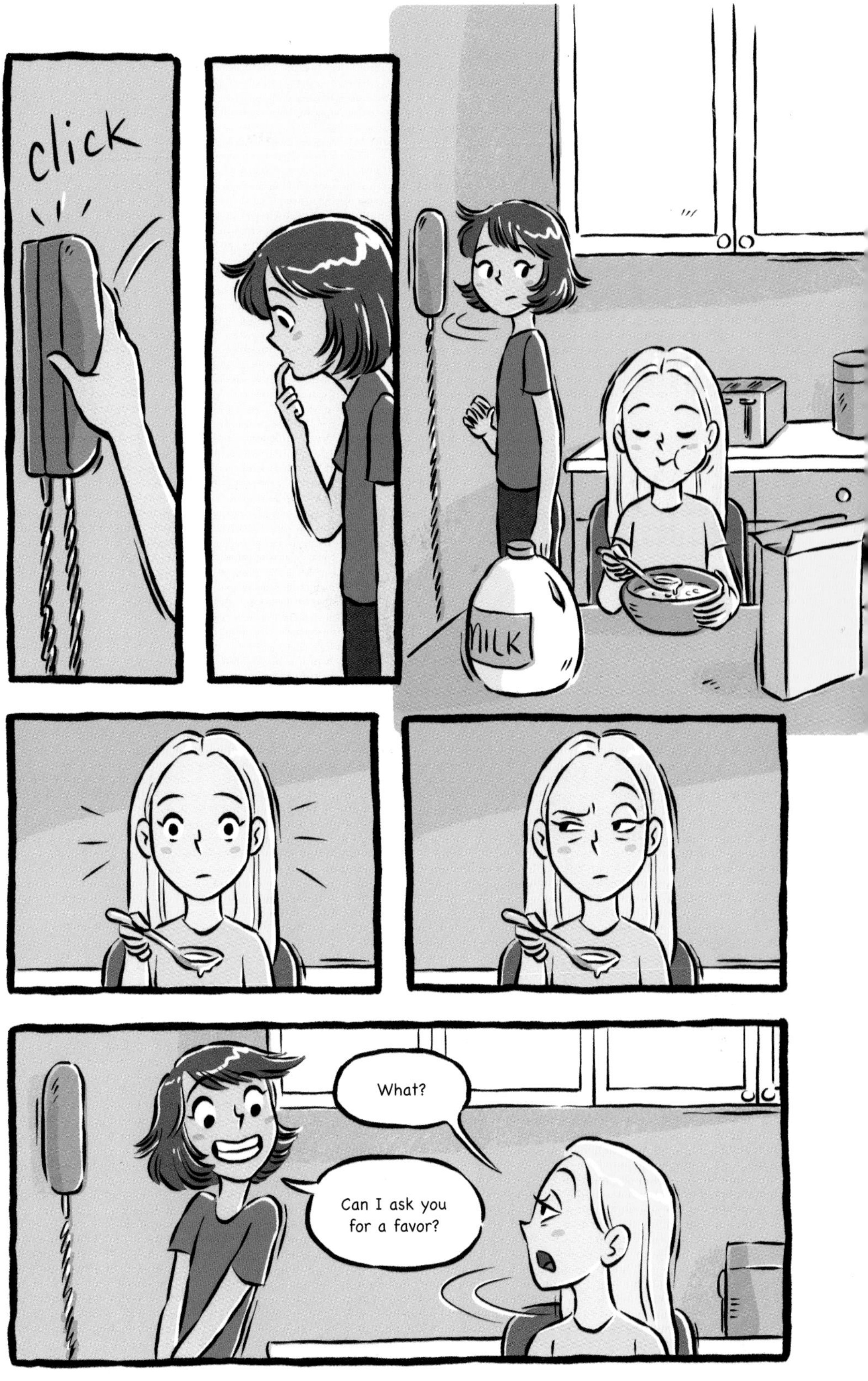
click
MILK
What?
Can I ask you for a favor?

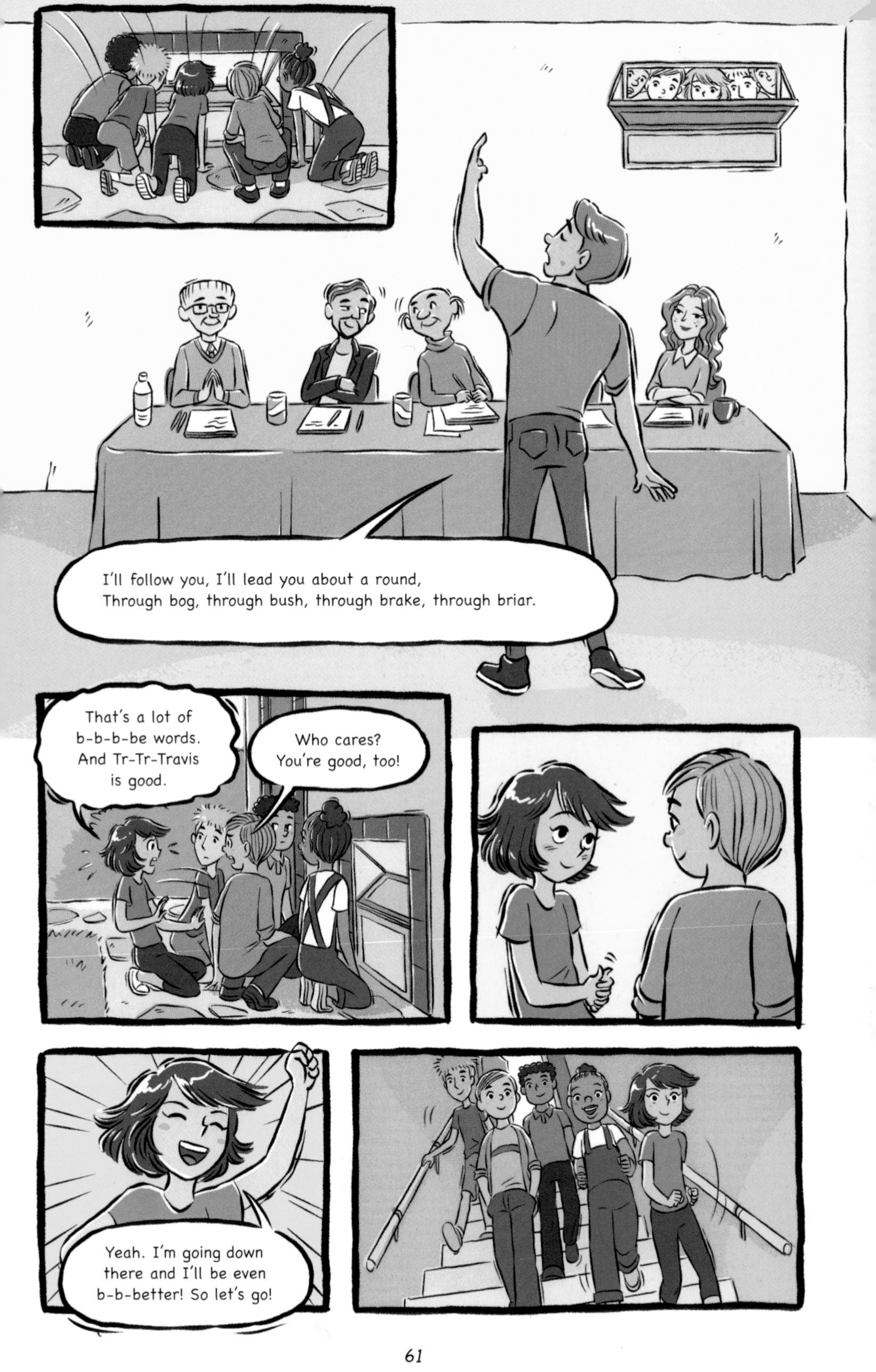

I'll follow you, I'll lead you about a round,
Through bog, through bush, through brake, through briar.
That's a lot of b-b-b-be words. And Tr-Tr-Travis is good.
Who cares? You're good, too!
Yeah. I'm going down there and I'll be even b-b-better! So let's go!

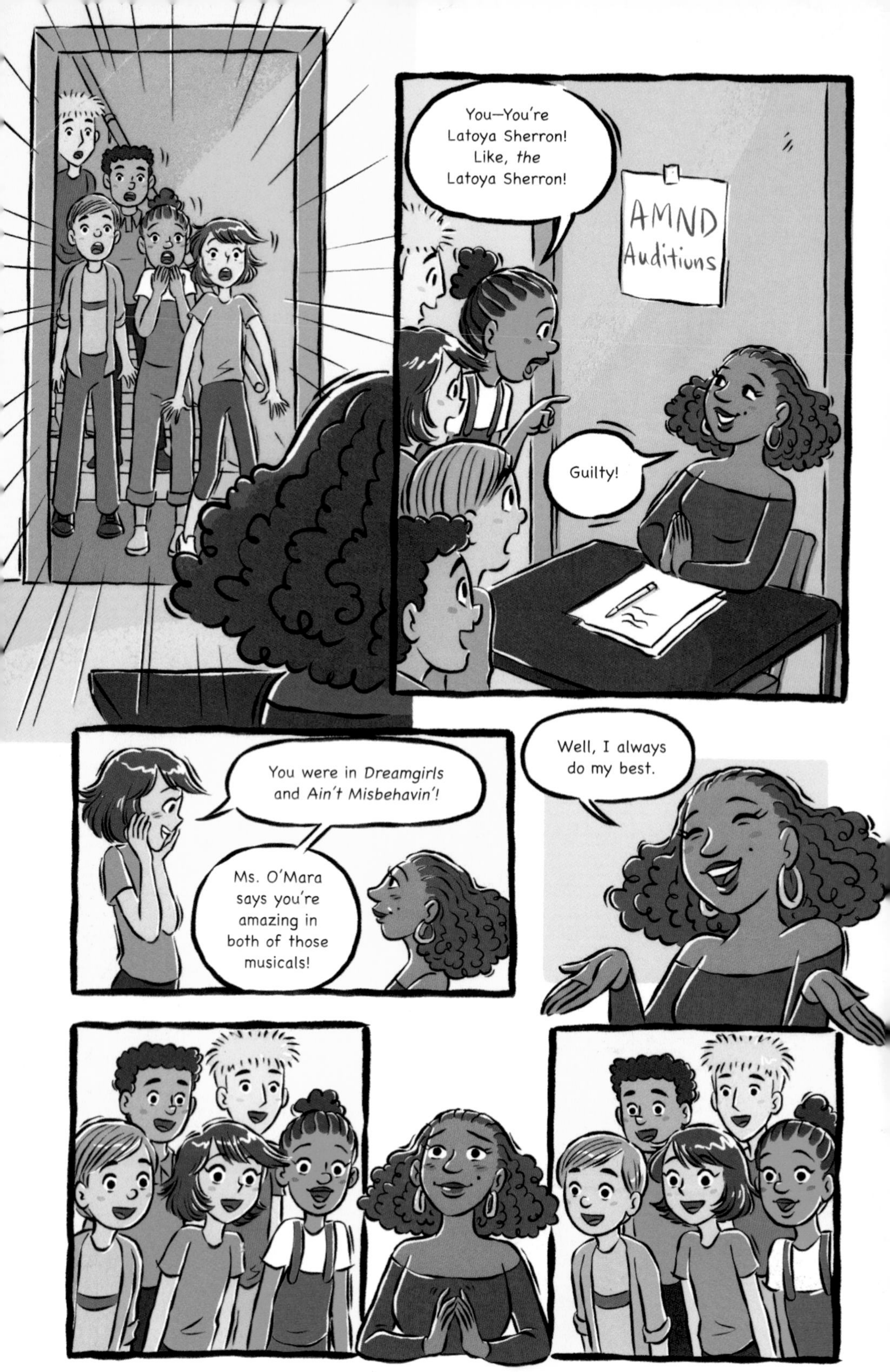
You—You're Latoya Sherron! Like, *the* Latoya Sherron!
AMND Auditions
Guilty!
You were in *Dreamgirls* and *Ain't Misbehavin'*!
Ms. O'Mara says you're amazing in both of those musicals!
Well, I always do my best.

63

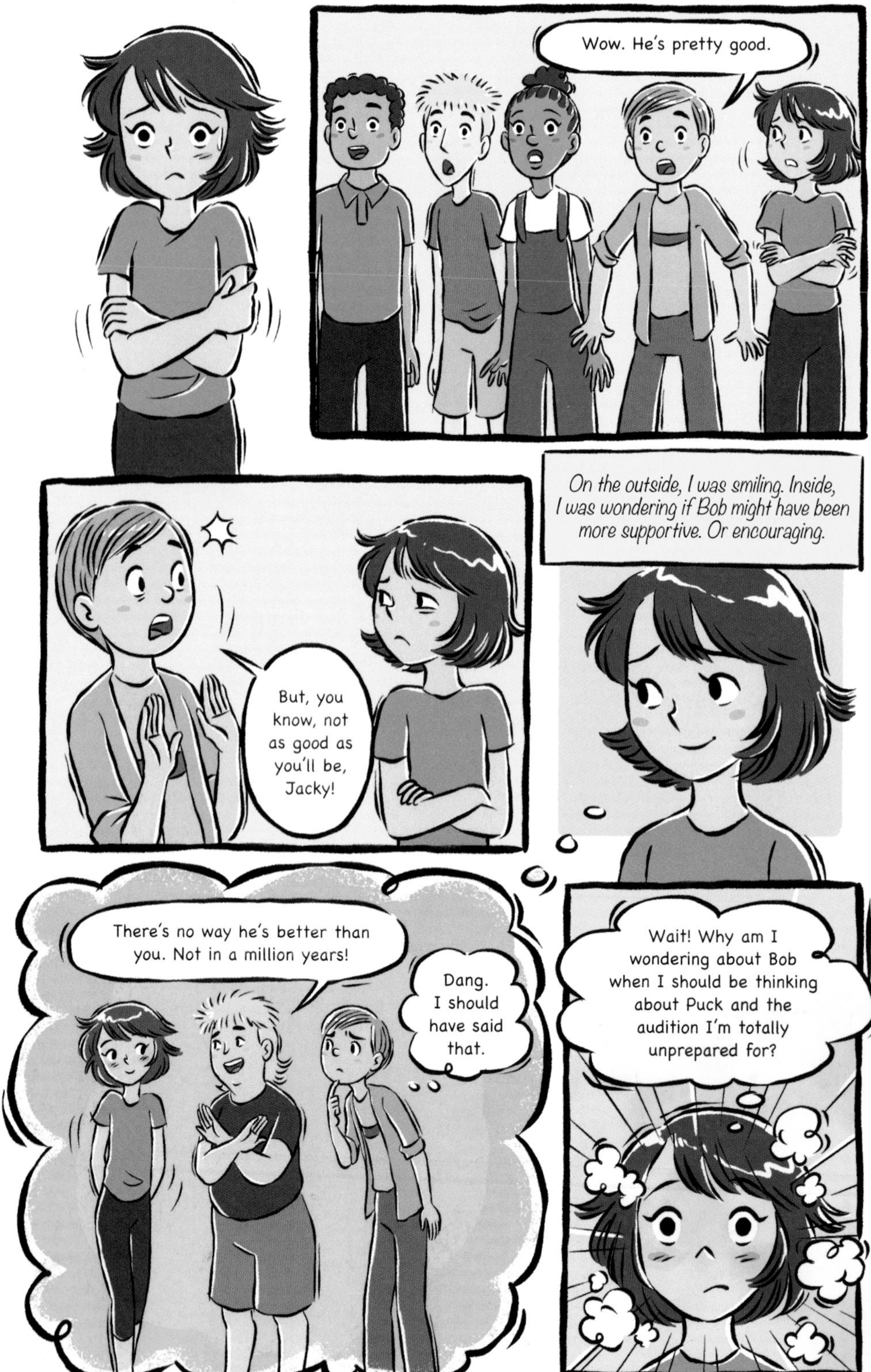
Wow. He's pretty good.
On the outside, I was smiling. Inside, I was wondering if Bob might have been more supportive. Or encouraging.
But, you know, not as good as you'll be, Jacky!
There's no way he's better than you. Not in a million years!
Dang. I should have said that.
Wait! Why am I wondering about Bob when I should be thinking about Puck and the audition I'm totally unprepared for?

67

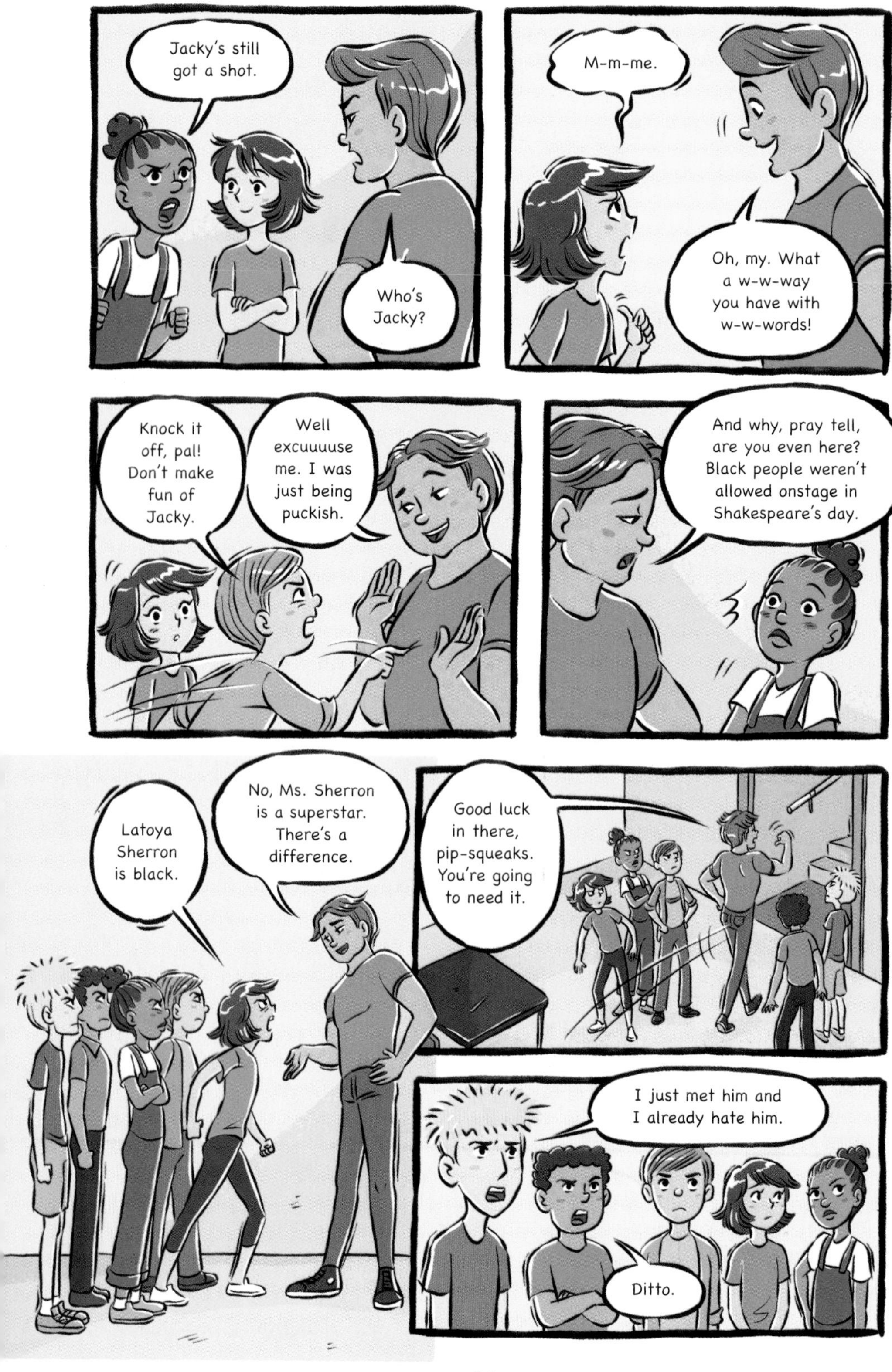

Jacky's still got a shot.
Who's Jacky?
M-m-me.
Oh, my. What a w-w-way you have with w-w-words!
Knock it off, pal! Don't make fun of Jacky.
Well excuuuuse me. I was just being puckish.
And why, pray tell, are you even here? Black people weren't allowed onstage in Shakespeare's day.
Latoya Sherron is black.
No, Ms. Sherron is a superstar. There's a difference.
Good luck in there, pip-squeaks. You're going to need it.
I just met him and I already hate him.
Ditto.

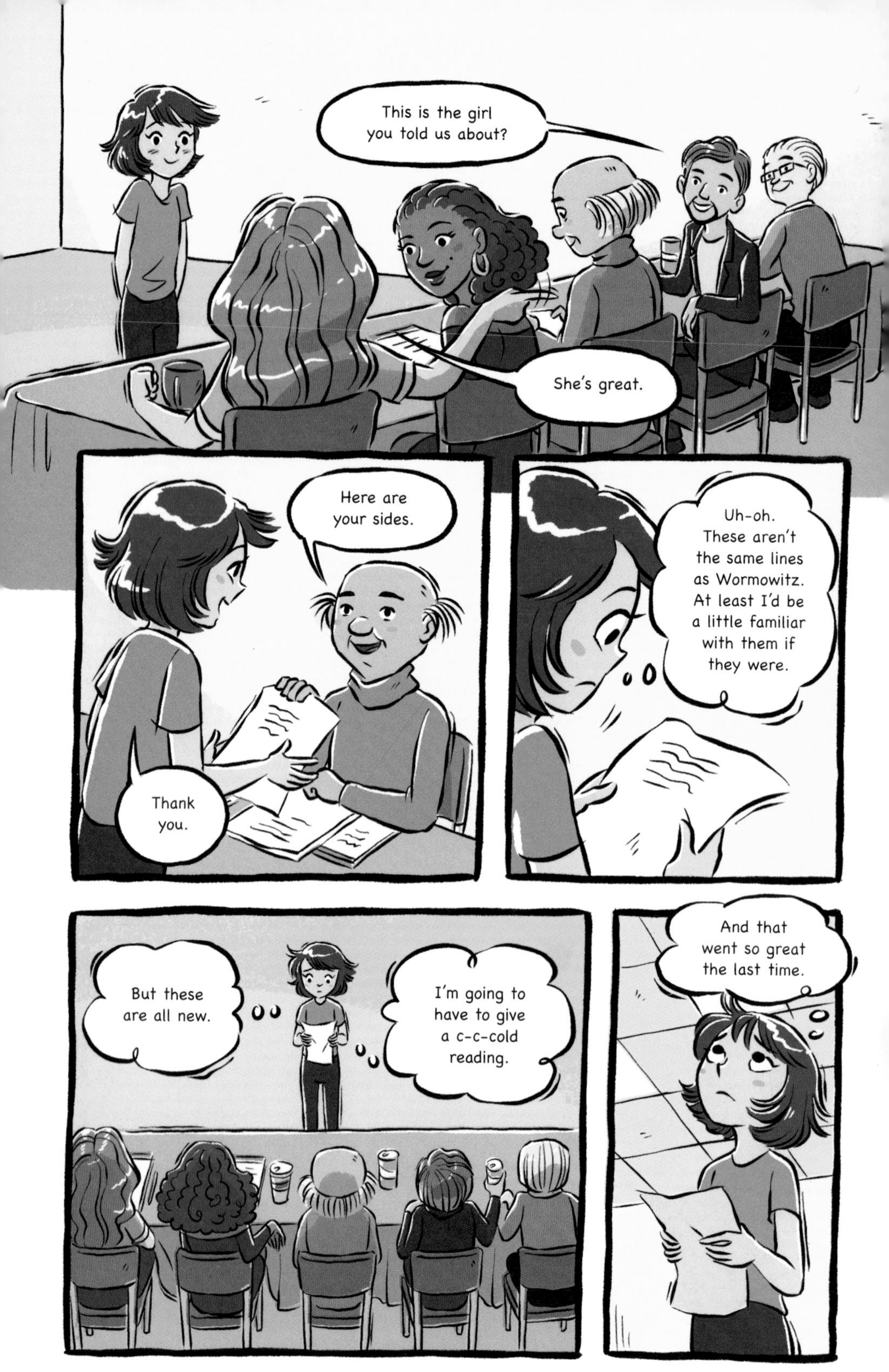
This is the girl you told us about?
She's great.
Here are your sides.
Thank you.
Uh-oh. These aren't the same lines as Wormowitz. At least I'd be a little familiar with them if they were.
But these are all new.
I'm going to have to give a c-c-cold reading.
And that went so great the last time.

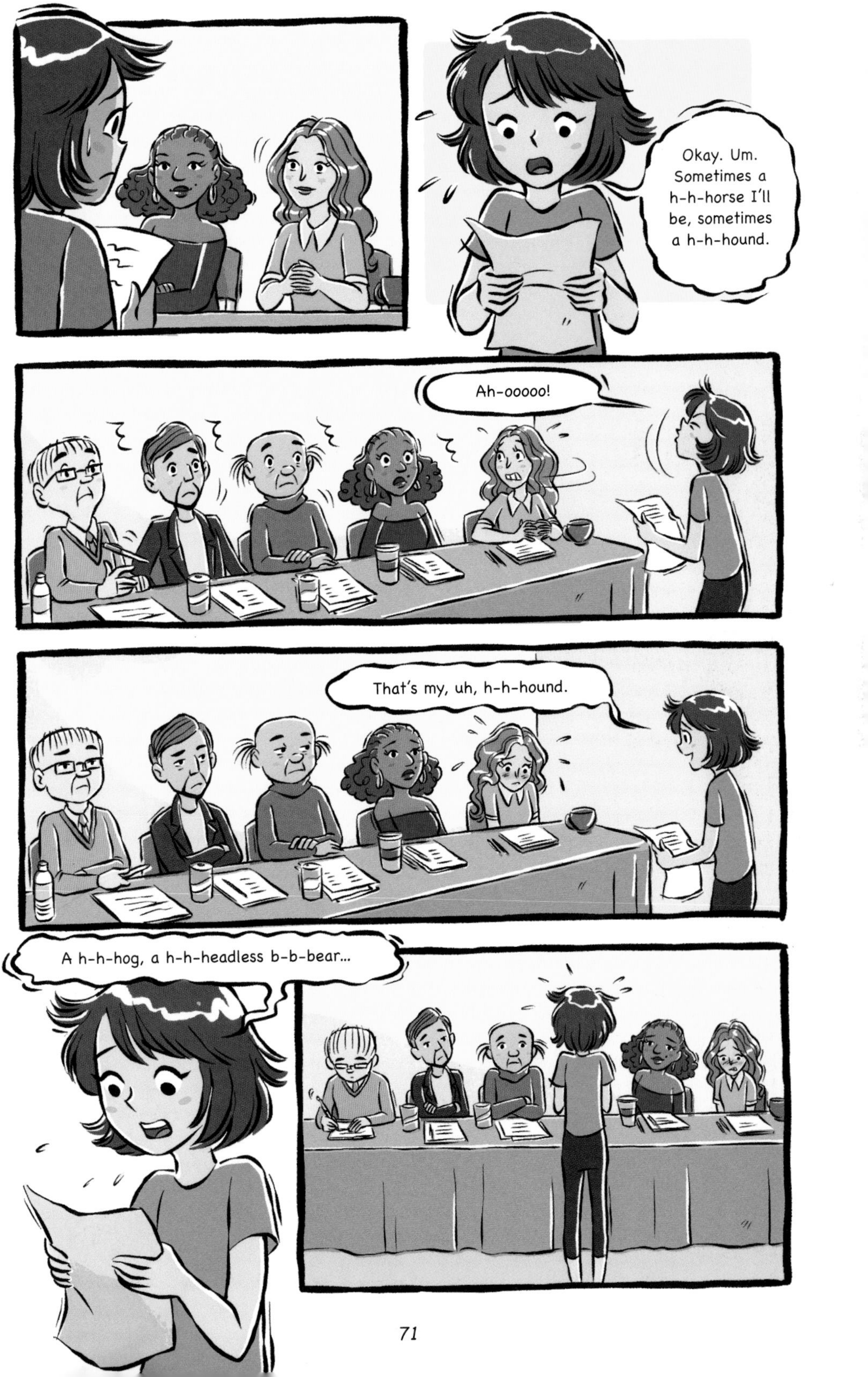
Okay. Um. Sometimes a h-h-horse I'll be, sometimes a h-h-hound.
Ah-ooooo!
That's my, uh, h-h-hound.
A h-h-hog, a h-h-headless b-b-bear...

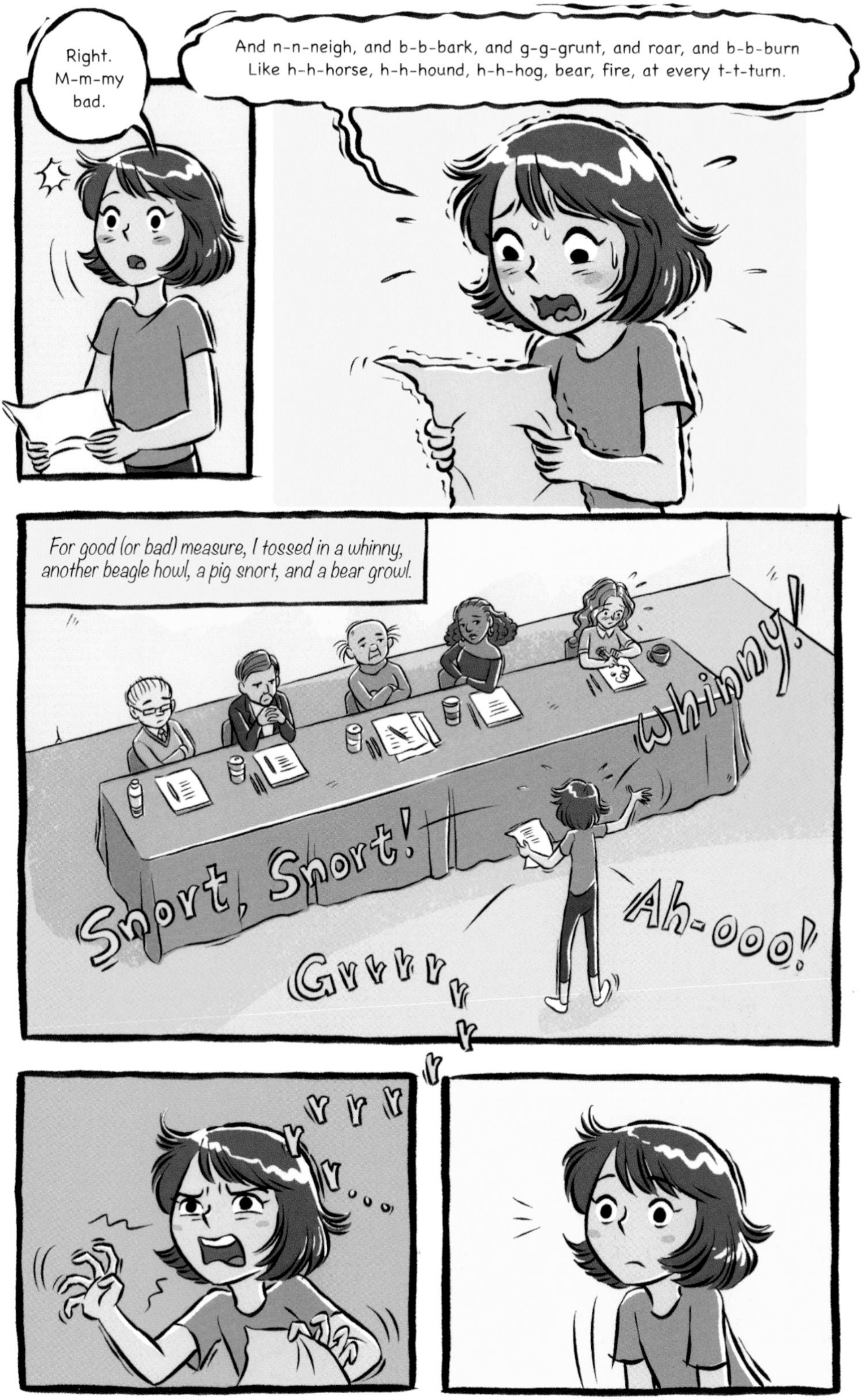
Right. M-m-my bad.
And n-n-neigh, and b-b-bark, and g-g-grunt, and roar, and b-b-burn
Like h-h-horse, h-h-hound, h-h-hog, bear, fire, at every t-t-turn.
For good (or bad) measure, I tossed in a whinny, another beagle howl, a pig snort, and a bear growl.
Whinny!
Snort, Snort!
Ah-ooo!
Grrrrrrrrrrrrr...

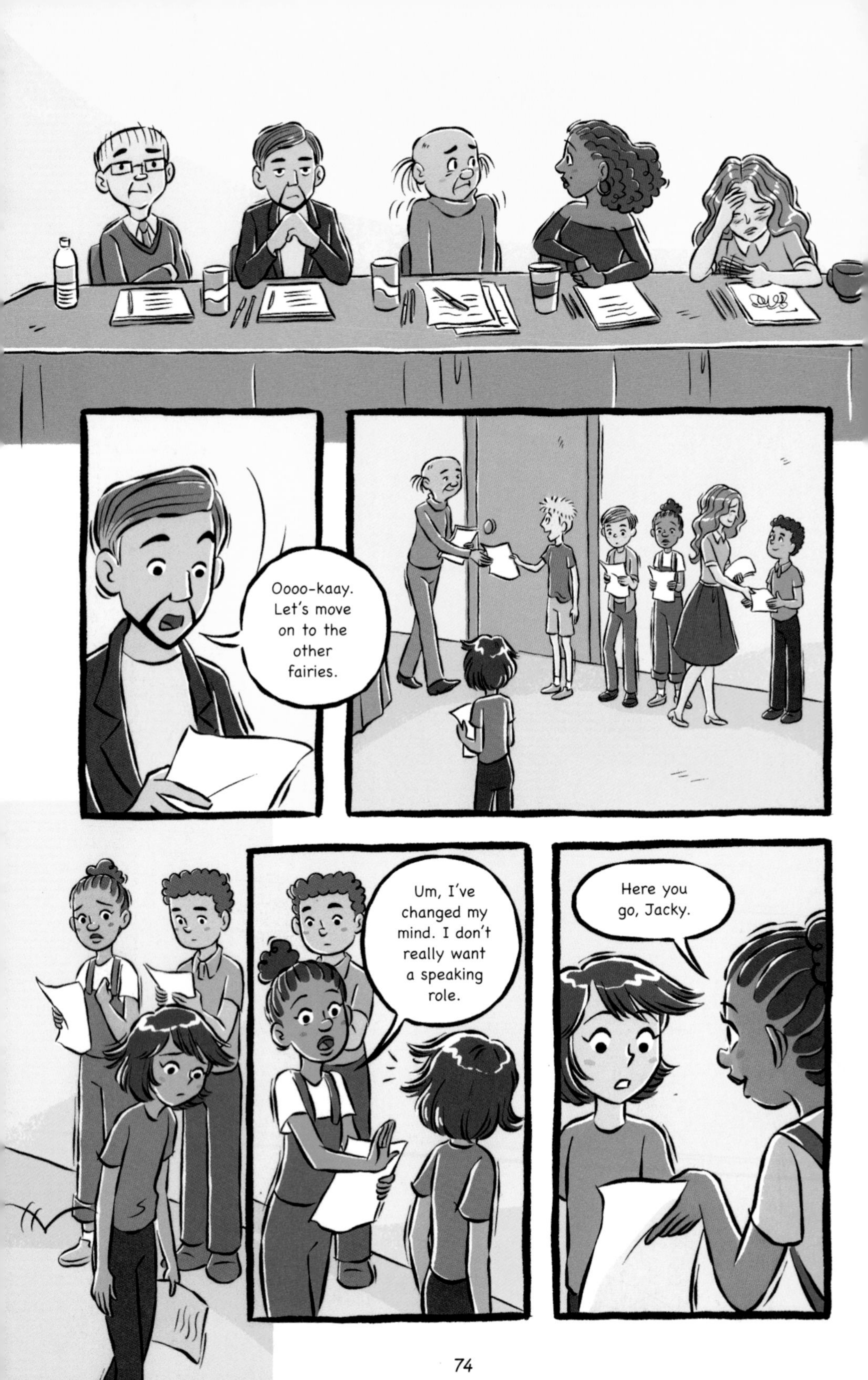
Oooo-kaay. Let's move on to the other fairies.
Um, I've changed my mind. I don't really want a speaking role.
Here you go, Jacky.

Wake up, why don't you? We've got potential customers here.

WATER BALLOON RACE

Sorry, Vinnie!

Ladies and gentlemen, boys and girls: it's time to neigh and bark and grunt and oink and burn. Step right up and take your turn!

What the... What's all them animal noises got to do with squirting guns down a clown's gullet?

Just trying to shake things up.

Well, I don't think—

Oink, oink!

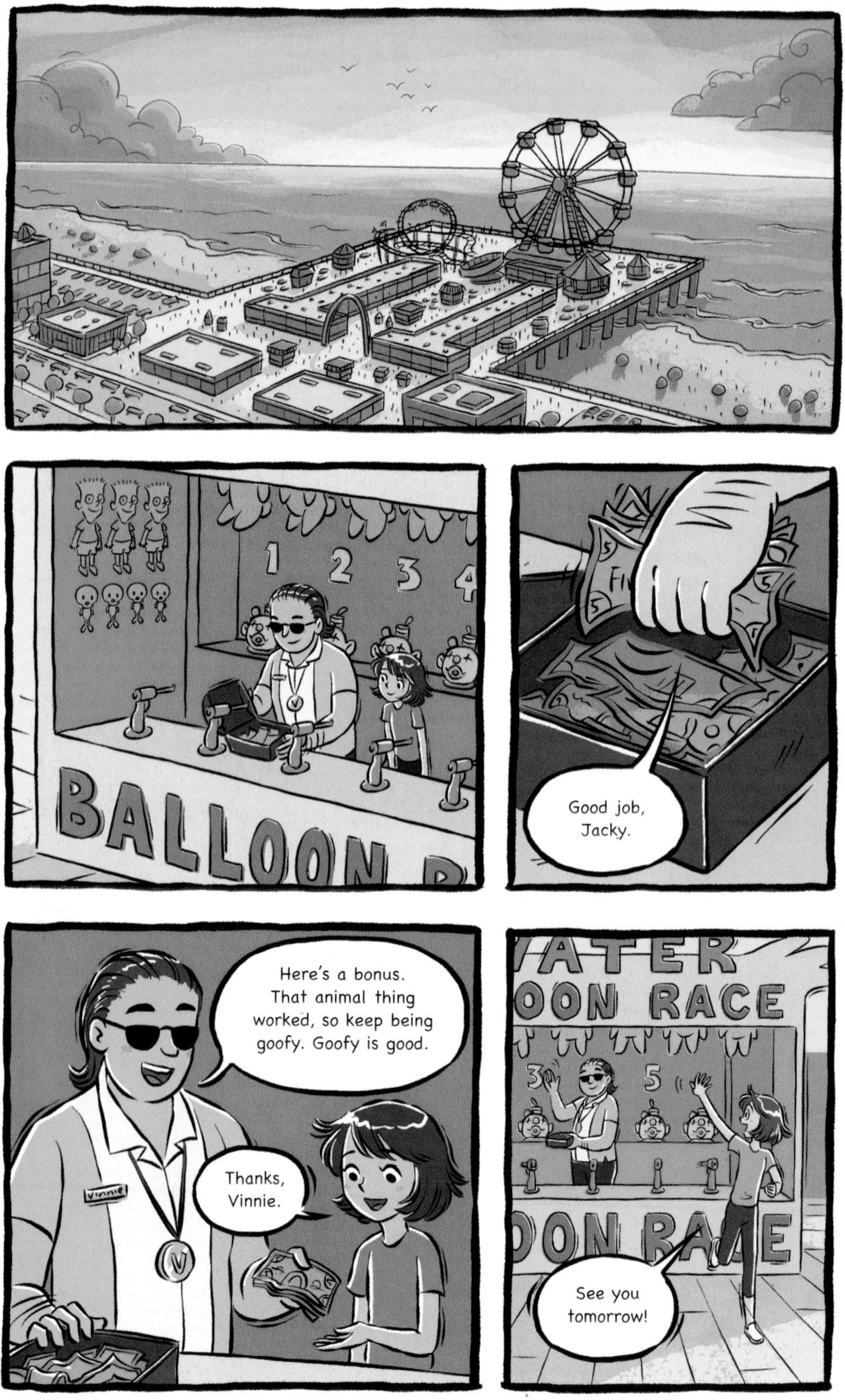
BALLOON
Good job, Jacky.
Here's a bonus. That animal thing worked, so keep being goofy. Goofy is good.
Vinnie
Thanks, Vinnie.
RACE
See you tomorrow!

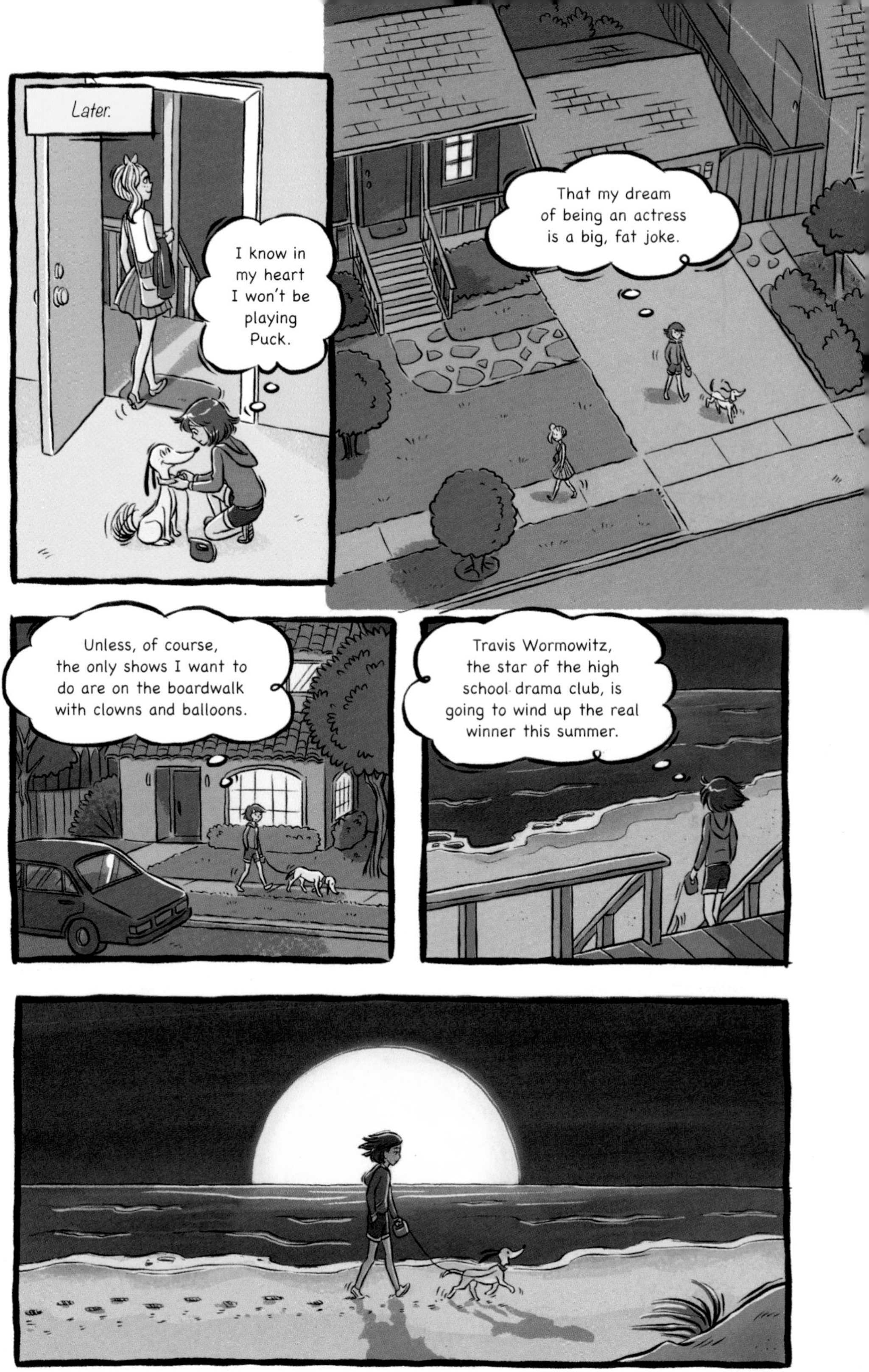
Later.
I know in my heart I won't be playing Puck.
That my dream of being an actress is a big, fat joke.
Unless, of course, the only shows I want to do are on the boardwalk with clowns and balloons.
Travis Wormowitz, the star of the high school drama club, is going to wind up the real winner this summer.

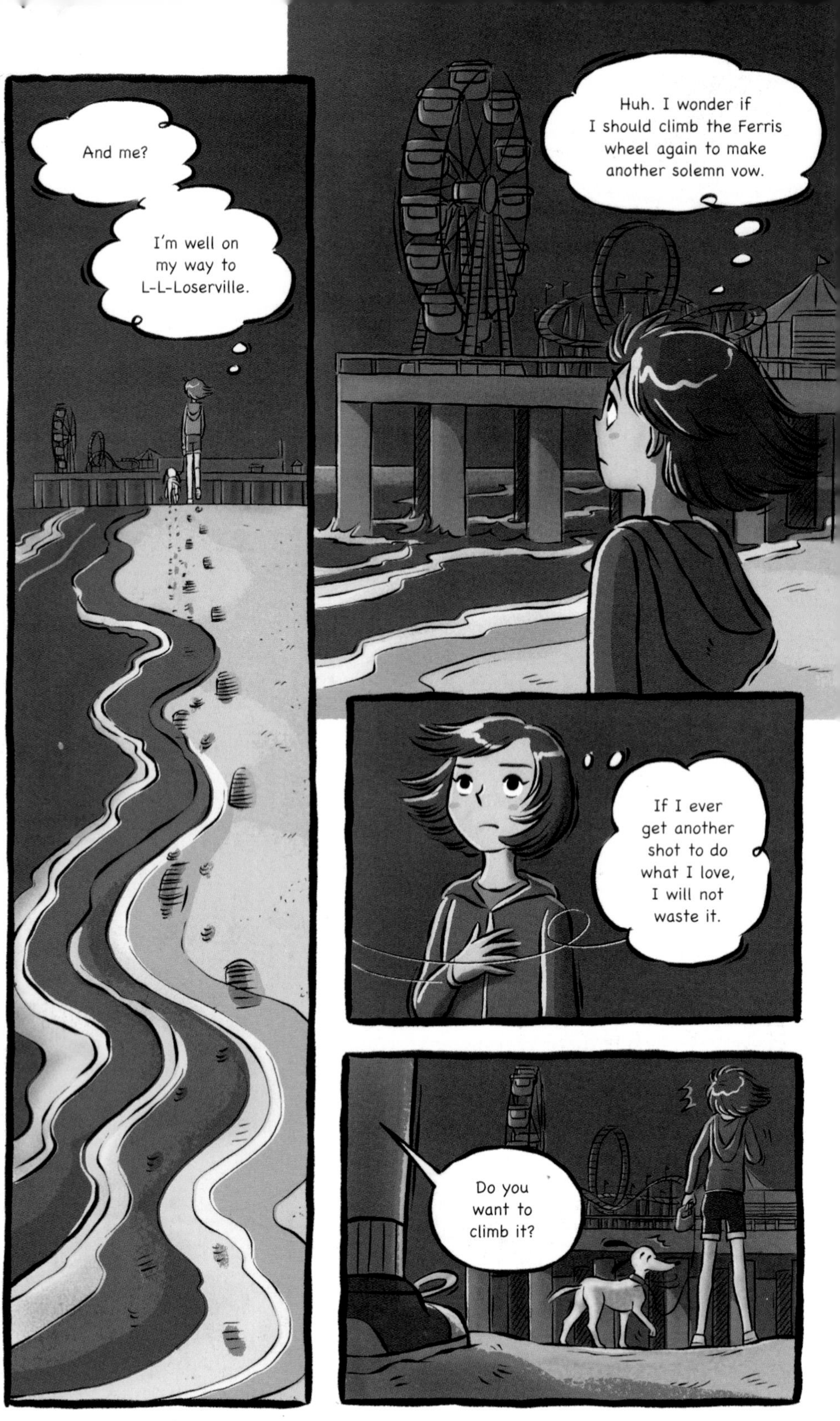
And me?
I'm well on my way to L-L-Loserville.
Huh. I wonder if I should climb the Ferris wheel again to make another solemn vow.
If I ever get another shot to do what I love, I will not waste it.
Do you want to climb it?

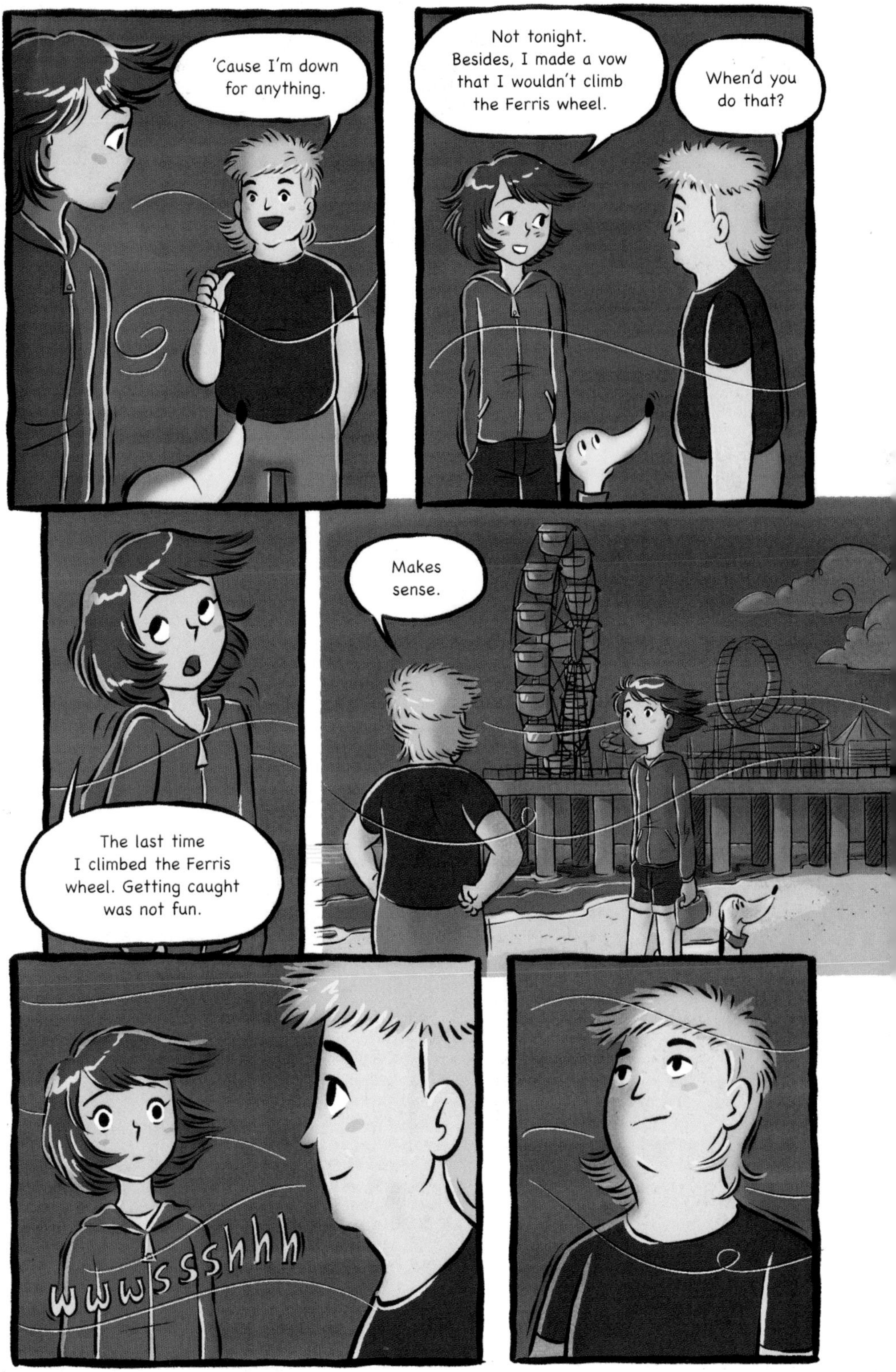
'Cause I'm down for anything.
Not tonight. Besides, I made a vow that I wouldn't climb the Ferris wheel.
When'd you do that?
The last time I climbed the Ferris wheel. Getting caught was not fun.
Makes sense.
wwwssshhh

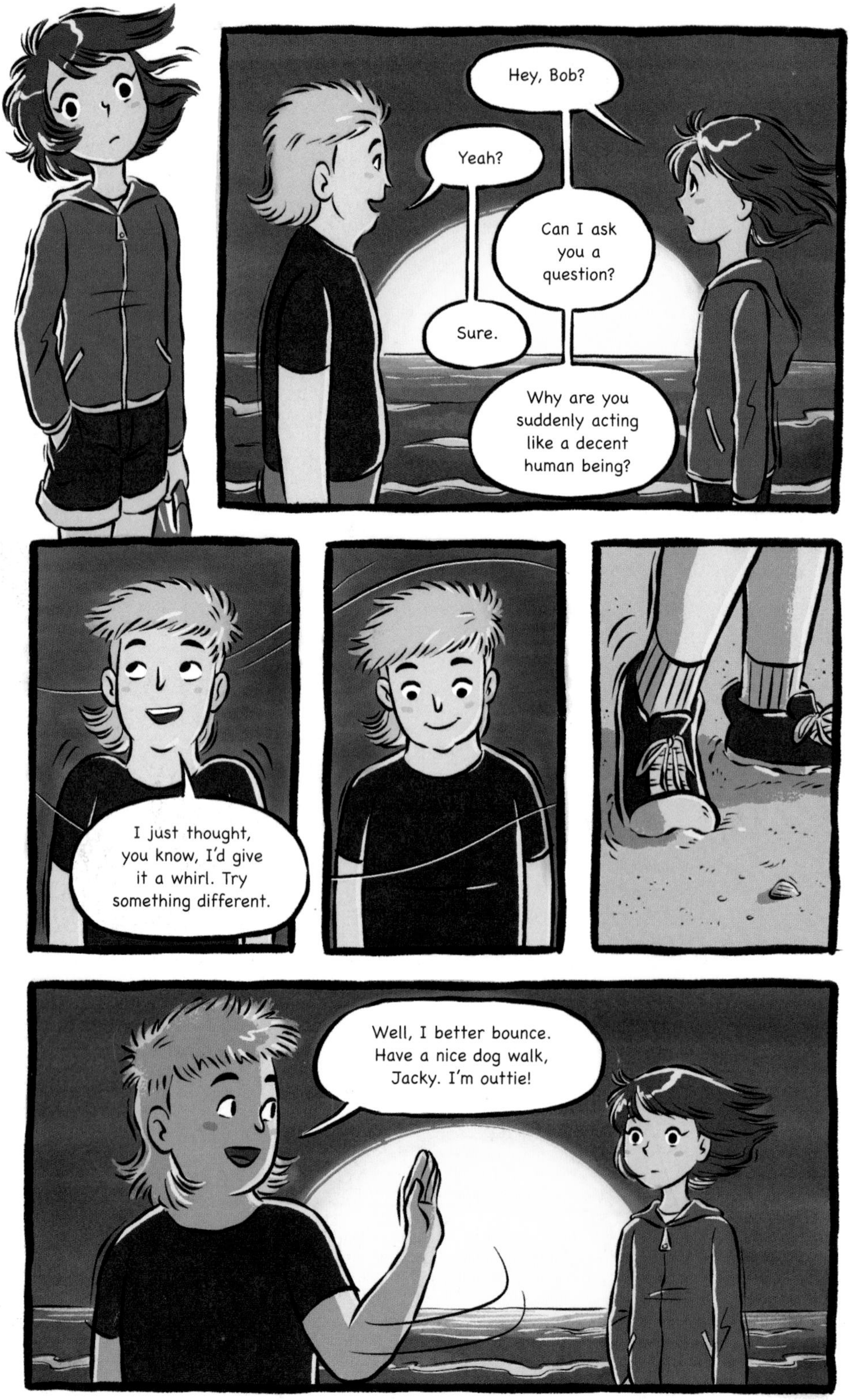
Hey, Bob?
Yeah?
Can I ask you a question?
Sure.
Why are you suddenly acting like a decent human being?
I just thought, you know, I'd give it a whirl. Try something different.
Well, I better bounce. Have a nice dog walk, Jacky. I'm outtie!

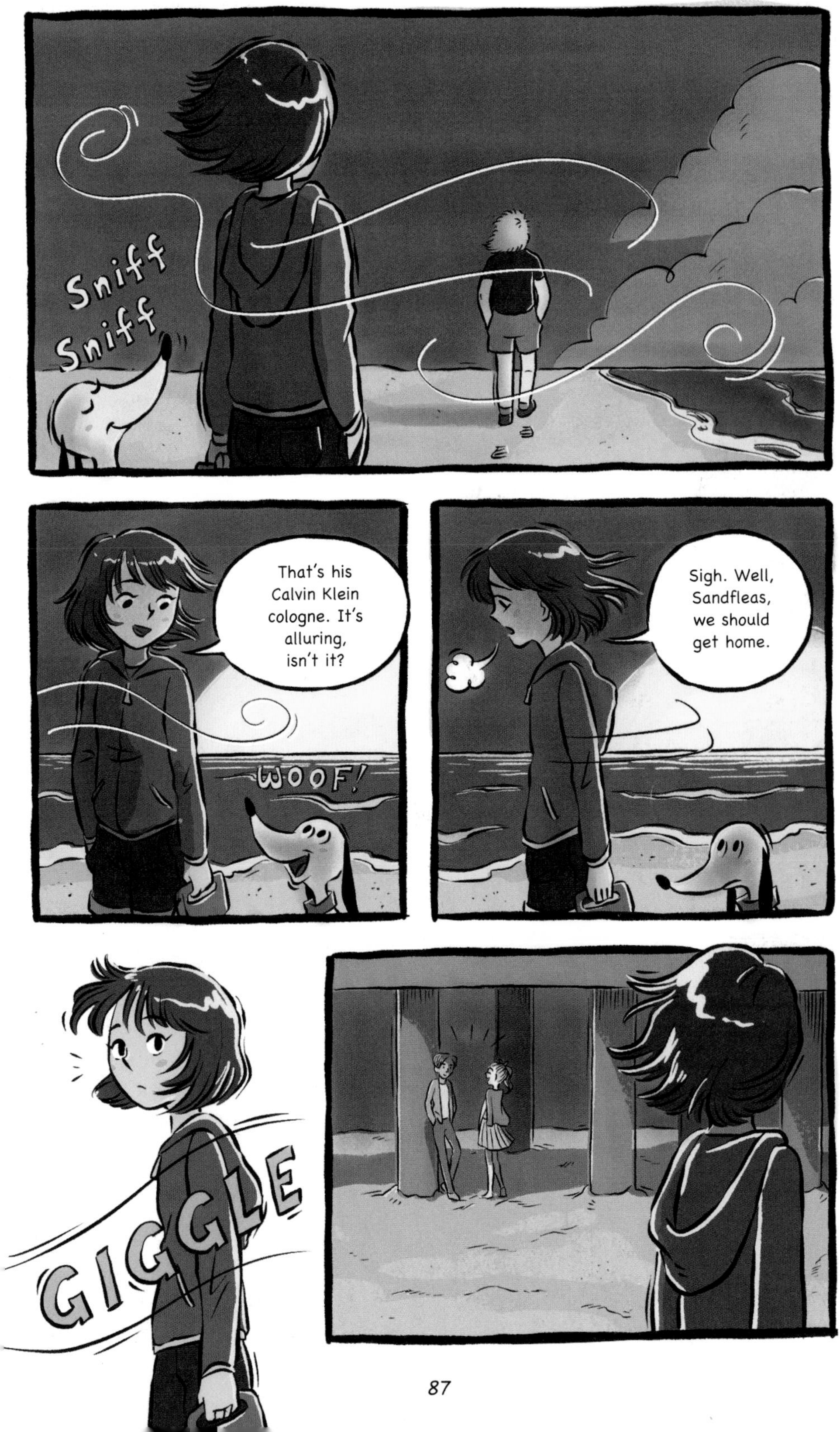
Sniff
Sniff
That's his Calvin Klein cologne. It's alluring, isn't it?
WOOF!
Sigh. Well, Sandfleas, we should get home.
GIGGLE

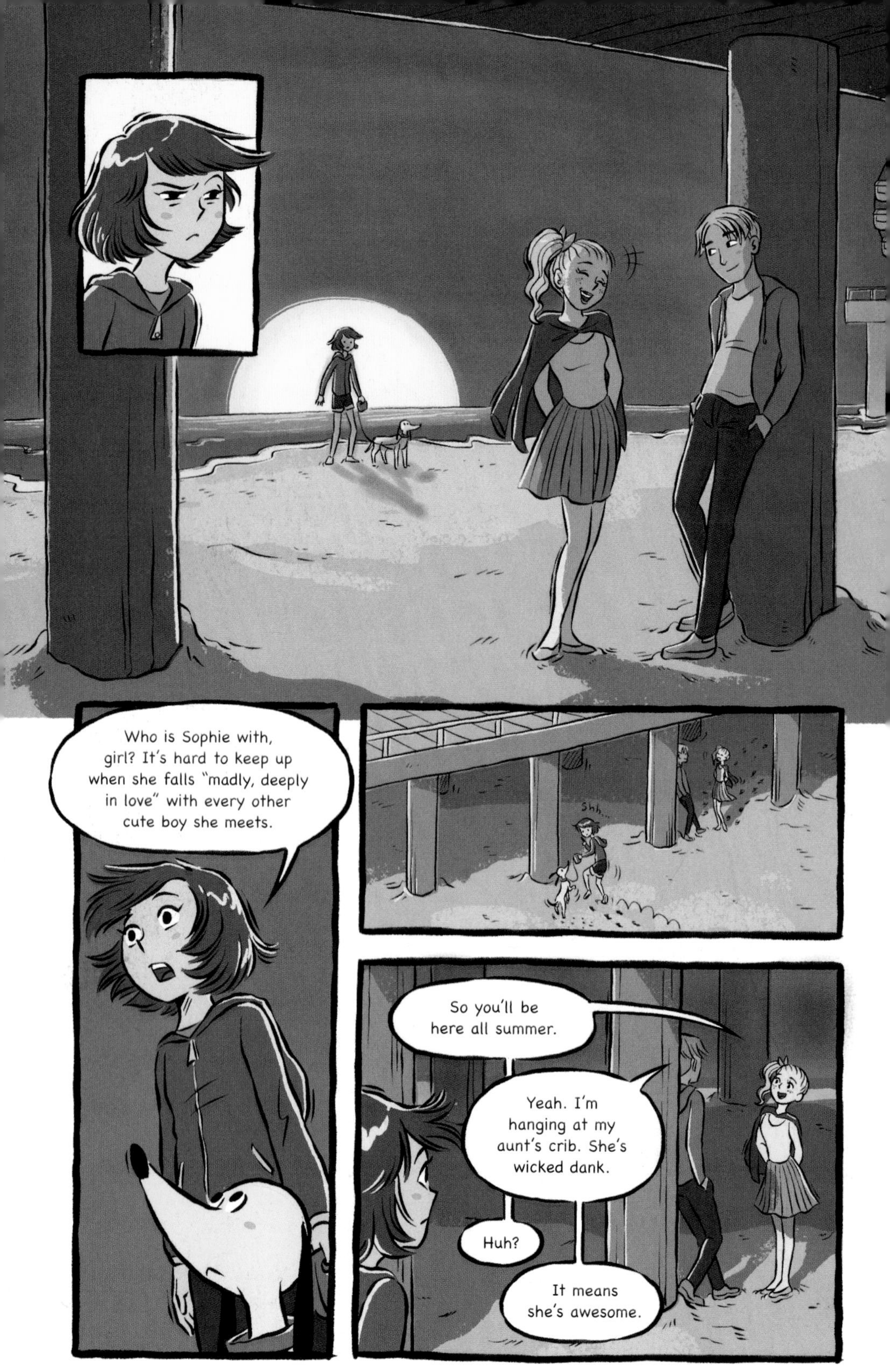
Who is Sophie with, girl? It's hard to keep up when she falls "madly, deeply in love" with every other cute boy she meets.
Shh..
So you'll be here all summer.
Yeah. I'm hanging at my aunt's crib. She's wicked dank.
Huh?
It means she's awesome.

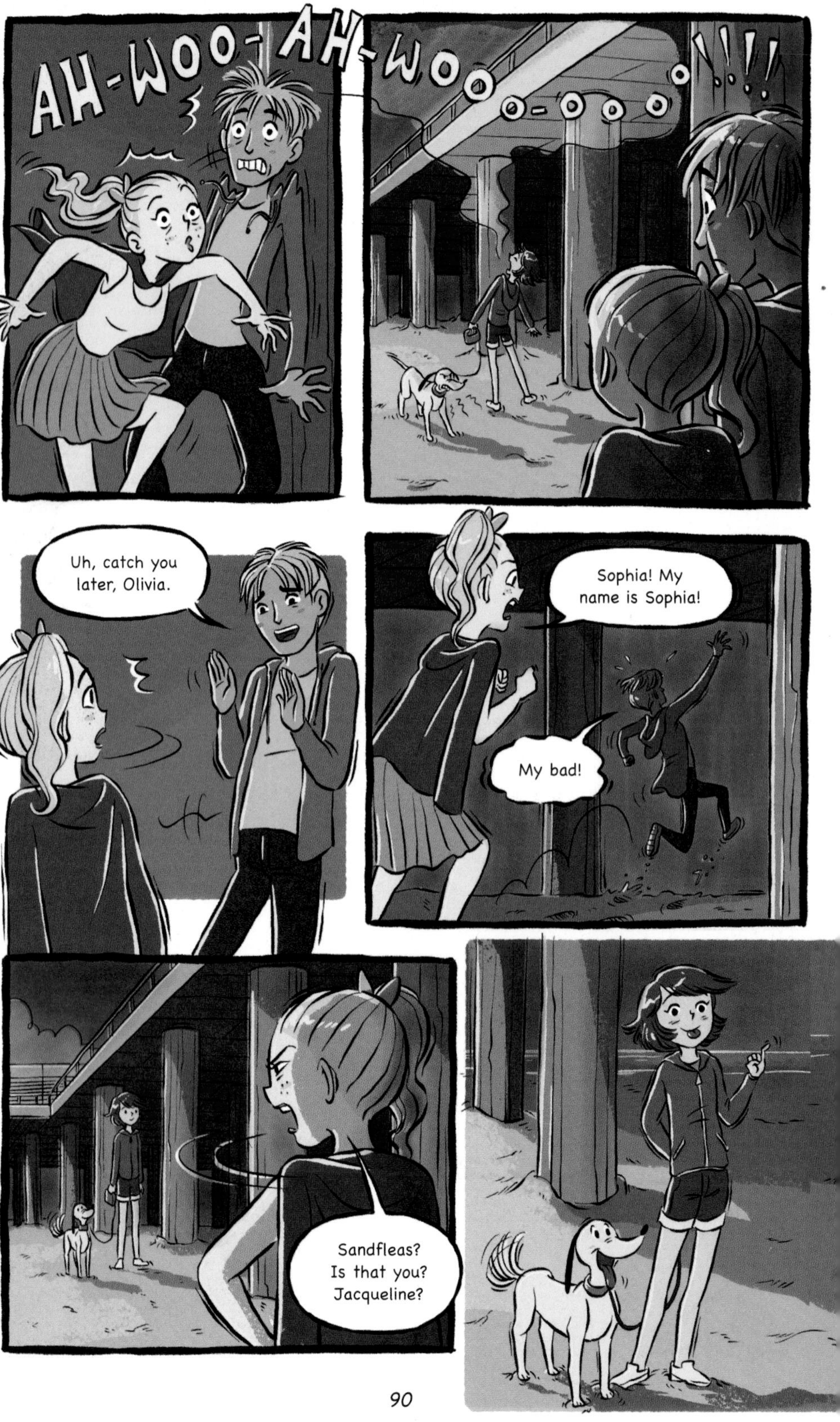
AH-WOO-AH-WOOO-O-O-O!!!!
Uh, catch you later, Olivia.
Sophia! My name is Sophia!
My bad!
Sandfleas? Is that you? Jacqueline?

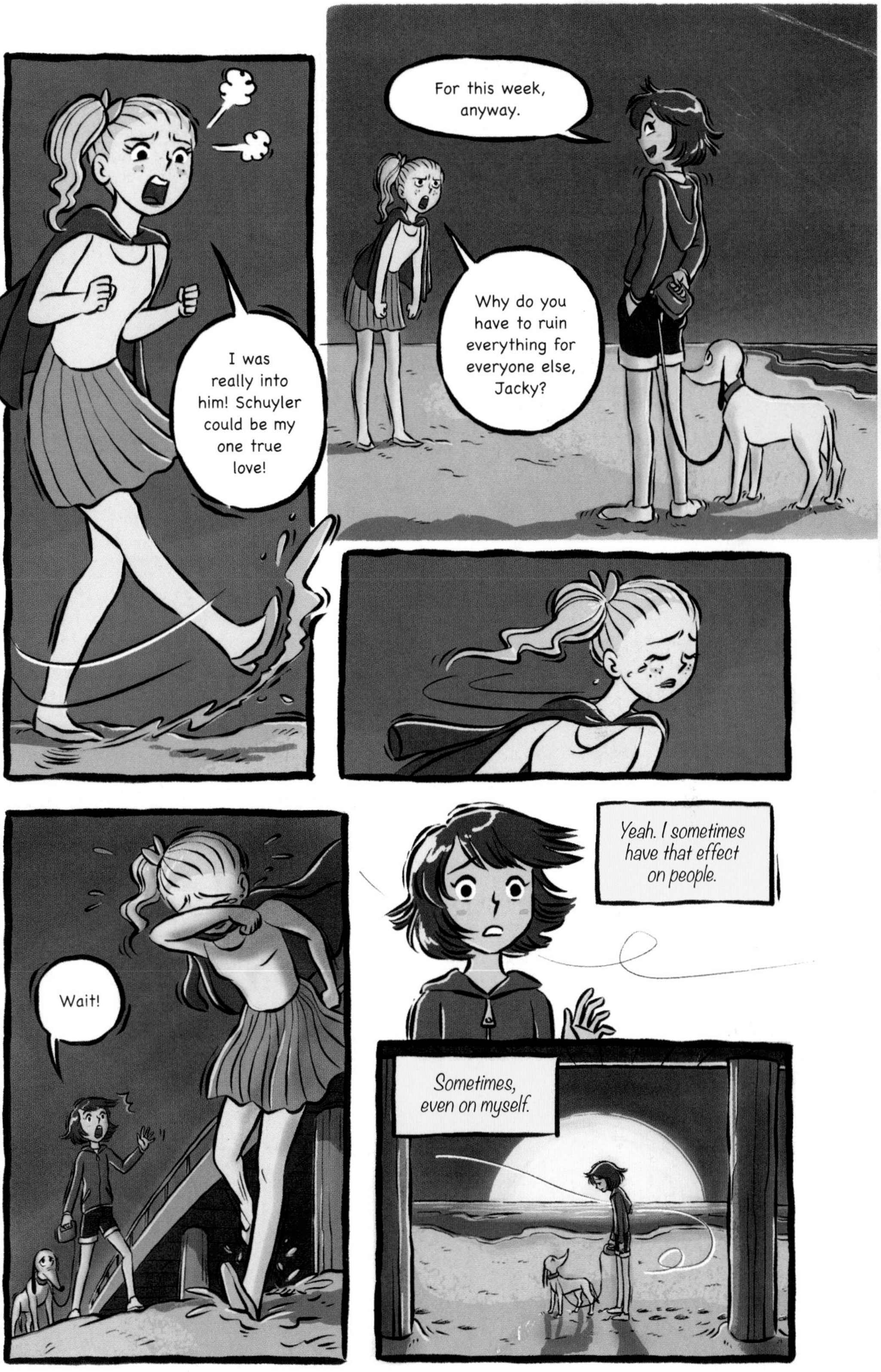
I was really into him! Schuyler could be my one true love!
For this week, anyway.
Why do you have to ruin everything for everyone else, Jacky?
Wait!
Yeah. I sometimes have that effect on people.
Sometimes, even on myself.

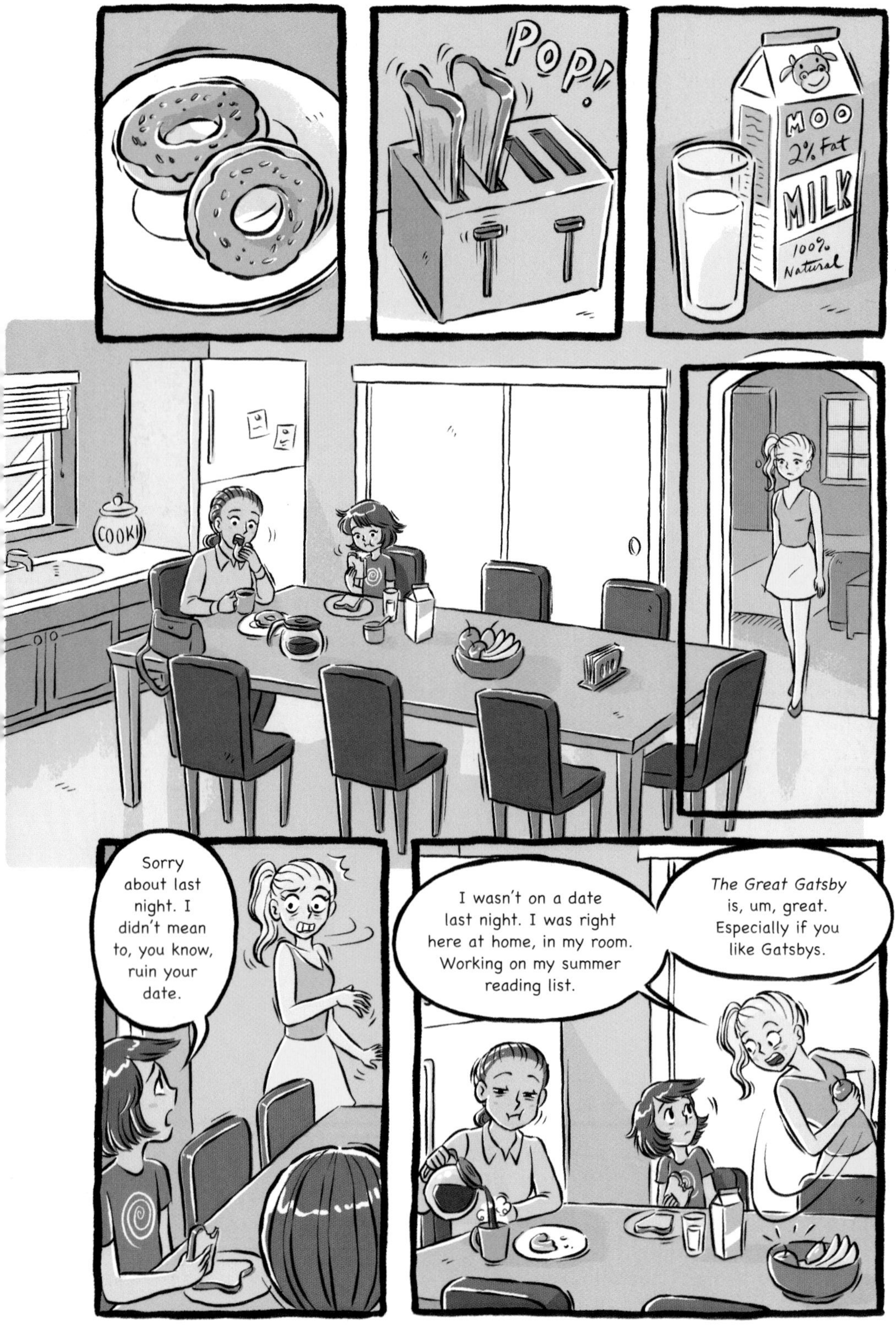
POP!
MOO
2% Fat
MILK
100% Natural
COOKI
Sorry about last night. I didn't mean to, you know, ruin your date.
I wasn't on a date last night. I was right here at home, in my room. Working on my summer reading list.
The Great Gatsby is, um, great. Especially if you like Gatsbys.

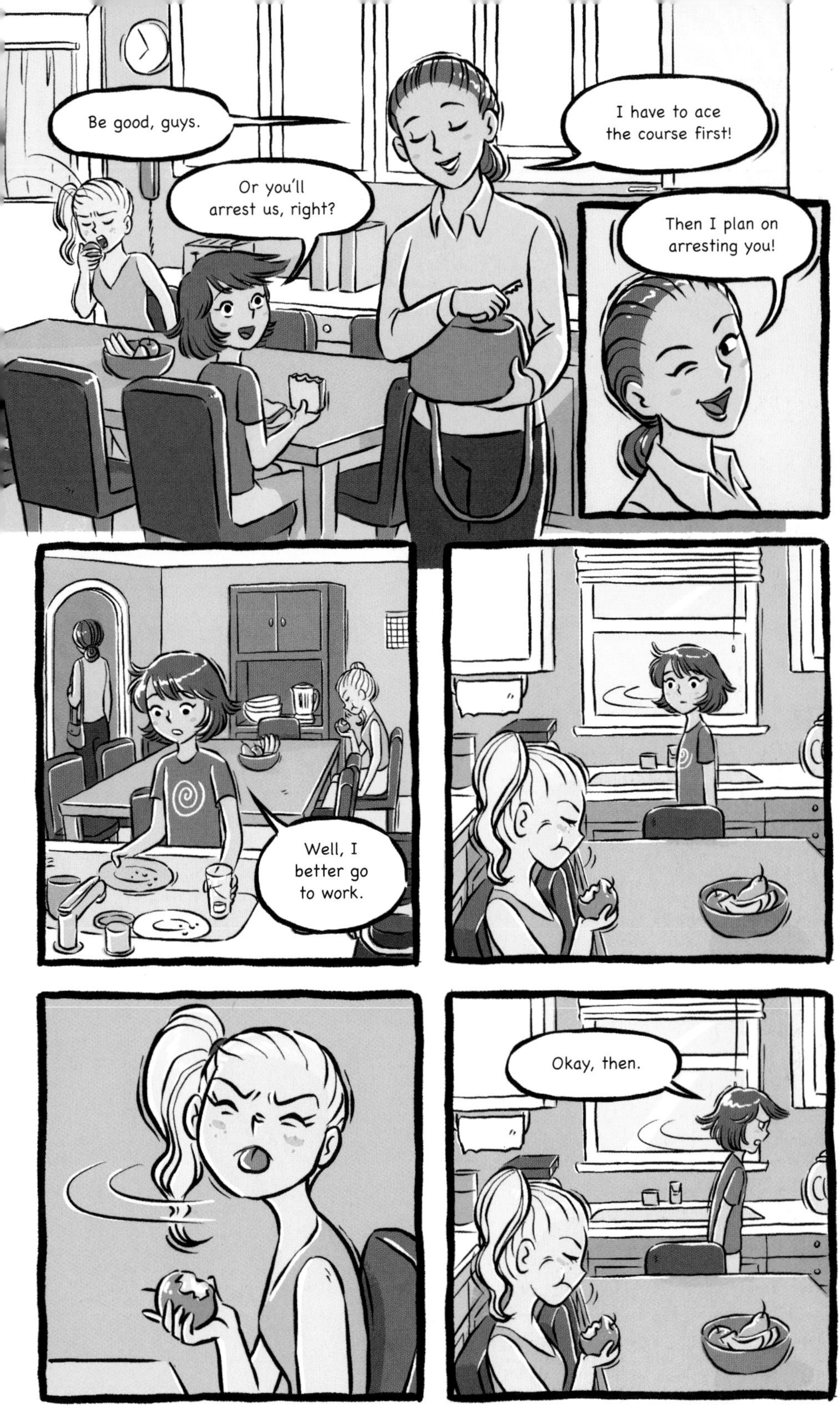
Be good, guys.
Or you'll arrest us, right?
I have to ace the course first!
Then I plan on arresting you!
Well, I better go to work.
Okay, then.

OBERON
About the wood go swifter than the wind,
And Helena of Athens look thou find:
All fancy-sick she is and pale of cheer,
With sighs of love, that costs the fresh blood
By some illusion see thou bring her here:
I'll charm his eyes against she do appear.

PUCK
I go, I go; look how I go,
Swifter than arrow from the Tartar's bow.

Exit

OBERON
Flower of this purple dye,
Hit with Cupid's archery,
Sink in apple of his eye.
When his love he doth espy,
Let her shine as gloriously
As the Venus of the sky.
When thou wakest, if she be by,
Beg of her for remedy.

If I ever get another chance to play Puck, I better make sure I know what all the words mean.

t costs the
hou bring her here:
ainst she do appear.

w I go,
w from the Tartar's bow.

What's a Tartar?
Someone who invented tartar sauce?
Look it up!

s purple dye,
id's archery,
e of his eye.
ove he doth espy,
ine as gloriously
f the sky.
if she be by,

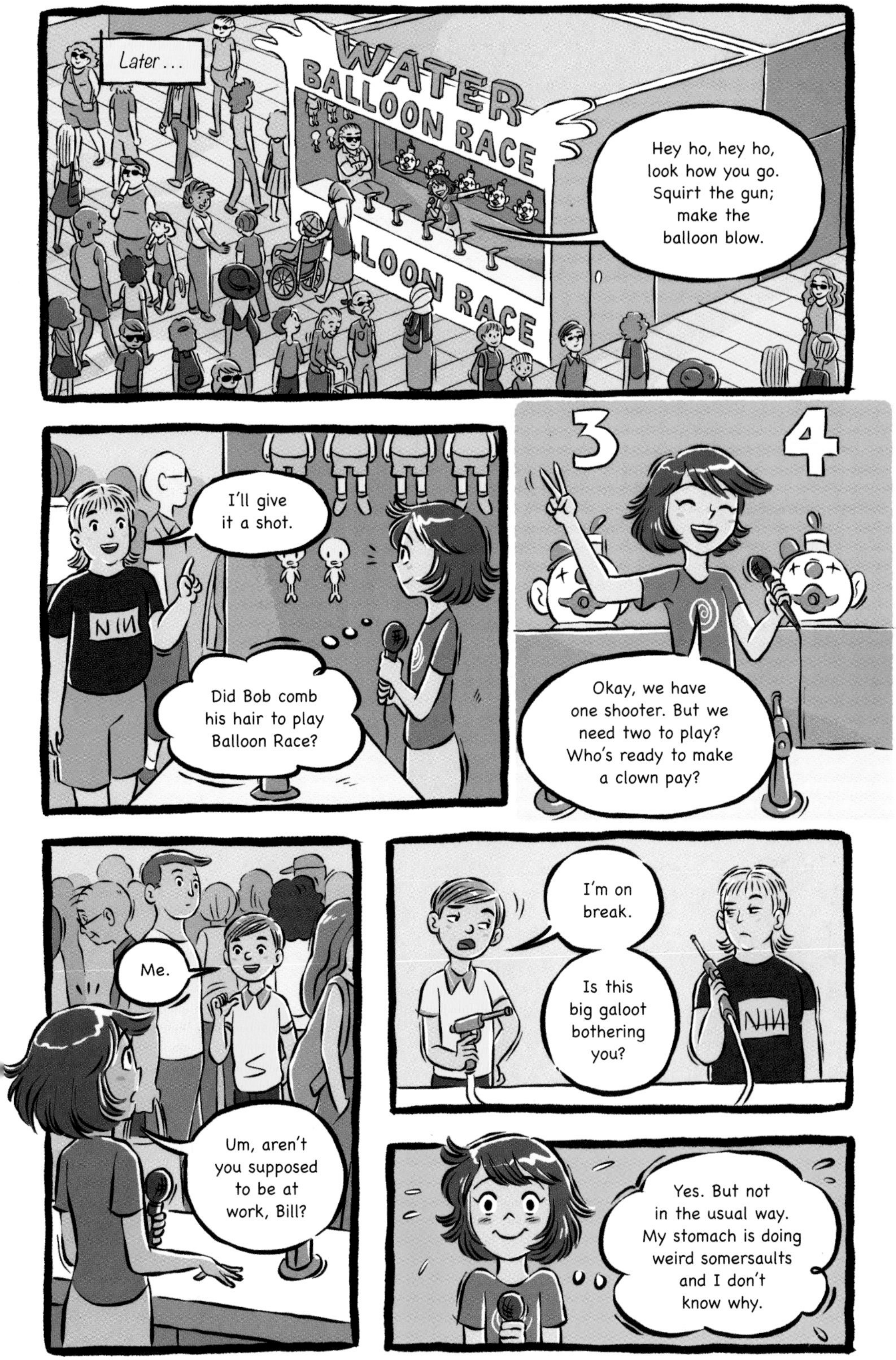
Later...
WATER BALLOON RACE
BALLOON RACE
Hey ho, hey ho, look how you go. Squirt the gun; make the balloon blow.
I'll give it a shot.
Did Bob comb his hair to play Balloon Race?
3
4
Okay, we have one shooter. But we need two to play? Who's ready to make a clown pay?
Me.
Um, aren't you supposed to be at work, Bill?
I'm on break.
Is this big galoot bothering you?
Yes. But not in the usual way. My stomach is doing weird somersaults and I don't know why.

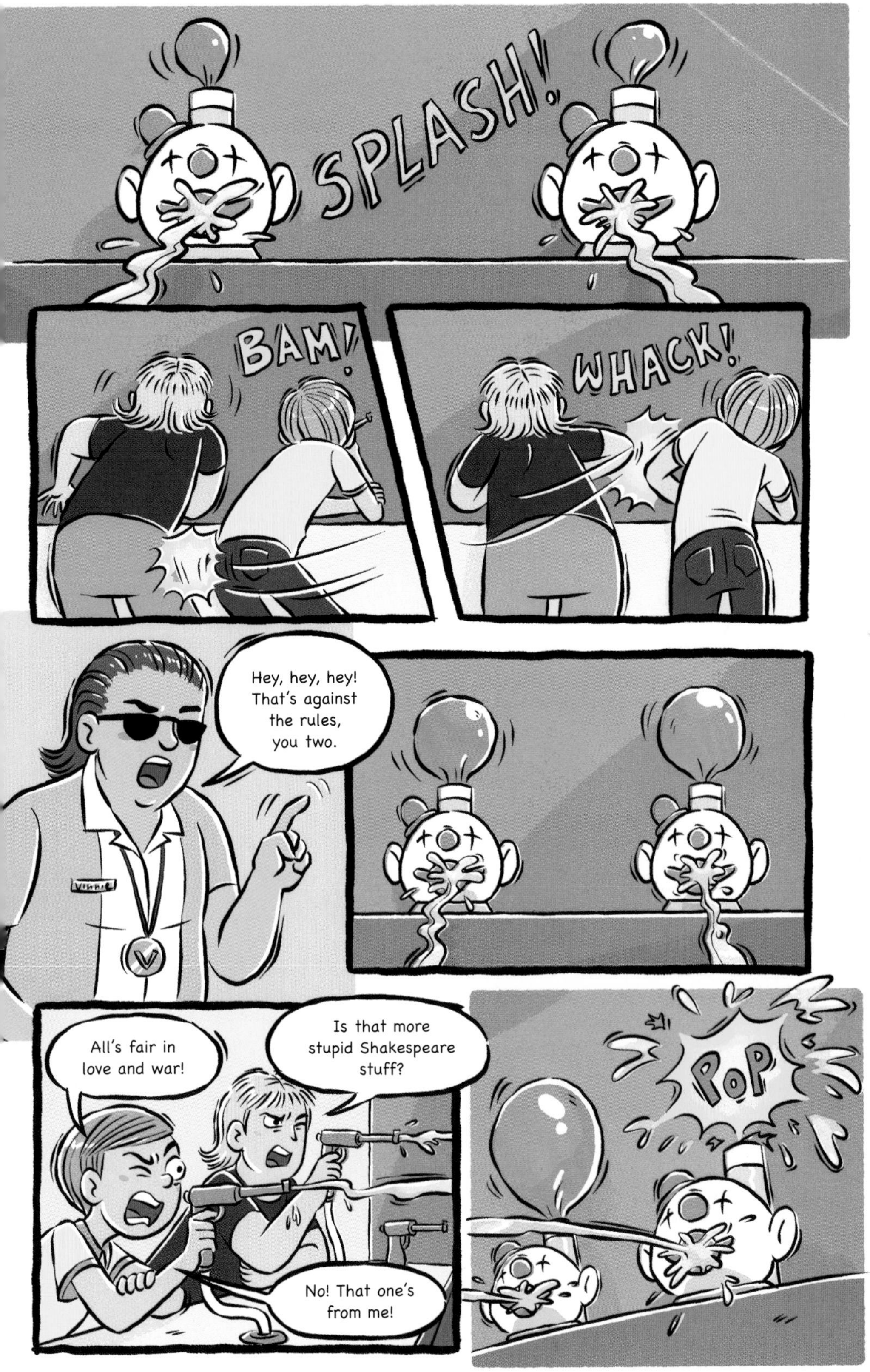
SPLASH!
BAM!
WHACK!
Hey, hey, hey! That's against the rules, you two.
VINNIE
All's fair in love and war!
Is that more stupid Shakespeare stuff?
No! That one's from me!
POP

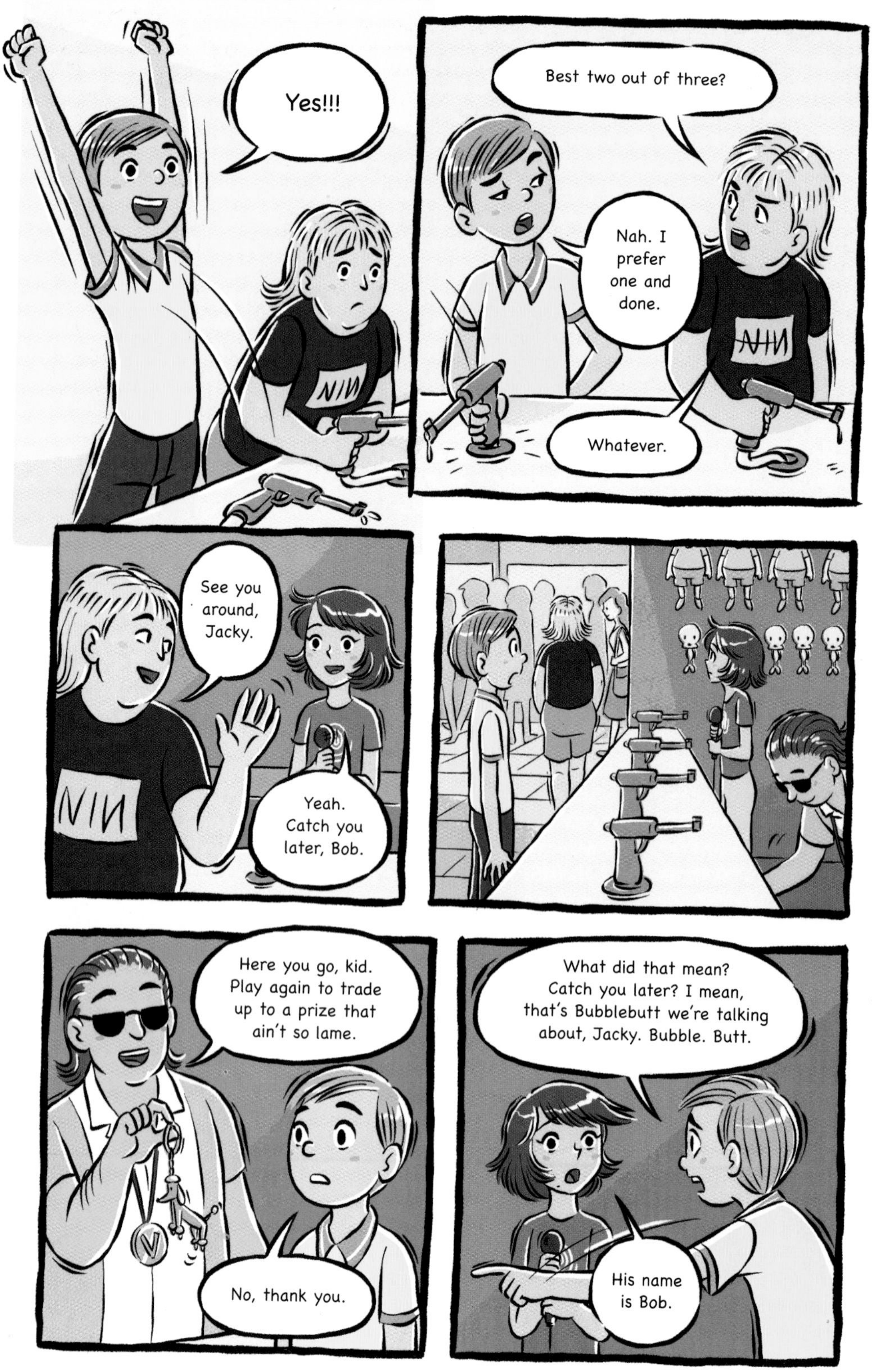
Yes!!!
Best two out of three?
Nah. I prefer one and done.
Whatever.
NIN
See you around, Jacky.
Yeah. Catch you later, Bob.
Here you go, kid. Play again to trade up to a prize that ain't so lame.
No, thank you.
What did that mean? Catch you later? I mean, that's Bubblebutt we're talking about, Jacky. Bubble. Butt.
His name is Bob.

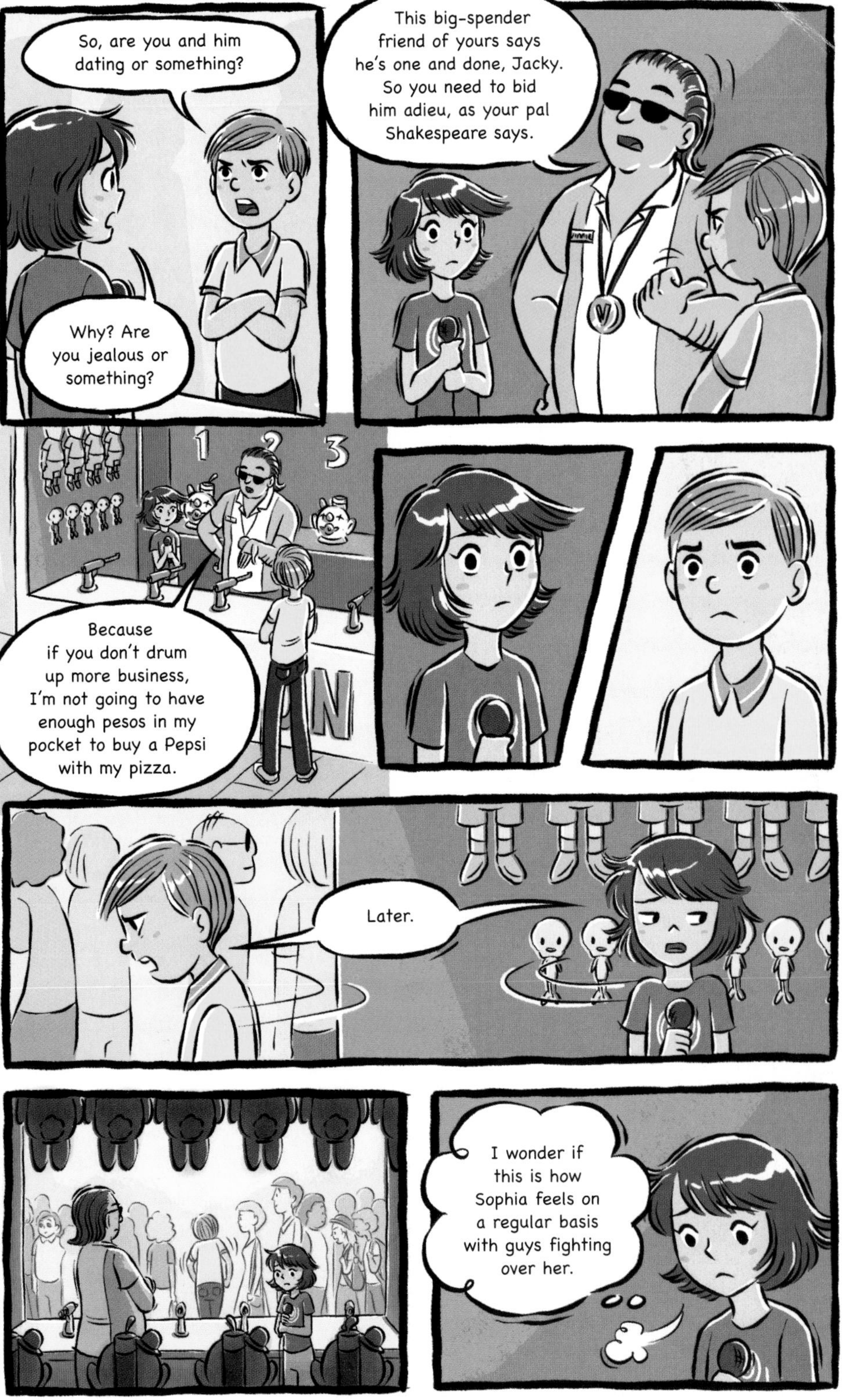

So, are you and him dating or something?
Why? Are you jealous or something?
This big-spender friend of yours says he's one and done, Jacky. So you need to bid him adieu, as your pal Shakespeare says.
1
2
3
N
Because if you don't drum up more business, I'm not going to have enough pesos in my pocket to buy a Pepsi with my pizza.
Later.
I wonder if this is how Sophia feels on a regular basis with guys fighting over her.

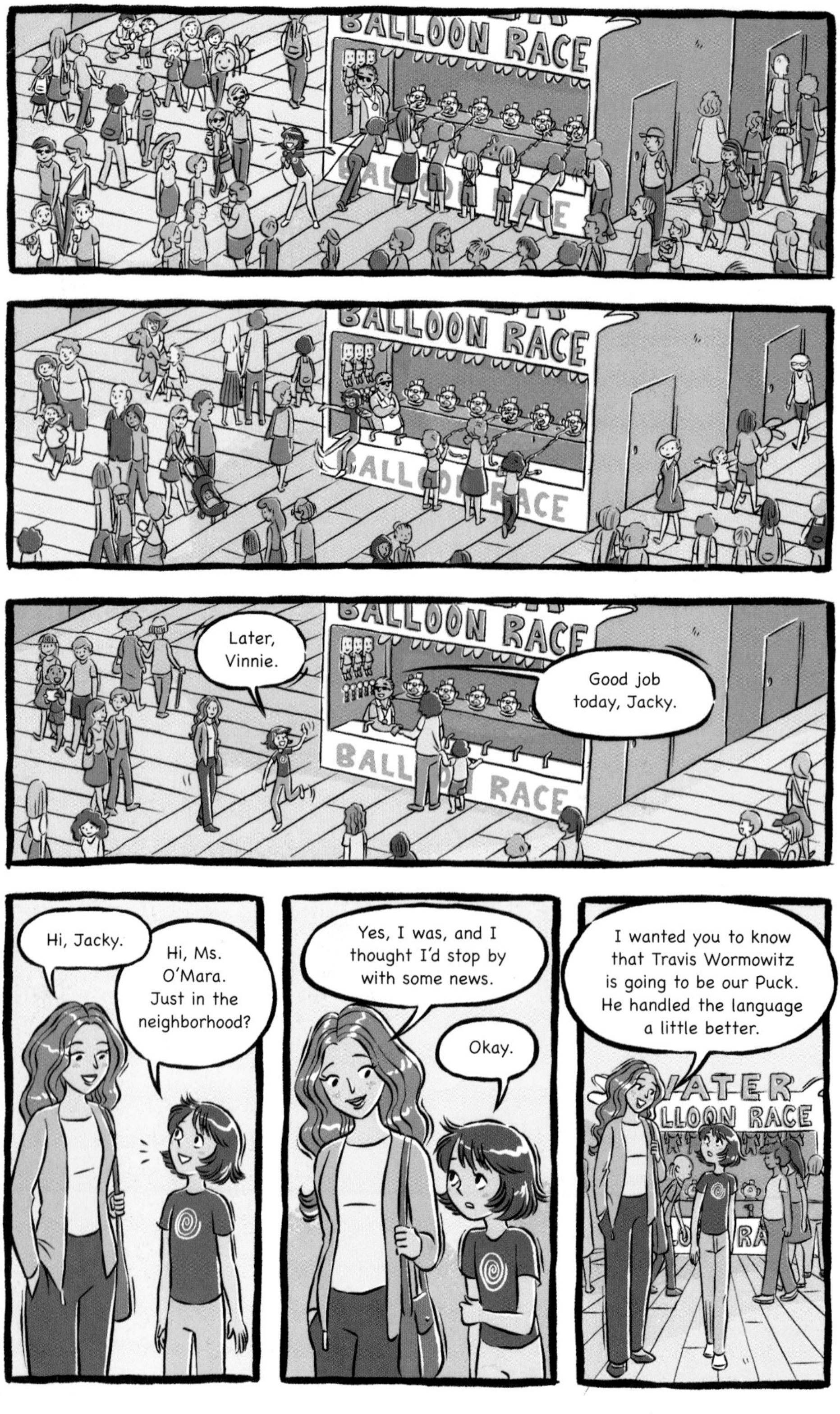
BALLOON RACE
BALLOON RACE
BALLOON RACE
Later, Vinnie.
Good job today, Jacky.
Hi, Jacky.
Hi, Ms. O'Mara. Just in the neighborhood?
Yes, I was, and I thought I'd stop by with some news.
Okay.
I wanted you to know that Travis Wormowitz is going to be our Puck. He handled the language a little better.

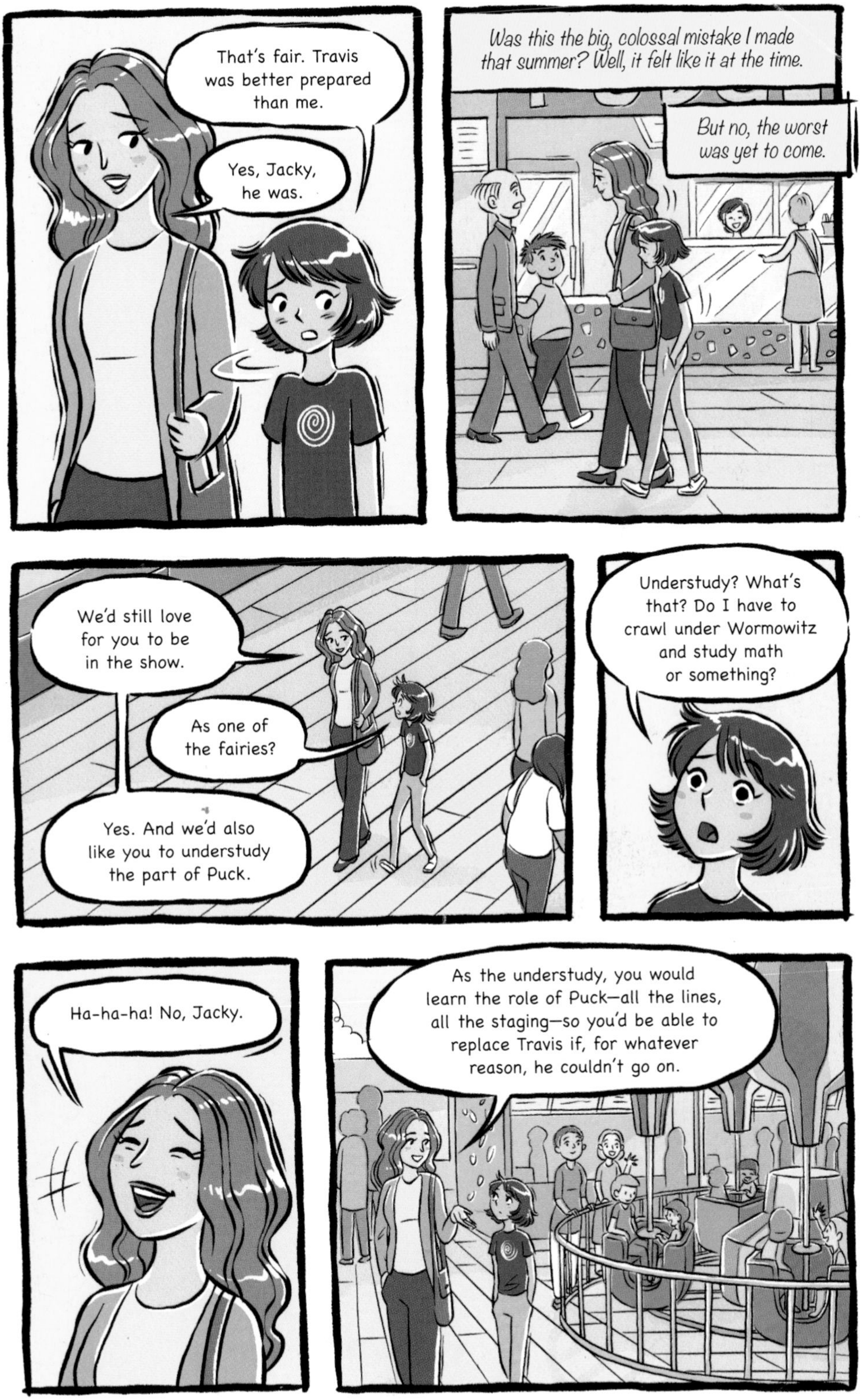
That's fair. Travis was better prepared than me.
Yes, Jacky, he was.
Was this the big, colossal mistake I made that summer? Well, it felt like it at the time.
But no, the worst was yet to come.
We'd still love for you to be in the show.
As one of the fairies?
Yes. And we'd also like you to understudy the part of Puck.
Understudy? What's that? Do I have to crawl under Wormowitz and study math or something?
Ha-ha-ha! No, Jacky.
As the understudy, you would learn the role of Puck—all the lines, all the staging—so you'd be able to replace Travis if, for whatever reason, he couldn't go on.

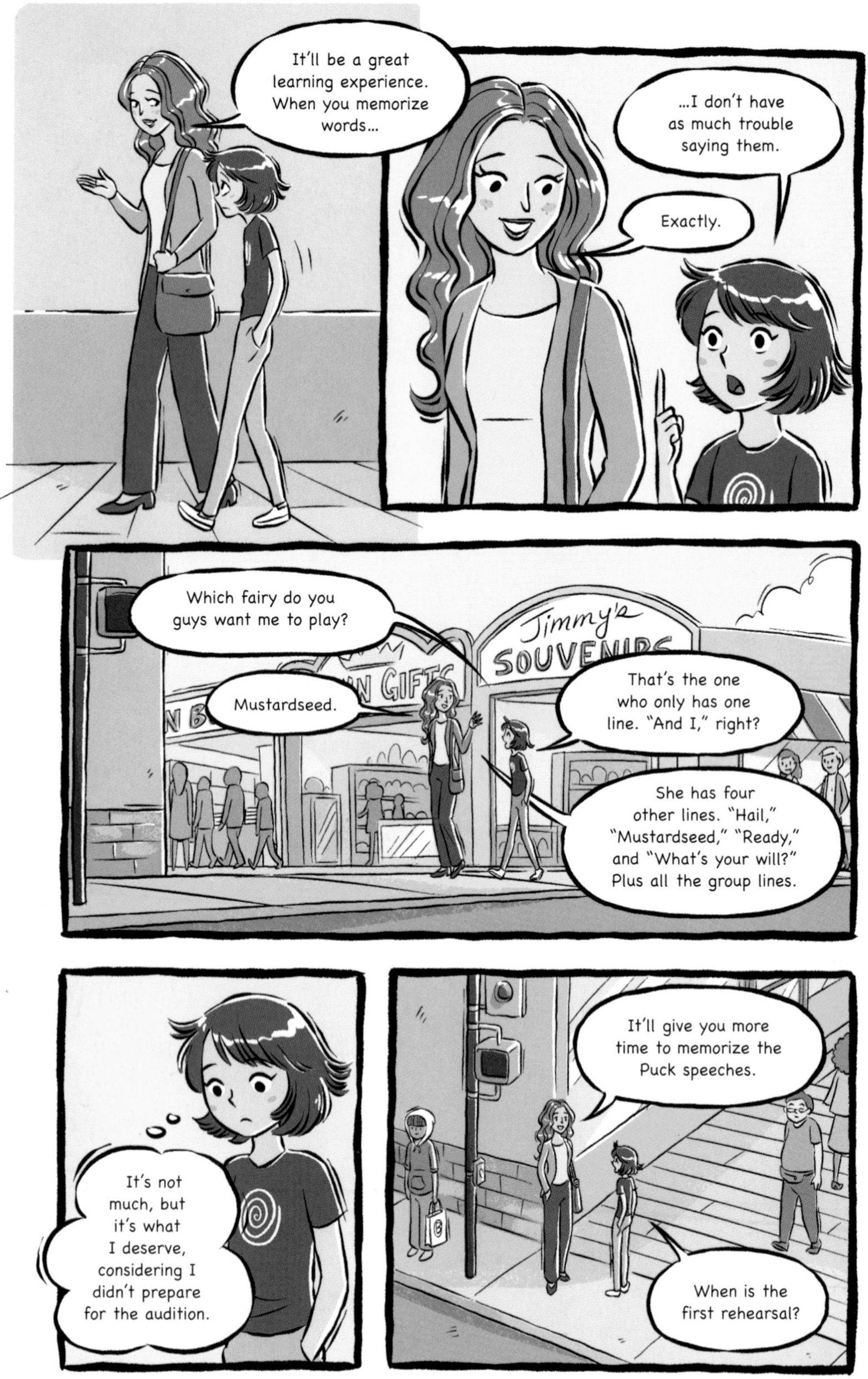
It'll be a great learning experience. When you memorize words...
...I don't have as much trouble saying them.
Exactly.
Which fairy do you guys want me to play?
Jimmy's SOUVENIRS
Mustardseed.
That's the one who only has one line. "And I," right?
She has four other lines. "Hail," "Mustardseed," "Ready," and "What's your will?" Plus all the group lines.
It's not much, but it's what I deserve, considering I didn't prepare for the audition.
It'll give you more time to memorize the Puck speeches.
When is the first rehearsal?

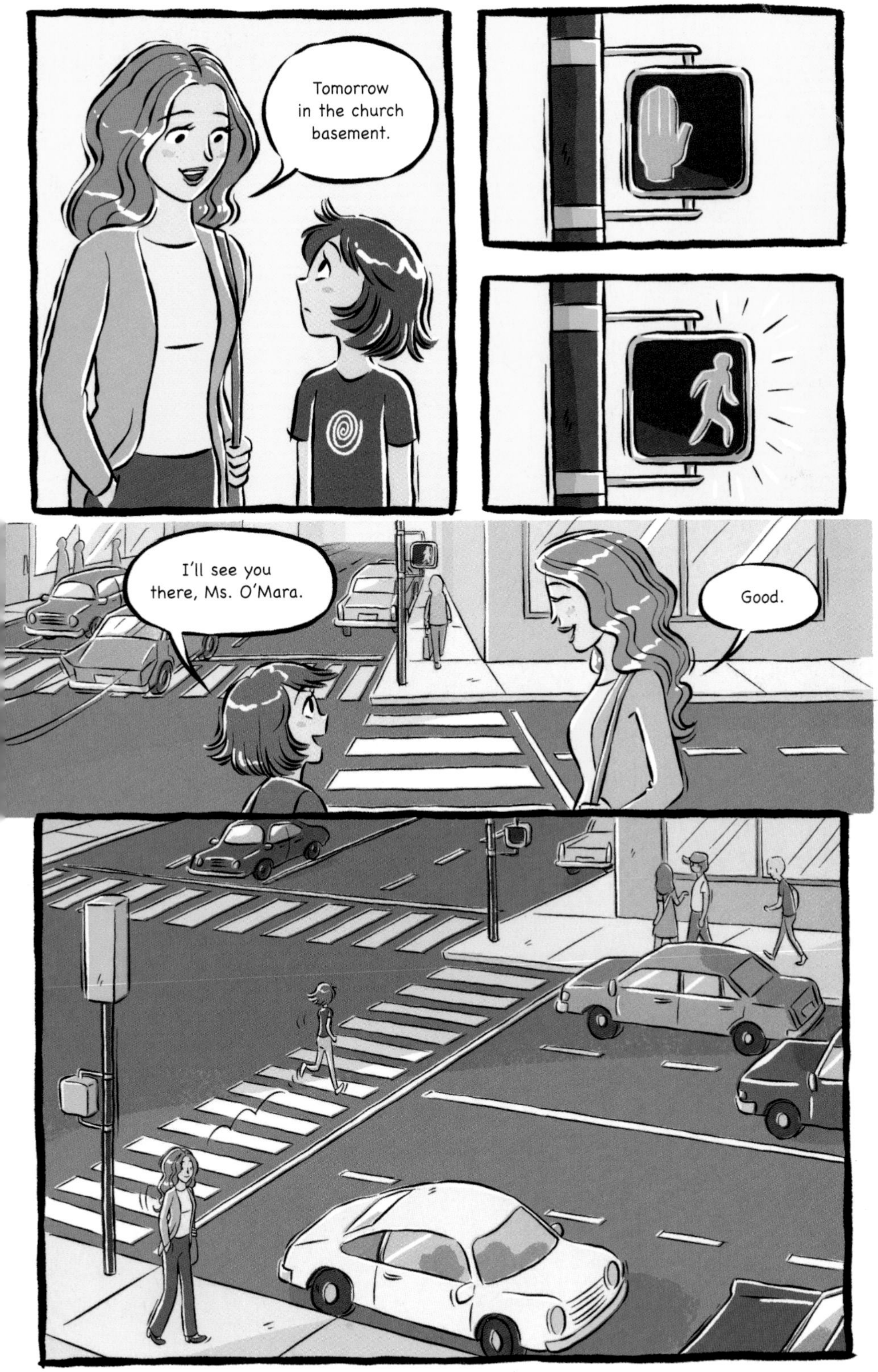
Tomorrow in the church basement.
I'll see you there, Ms. O'Mara.
Good.

The next day...

T-SHIRT HUT

SALE

You ready for the first rehearsal?

As I'll ever be!

Sorry for saying that stuff about you being jealous.

No, I'm sorry.

RDWARE STORE

OPEN

Bob is turning into a decent human being. I think we should encourage that.

Definitely. The more decent humans, the better. Does this mean we can't call him Bubblebutt anymore?

Not if we want to be, you know, decent human beings.

What about Ringworm?

I guess that's okay for now. I don't even know his real name.

Cool.

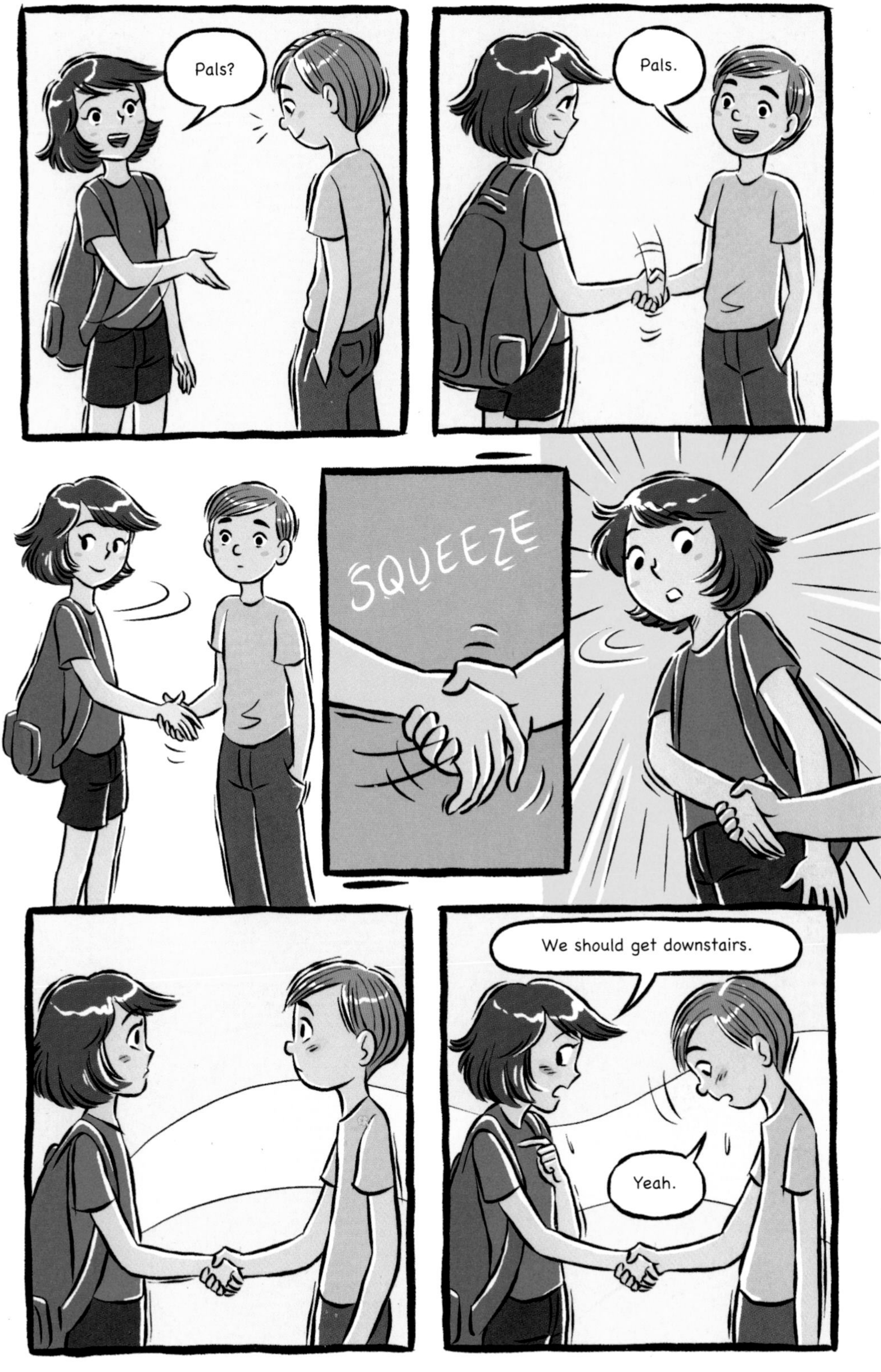
Pals?
Pals.
SQUEEZE
We should get downstairs.
Yeah.

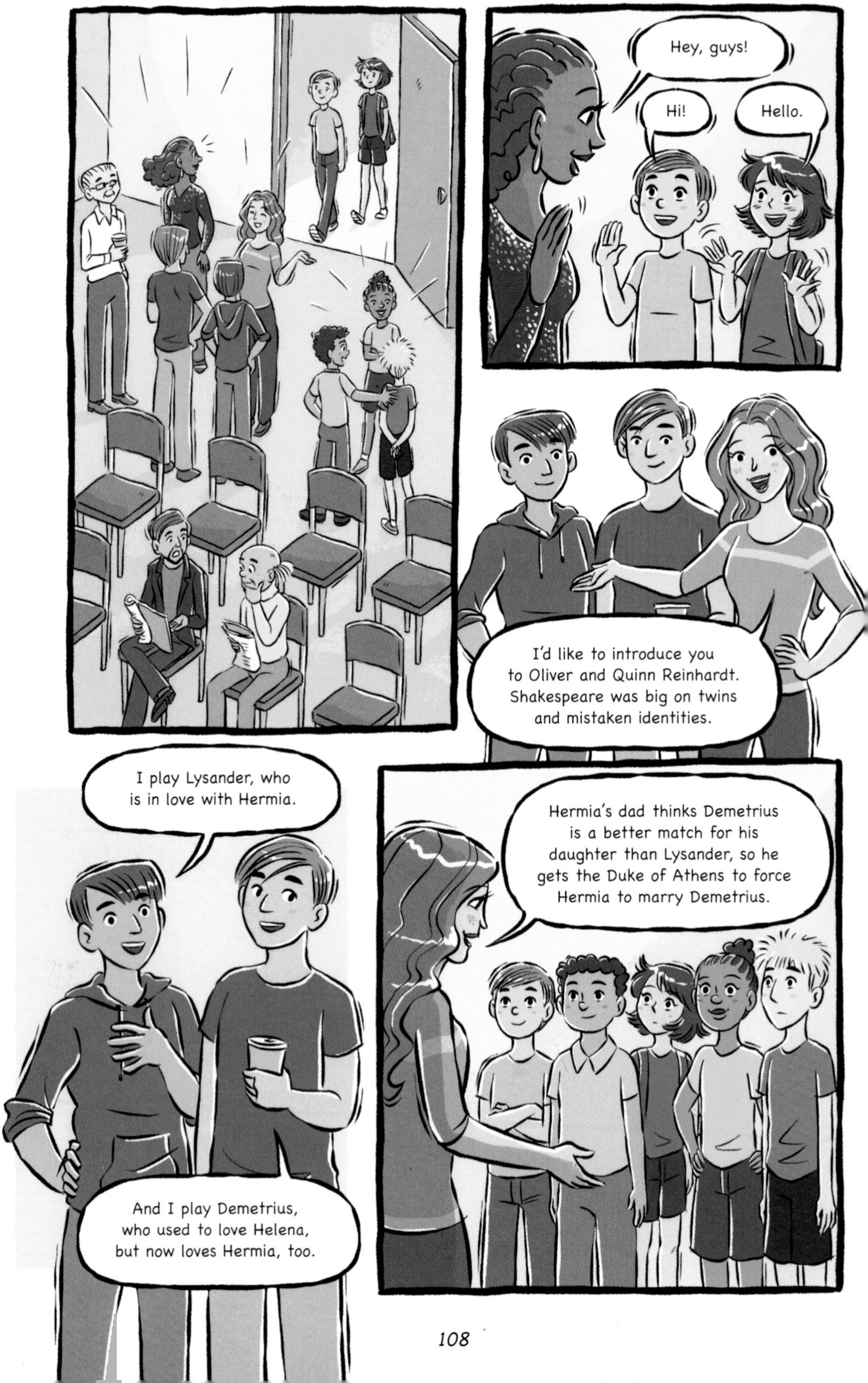
Hey, guys!
Hi!
Hello.
I'd like to introduce you to Oliver and Quinn Reinhardt. Shakespeare was big on twins and mistaken identities.
I play Lysander, who is in love with Hermia.
And I play Demetrius, who used to love Helena, but now loves Hermia, too.
Hermia's dad thinks Demetrius is a better match for his daughter than Lysander, so he gets the Duke of Athens to force Hermia to marry Demetrius.

109

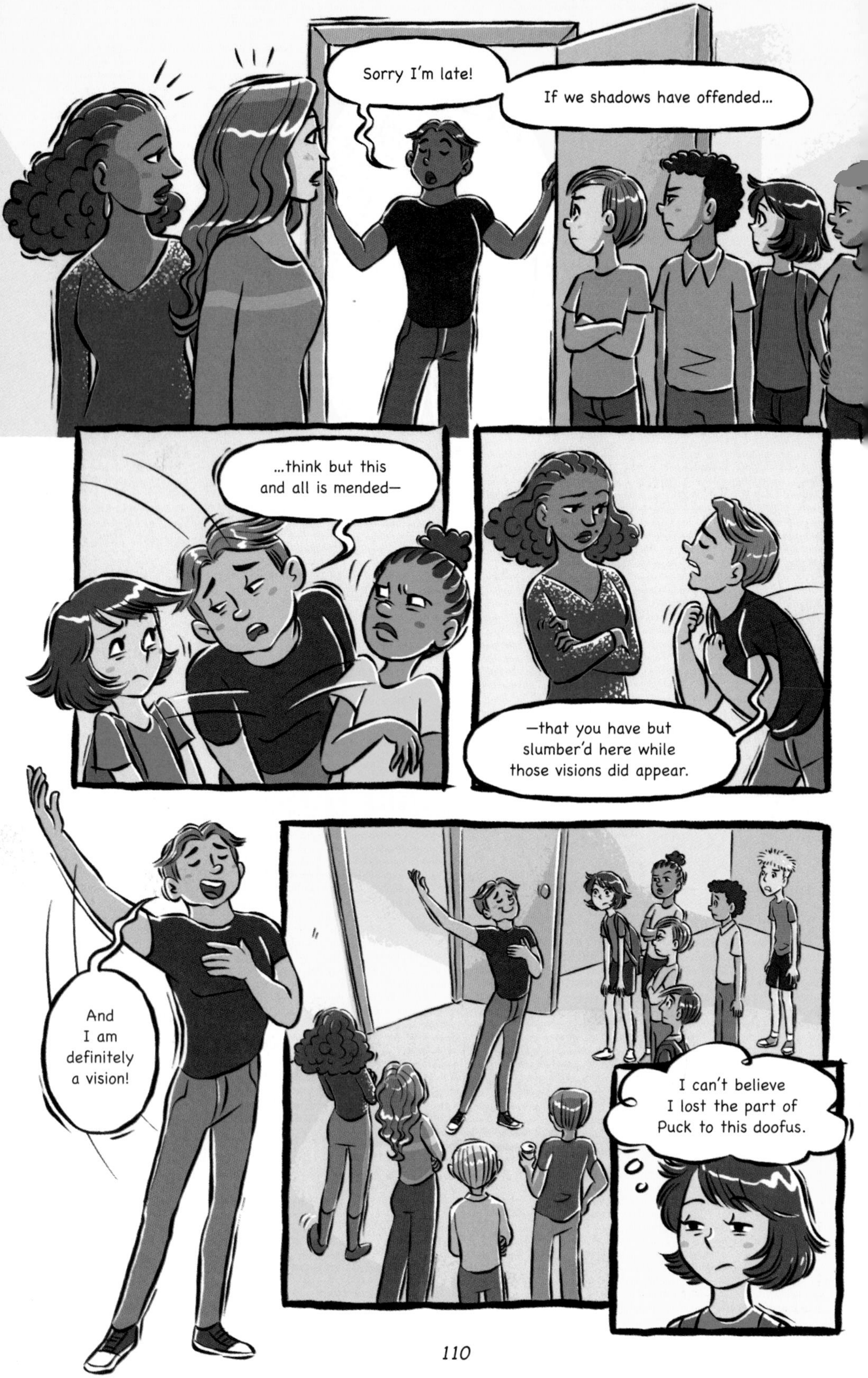
Sorry I'm late!
If we shadows have offended...
...think but this and all is mended—
—that you have but slumber'd here while those visions did appear.
And I am definitely a vision!
I can't believe I lost the part of Puck to this doofus.

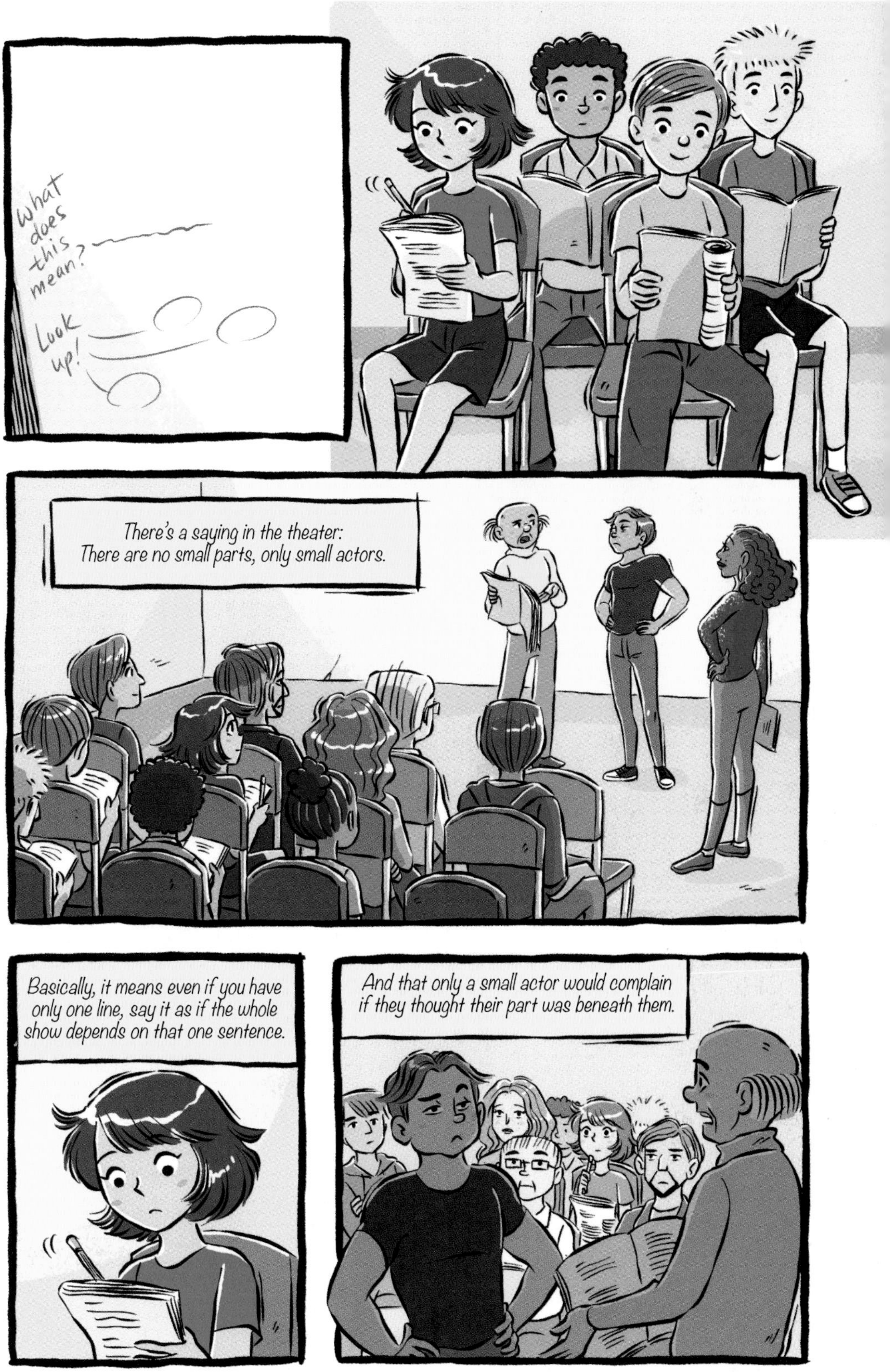

What does this mean?
Look up!
There's a saying in the theater: There are no small parts, only small actors.
Basically, it means even if you have only one line, say it as if the whole show depends on that one sentence.
And that only a small actor would complain if they thought their part was beneath them.

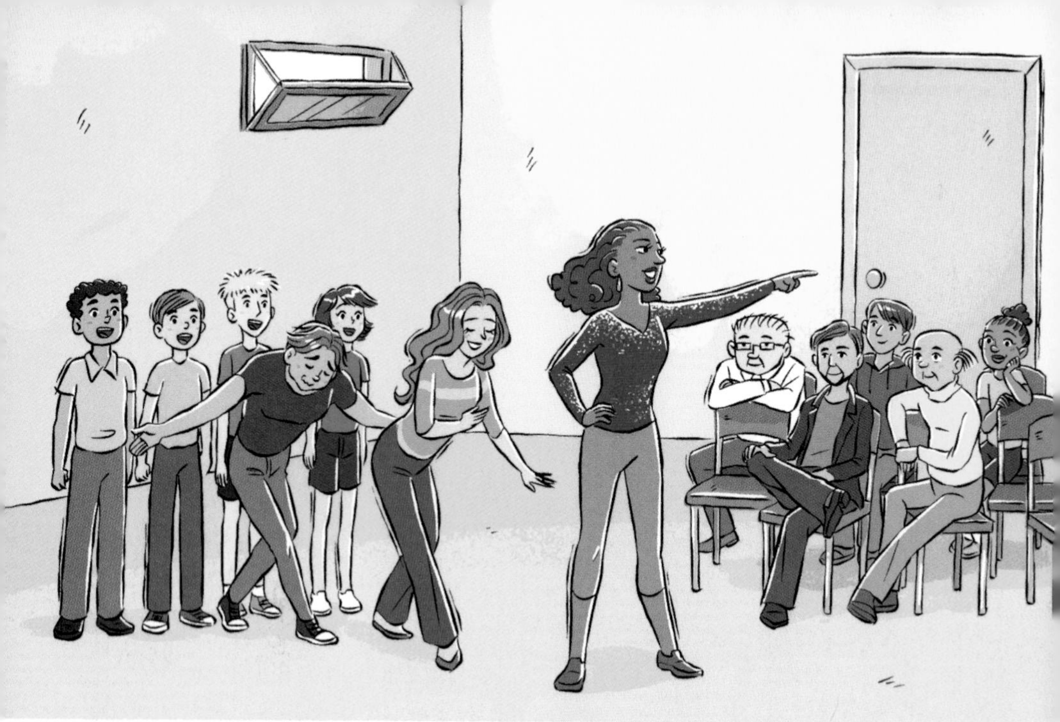

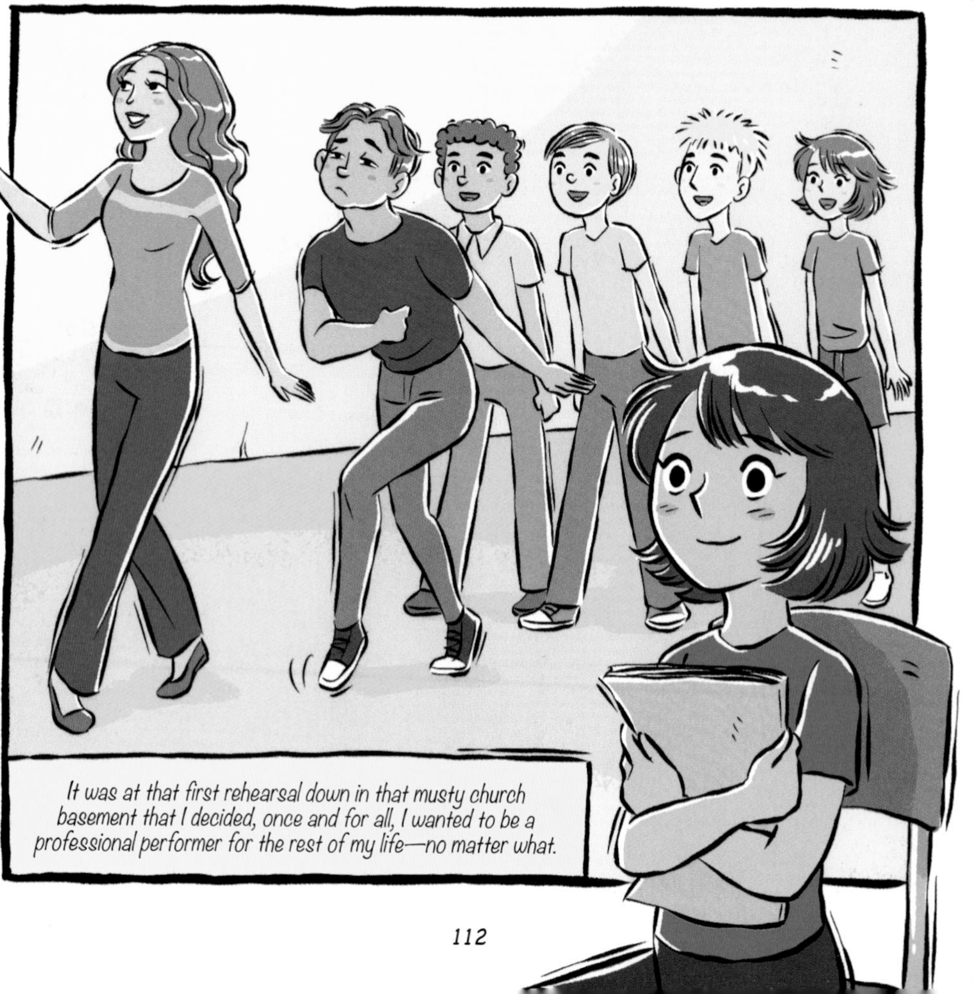
It was at that first rehearsal down in that musty church basement that I decided, once and for all, I wanted to be a professional performer for the rest of my life—no matter what.

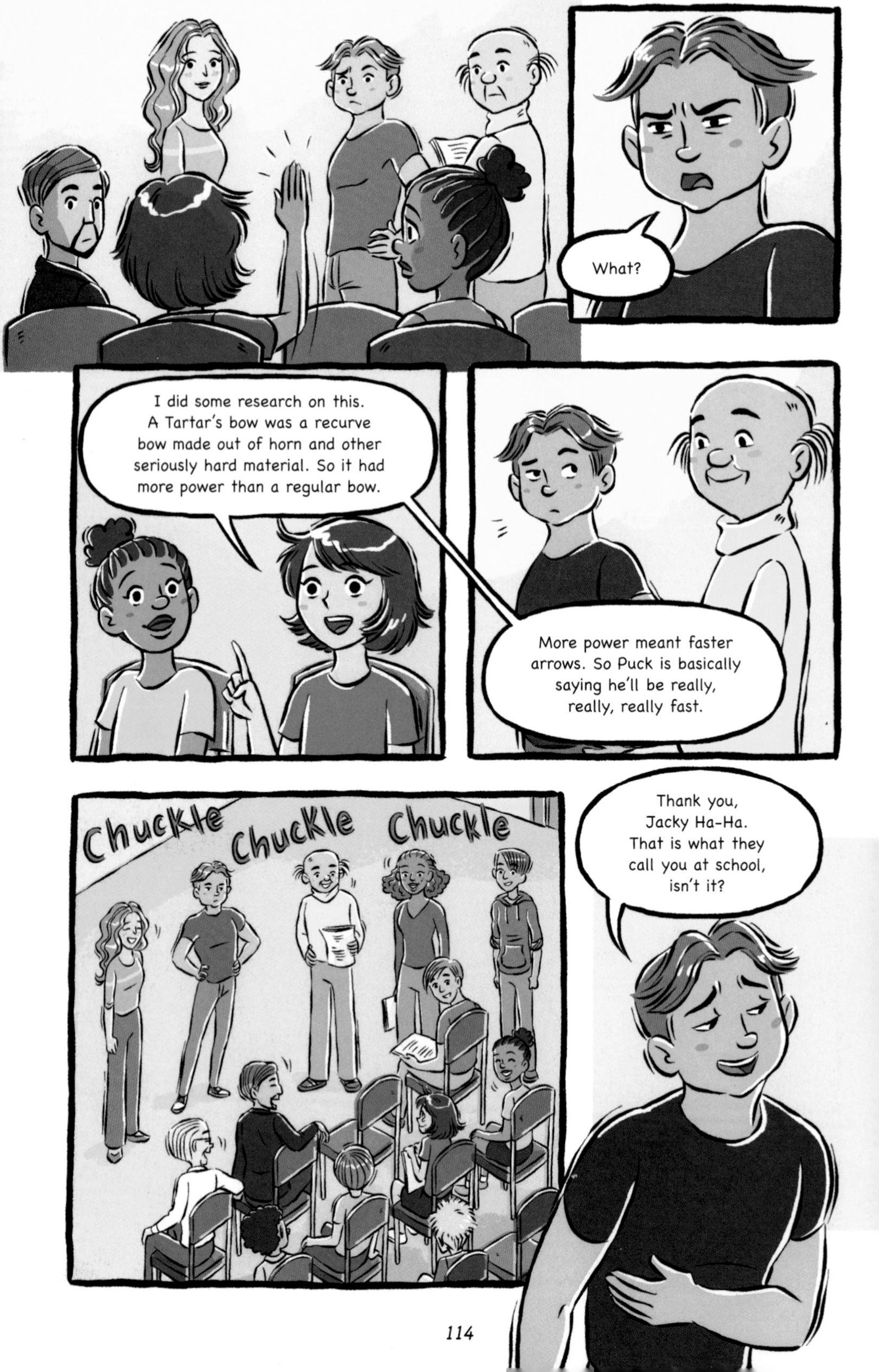
What?
I did some research on this. A Tartar's bow was a recurve bow made out of horn and other seriously hard material. So it had more power than a regular bow.
More power meant faster arrows. So Puck is basically saying he'll be really, really, really fast.
Chuckle Chuckle Chuckle
Thank you, Jacky Ha-Ha. That is what they call you at school, isn't it?

Because she's funny.

Jacky is doing her job like a pro. After all, she is understudying the role of Puck.

Hysterical. Tell you what, Jacky. Since your part is so teensy tiny, you can do all of my homework for me.

What? Why?

For the same reason I'm understudying Latoya's part. The show must go on, even if one of our leads can't.

Well, if you play her part, who plays yours?

My understudy.

It seems sort of stupid. All these people learning all these different parts. Everybody just don't get sick.

I know I won't.

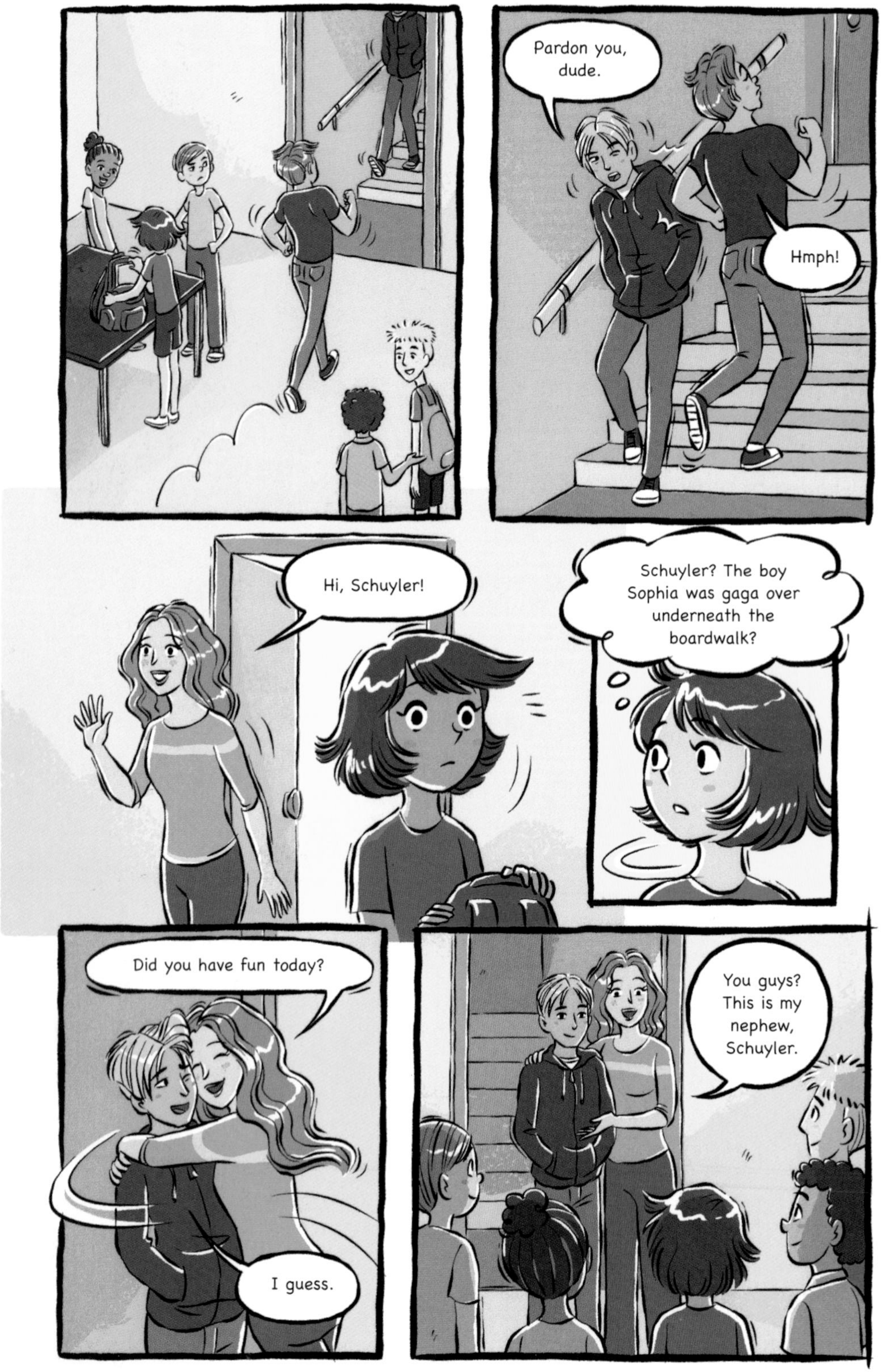

Pardon you, dude.
Hmph!
Hi, Schuyler!
Schuyler? The boy Sophia was gaga over underneath the boardwalk?
Did you have fun today?
I guess.
You guys? This is my nephew, Schuyler.

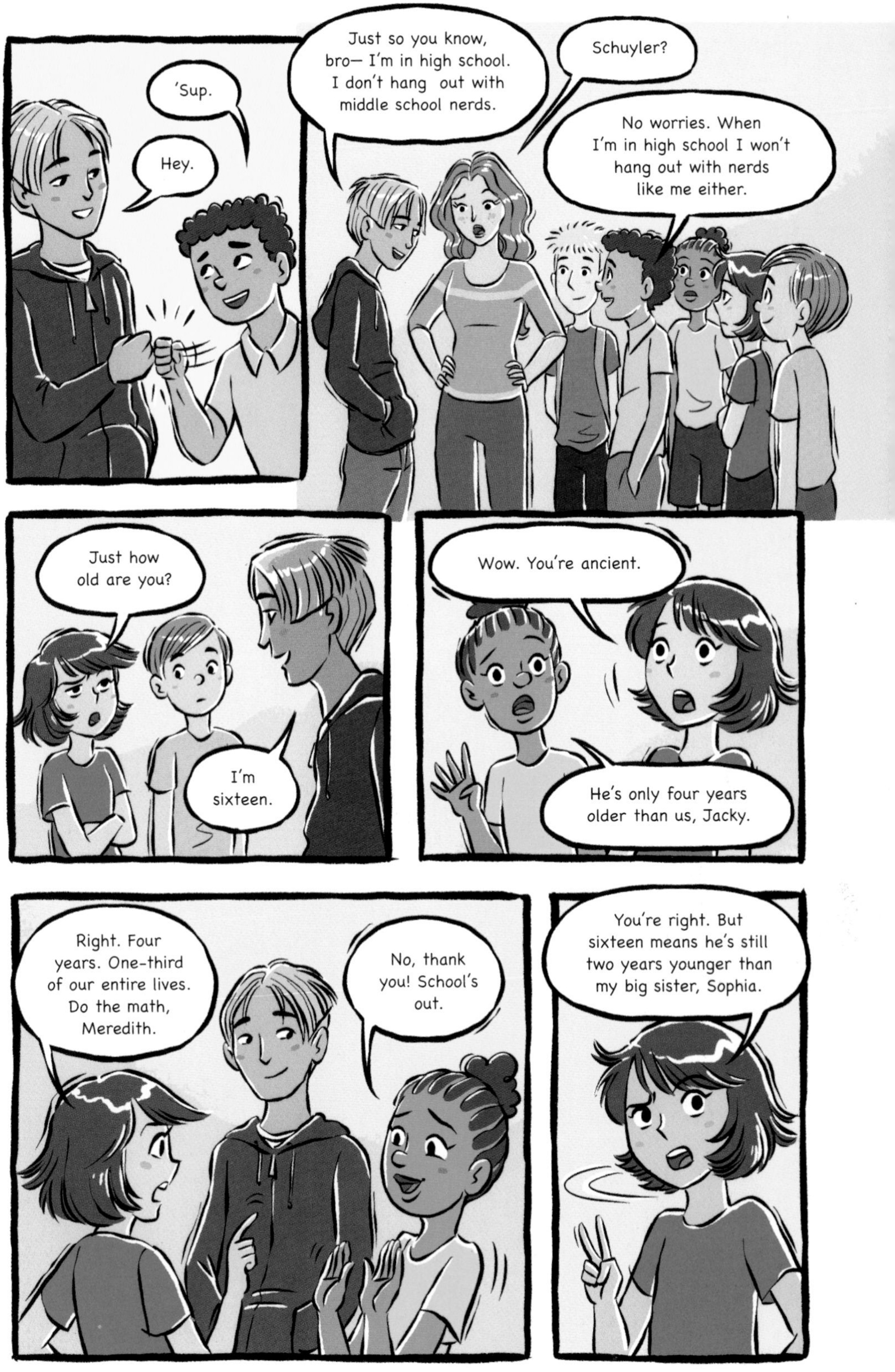
'Sup.
Hey.
Just so you know, bro— I'm in high school. I don't hang out with middle school nerds.
Schuyler?
No worries. When I'm in high school I won't hang out with nerds like me either.
Just how old are you?
I'm sixteen.
Wow. You're ancient.
He's only four years older than us, Jacky.
Right. Four years. One-third of our entire lives. Do the math, Meredith.
No, thank you! School's out.
You're right. But sixteen means he's still two years younger than my big sister, Sophia.

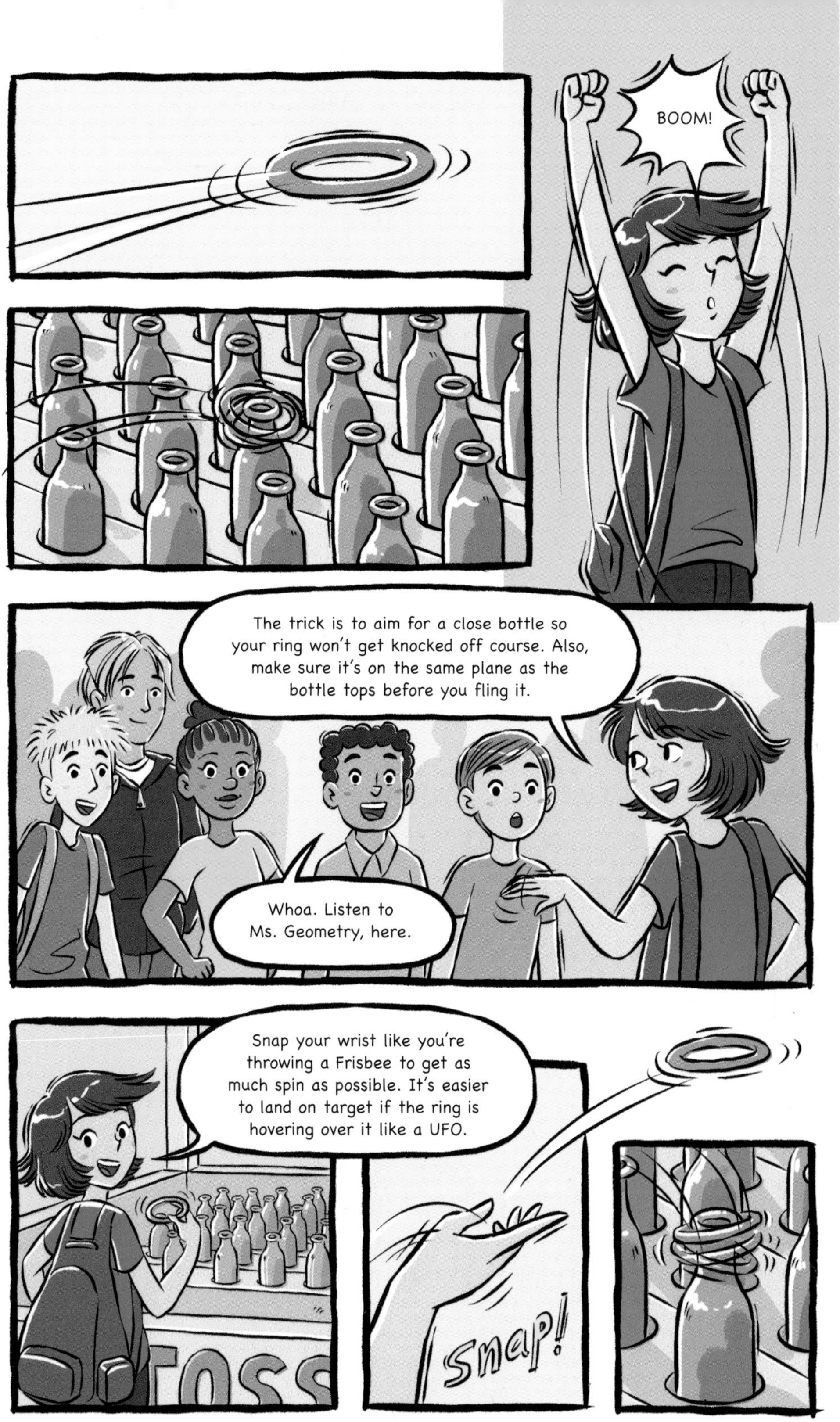
BOOM!
The trick is to aim for a close bottle so your ring won't get knocked off course. Also, make sure it's on the same plane as the bottle tops before you fling it.
Whoa. Listen to Ms. Geometry, here.
Snap your wrist like you're throwing a Frisbee to get as much spin as possible. It's easier to land on target if the ring is hovering over it like a UFO.
TOSS
Snap!

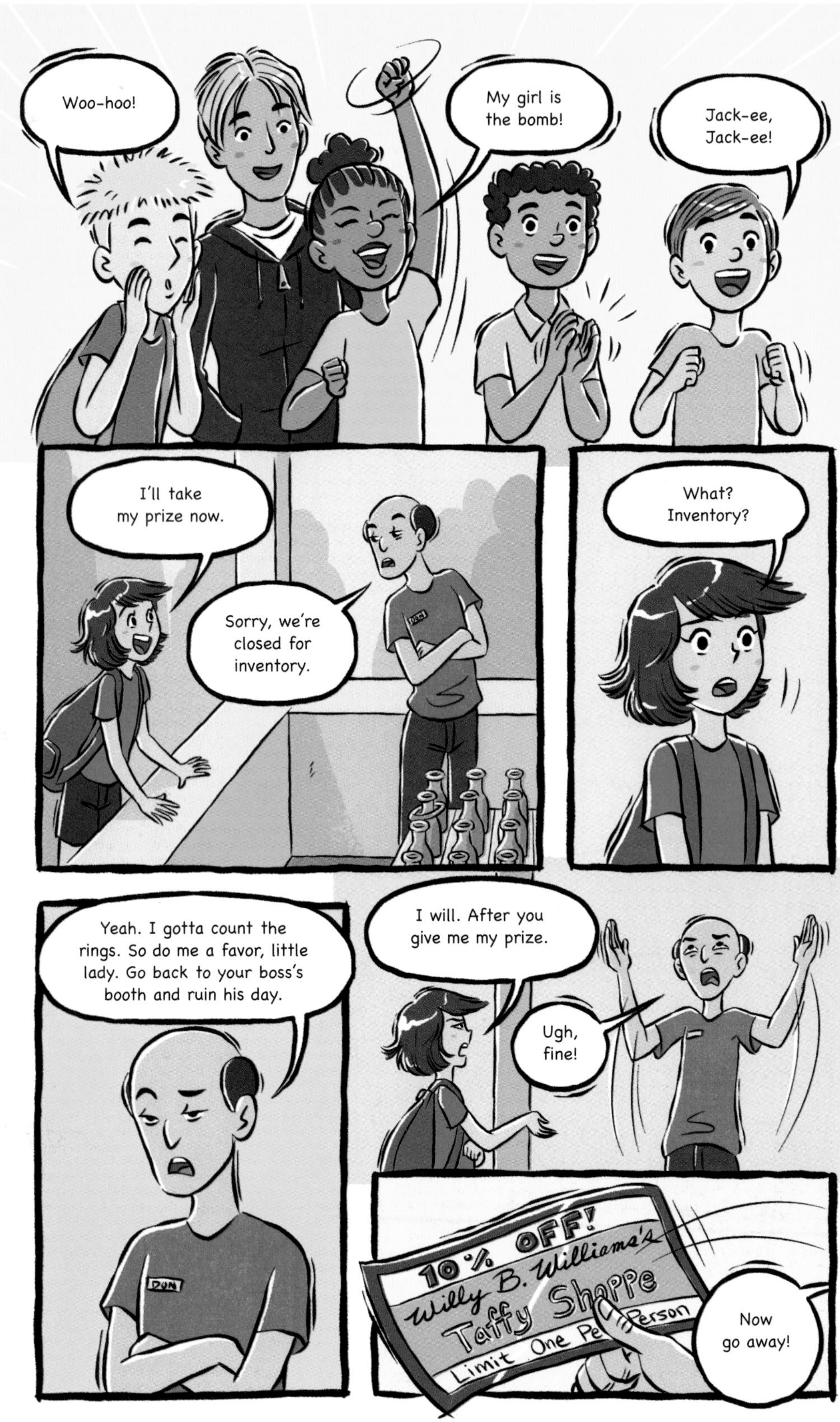
Woo-hoo!
My girl is the bomb!
Jack-ee, Jack-ee!
I'll take my prize now.
Sorry, we're closed for inventory.
What? Inventory?
Yeah. I gotta count the rings. So do me a favor, little lady. Go back to your boss's booth and ruin his day.
I will. After you give me my prize.
Ugh, fine!
10% OFF!
Willy B. Williams's
Taffy Shoppe
Now go away!

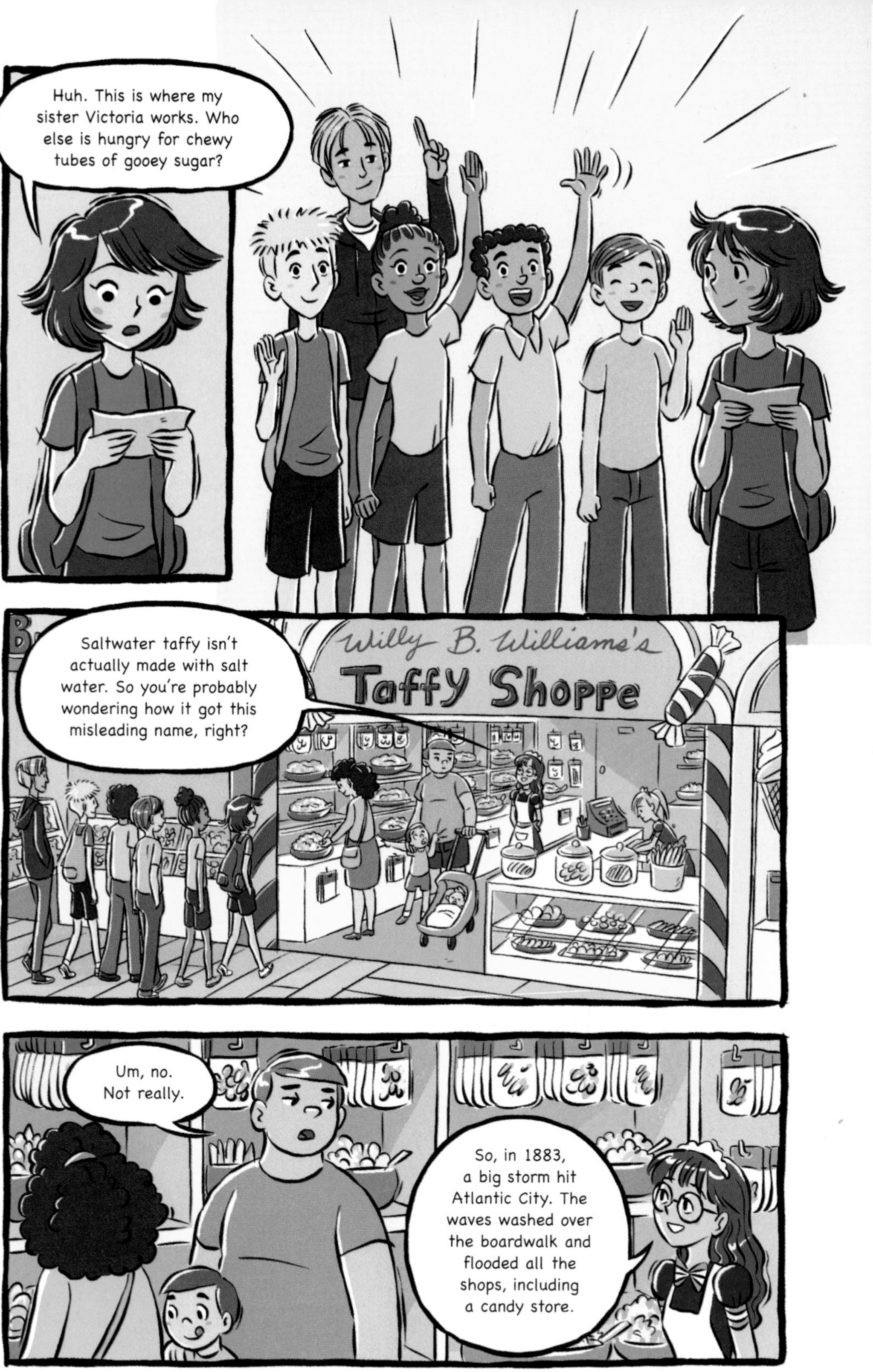
Huh. This is where my sister Victoria works. Who else is hungry for chewy tubes of gooey sugar?
Willy B. Williams's Taffy Shoppe
Saltwater taffy isn't actually made with salt water. So you're probably wondering how it got this misleading name, right?
Um, no. Not really.
So, in 1883, a big storm hit Atlantic City. The waves washed over the boardwalk and flooded all the shops, including a candy store.

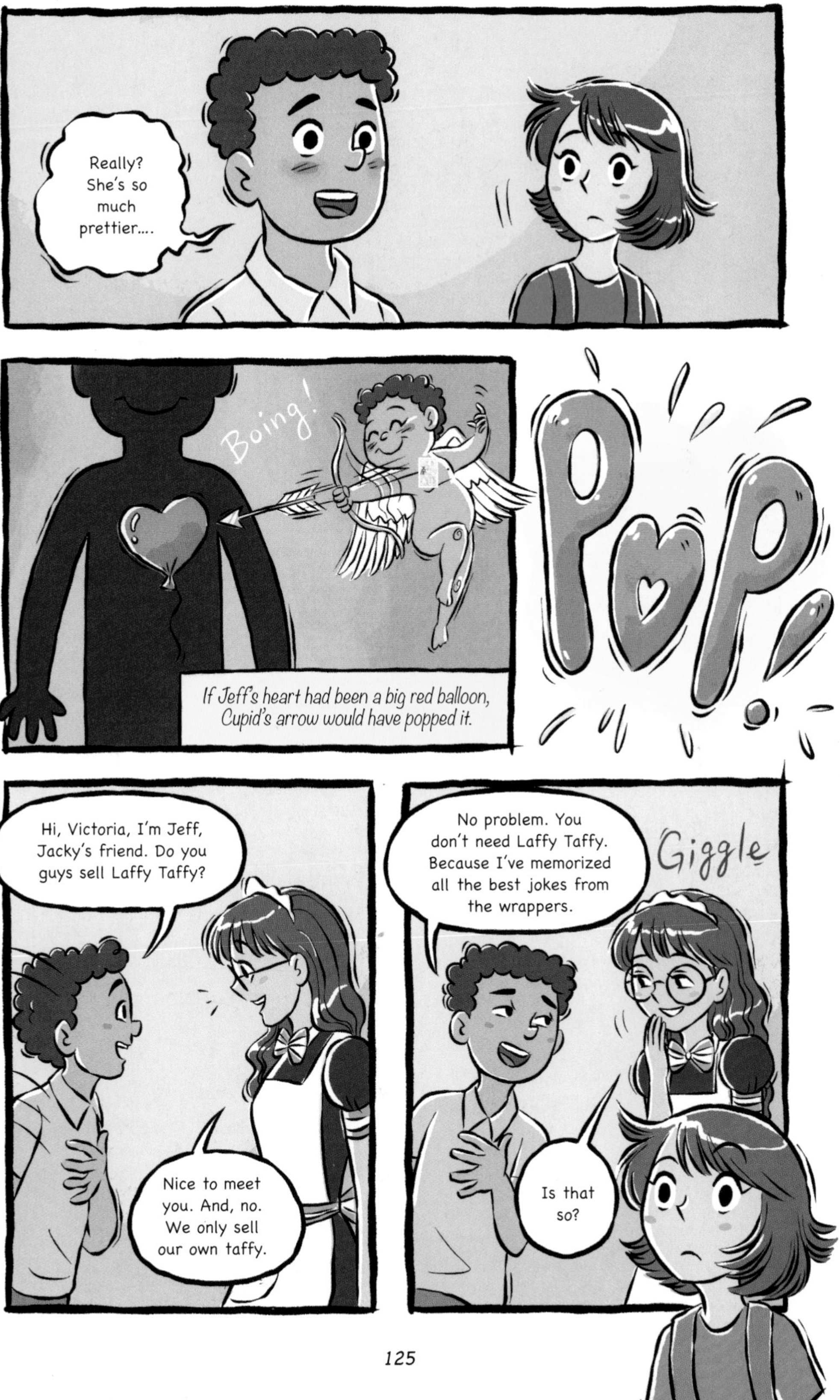
Really? She's so much prettier....
Boing!
If Jeff's heart had been a big red balloon, Cupid's arrow would have popped it.
POP!
Hi, Victoria, I'm Jeff, Jacky's friend. Do you guys sell Laffy Taffy?
Nice to meet you. And, no. We only sell our own taffy.
No problem. You don't need Laffy Taffy. Because I've memorized all the best jokes from the wrappers.
Giggle
Is that so?

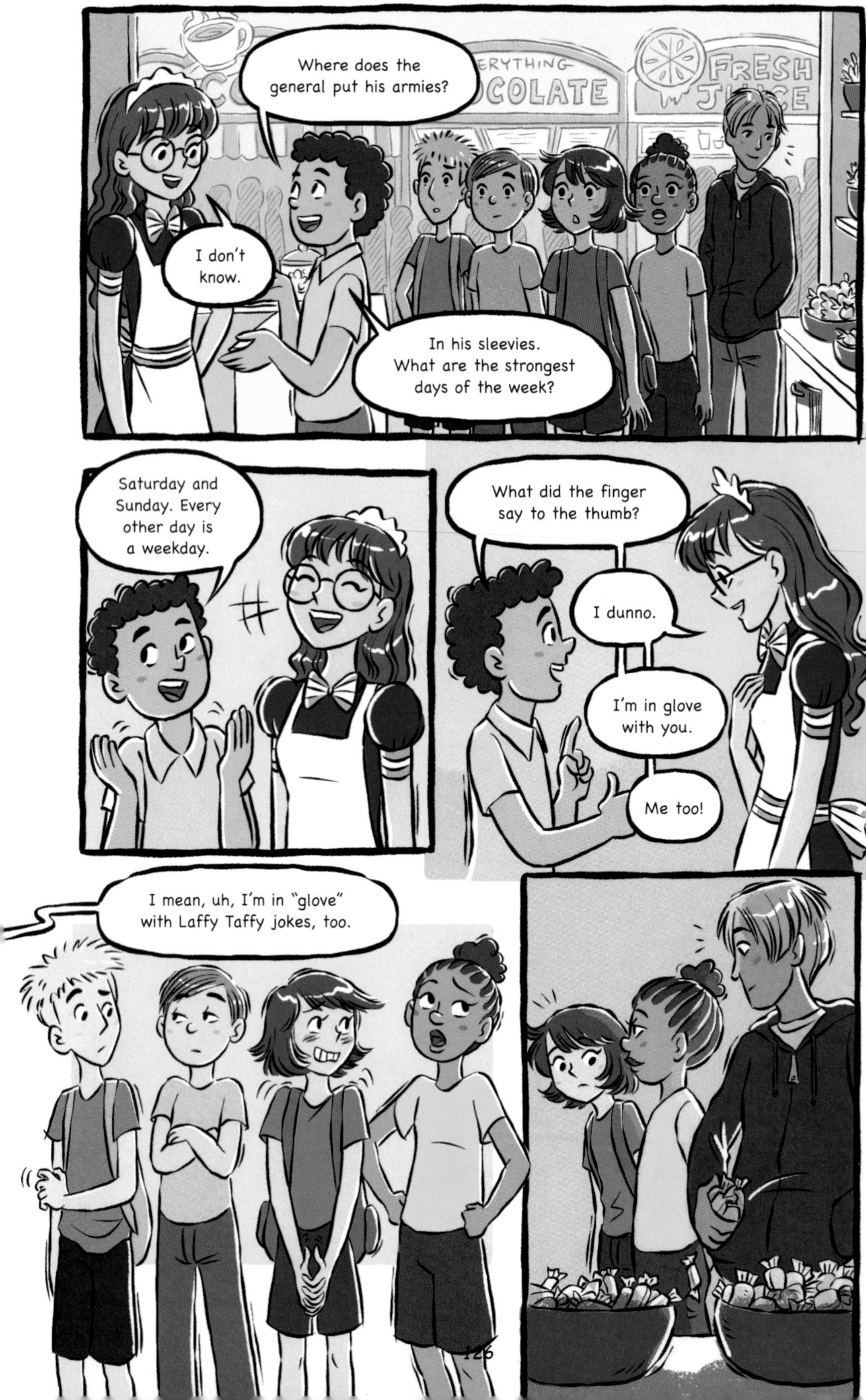
ERYTHING
OCOLATE
FRESH JUICE
Where does the general put his armies?
I don't know.
In his sleevies. What are the strongest days of the week?
Saturday and Sunday. Every other day is a weekday.
What did the finger say to the thumb?
I dunno.
I'm in glove with you.
Me too!
I mean, uh, I'm in "glove" with Laffy Taffy jokes, too.

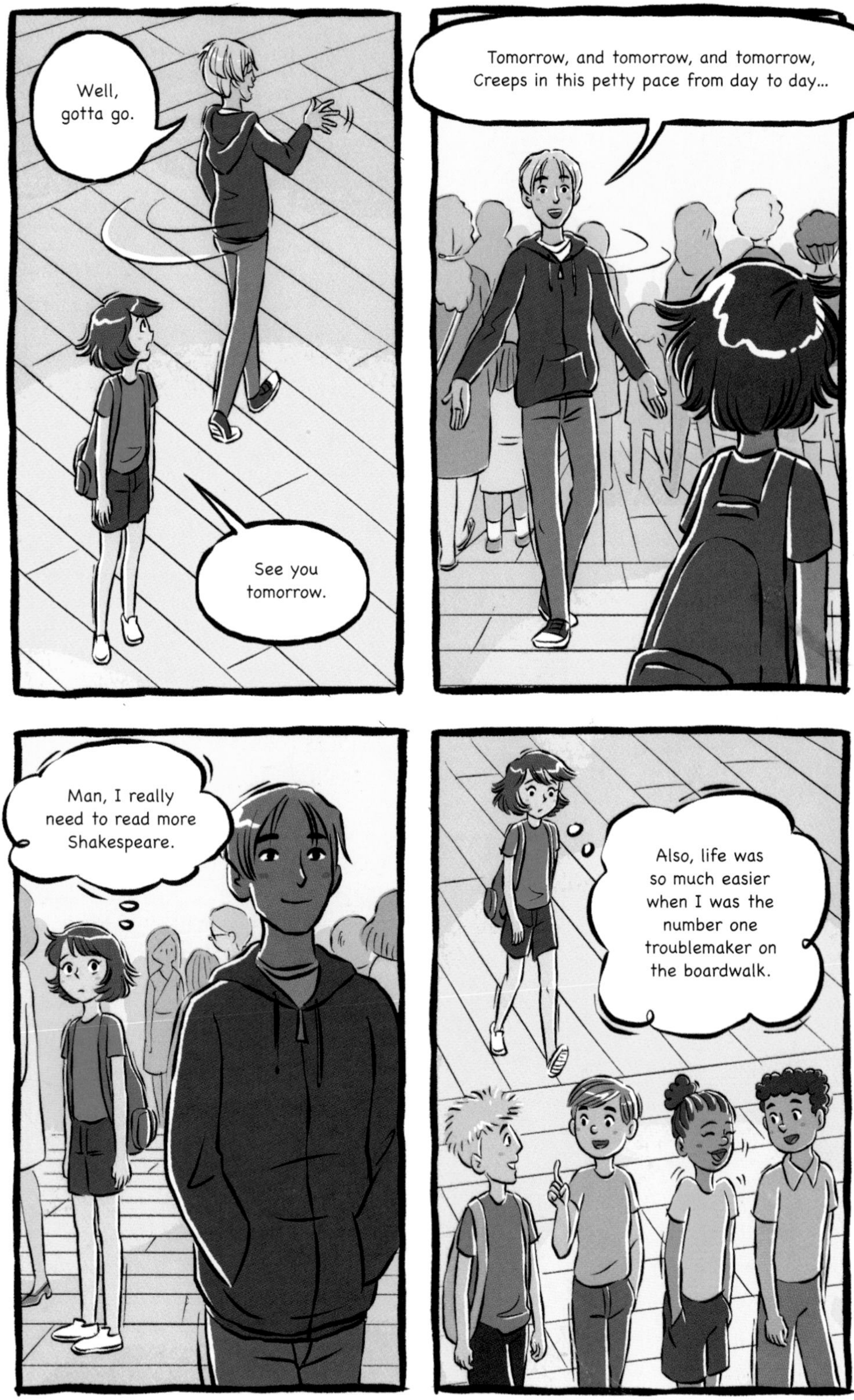
Well, gotta go.
See you tomorrow.
Tomorrow, and tomorrow, and tomorrow, Creeps in this petty pace from day to day...
Man, I really need to read more Shakespeare.
Also, life was so much easier when I was the number one troublemaker on the boardwalk.

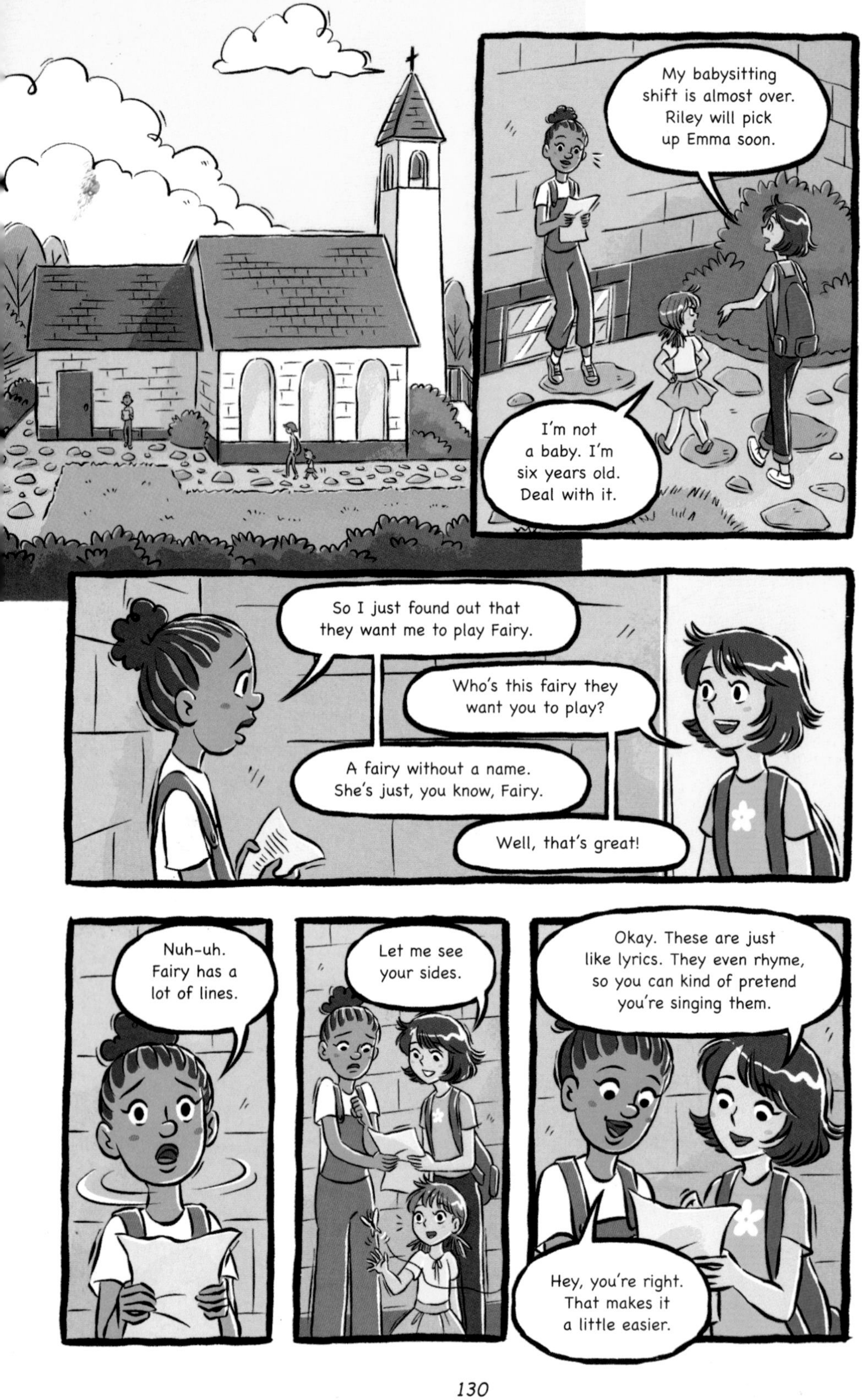
My babysitting shift is almost over. Riley will pick up Emma soon.
I'm not a baby. I'm six years old. Deal with it.
So I just found out that they want me to play Fairy.
Who's this fairy they want you to play?
A fairy without a name. She's just, you know, Fairy.
Well, that's great!
Nuh-uh. Fairy has a lot of lines.
Let me see your sides.
Okay. These are just like lyrics. They even rhyme, so you can kind of pretend you're singing them.
Hey, you're right. That makes it a little easier.

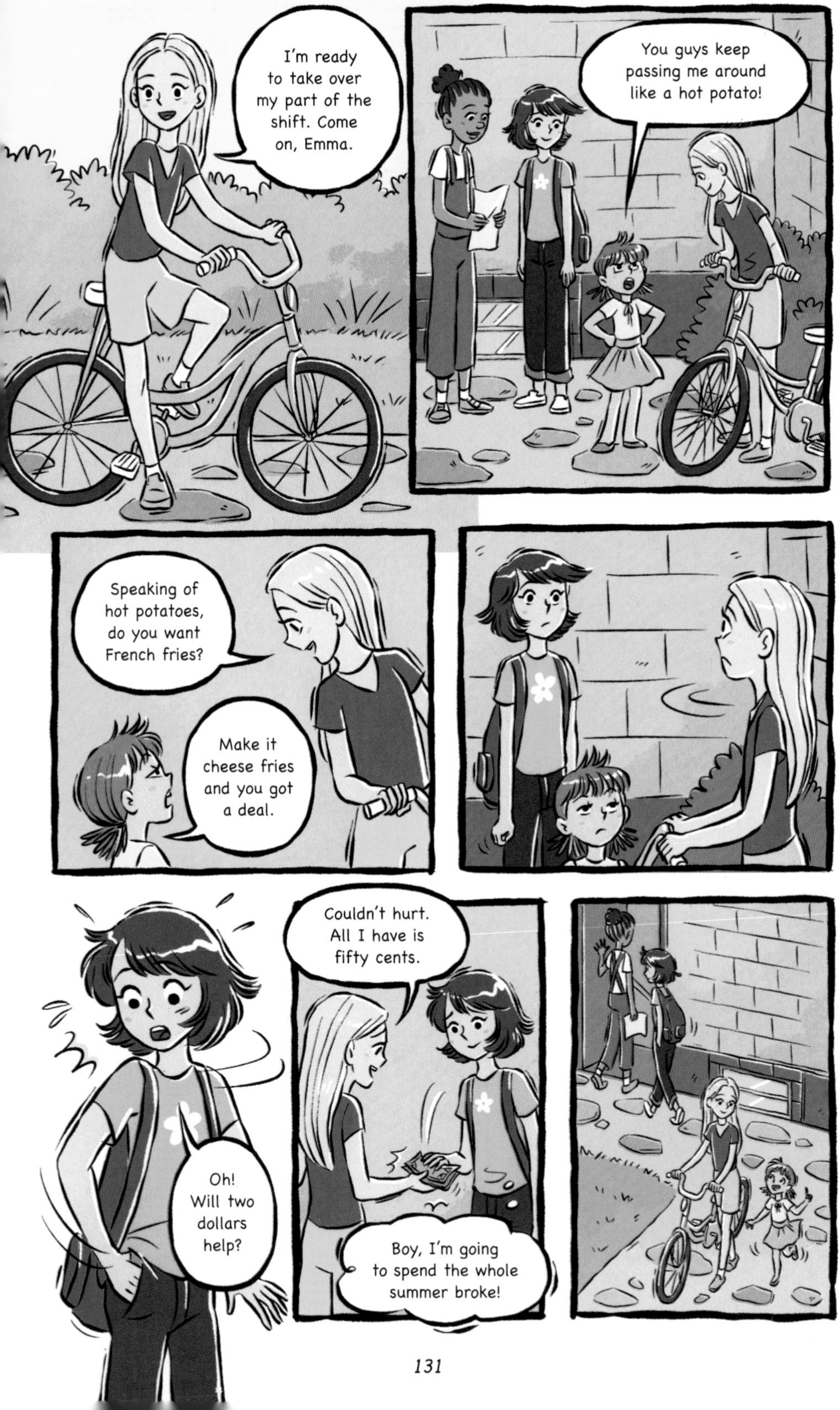
I'm ready to take over my part of the shift. Come on, Emma.
You guys keep passing me around like a hot potato!
Speaking of hot potatoes, do you want French fries?
Make it cheese fries and you got a deal.
Oh! Will two dollars help?
Couldn't hurt. All I have is fifty cents.
Boy, I'm going to spend the whole summer broke!

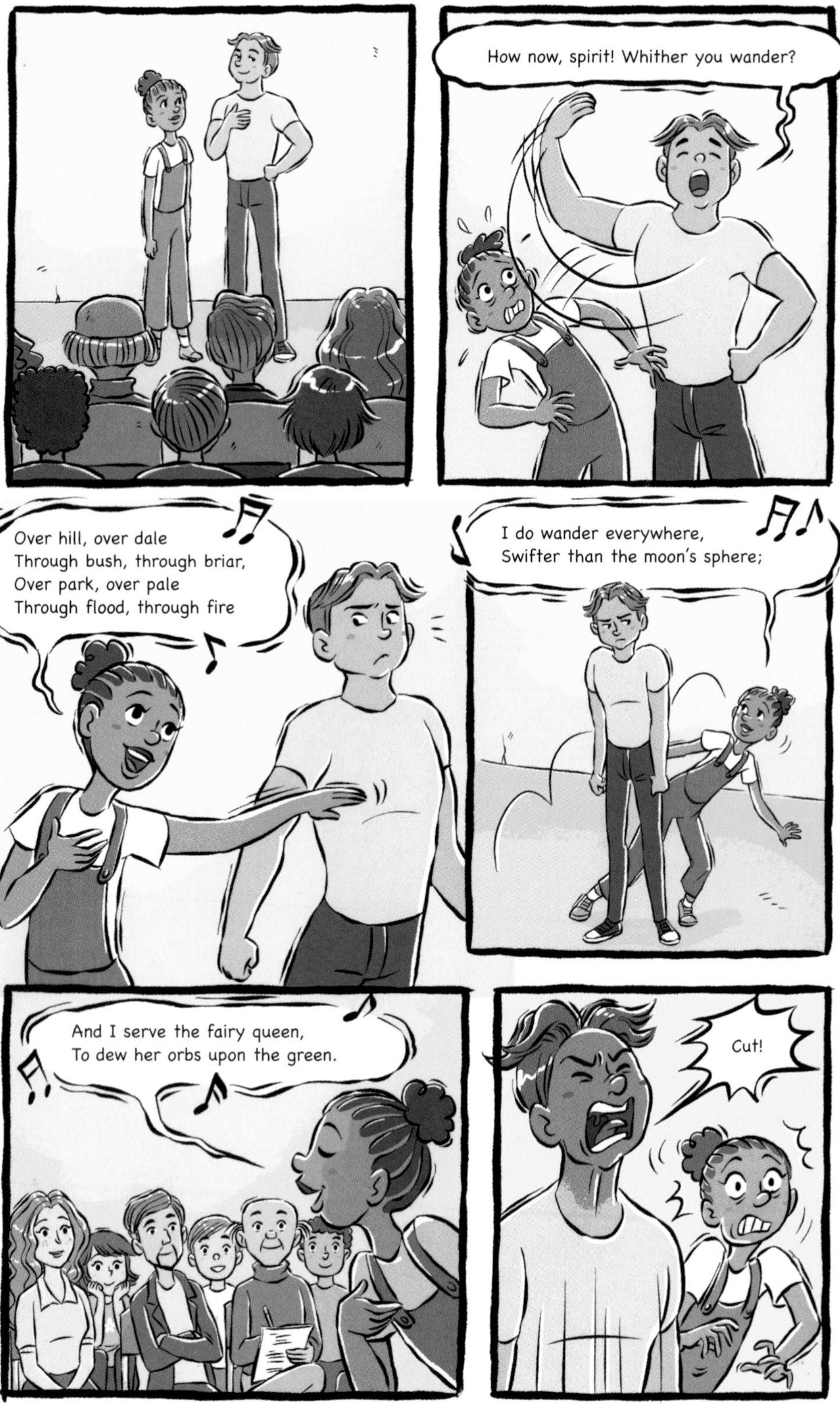
How now, spirit! Whither you wander?
Over hill, over dale
Through bush, through briar,
Over park, over pale
Through flood, through fire
I do wander everywhere,
Swifter than the moon's sphere;
And I serve the fairy queen,
To dew her orbs upon the green.
Cut!

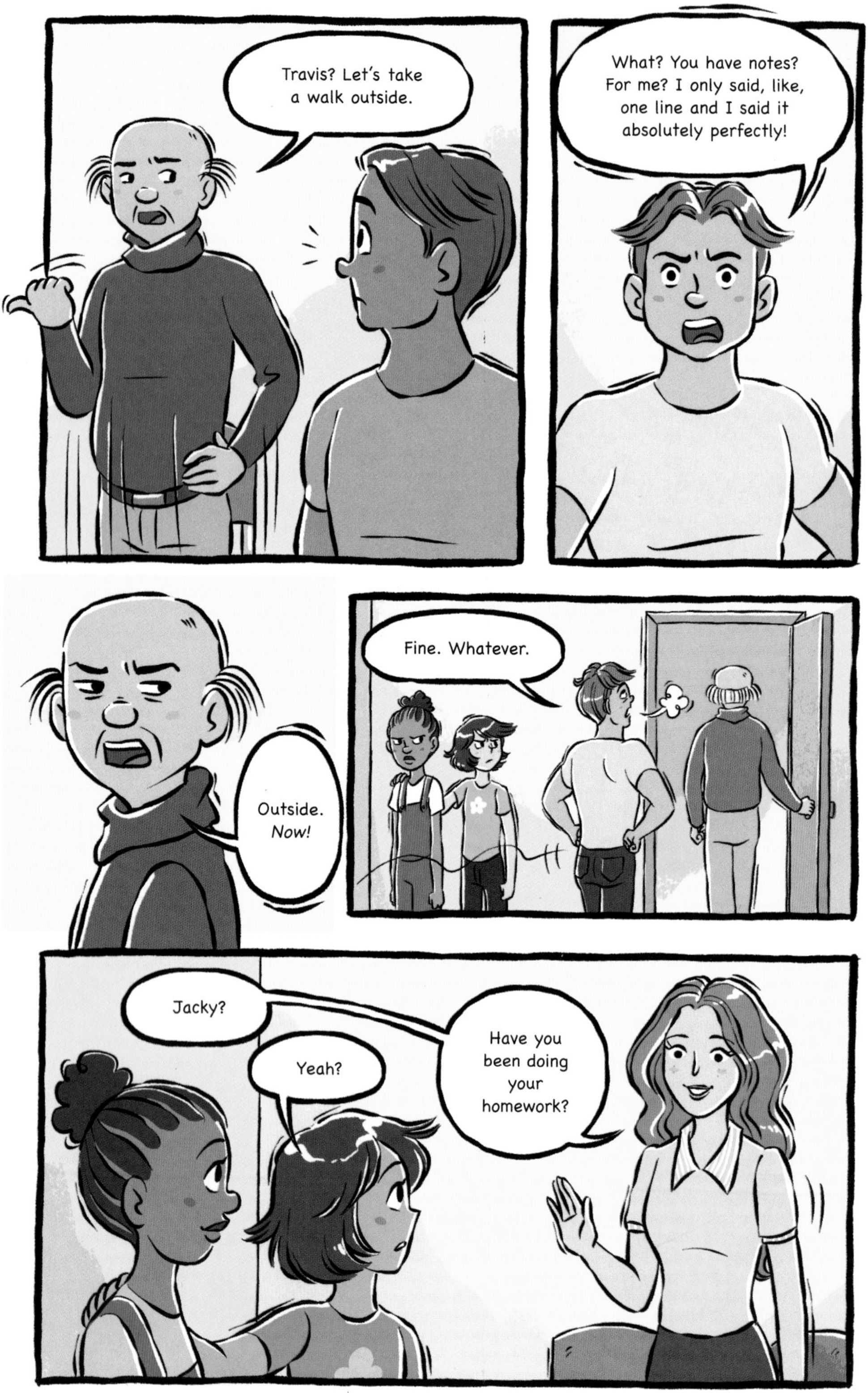
Travis? Let's take a walk outside.
What? You have notes? For me? I only said, like, one line and I said it absolutely perfectly!
Outside. Now!
Fine. Whatever.
Jacky?
Yeah?
Have you been doing your homework?

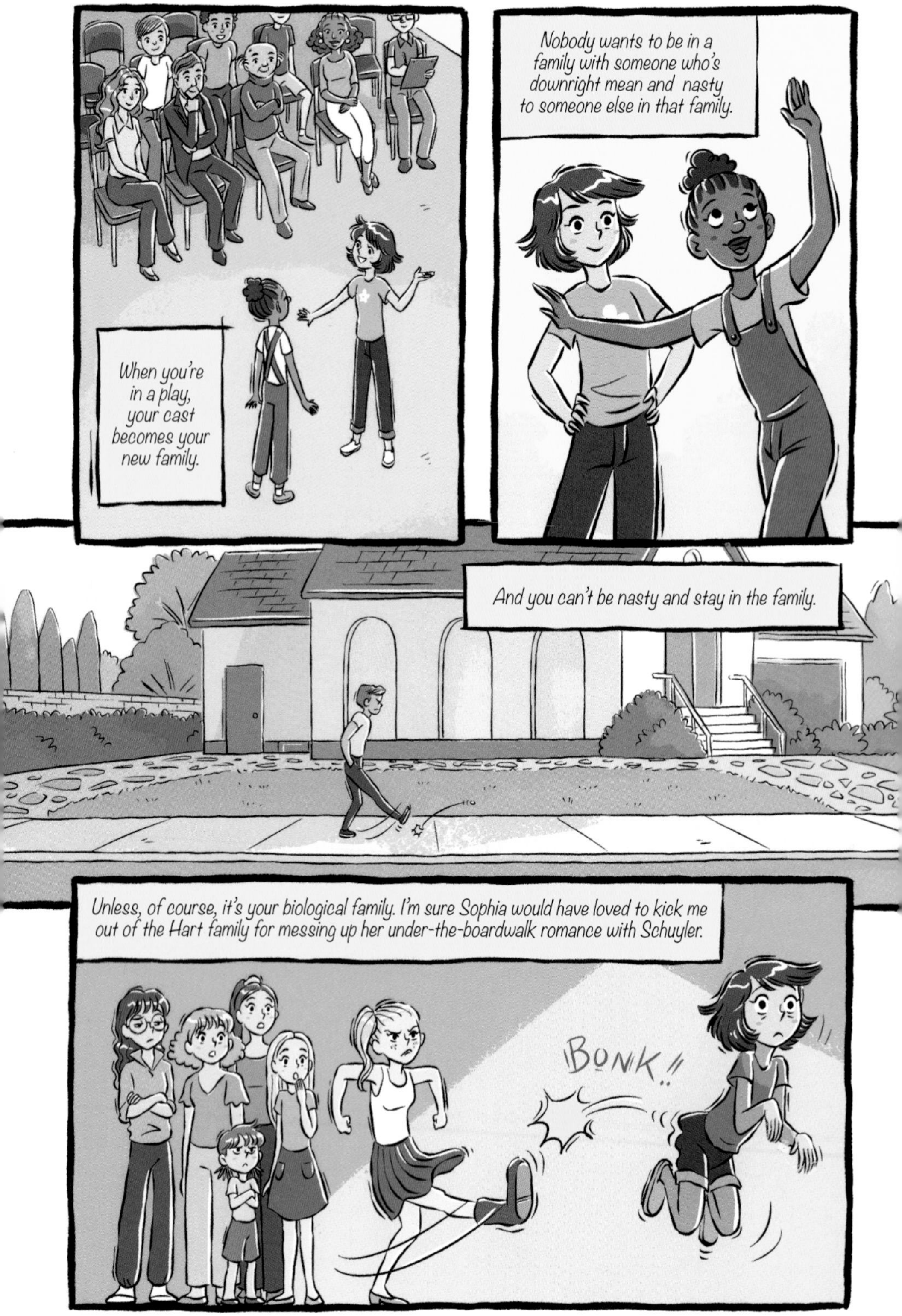
When you're in a play, your cast becomes your new family.
Nobody wants to be in a family with someone who's downright mean and nasty to someone else in that family.
And you can't be nasty and stay in the family.
Unless, of course, it's your biological family. I'm sure Sophia would have loved to kick me out of the Hart family for messing up her under-the-boardwalk romance with Schuyler.
BONK!!

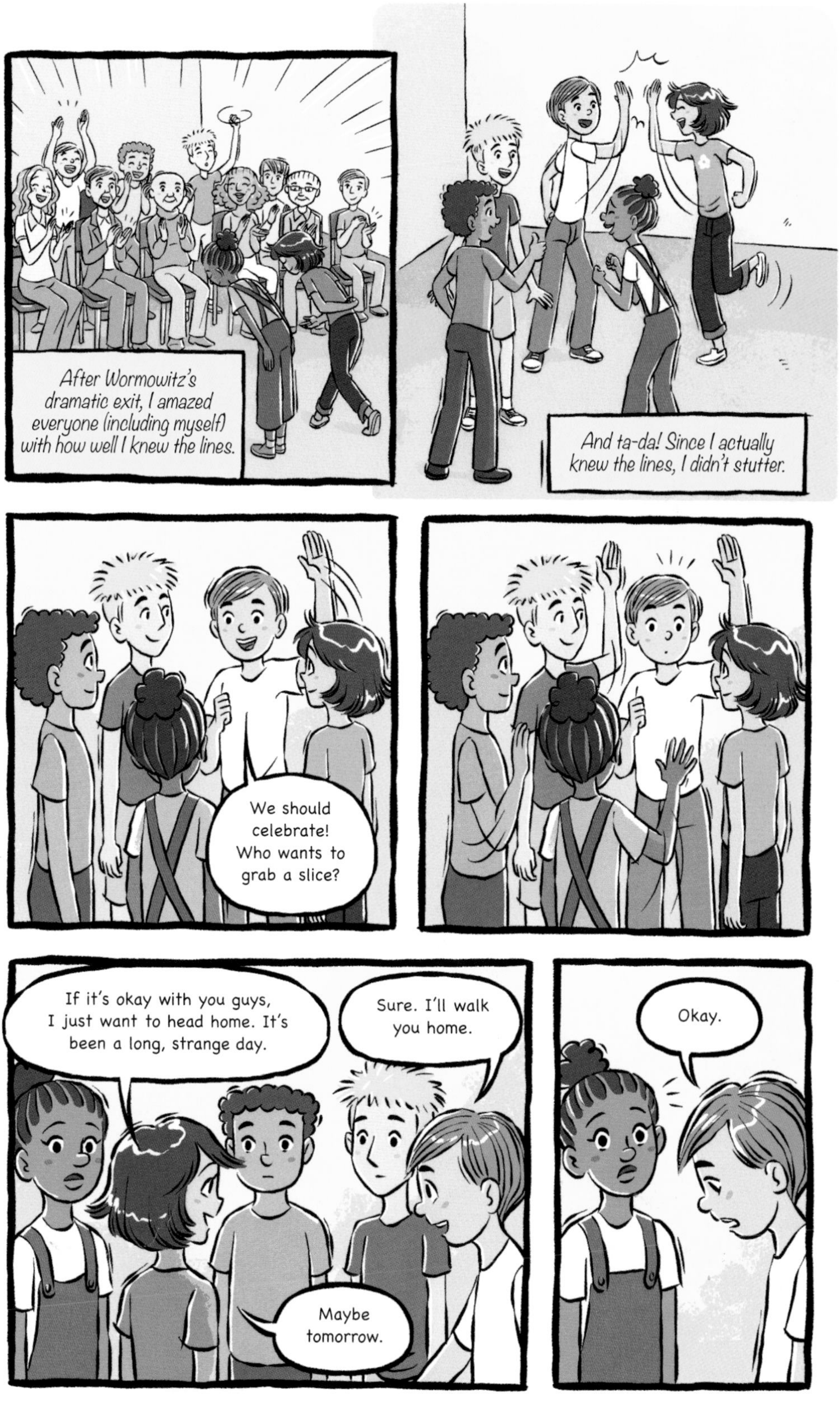
After Wormowitz's dramatic exit, I amazed everyone (including myself) with how well I knew the lines.
And ta-da! Since I actually knew the lines, I didn't stutter.
We should celebrate! Who wants to grab a slice?
If it's okay with you guys, I just want to head home. It's been a long, strange day.
Sure. I'll walk you home.
Maybe tomorrow.
Okay.

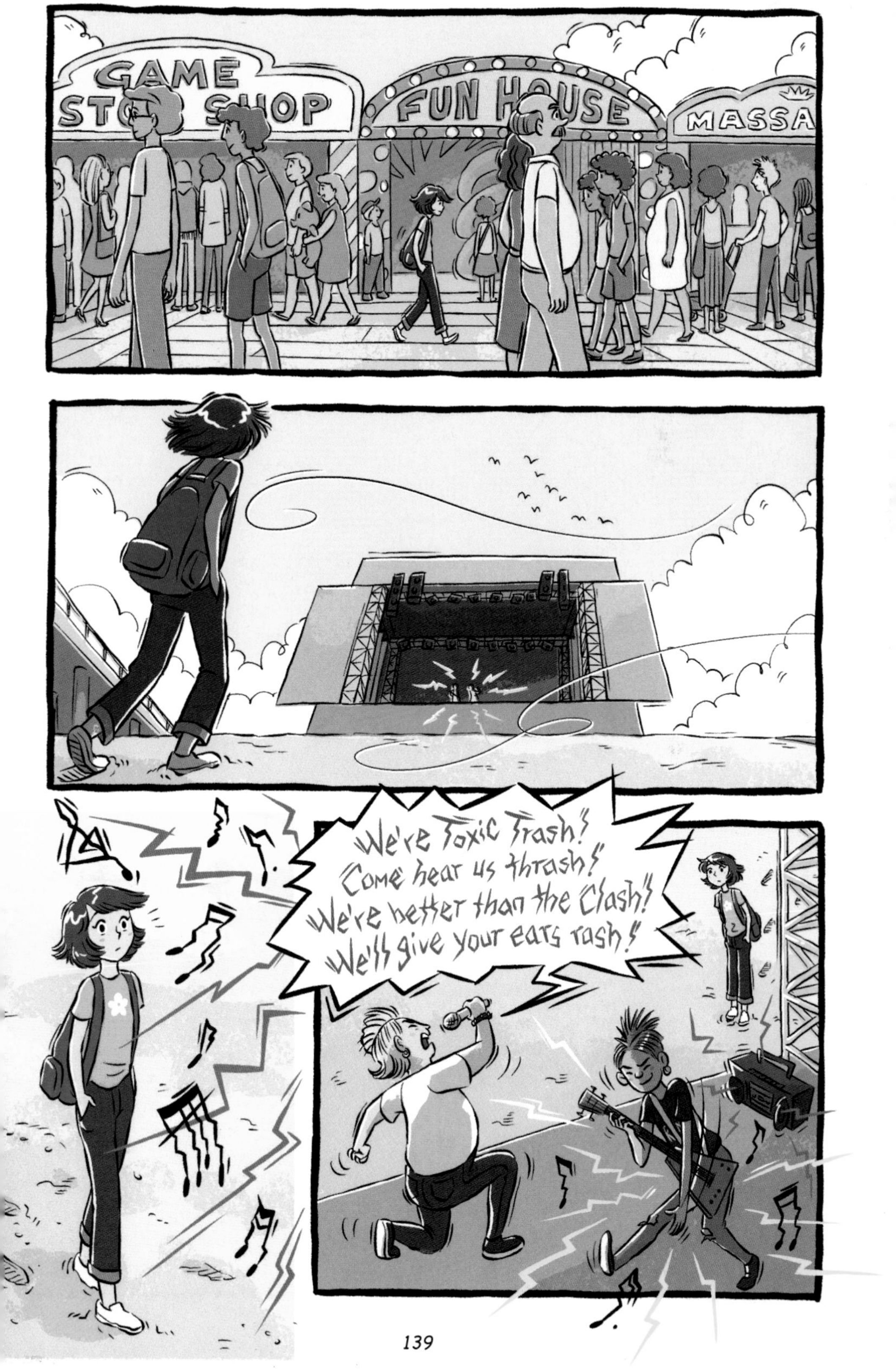
GAME
STO SHOP
FUN HOUSE
MASSA
We're Toxic Trash!
Come hear us thrash!
We're better than the Clash!
We'll give your ears rash!

Aren't we awesome?

Well, your hair sure is.

Thanks. We're going for the whole punk look. I might dye mine pink for the show.

What show?

The Battle of the Bands! It's going to be here on the beach.

Seaside Heights
BATTLE
of the BANDS
Rock the Beach!

FIRST PRIZE $1000

The battle takes place right here on this stage. Right before your stupid Shakespeare show.

Um, our Shakespeare show isn't stupid.

Sure it is. It's Sh-Sh-Shakespeare, isn't it?

143

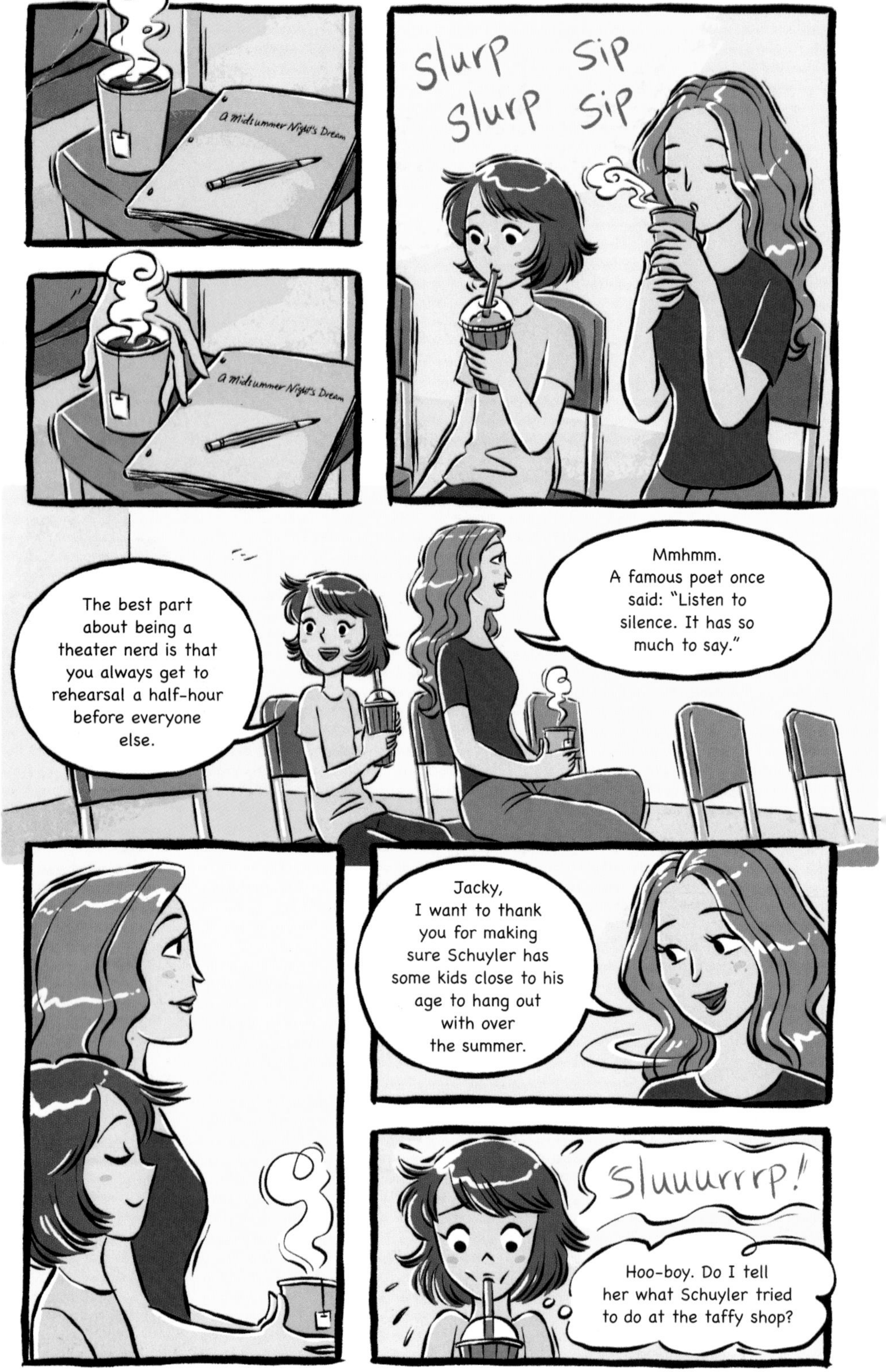
A Midsummer Night's Dream
A Midsummer Night's Dream
Slurp Slurp
Sip Sip
The best part about being a theater nerd is that you always get to rehearsal a half-hour before everyone else.
Mmhmm. A famous poet once said: "Listen to silence. It has so much to say."
Jacky, I want to thank you for making sure Schuyler has some kids close to his age to hang out with over the summer.
Sluuurrrp!
Hoo-boy. Do I tell her what Schuyler tried to do at the taffy shop?

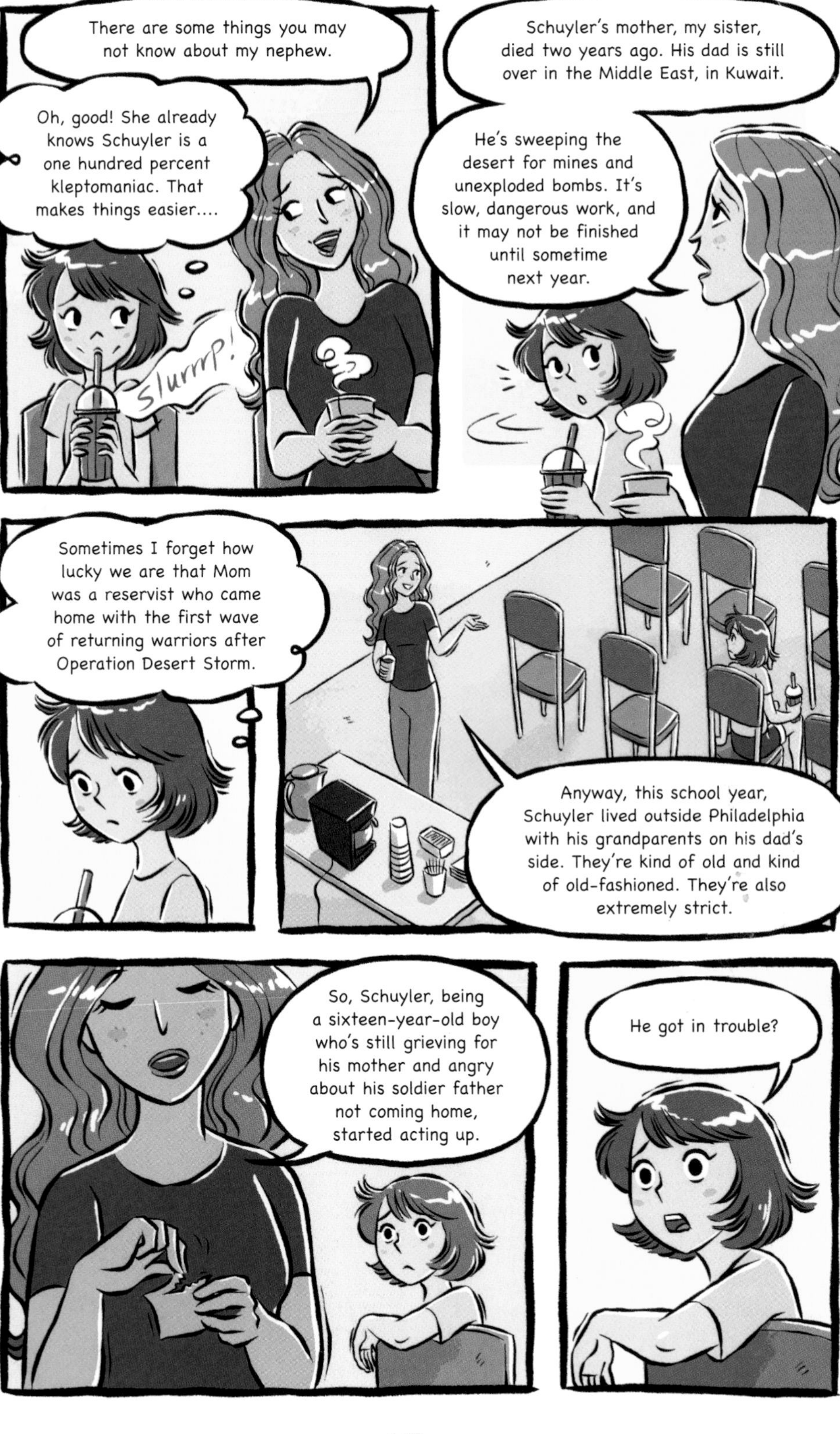
There are some things you may not know about my nephew.
Oh, good! She already knows Schuyler is a one hundred percent kleptomaniac. That makes things easier....
Slurrrp!
Schuyler's mother, my sister, died two years ago. His dad is still over in the Middle East, in Kuwait.
He's sweeping the desert for mines and unexploded bombs. It's slow, dangerous work, and it may not be finished until sometime next year.
Sometimes I forget how lucky we are that Mom was a reservist who came home with the first wave of returning warriors after Operation Desert Storm.
Anyway, this school year, Schuyler lived outside Philadelphia with his grandparents on his dad's side. They're kind of old and kind of old-fashioned. They're also extremely strict.
So, Schuyler, being a sixteen-year-old boy who's still grieving for his mother and angry about his soldier father not coming home, started acting up.
He got in trouble?

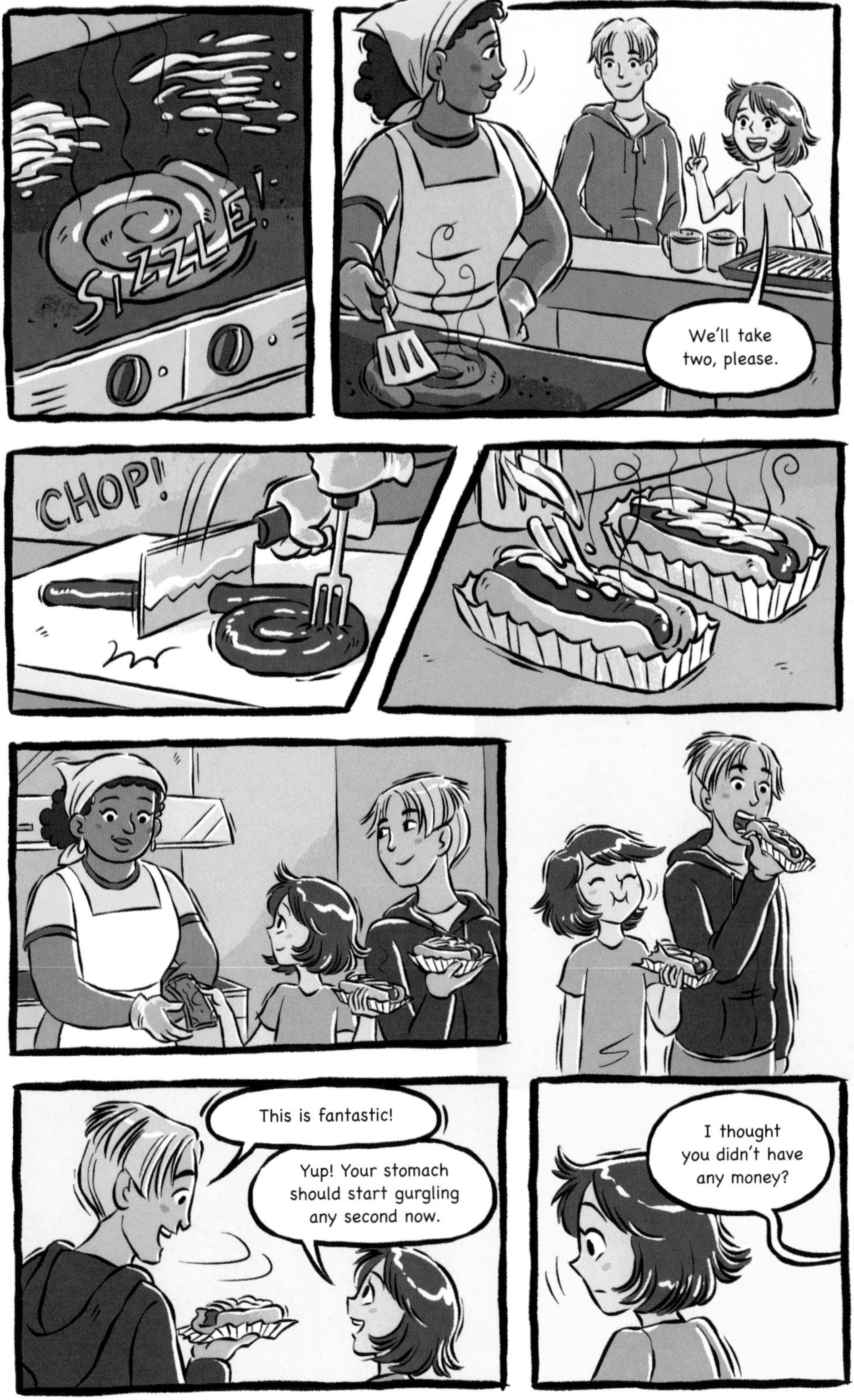
SIZZLE!
We'll take two, please.
CHOP!
This is fantastic!
Yup! Your stomach should start gurgling any second now.
I thought you didn't have any money?

152

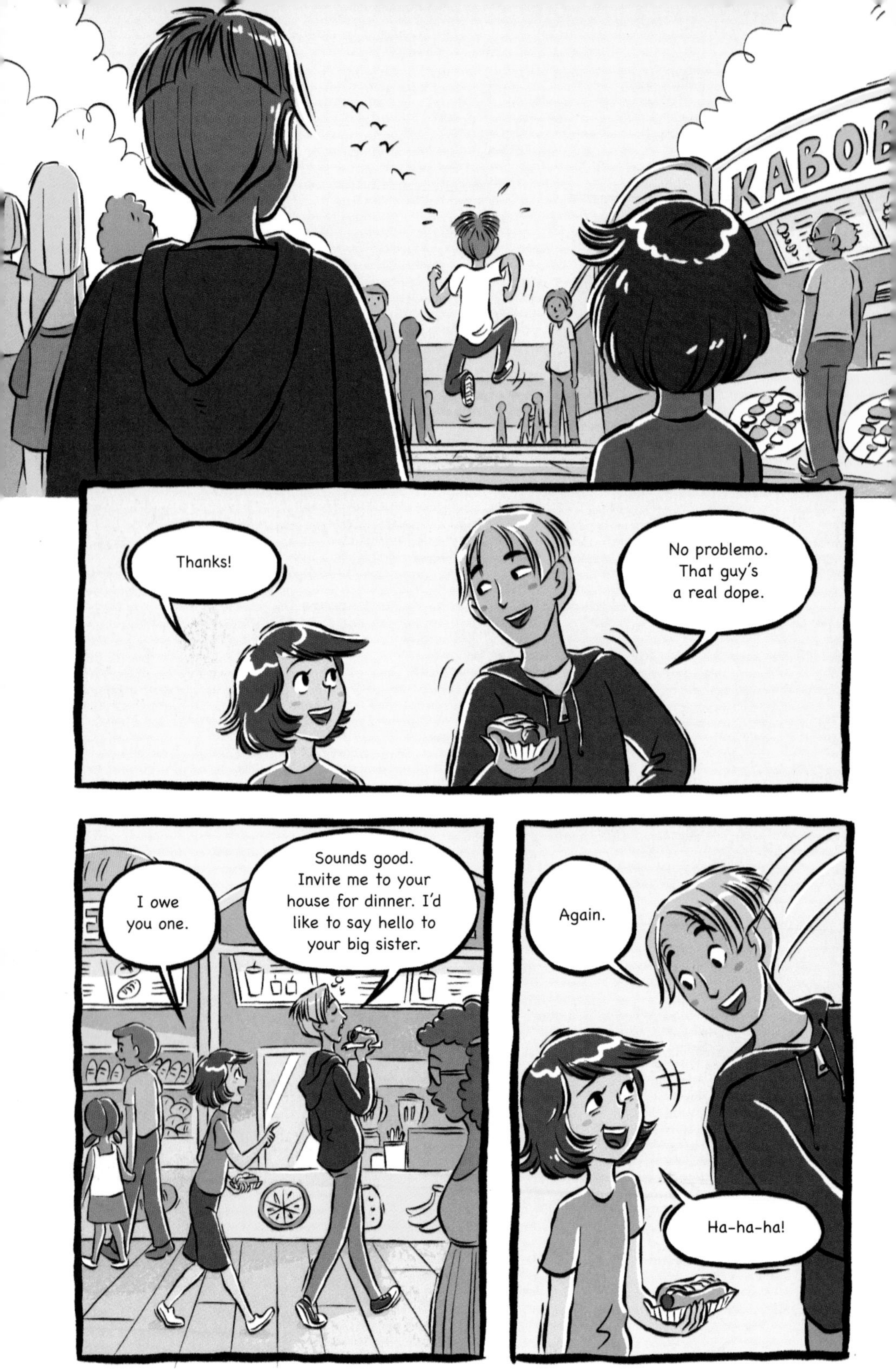
KABOB
Thanks!
No problemo. That guy's a real dope.
I owe you one.
Sounds good. Invite me to your house for dinner. I'd like to say hello to your big sister.
Again.
Ha-ha-ha!

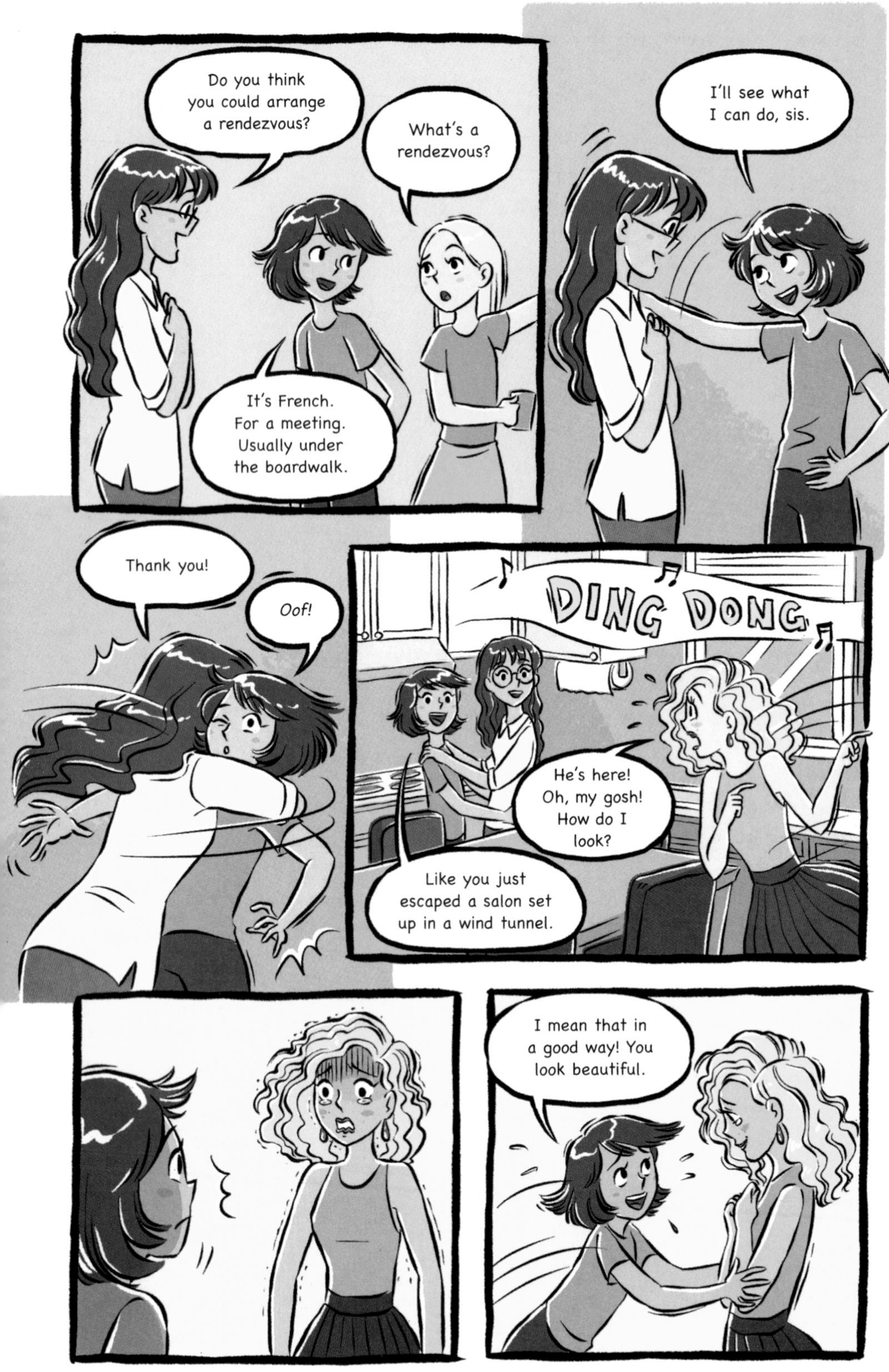
Do you think you could arrange a rendezvous?
What's a rendezvous?
It's French. For a meeting. Usually under the boardwalk.
I'll see what I can do, sis.
Thank you!
Oof!
DING DONG
He's here! Oh, my gosh! How do I look?
Like you just escaped a salon set up in a wind tunnel.
I mean that in a good way! You look beautiful.

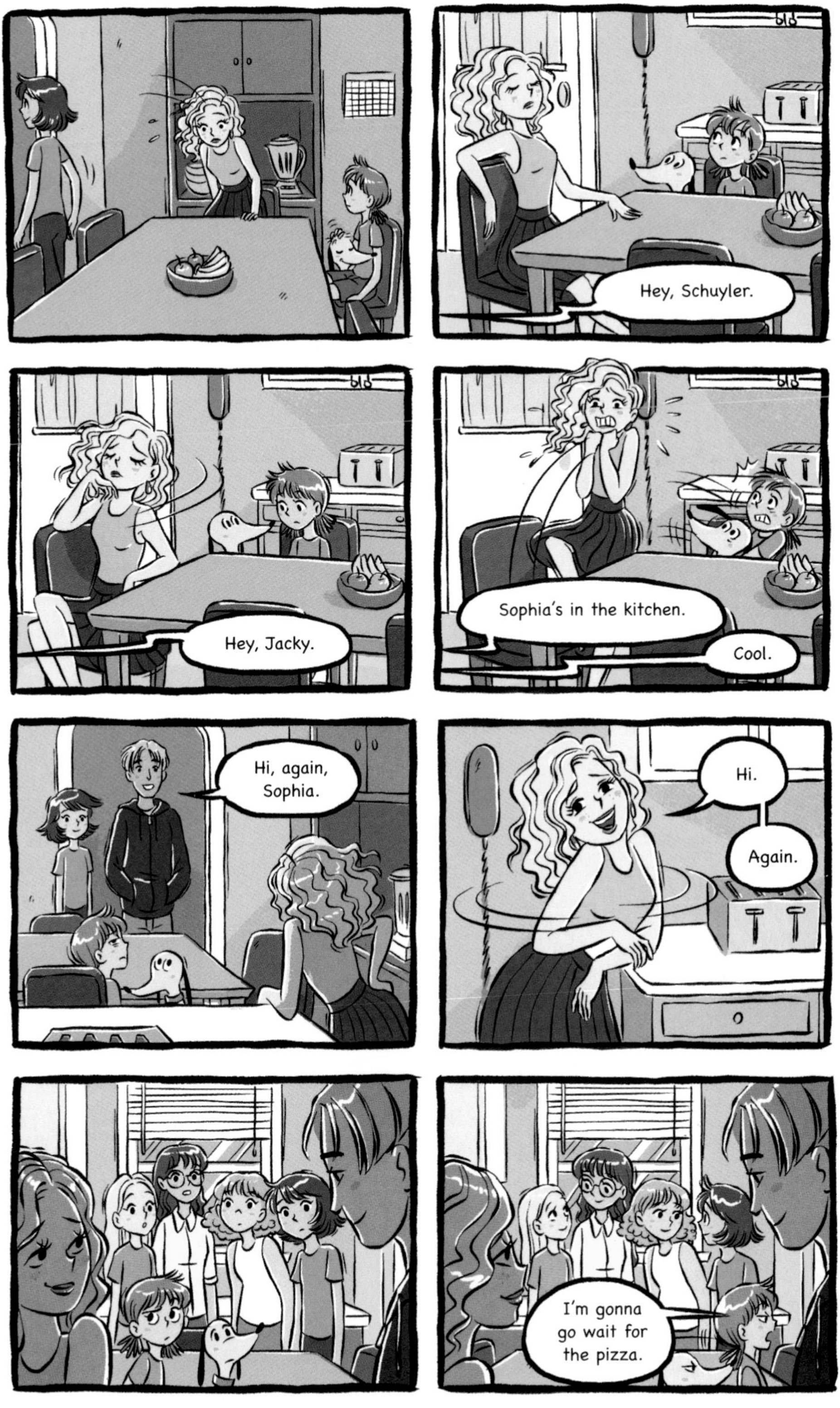
Hey, Schuyler.
Hey, Jacky.
Sophia's in the kitchen.
Cool.
Hi, again, Sophia.
Hi.
Again.
I'm gonna go wait for the pizza.

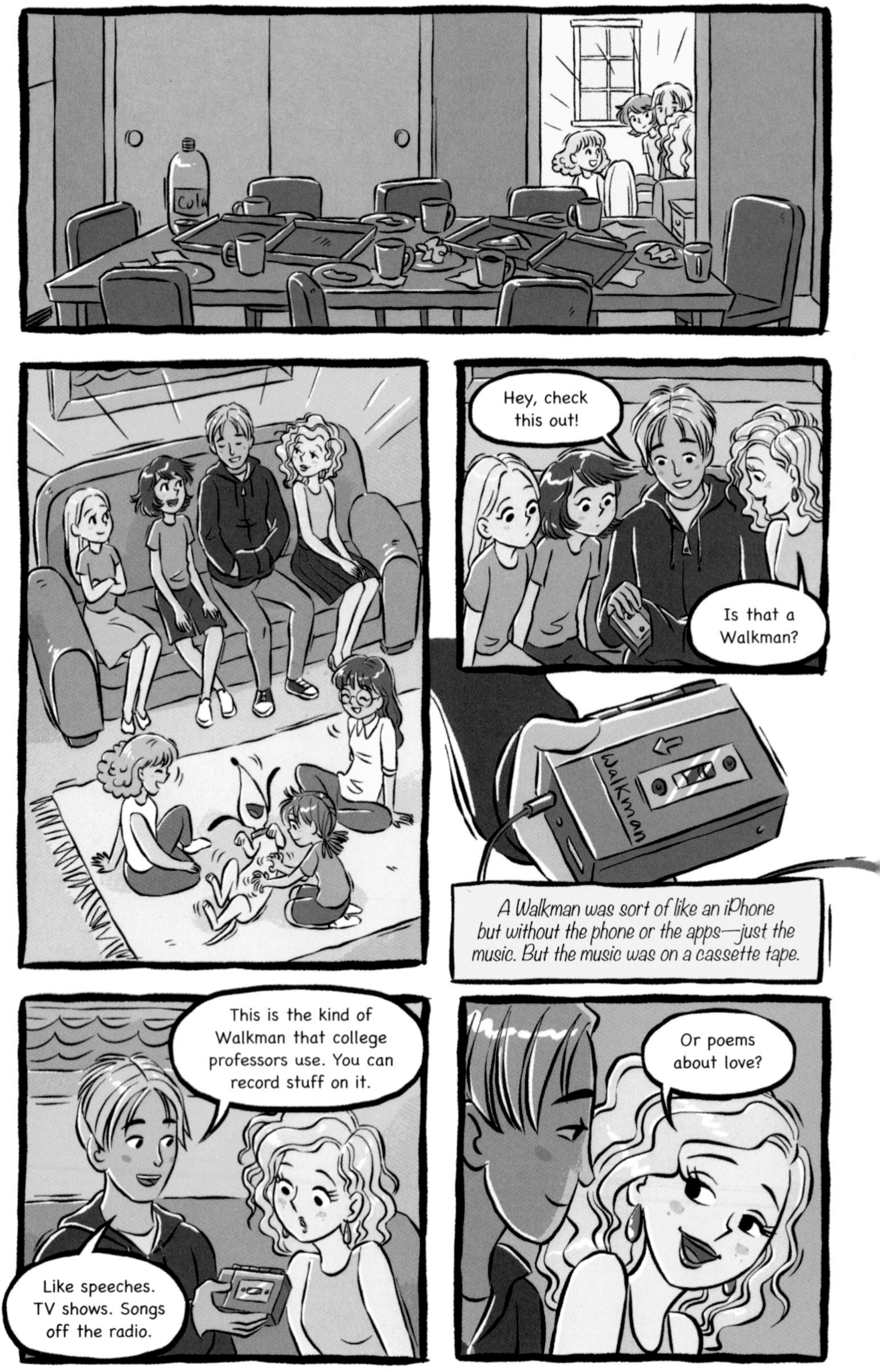
Cola
Hey, check this out!
Is that a Walkman?
Walkman
A Walkman was sort of like an iPhone but without the phone or the apps—just the music. But the music was on a cassette tape.
This is the kind of Walkman that college professors use. You can record stuff on it.
Like speeches. TV shows. Songs off the radio.
Or poems about love?

How about music? Can you play music on your Walkman?

Like right now?

Sure, yeah. Go ahead.

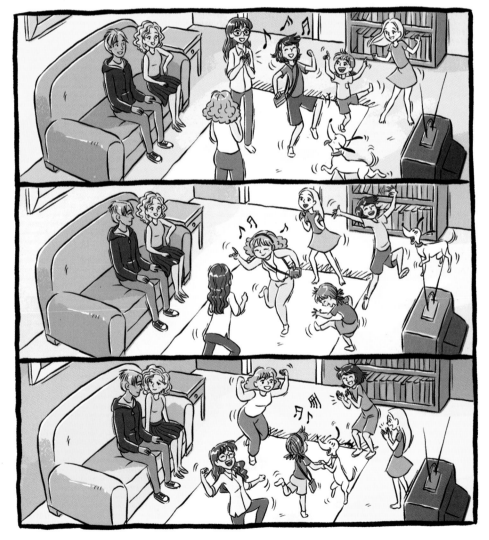

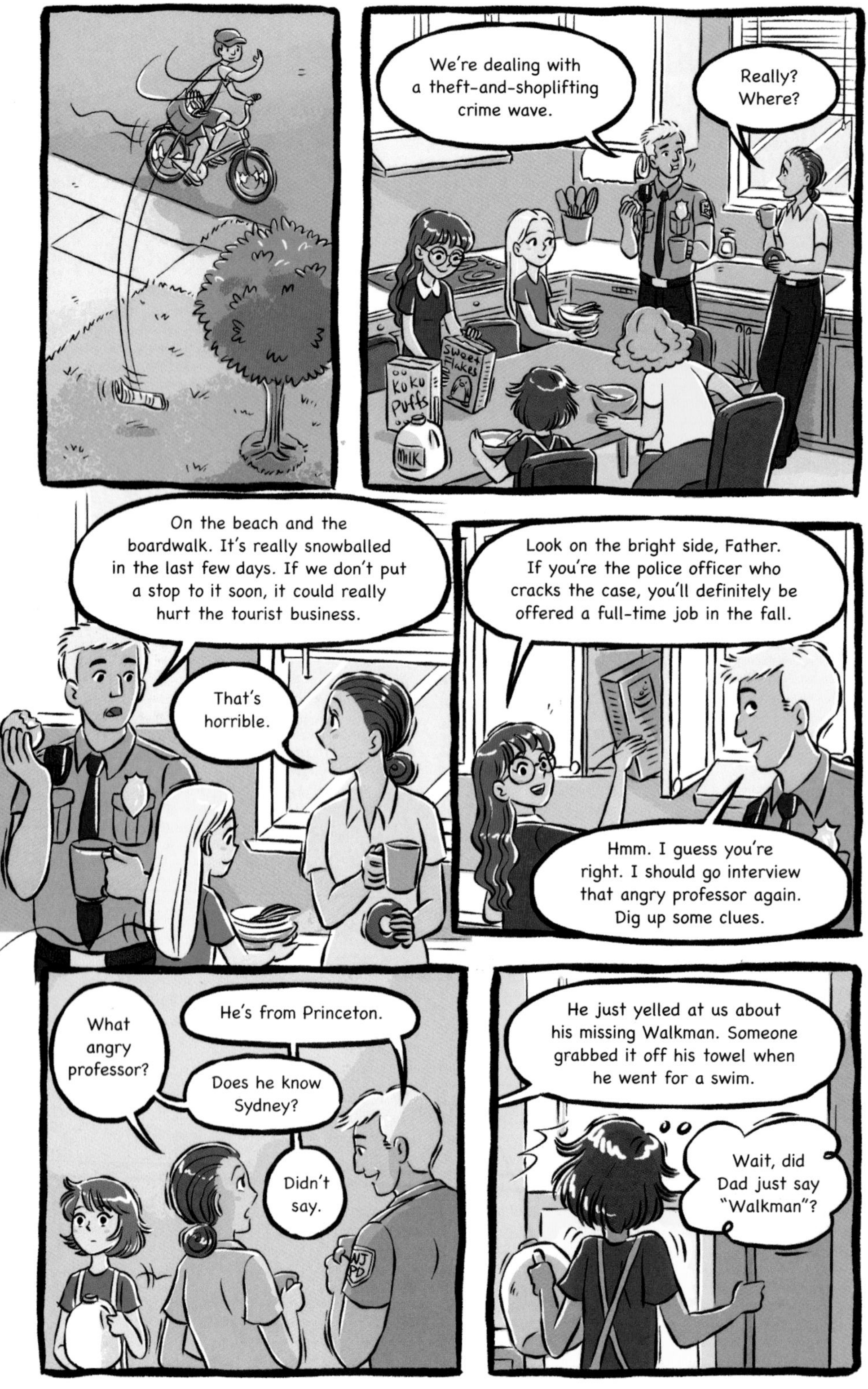
We're dealing with a theft-and-shoplifting crime wave.
Really? Where?
Kuku Puffs
Sweet Flakes
MILK
On the beach and the boardwalk. It's really snowballed in the last few days. If we don't put a stop to it soon, it could really hurt the tourist business.
That's horrible.
Look on the bright side, Father. If you're the police officer who cracks the case, you'll definitely be offered a full-time job in the fall.
Hmm. I guess you're right. I should go interview that angry professor again. Dig up some clues.
What angry professor?
He's from Princeton.
Does he know Sydney?
Didn't say.
WJPD
He just yelled at us about his missing Walkman. Someone grabbed it off his towel when he went for a swim.
Wait, did Dad just say "Walkman"?

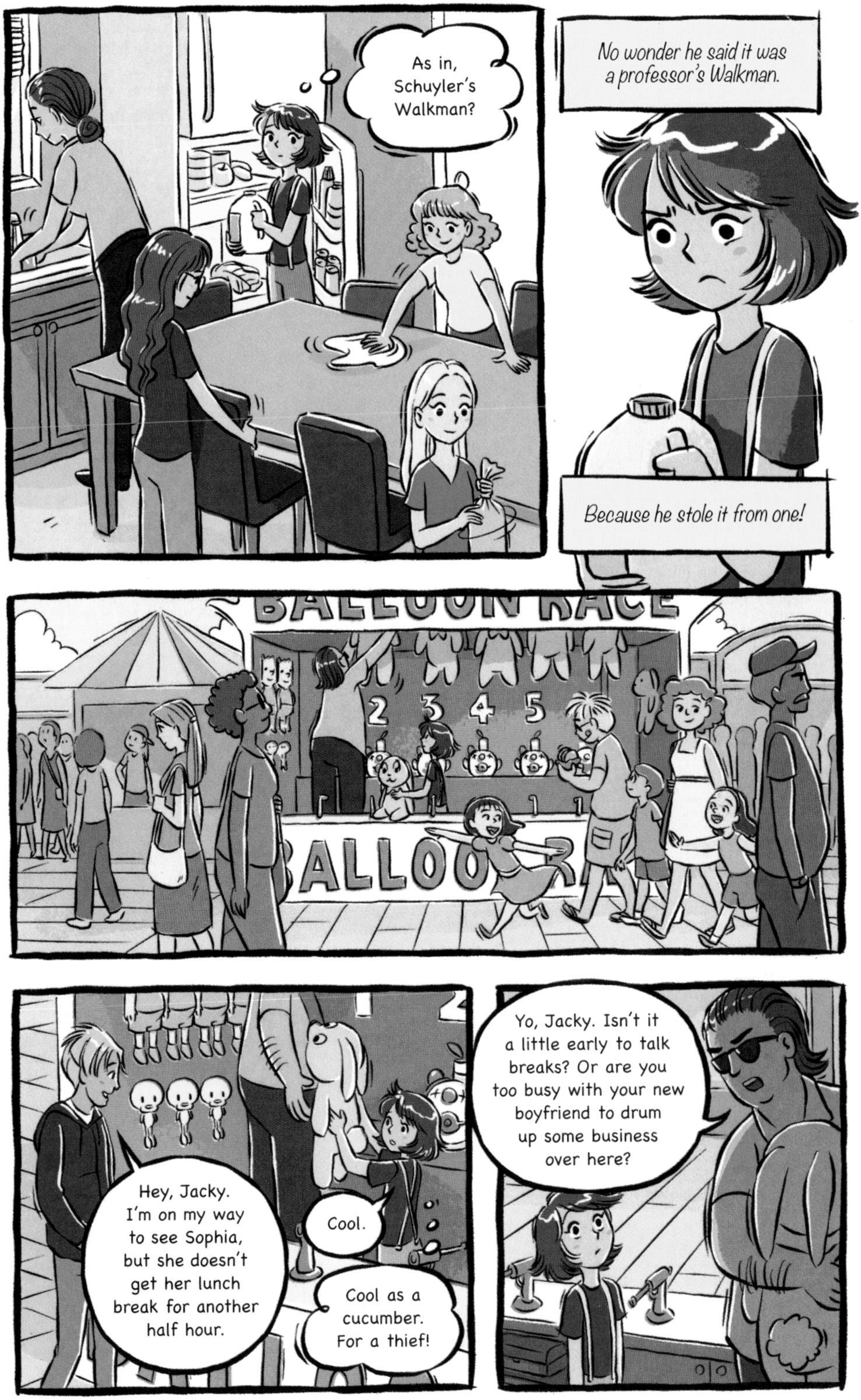
As in, Schuyler's Walkman?
No wonder he said it was a professor's Walkman.
Because he stole it from one!
BALLOON RACE
2 3 4 5
BALLOO RA
Hey, Jacky. I'm on my way to see Sophia, but she doesn't get her lunch break for another half hour.
Cool.
Cool as a cucumber. For a thief!
Yo, Jacky. Isn't it a little early to talk breaks? Or are you too busy with your new boyfriend to drum up some business over here?

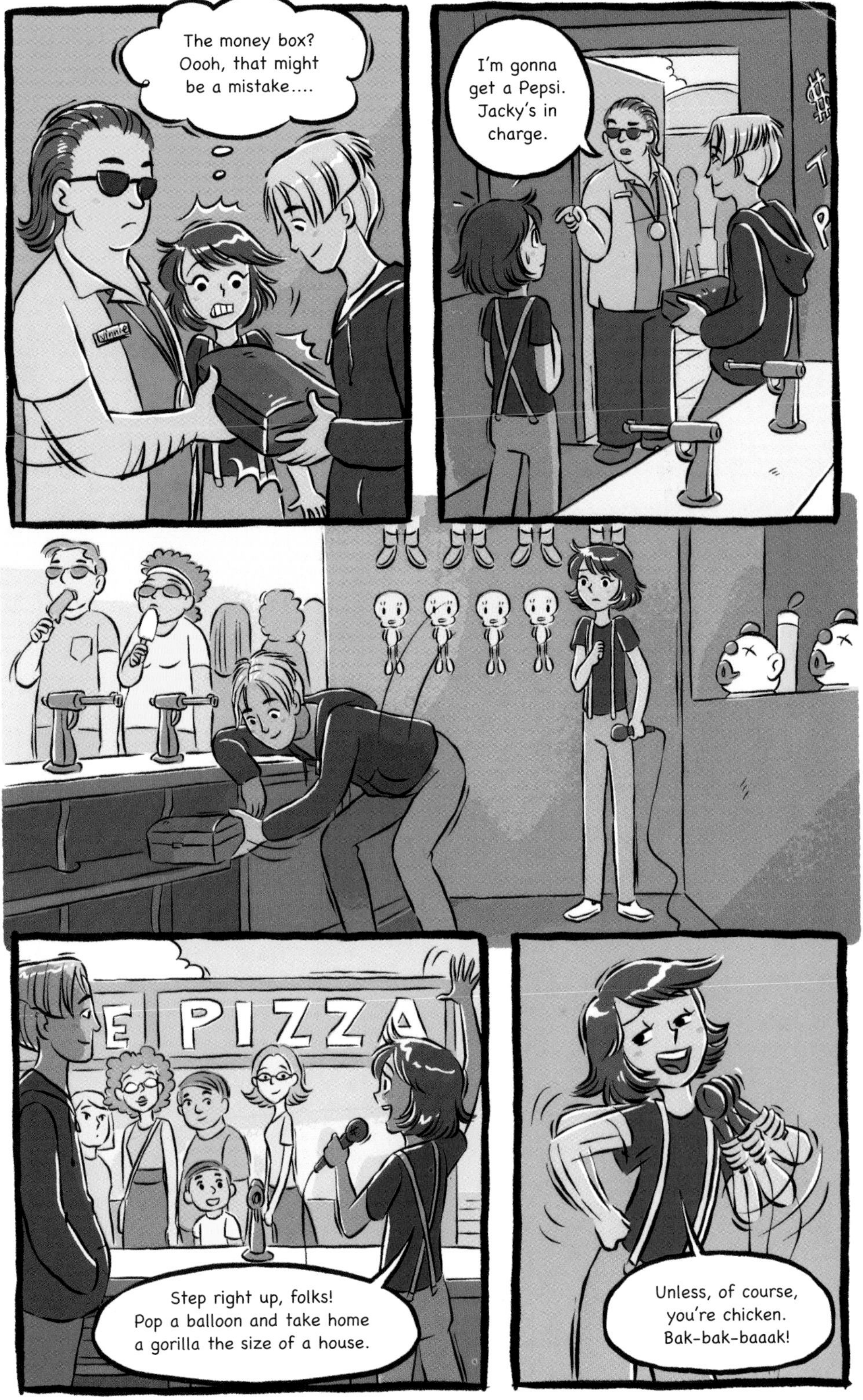
The money box?
Oooh, that might
be a mistake....
Winnie
I'm gonna
get a Pepsi.
Jacky's in
charge.
PIZZA
Step right up, folks!
Pop a balloon and take home
a gorilla the size of a house.
Unless, of course,
you're chicken.
Bak-bak-baaak!

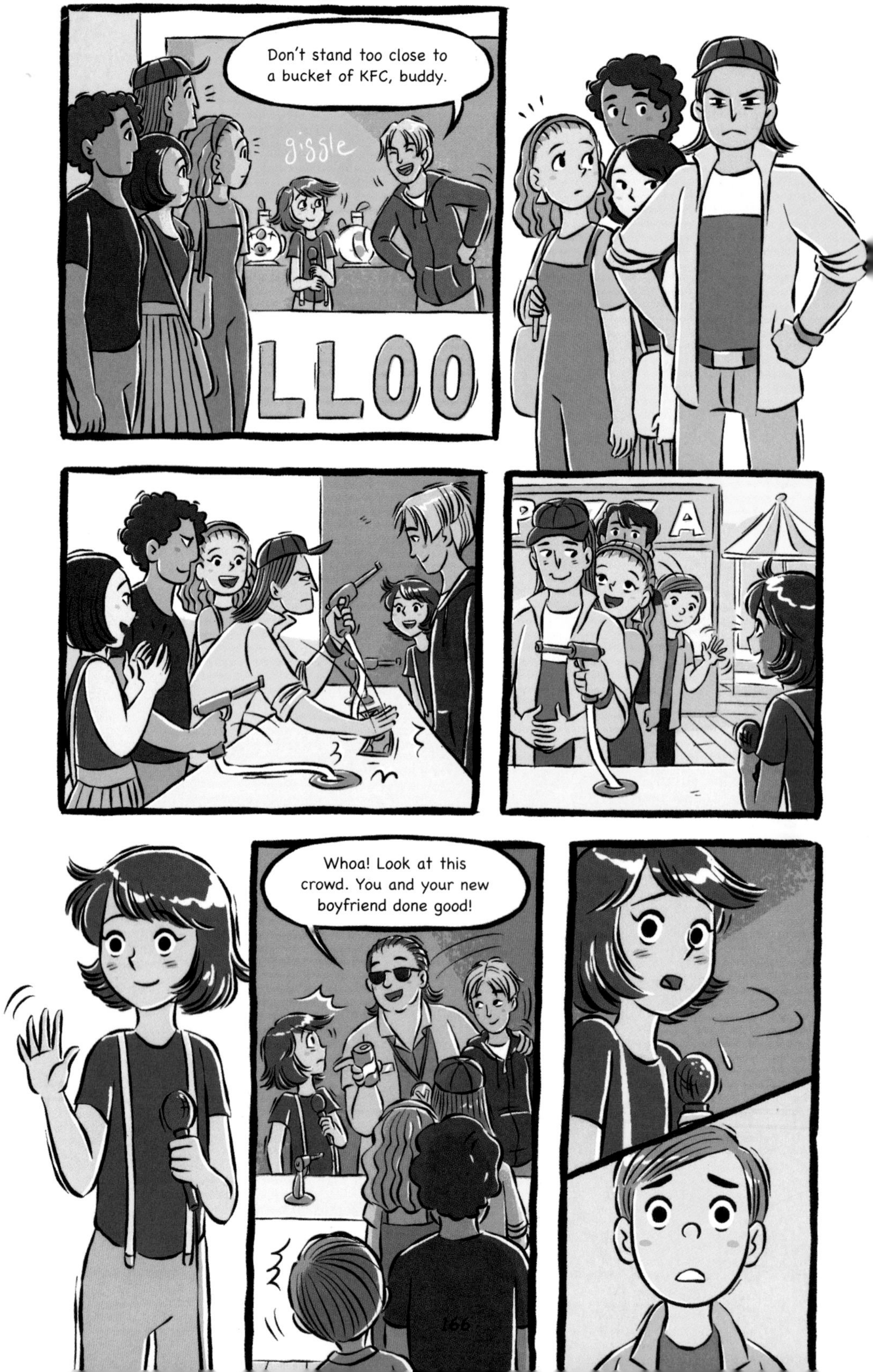
Don't stand too close to a bucket of KFC, buddy.
giggle
LLOO
Whoa! Look at this crowd. You and your new boyfriend done good!

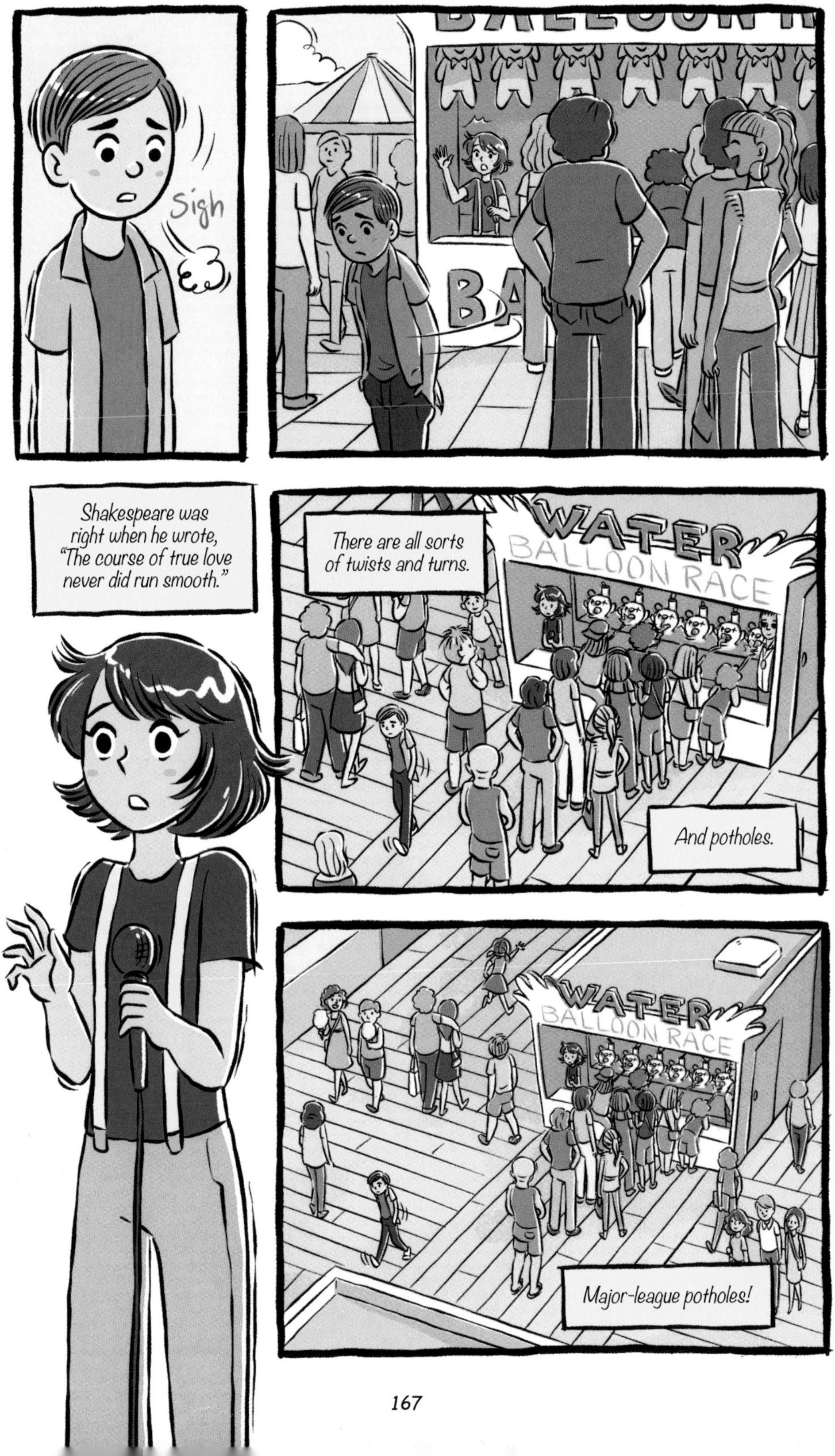
Sigh
Shakespeare was right when he wrote, "The course of true love never did run smooth."
There are all sorts of twists and turns.
WATER
BALLOON RACE
And potholes.
WATER
BALLOON RACE
Major-league potholes!

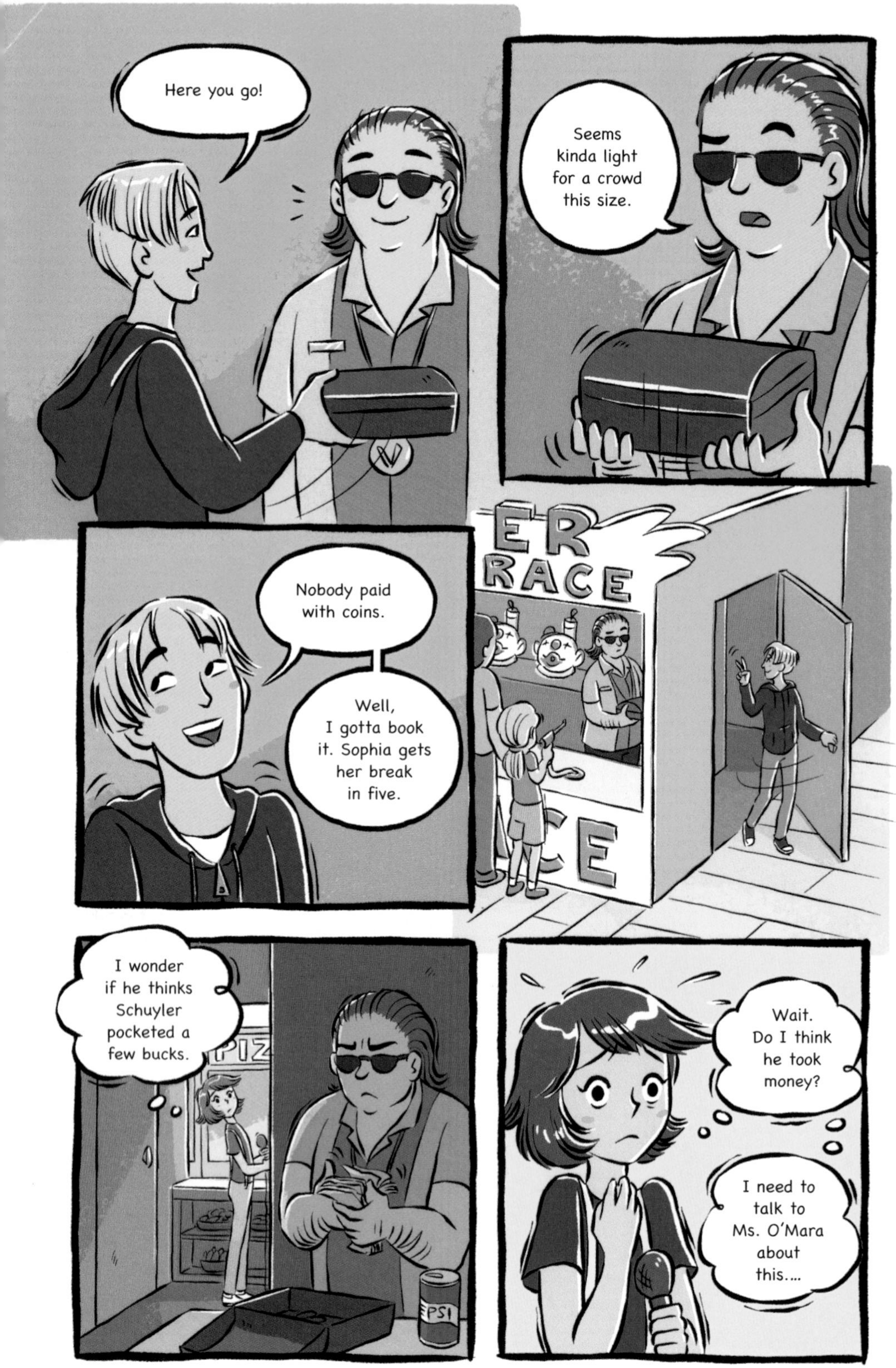
Here you go!
Seems kinda light for a crowd this size.
Nobody paid with coins.
Well, I gotta book it. Sophia gets her break in five.
ER
RACE
CE
I wonder if he thinks Schuyler pocketed a few bucks.
PIZ
PSI
Wait. Do I think he took money?
I need to talk to Ms. O'Mara about this....

170

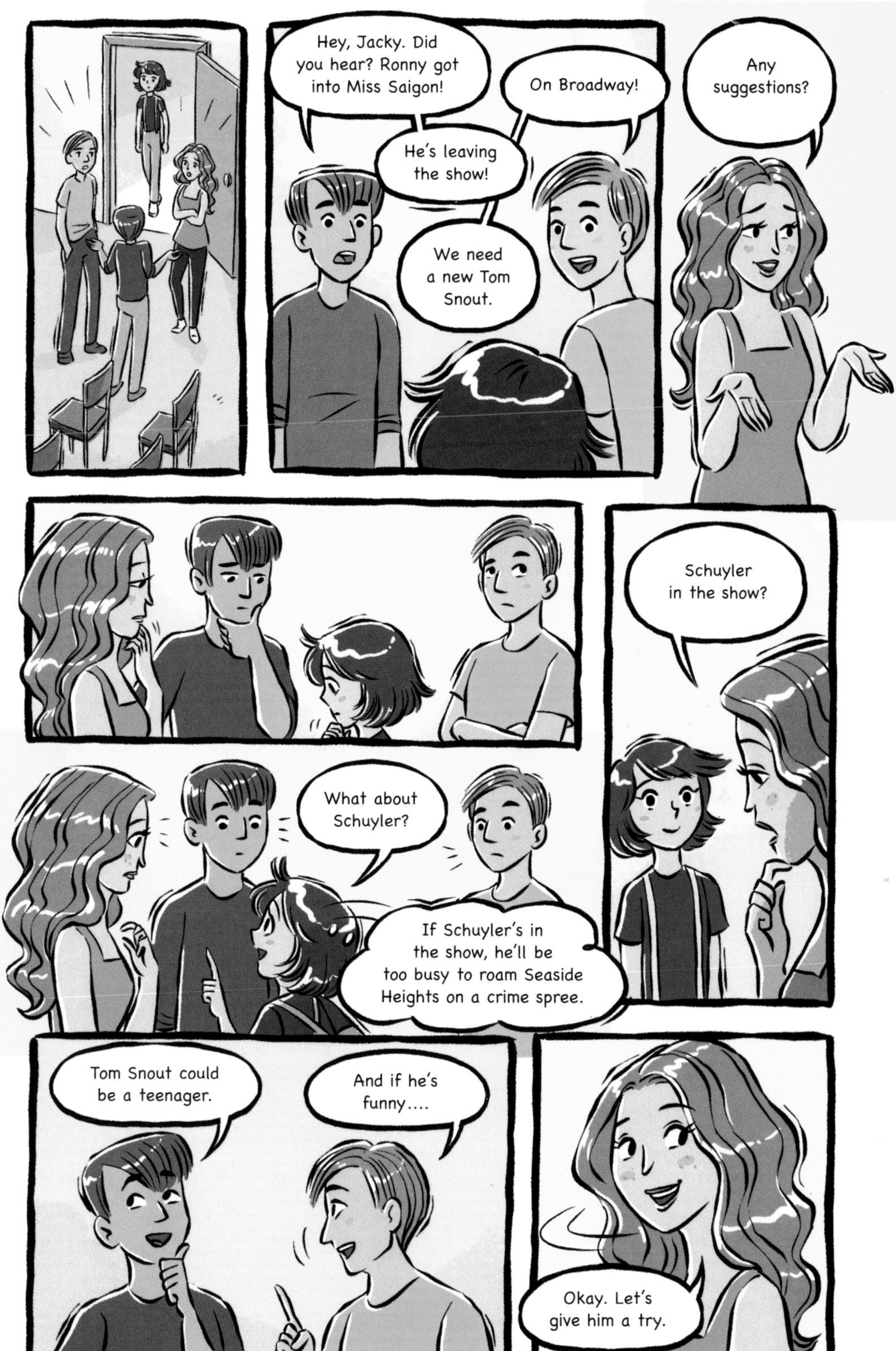
Hey, Jacky. Did you hear? Ronny got into Miss Saigon!
On Broadway!
He's leaving the show!
We need a new Tom Snout.
Any suggestions?
What about Schuyler?
Schuyler in the show?
If Schuyler's in the show, he'll be too busy to roam Seaside Heights on a crime spree.
Tom Snout could be a teenager.
And if he's funny....
Okay. Let's give him a try.

I'd be playing a wall?

Right. It's a joke. There are two lovers who have to talk through your fingers like it's a hole in the bricks.

Cool.

Schuyler played a scene with the adult actors, including Tony Keefer.

Tony used to star on the TV sitcom *Who's in Charge?*

His face was on the cover of *TV Guide* three different times.

Guess who this is?

If you ever met him, he'd tell you. At least twice.

172

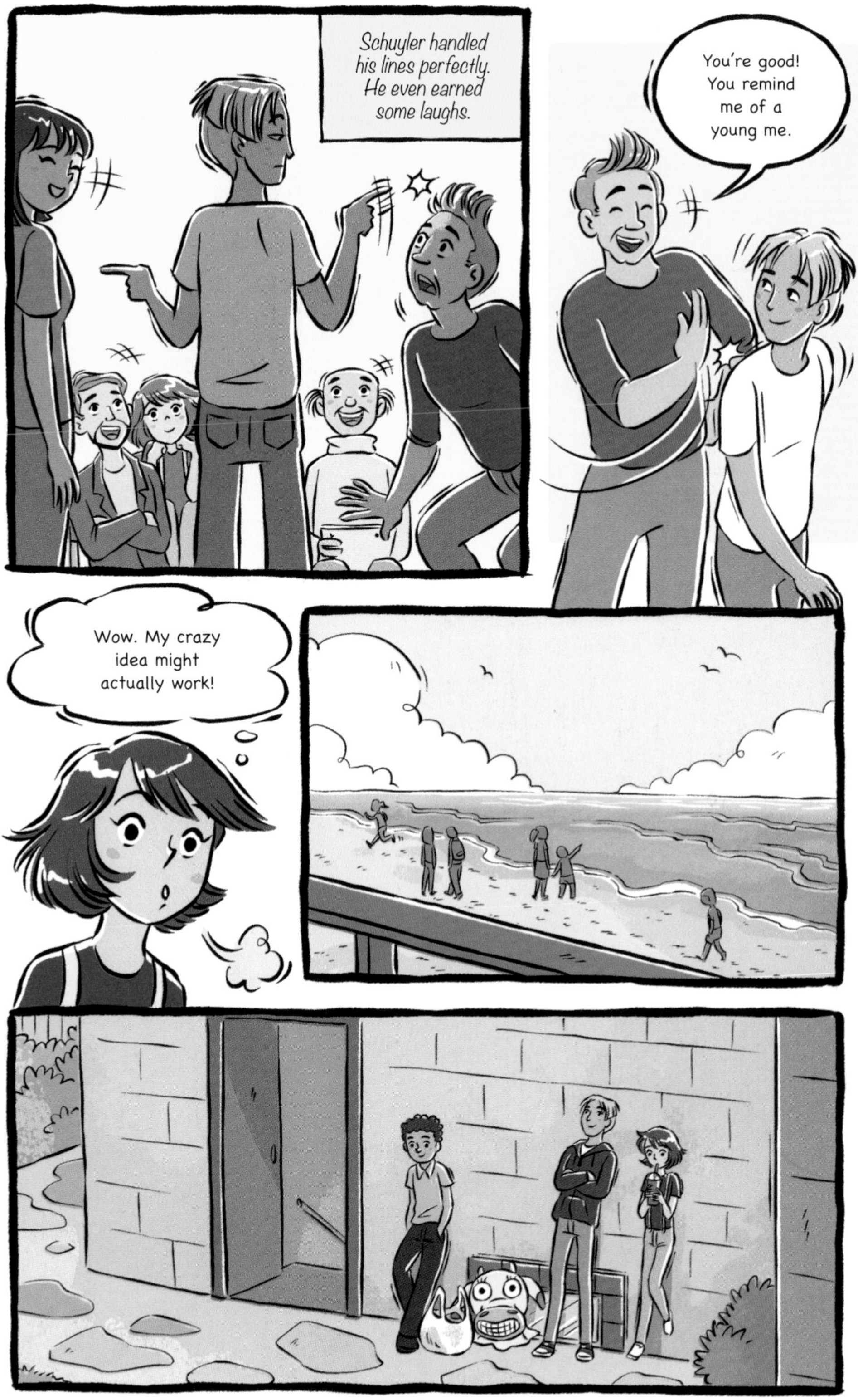
Schuyler handled his lines perfectly. He even earned some laughs.
You're good! You remind me of a young me.
Wow. My crazy idea might actually work!

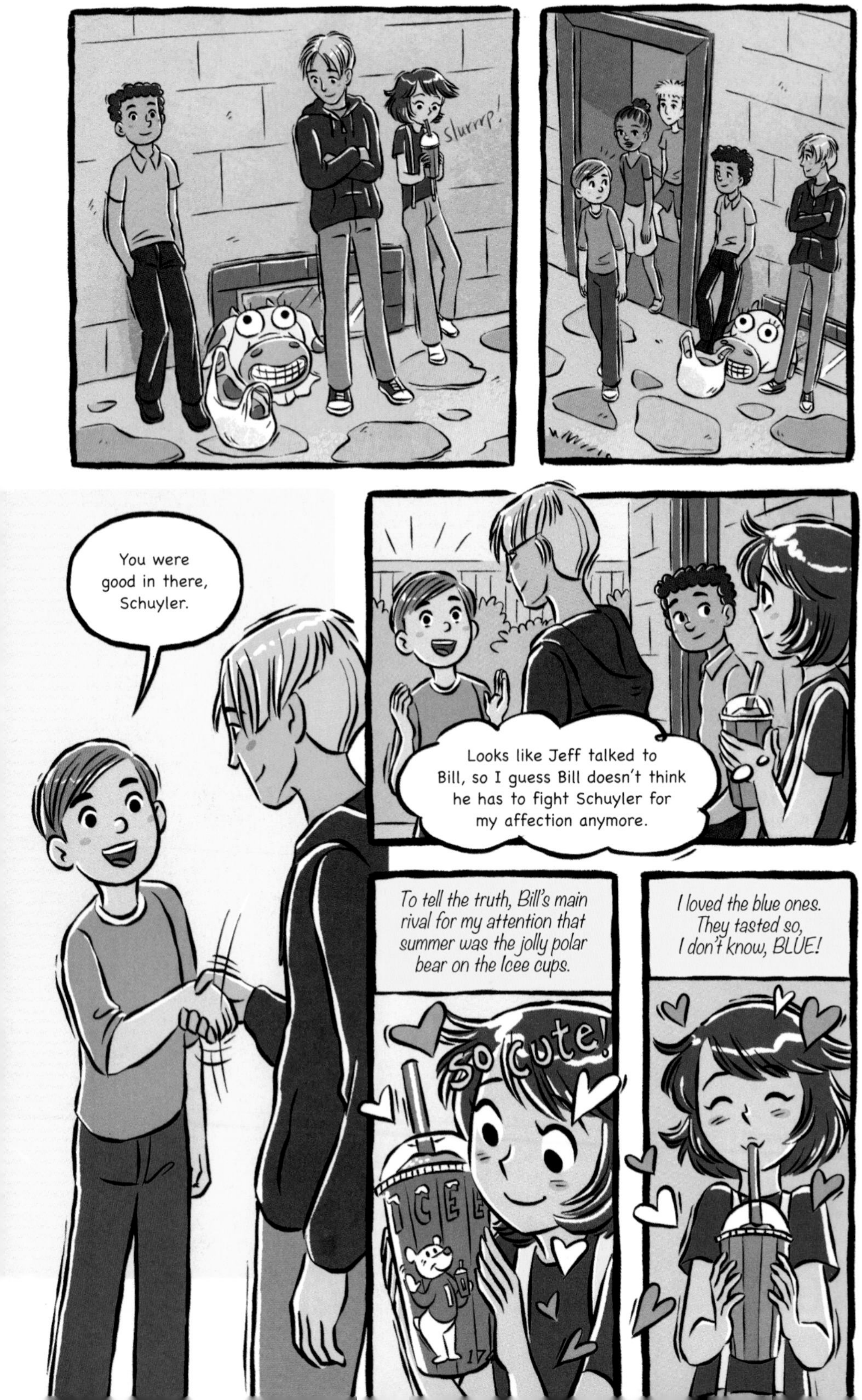
slurrrp!
You were good in there, Schuyler.
Looks like Jeff talked to Bill, so I guess Bill doesn't think he has to fight Schuyler for my affection anymore.
To tell the truth, Bill's main rival for my attention that summer was the jolly polar bear on the Icee cups.
SO CUTE!
ICEE
I loved the blue ones. They tasted so, I don't know, BLUE!

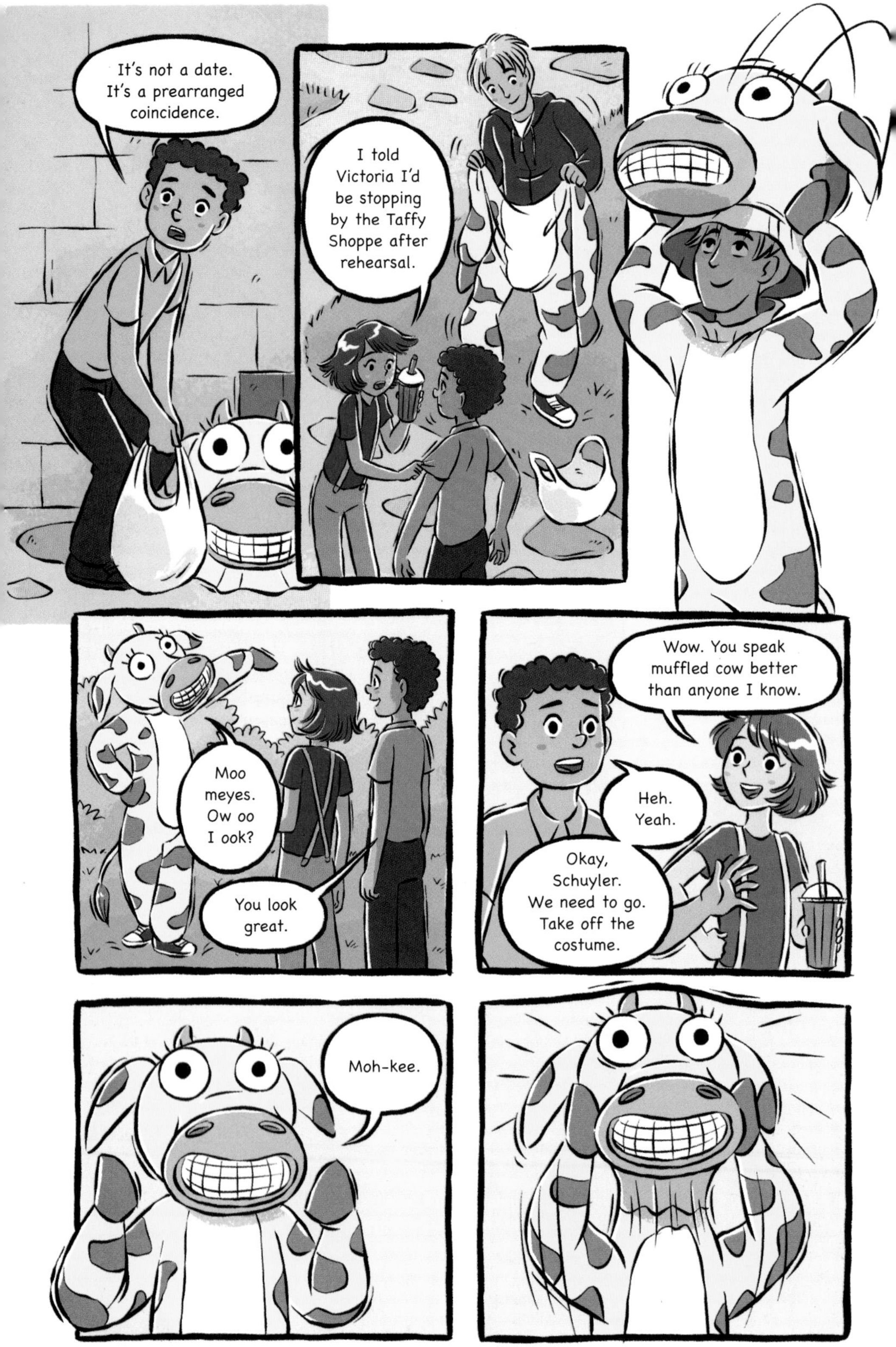
It's not a date. It's a prearranged coincidence.
I told Victoria I'd be stopping by the Taffy Shoppe after rehearsal.
Moo meyes. Ow oo I ook?
You look great.
Wow. You speak muffled cow better than anyone I know.
Heh. Yeah.
Okay, Schuyler. We need to go. Take off the costume.
Moh-kee.

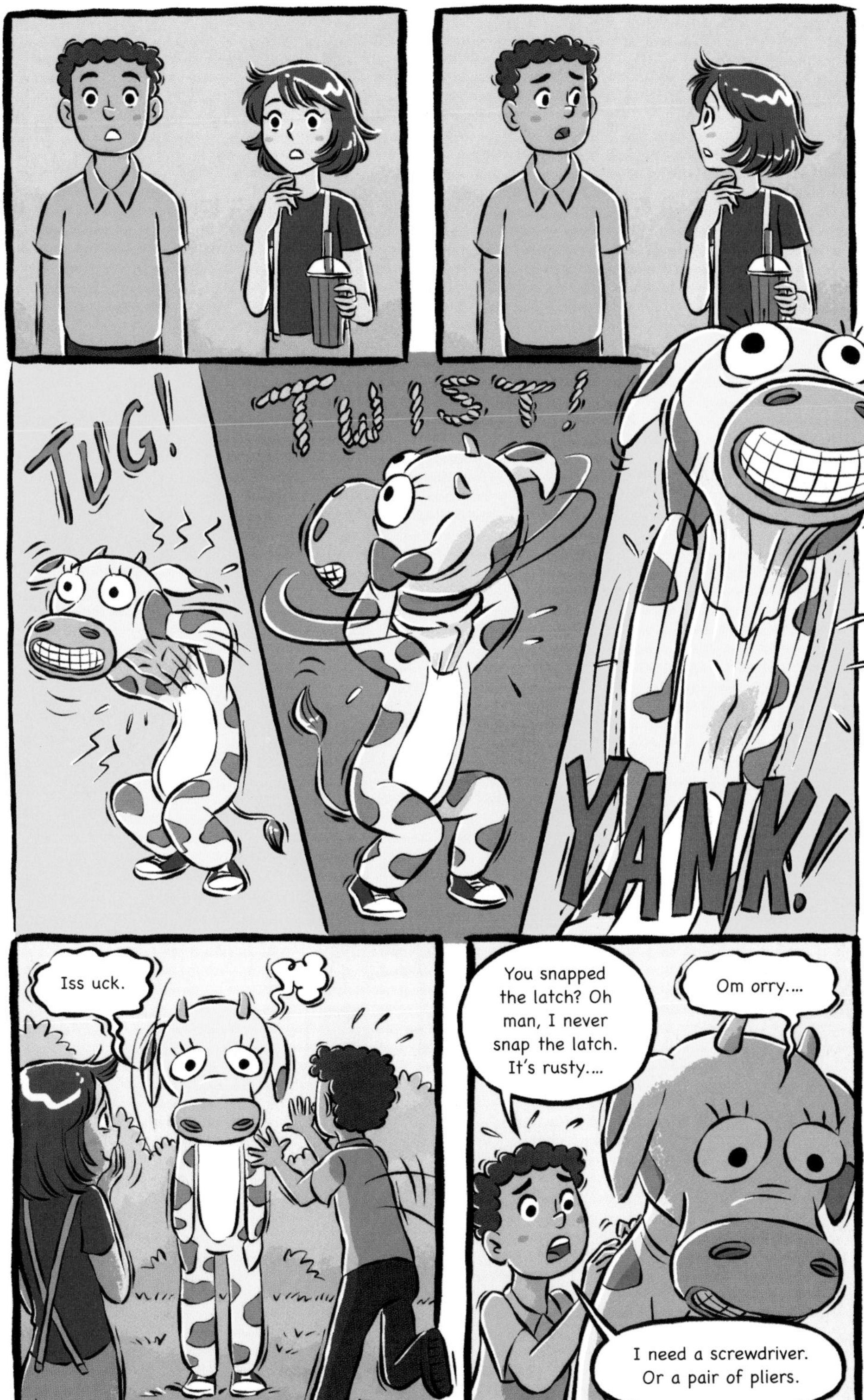
TUG!
TWIST!
YANK!
Iss uck.
You snapped the latch? Oh man, I never snap the latch. It's rusty....
Om orry....
I need a screwdriver. Or a pair of pliers.

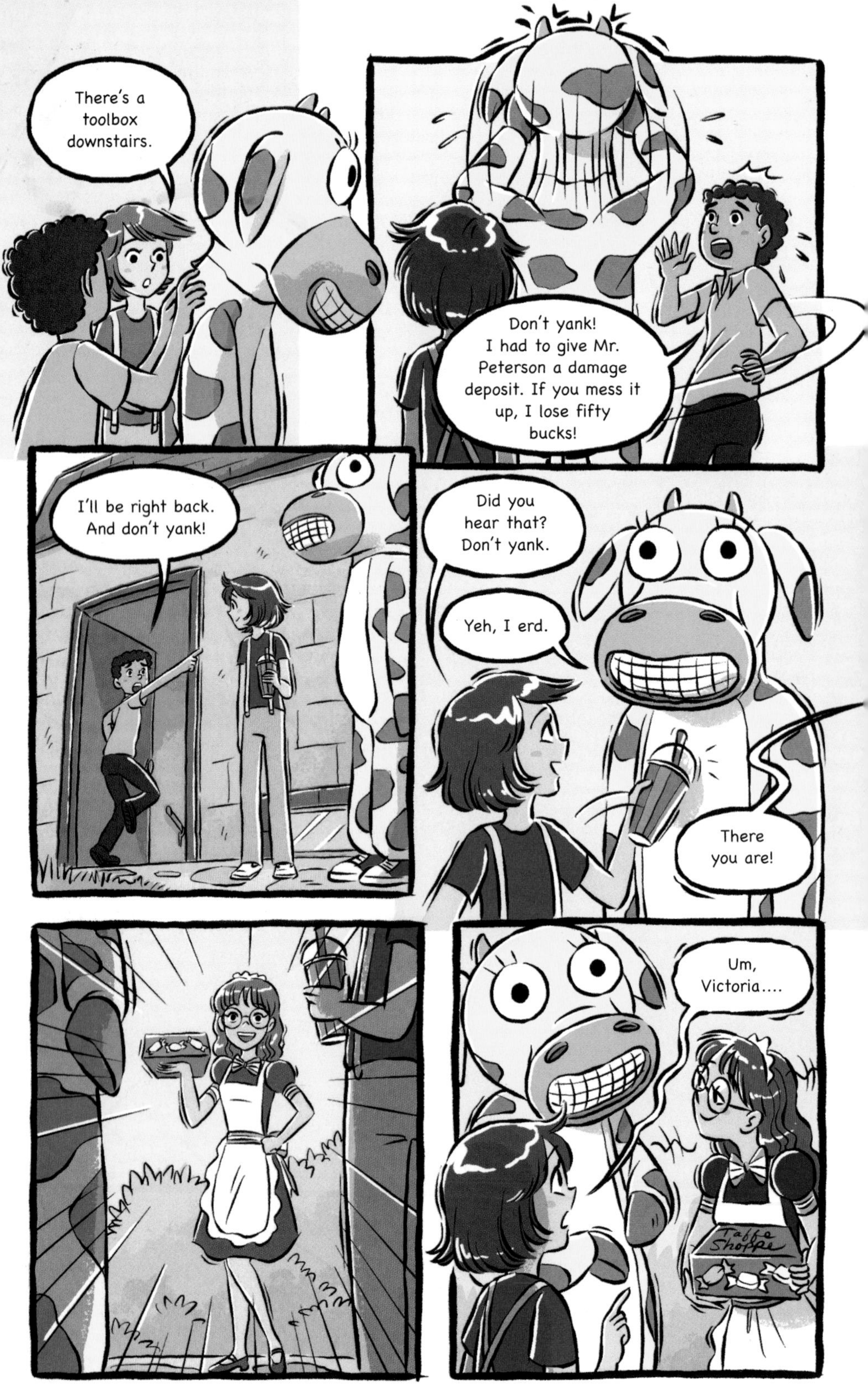
There's a toolbox downstairs.
Don't yank! I had to give Mr. Peterson a damage deposit. If you mess it up, I lose fifty bucks!
I'll be right back. And don't yank!
Did you hear that? Don't yank.
Yeh, I erd.
There you are!
Um, Victoria....
Taffee Shoppe

If you get a second, send me a reply.
You don't need to waste a stamp.
You can just slip it under my door. I'll probably be in my room. Crying.
Because I've messed up my summer and everybody else's.
Sincerely,
Your daughter Jacky

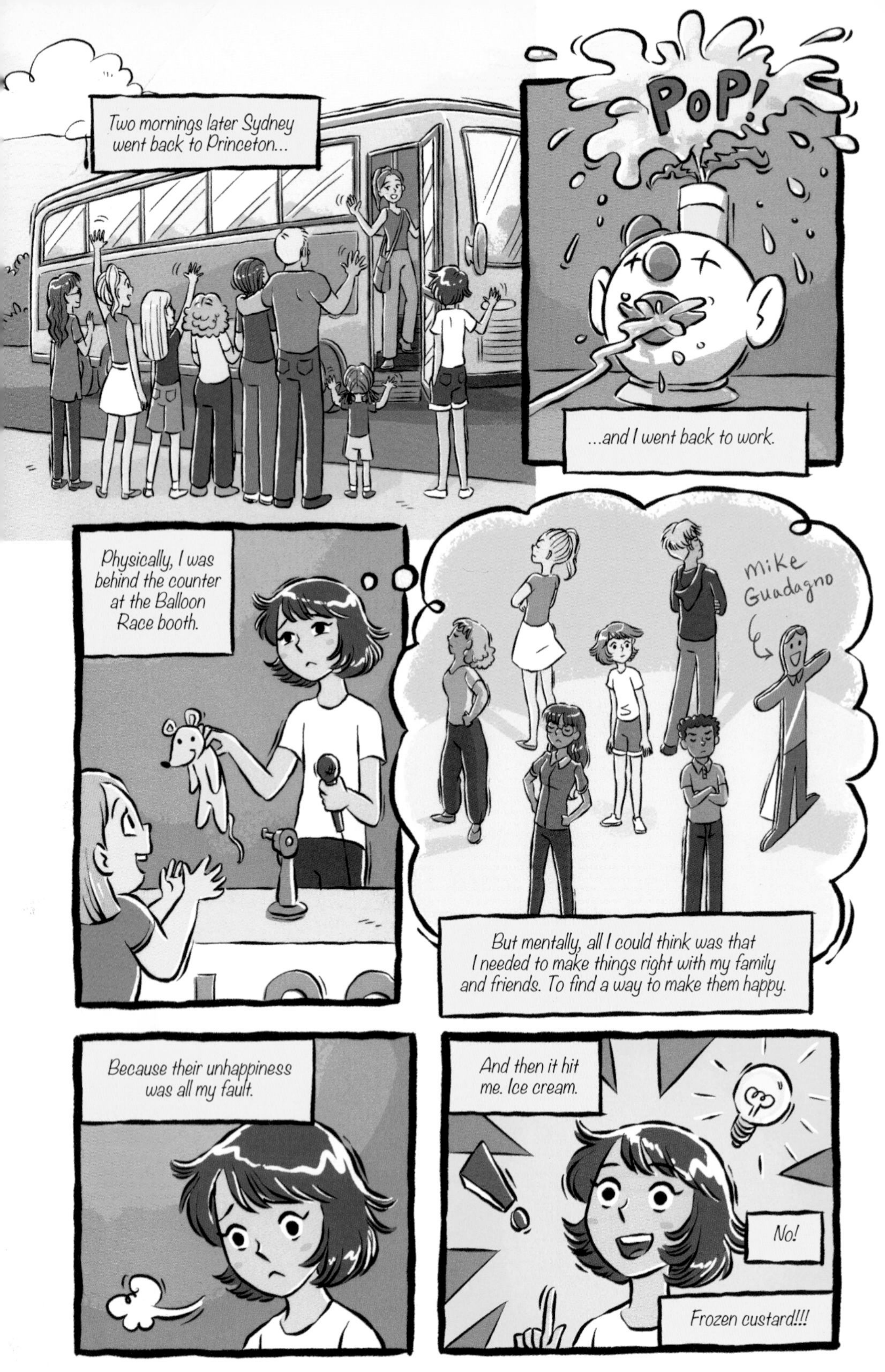
Two mornings later Sydney went back to Princeton...
POP!
...and I went back to work.
Physically, I was behind the counter at the Balloon Race booth.
Mike Guadagno
But mentally, all I could think was that I needed to make things right with my family and friends. To find a way to make them happy.
Because their unhappiness was all my fault.
And then it hit me. Ice cream.
No!
Frozen custard!!!

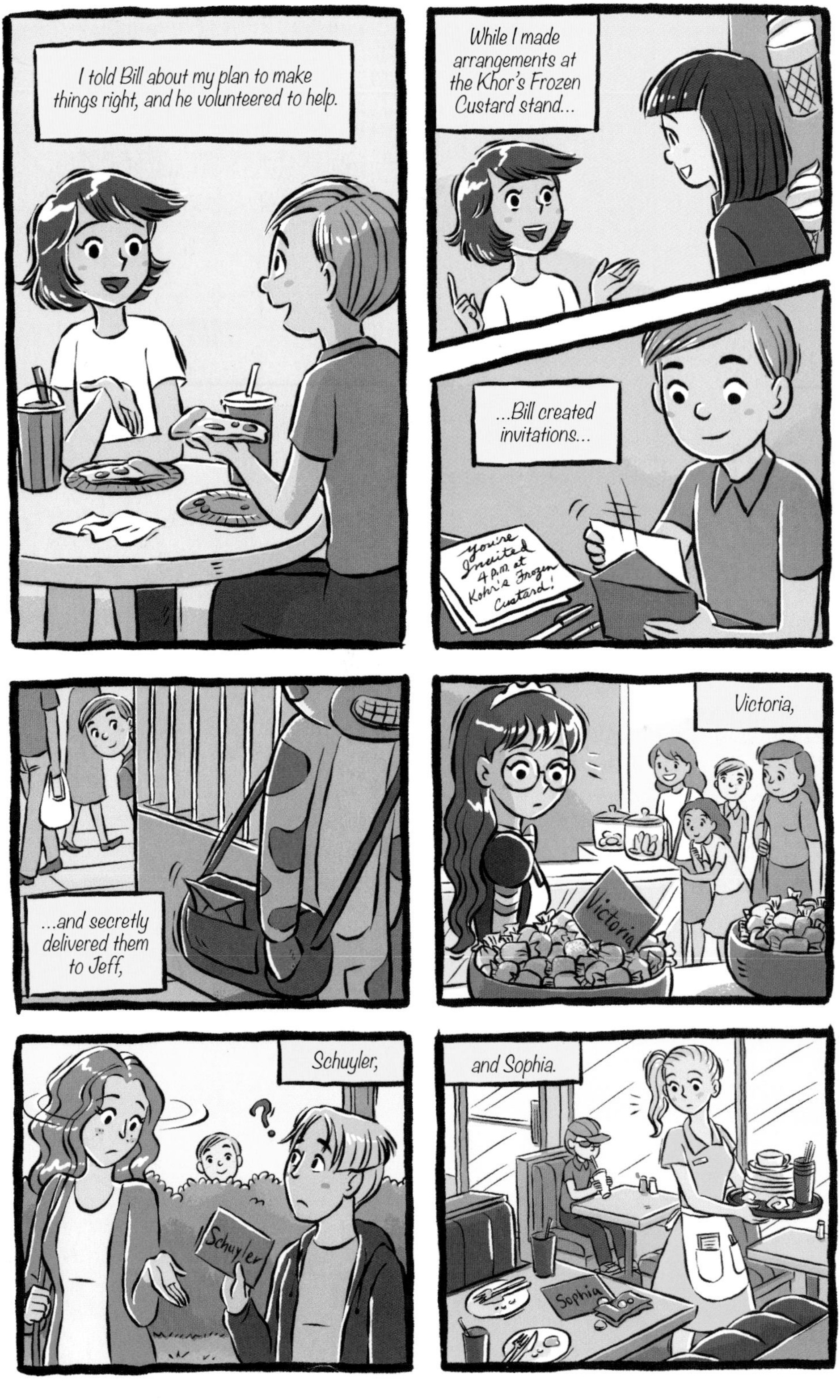
I told Bill about my plan to make things right, and he volunteered to help.
While I made arrangements at the Khor's Frozen Custard stand...
...Bill created invitations...
You're Invited 4 P.M. at Kohr's Frozen Custard!
...and secretly delivered them to Jeff,
Victoria,
Victoria
Schuyler,
Schuyler
and Sophia.
Sophia

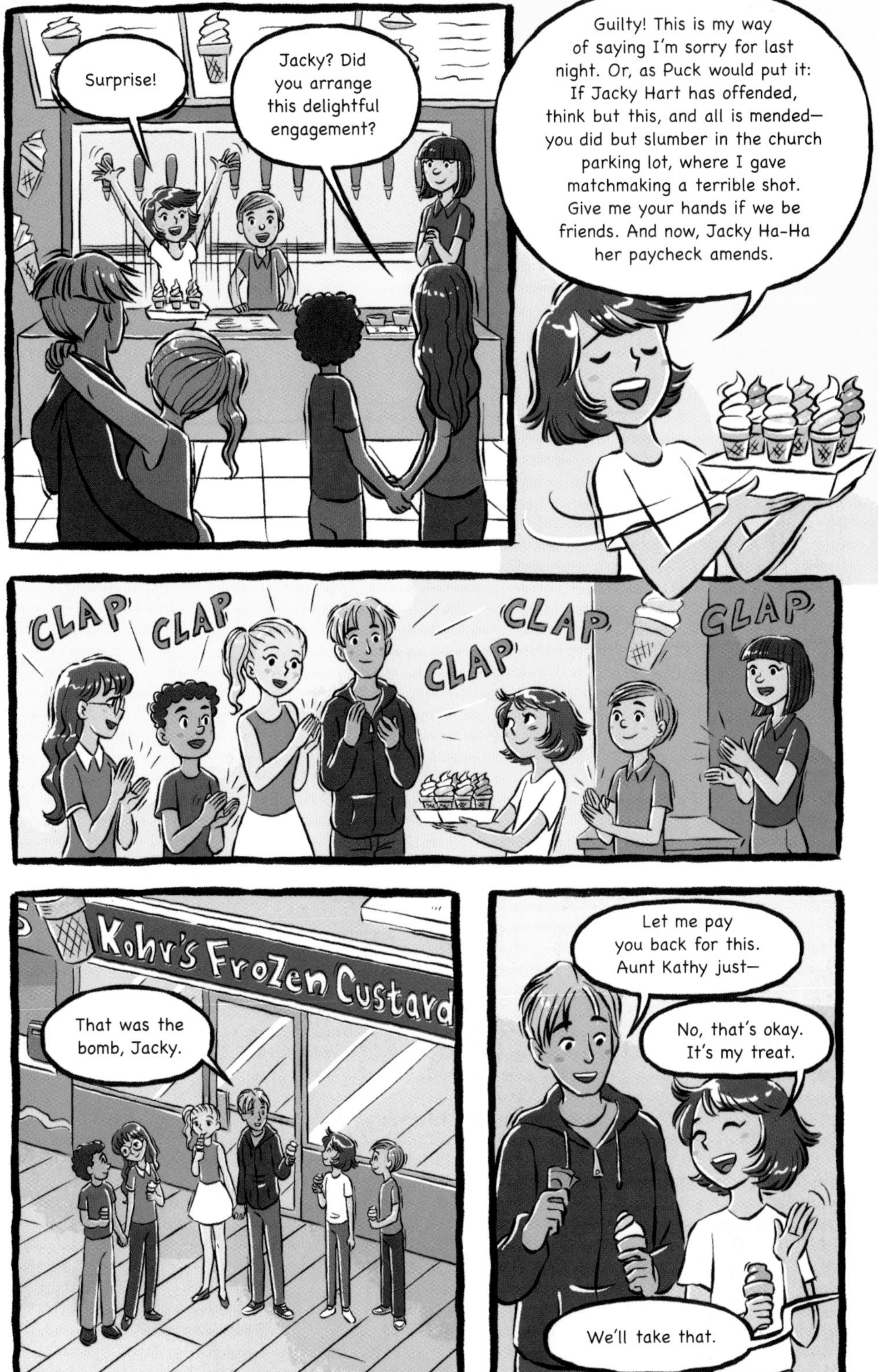
Surprise!
Jacky? Did you arrange this delightful engagement?
Guilty! This is my way of saying I'm sorry for last night. Or, as Puck would put it: If Jacky Hart has offended, think but this, and all is mended— you did but slumber in the church parking lot, where I gave matchmaking a terrible shot. Give me your hands if we be friends. And now, Jacky Ha-Ha her paycheck amends.
CLAP CLAP CLAP CLAP CLAP
Kohr's FroZen Custard
That was the bomb, Jacky.
Let me pay you back for this. Aunt Kathy just—
No, that's okay. It's my treat.
We'll take that.

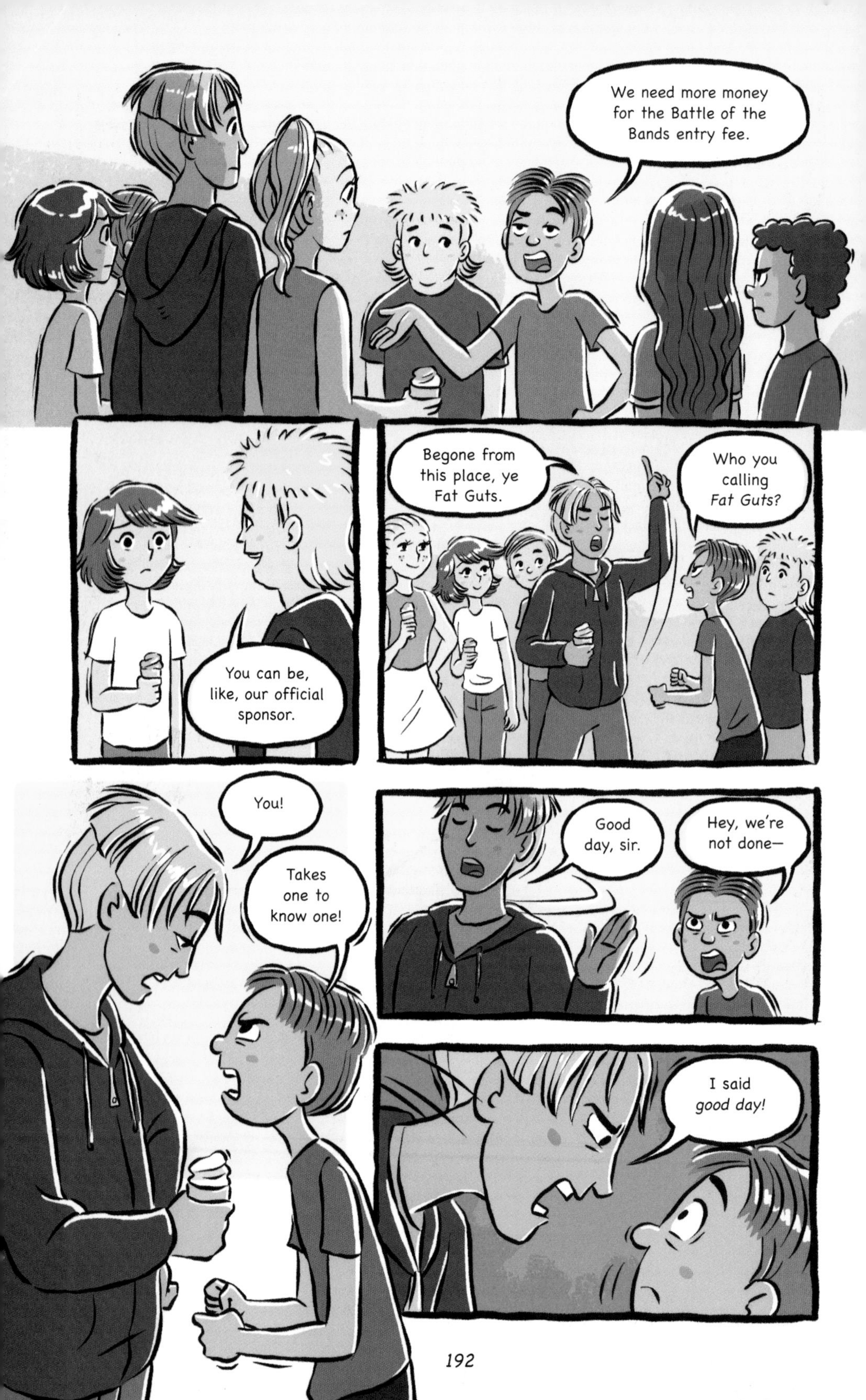
We need more money for the Battle of the Bands entry fee.
You can be, like, our official sponsor.
Begone from this place, ye Fat Guts.
Who you calling *Fat Guts?*
You!
Takes one to know one!
Good day, sir.
Hey, we're not done—
I said *good day!*

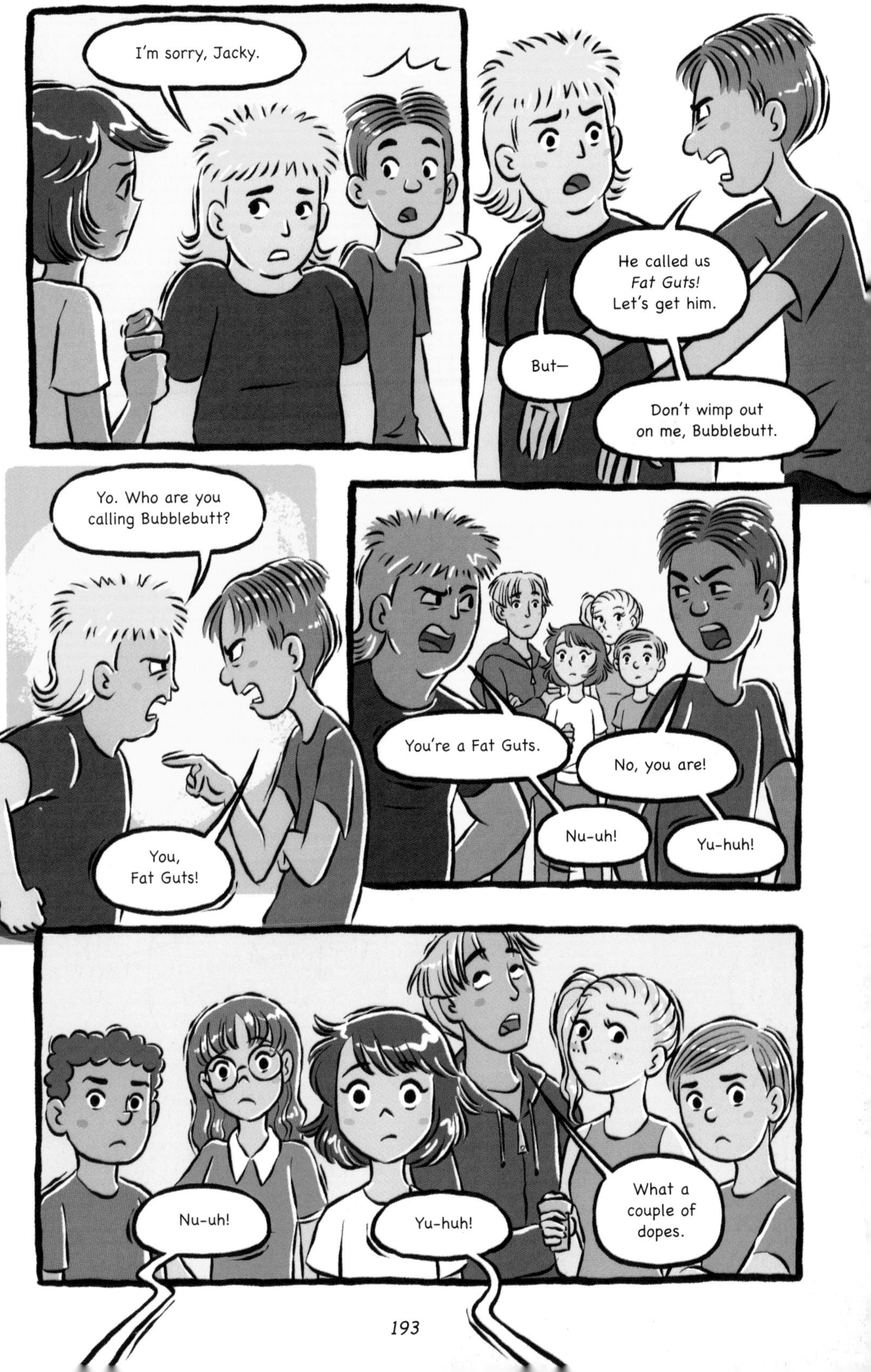
I'm sorry, Jacky.
He called us *Fat Guts!* Let's get him.
But—
Don't wimp out on me, Bubblebutt.
Yo. Who are you calling Bubblebutt?
You, Fat Guts!
You're a Fat Guts.
No, you are!
Nu-uh!
Yu-huh!
Nu-uh!
Yu-huh!
What a couple of dopes.

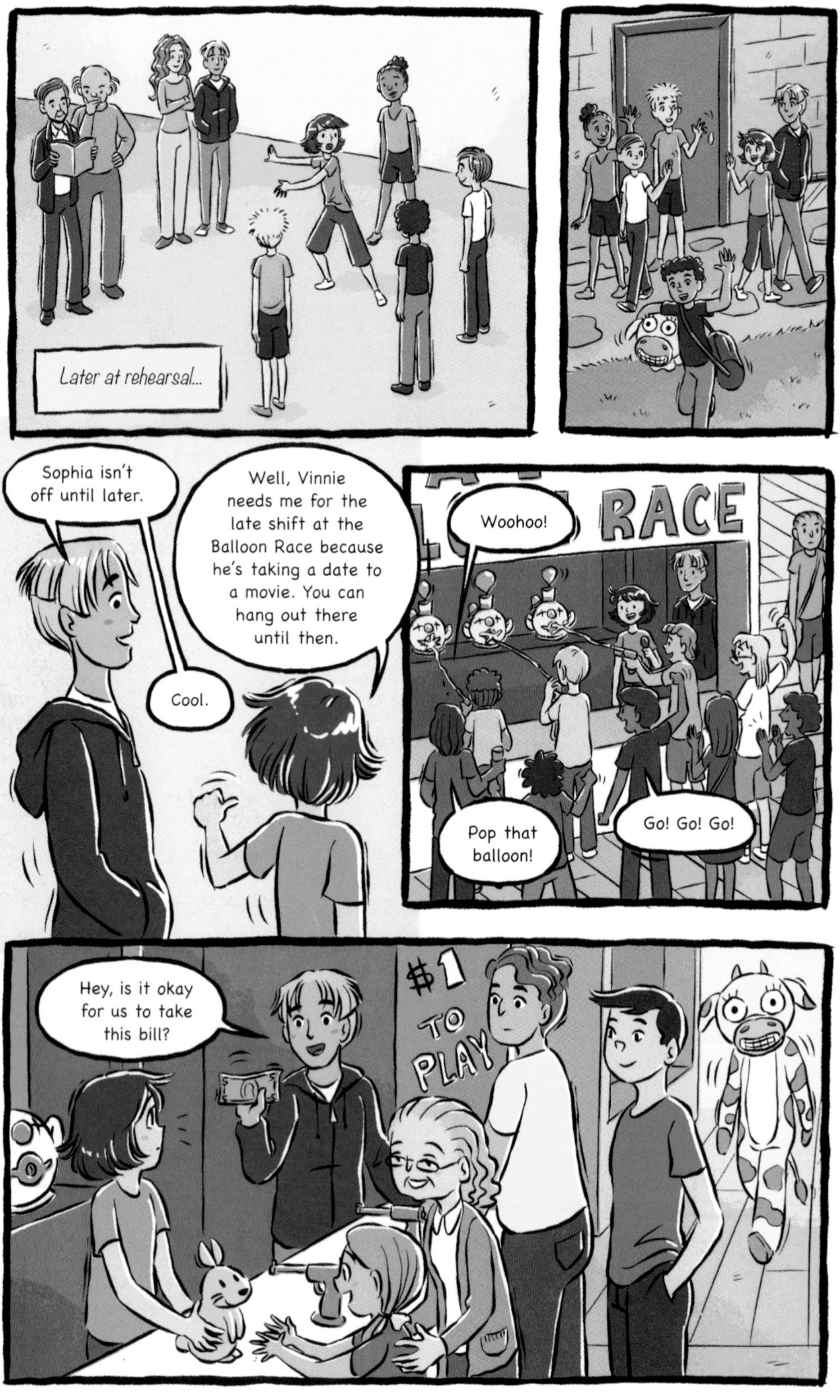
Later at rehearsal...
Sophia isn't off until later.
Well, Vinnie needs me for the late shift at the Balloon Race because he's taking a date to a movie. You can hang out there until then.
Cool.
RACE
Woohoo!
Pop that balloon!
Go! Go! Go!
Hey, is it okay for us to take this bill?
$1 TO PLAY

It's fine. Vinnie will sort it out with his bank.

THE UNITED STATES OF AMERICA
5 5
I 532521190
FIVE
FIVE DOLLARS
5 5

Okay.

I can't believe how busy it is!

Vinnie's going to be super happy.

POP!

Looks like we got another winner!

$1 TO PLAY

$1 TO PLA

Uh ee a ittle elp, acky. It's uck.

Can you watch the booth for a moment?

No problemo.

$1 TO PLAY

Come on. Head around back so no kids see you.

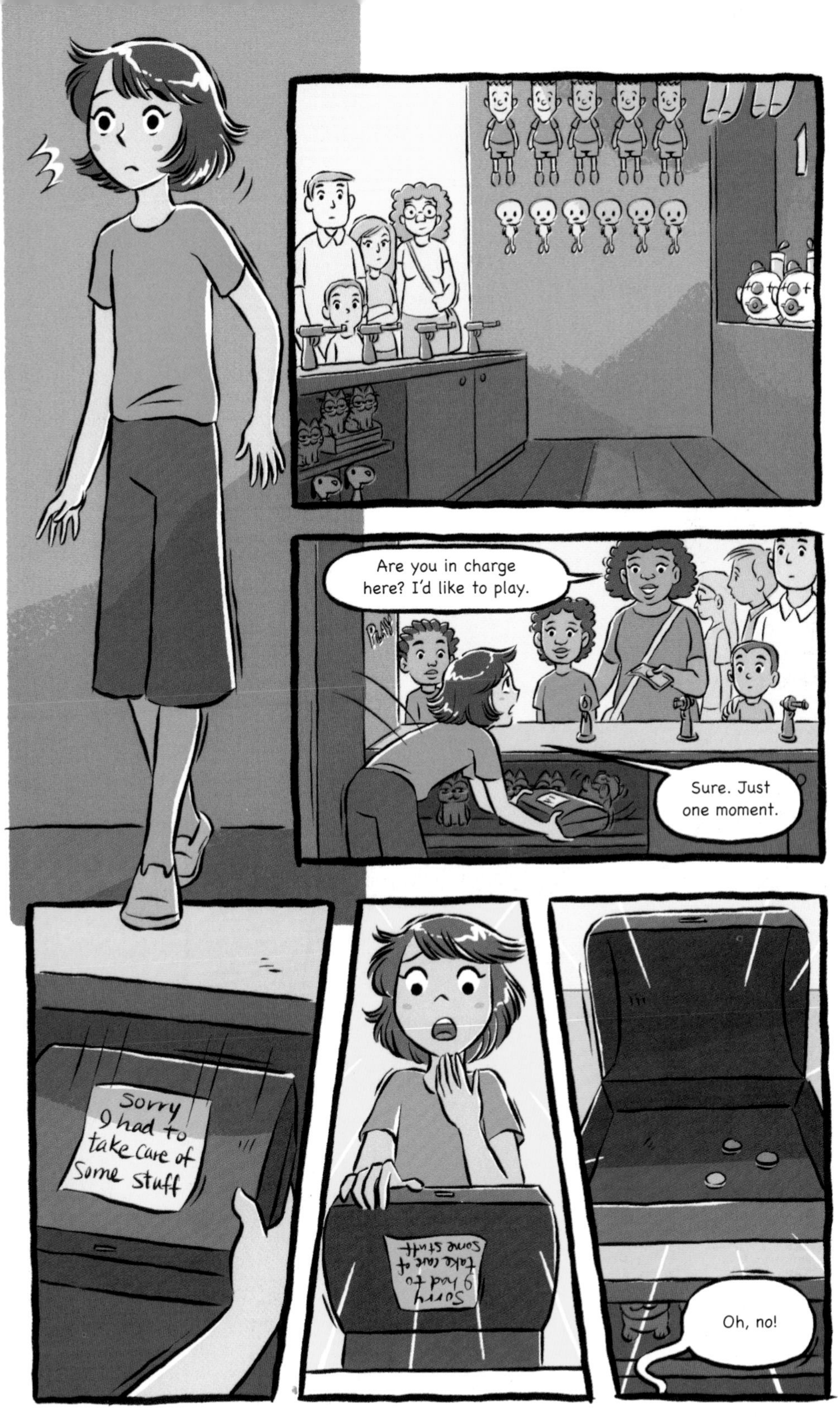
Are you in charge here? I'd like to play.
Sure. Just one moment.
Sorry I had to take care of some stuff
Oh, no!

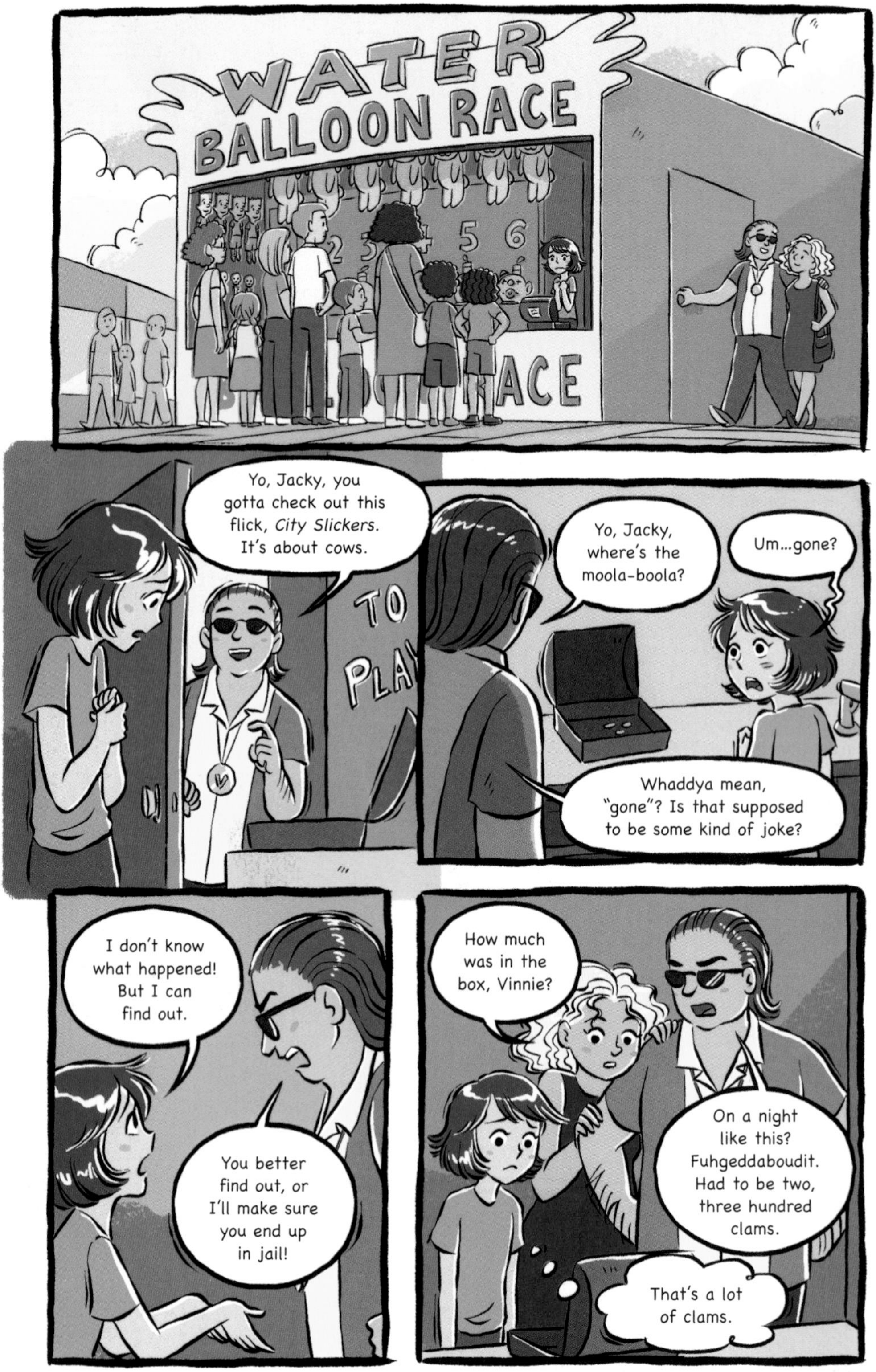
WATER BALLOON RACE
1 2 3 4 5 6
ACE
Yo, Jacky, you gotta check out this flick, *City Slickers*. It's about cows.
TO PLAY
Yo, Jacky, where's the moola-boola?
Um...gone?
Whaddya mean, "gone"? Is that supposed to be some kind of joke?
I don't know what happened! But I can find out.
You better find out, or I'll make sure you end up in jail!
How much was in the box, Vinnie?
On a night like this? Fuhgeddaboudit. Had to be two, three hundred clams.
That's a lot of clams.

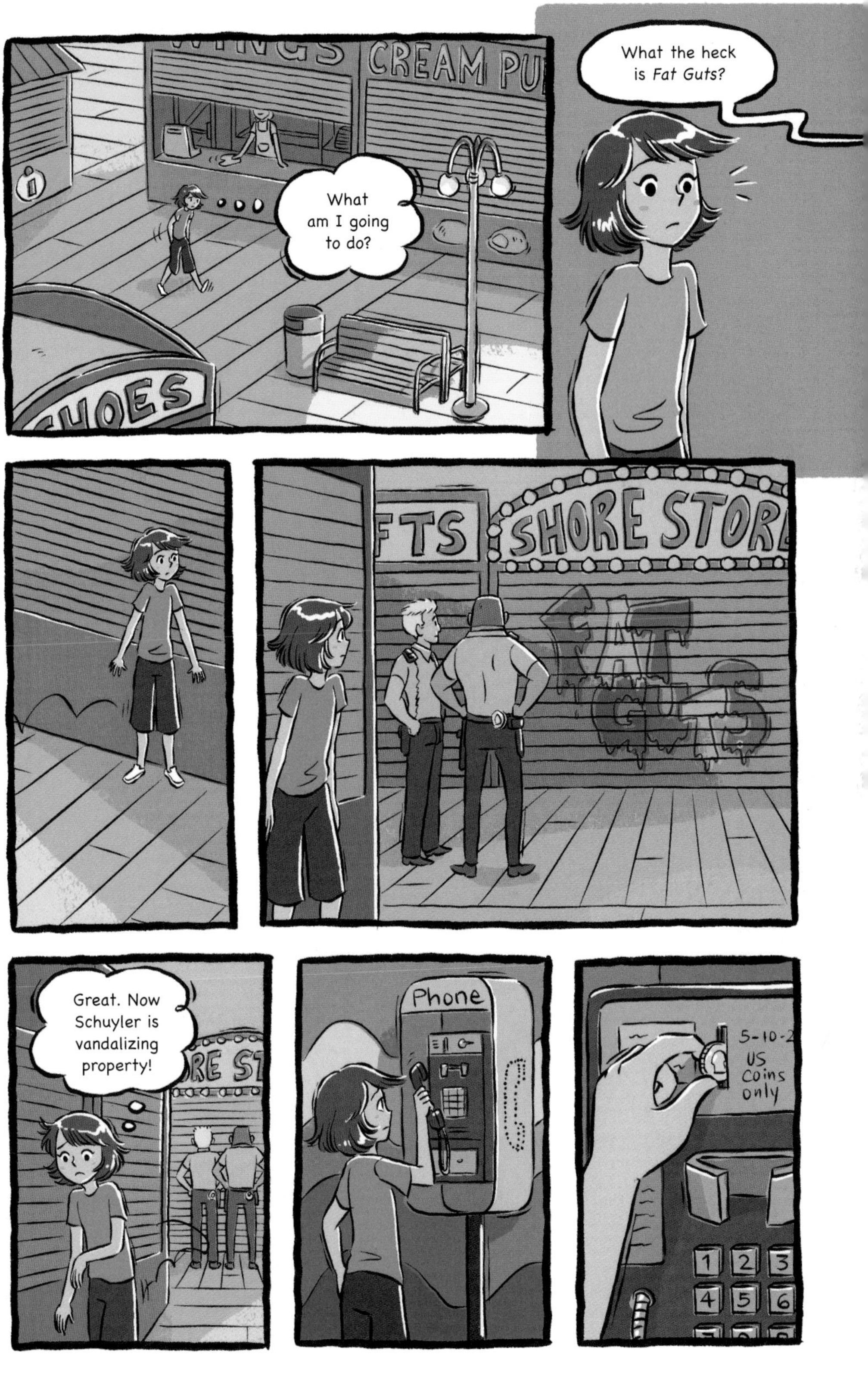

WINGS
CREAM PU
SHOES
What am I going to do?
What the heck is *Fat Guts*?
FTS
SHORE STOR
FAT GUTS
Great. Now Schuyler is vandalizing property!
RE ST
Phone
5-10-2
US Coins only
1 2 3
4 5 6

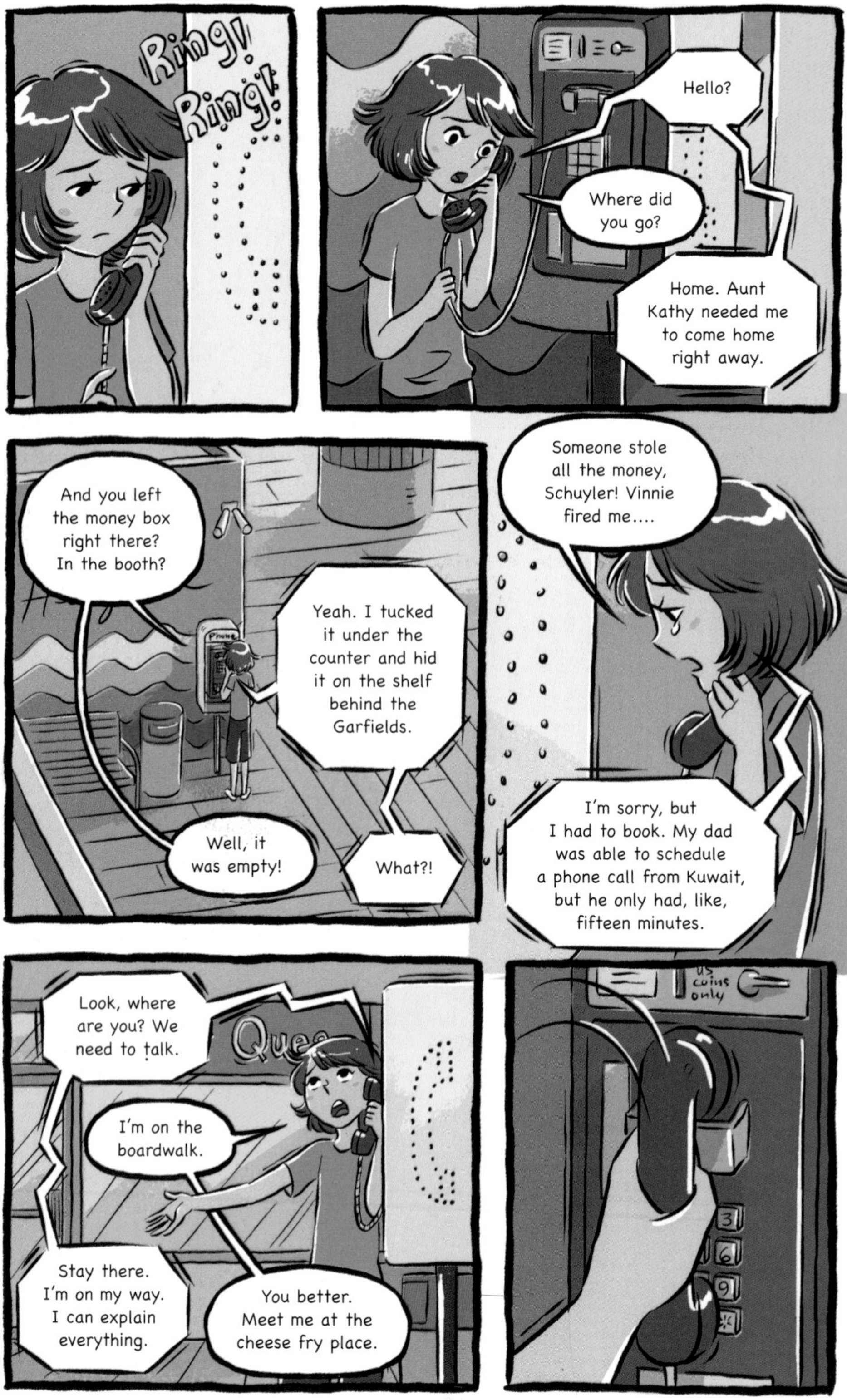
Ring! Ring!
Hello?
Where did you go?
Home. Aunt Kathy needed me to come home right away.
And you left the money box right there? In the booth?
Yeah. I tucked it under the counter and hid it on the shelf behind the Garfields.
Well, it was empty!
What?!
Someone stole all the money, Schuyler! Vinnie fired me....
I'm sorry, but I had to book. My dad was able to schedule a phone call from Kuwait, but he only had, like, fifteen minutes.
Look, where are you? We need to talk.
I'm on the boardwalk.
Stay there. I'm on my way. I can explain everything.
You better. Meet me at the cheese fry place.
US coins only

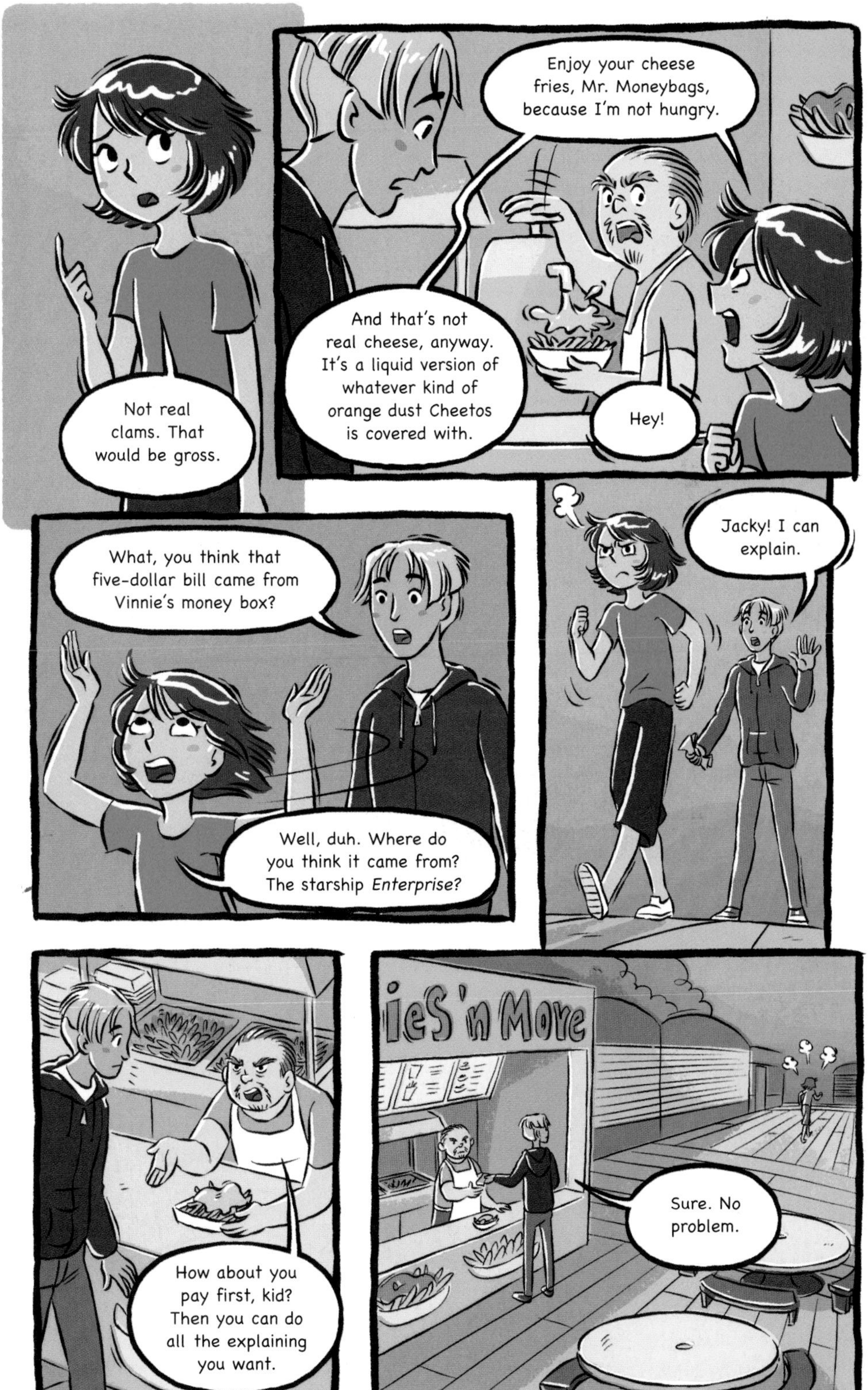
Not real clams. That would be gross.
Enjoy your cheese fries, Mr. Moneybags, because I'm not hungry.
And that's not real cheese, anyway. It's a liquid version of whatever kind of orange dust Cheetos is covered with.
Hey!
What, you think that five-dollar bill came from Vinnie's money box?
Well, duh. Where do you think it came from? The starship *Enterprise*?
Jacky! I can explain.
How about you pay first, kid? Then you can do all the explaining you want.
ieS 'n More
Sure. No problem.

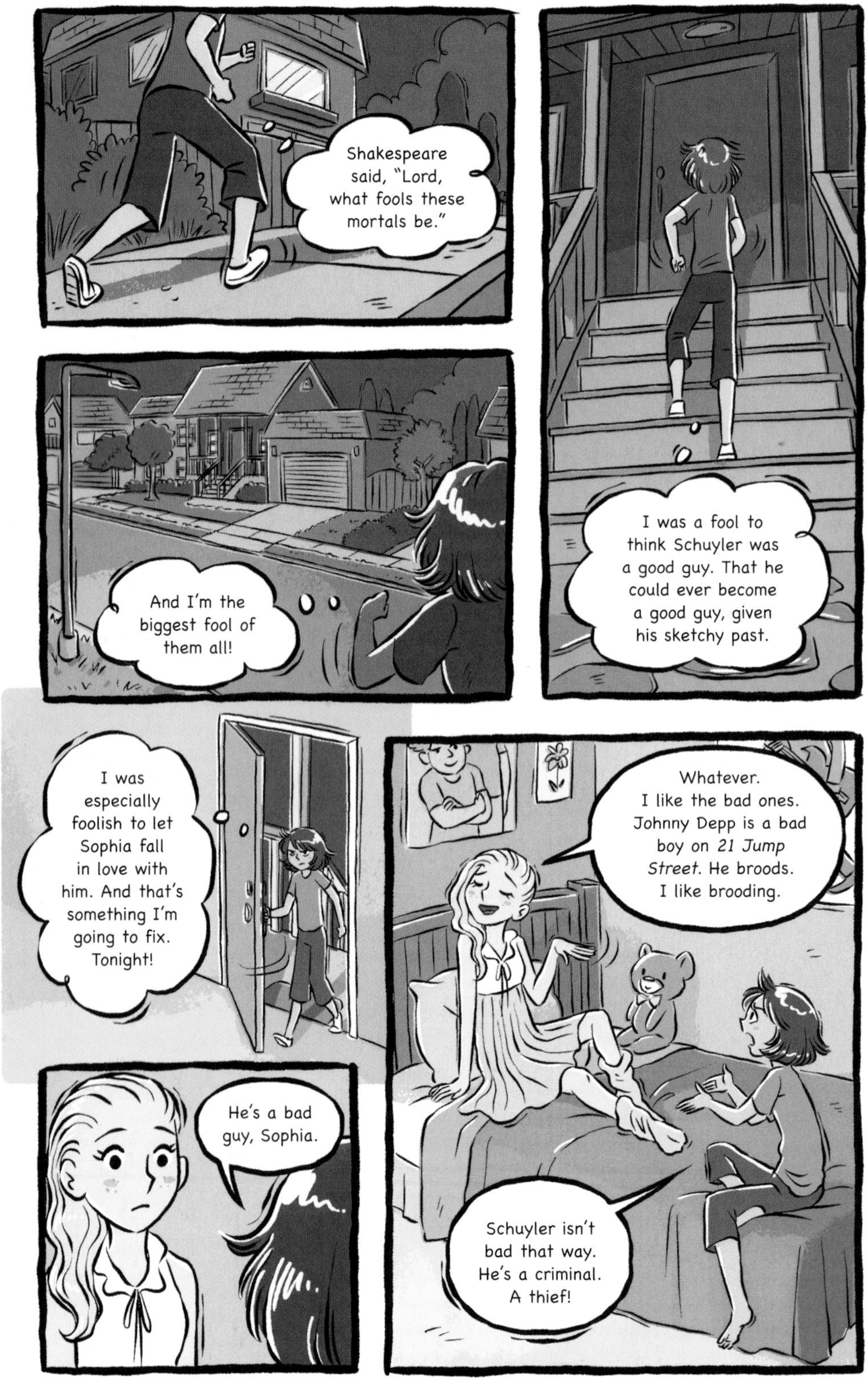

Shakespeare said, "Lord, what fools these mortals be."
I was a fool to think Schuyler was a good guy. That he could ever become a good guy, given his sketchy past.
And I'm the biggest fool of them all!
I was especially foolish to let Sophia fall in love with him. And that's something I'm going to fix. Tonight!
Whatever. I like the bad ones. Johnny Depp is a bad boy on *21 Jump Street*. He broods. I like brooding.
He's a bad guy, Sophia.
Schuyler isn't bad that way. He's a criminal. A thief!

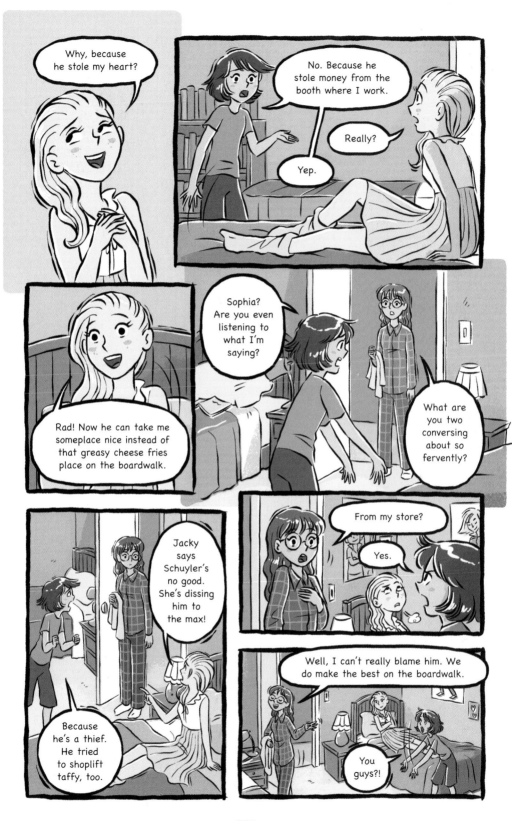

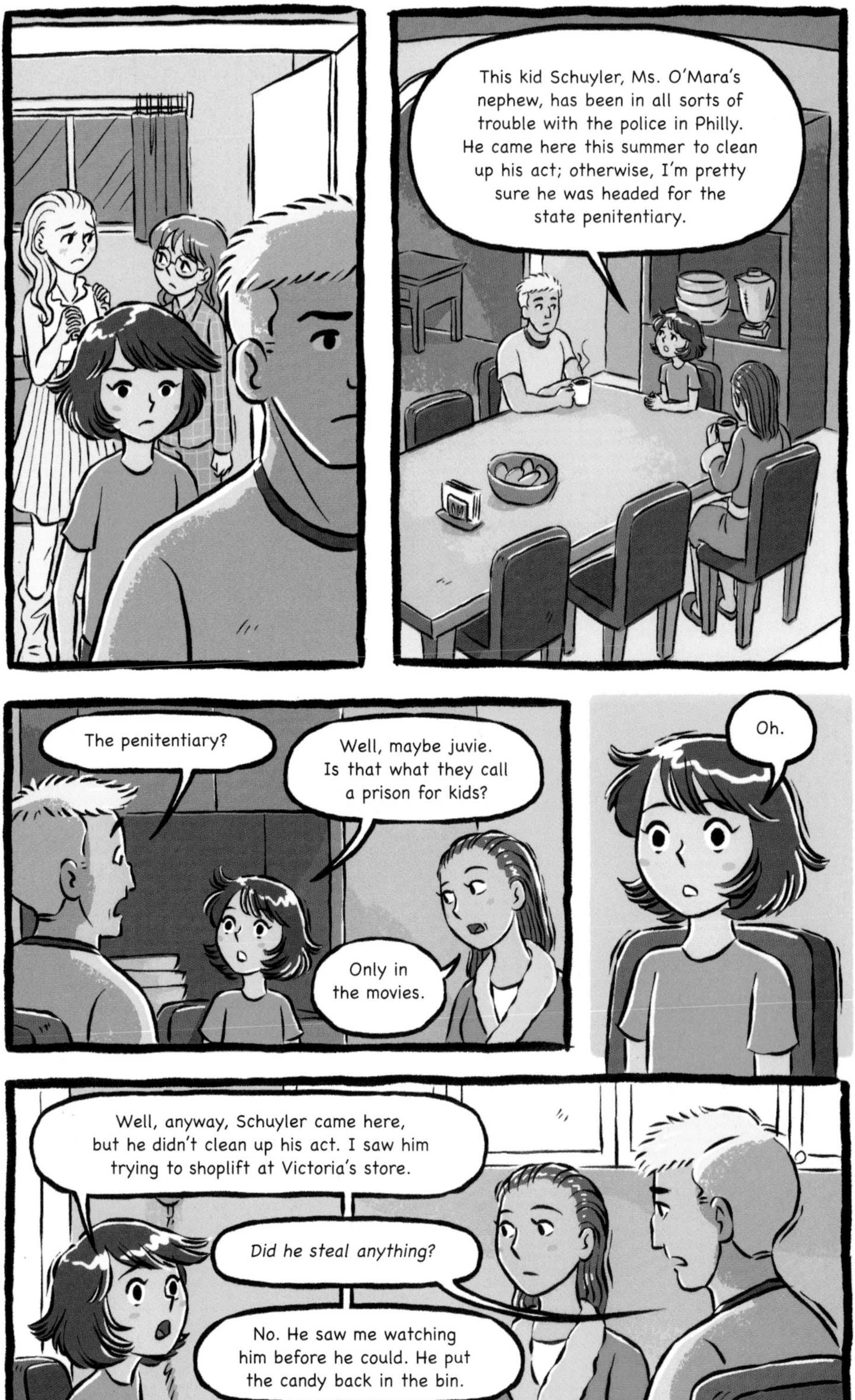
This kid Schuyler, Ms. O'Mara's nephew, has been in all sorts of trouble with the police in Philly. He came here this summer to clean up his act; otherwise, I'm pretty sure he was headed for the state penitentiary.
The penitentiary?
Well, maybe juvie. Is that what they call a prison for kids?
Only in the movies.
Oh.
Well, anyway, Schuyler came here, but he didn't clean up his act. I saw him trying to shoplift at Victoria's store.
Did he steal anything?
No. He saw me watching him before he could. He put the candy back in the bin.

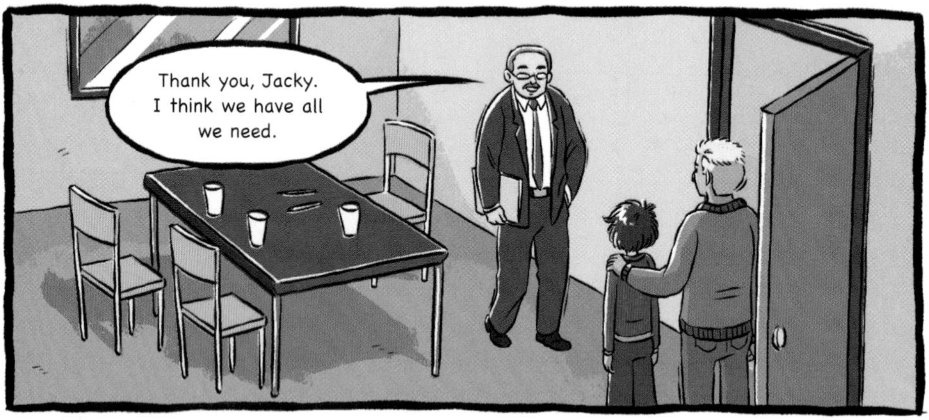
Thank you, Jacky.
I think we have all
we need.

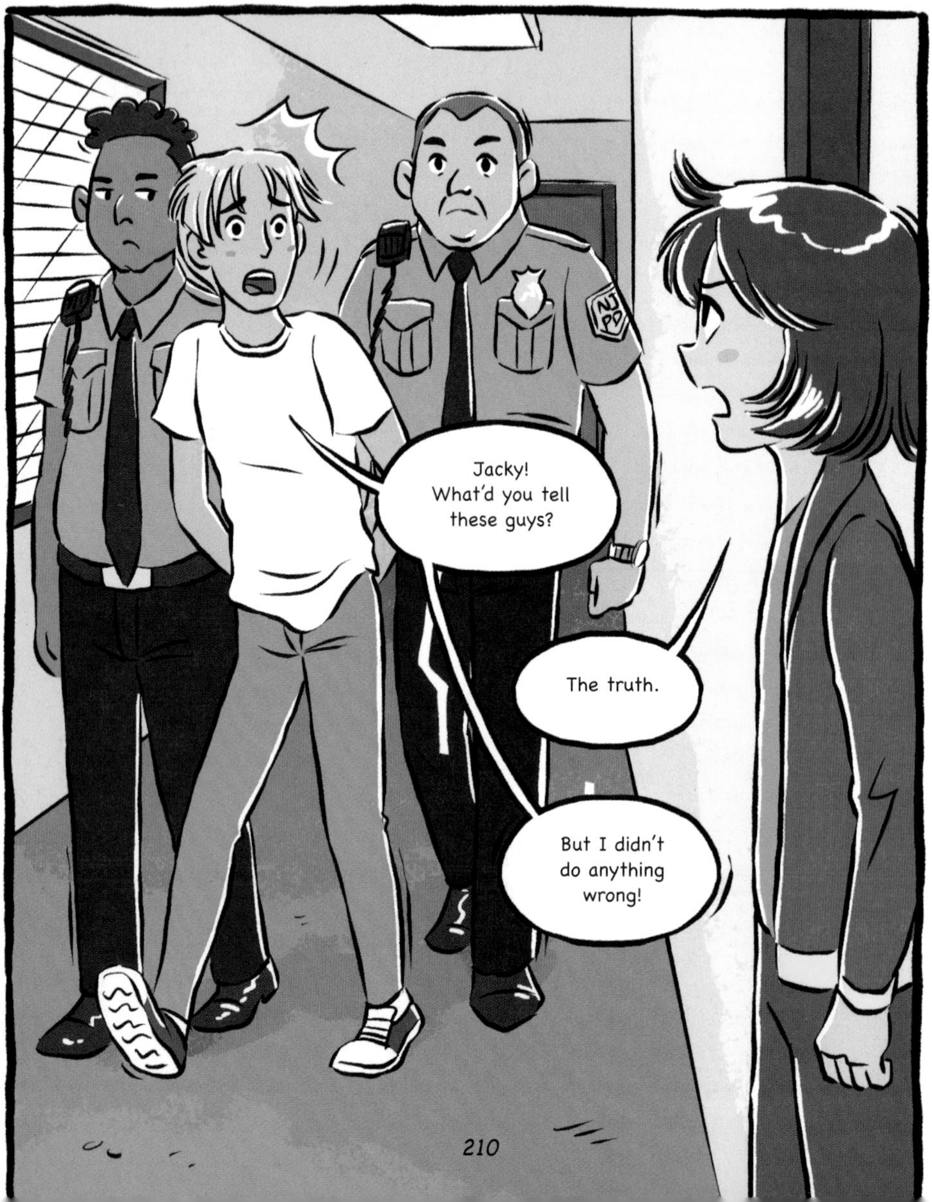
NJPD
Jacky!
What'd you tell
these guys?
The truth.
But I didn't
do anything
wrong!

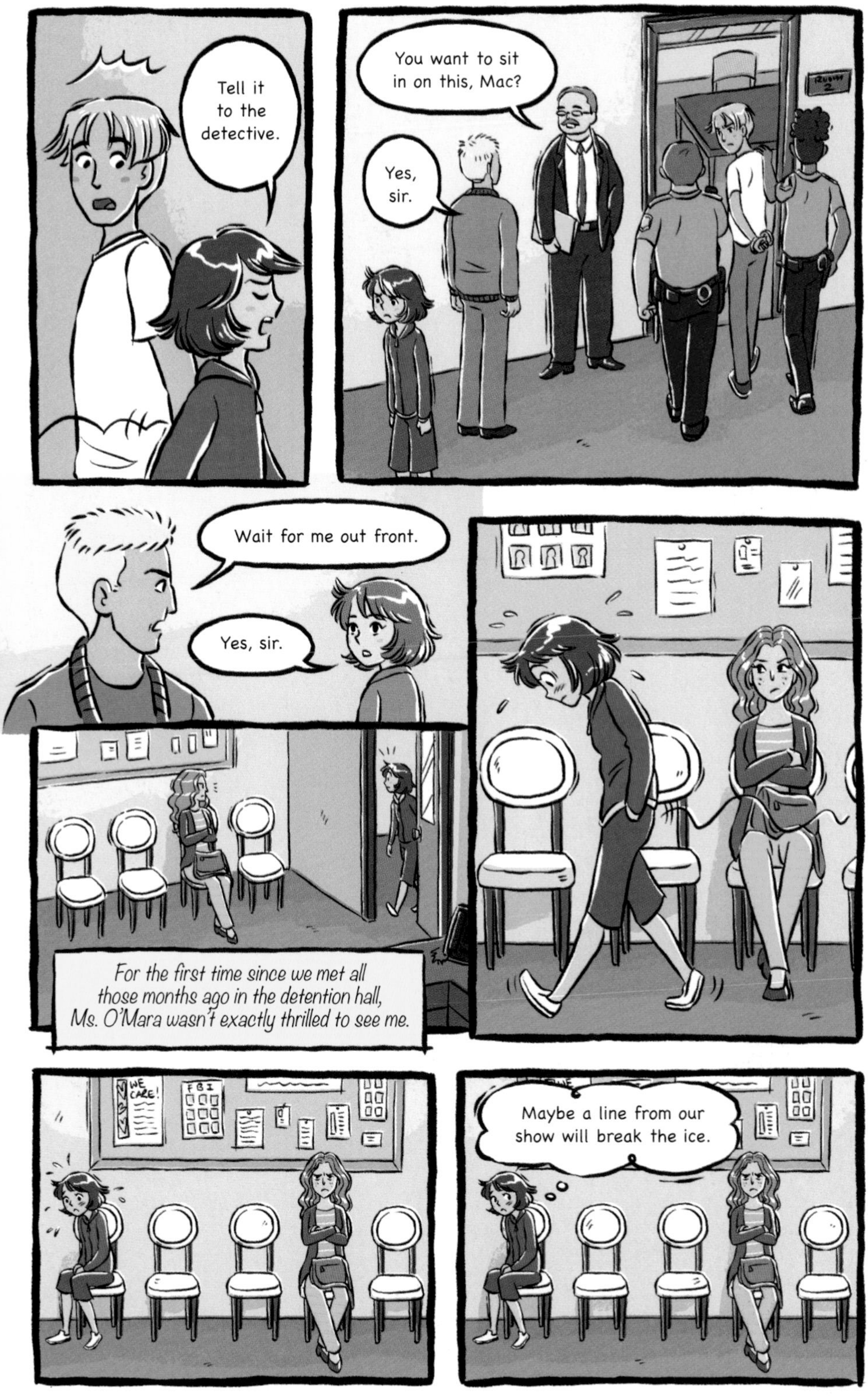
Tell it to the detective.
You want to sit in on this, Mac?
Yes, sir.
Wait for me out front.
Yes, sir.
For the first time since we met all those months ago in the detention hall, Ms. O'Mara wasn't exactly thrilled to see me.
Maybe a line from our show will break the ice.

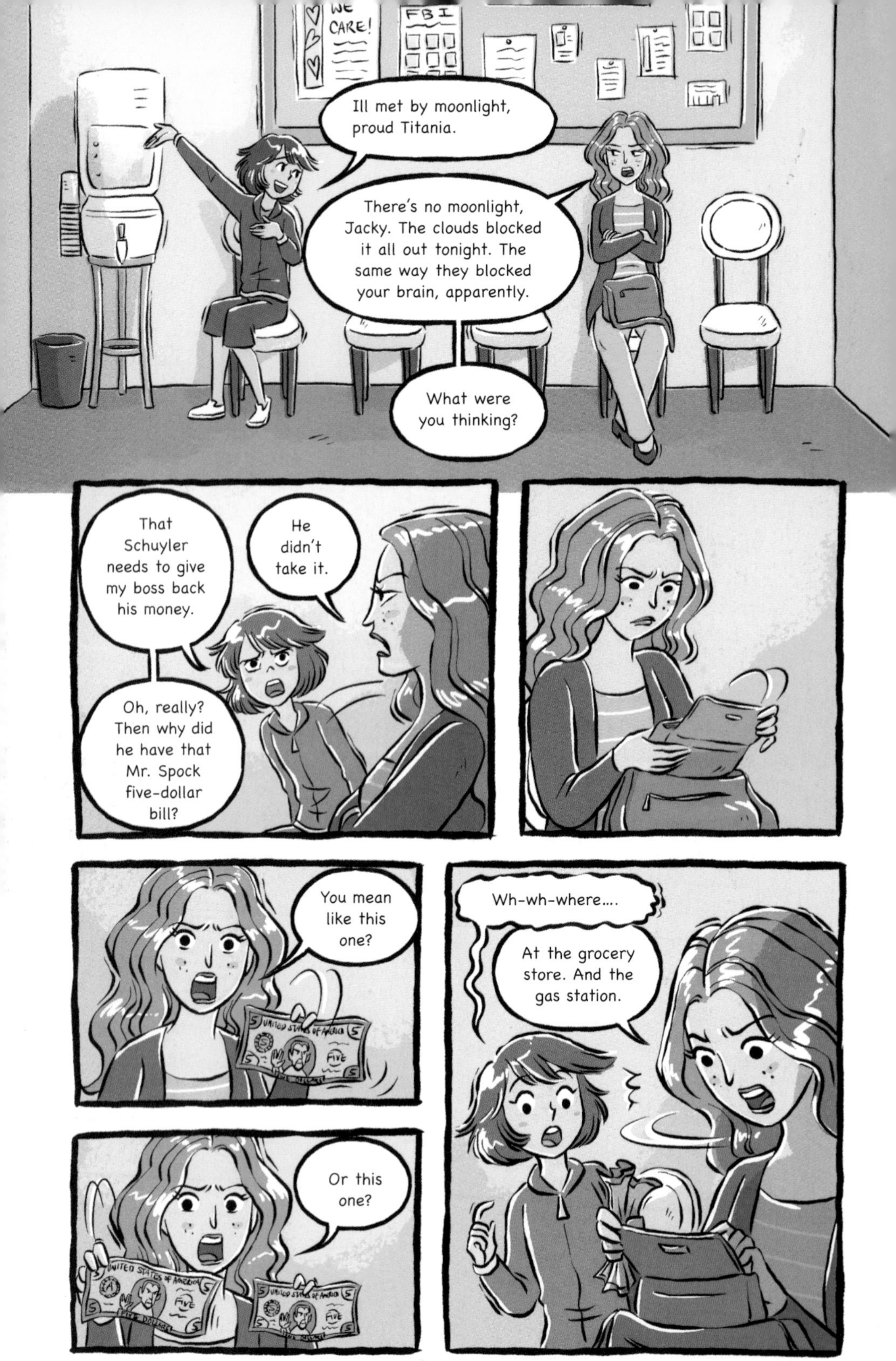
WE CARE!
FBI
Ill met by moonlight, proud Titania.
There's no moonlight, Jacky. The clouds blocked it all out tonight. The same way they blocked your brain, apparently.
What were you thinking?
That Schuyler needs to give my boss back his money.
He didn't take it.
Oh, really? Then why did he have that Mr. Spock five-dollar bill?
You mean like this one?
Or this one?
Wh-wh-where....
At the grocery store. And the gas station.

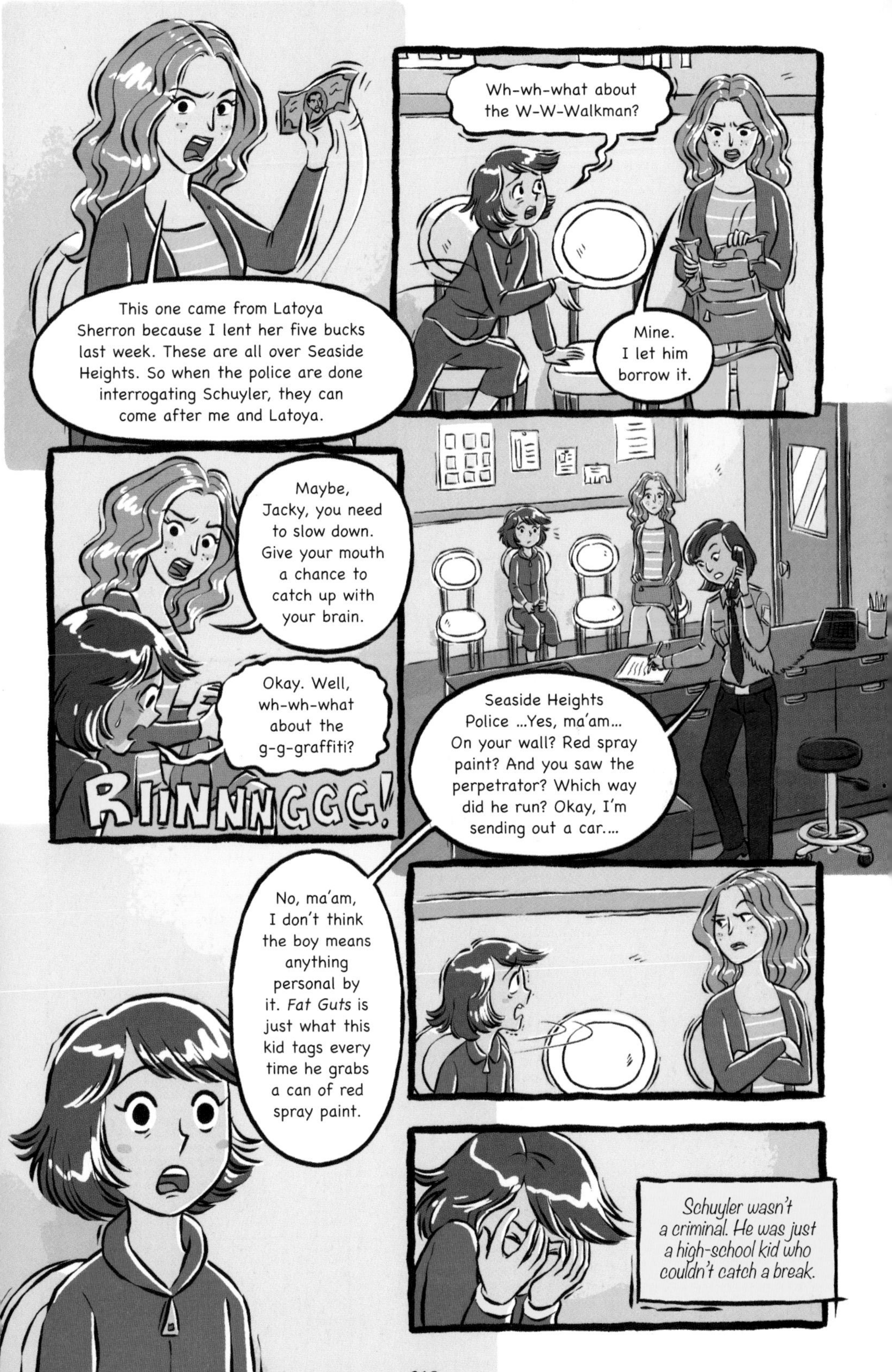
This one came from Latoya Sherron because I lent her five bucks last week. These are all over Seaside Heights. So when the police are done interrogating Schuyler, they can come after me and Latoya.
Wh-wh-what about the W-W-Walkman?
Mine. I let him borrow it.
Maybe, Jacky, you need to slow down. Give your mouth a chance to catch up with your brain.
Okay. Well, wh-wh-what about the g-g-graffiti?
RIINNNGGG!
Seaside Heights Police ...Yes, ma'am... On your wall? Red spray paint? And you saw the perpetrator? Which way did he run? Okay, I'm sending out a car....
No, ma'am, I don't think the boy means anything personal by it. *Fat Guts* is just what this kid tags every time he grabs a can of red spray paint.
Schuyler wasn't a criminal. He was just a high-school kid who couldn't catch a break.

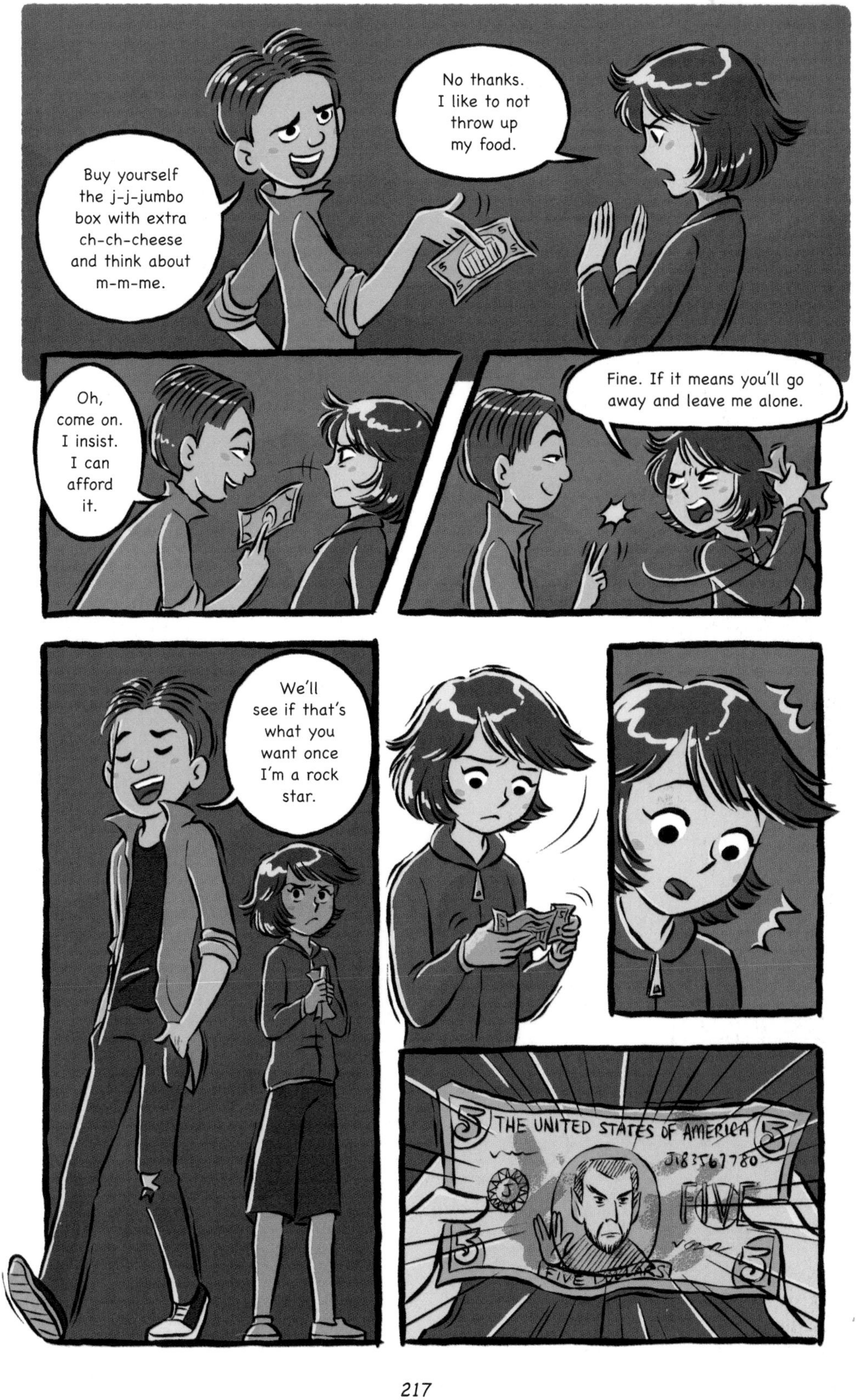
No thanks.
I like to not
throw up
my food.
Buy yourself
the j-j-jumbo
box with extra
ch-ch-cheese
and think about
m-m-me.
Oh,
come on.
I insist.
I can
afford
it.
Fine. If it means you'll go
away and leave me alone.
We'll
see if that's
what you
want once
I'm a rock
star.
THE UNITED STATES OF AMERICA
FIVE
FIVE DOLLARS

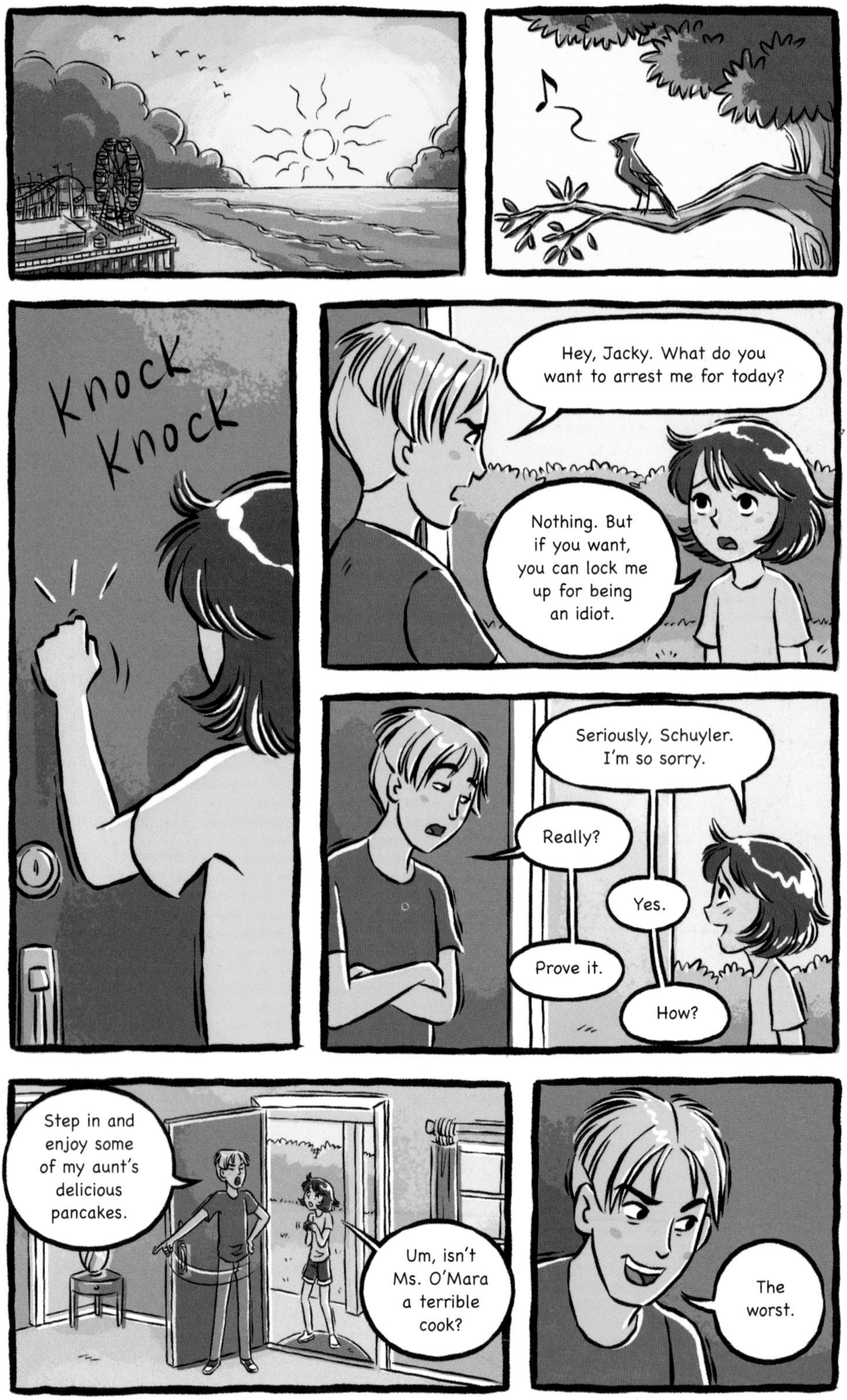
Knock
Knock
Hey, Jacky. What do you want to arrest me for today?
Nothing. But if you want, you can lock me up for being an idiot.
Seriously, Schuyler. I'm so sorry.
Really?
Yes.
Prove it.
How?
Step in and enjoy some of my aunt's delicious pancakes.
Um, isn't Ms. O'Mara a terrible cook?
The worst.

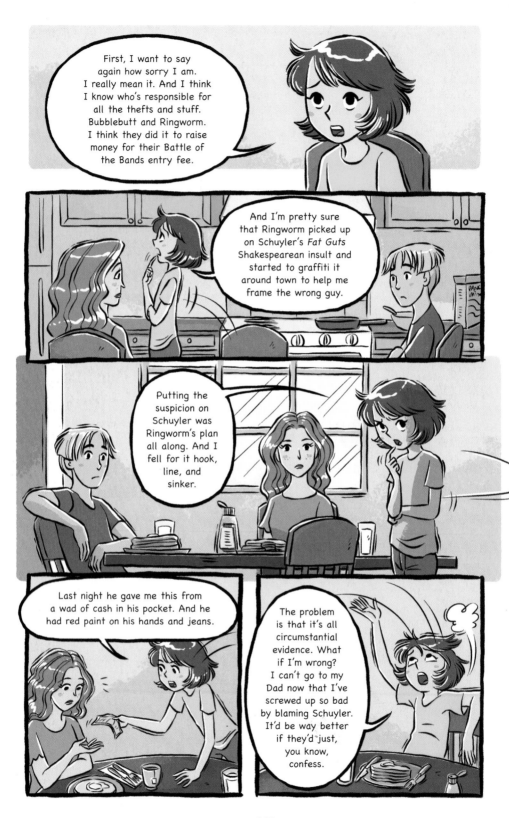

First, I want to say again how sorry I am. I really mean it. And I think I know who's responsible for all the thefts and stuff. Bubblebutt and Ringworm. I think they did it to raise money for their Battle of the Bands entry fee.

And I'm pretty sure that Ringworm picked up on Schuyler's *Fat Guts* Shakespearean insult and started to graffiti it around town to help me frame the wrong guy.

Putting the suspicion on Schuyler was Ringworm's plan all along. And I fell for it hook, line, and sinker.

Last night he gave me this from a wad of cash in his pocket. And he had red paint on his hands and jeans.

The problem is that it's all circumstantial evidence. What if I'm wrong? I can't go to my Dad now that I've screwed up so bad by blaming Schuyler. It'd be way better if they'd just, you know, confess.

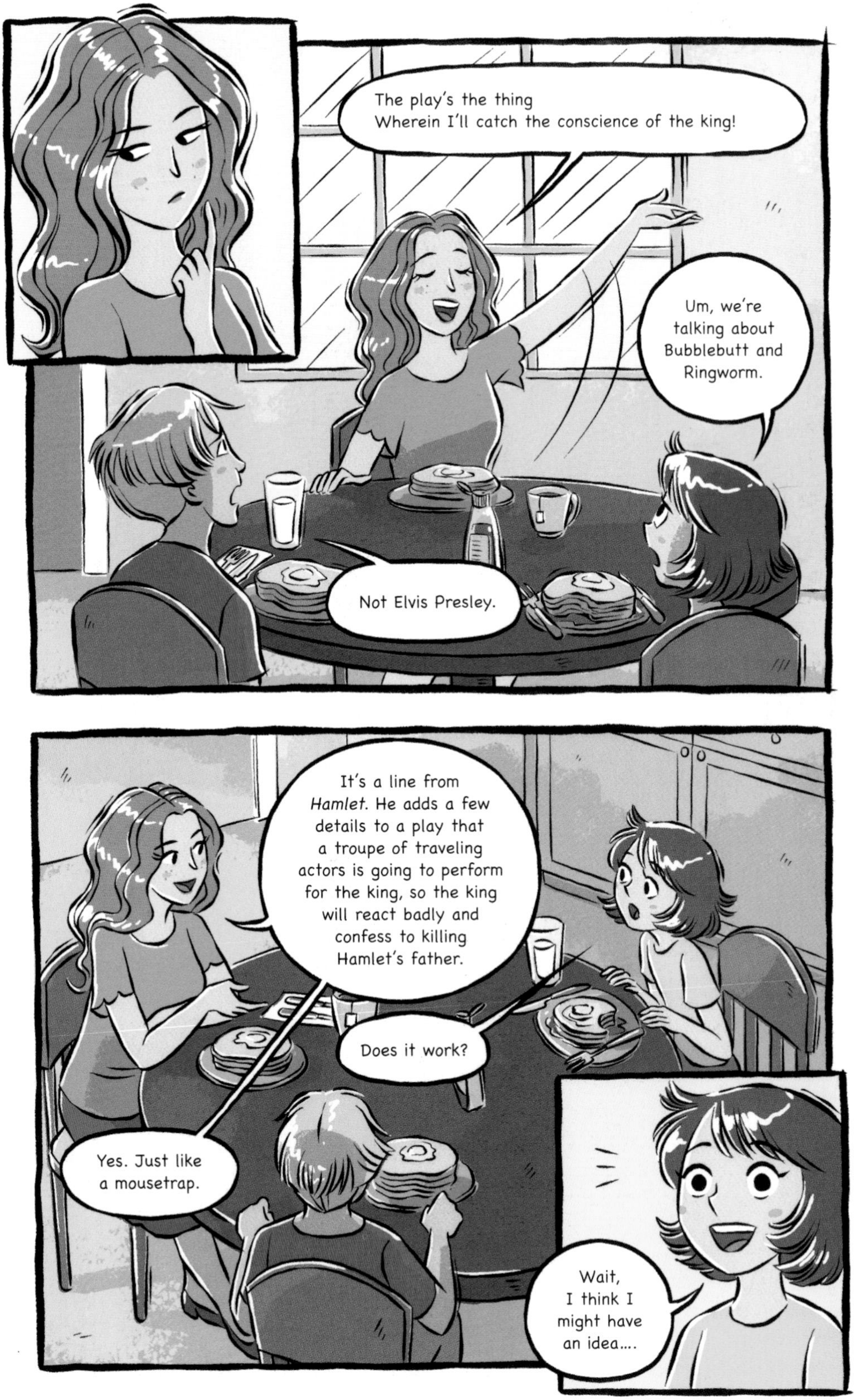
The play's the thing
Wherein I'll catch the conscience of the king!
Um, we're talking about Bubblebutt and Ringworm.
Not Elvis Presley.
It's a line from *Hamlet*. He adds a few details to a play that a troupe of traveling actors is going to perform for the king, so the king will react badly and confess to killing Hamlet's father.
Does it work?
Yes. Just like a mousetrap.
Wait, I think I might have an idea….

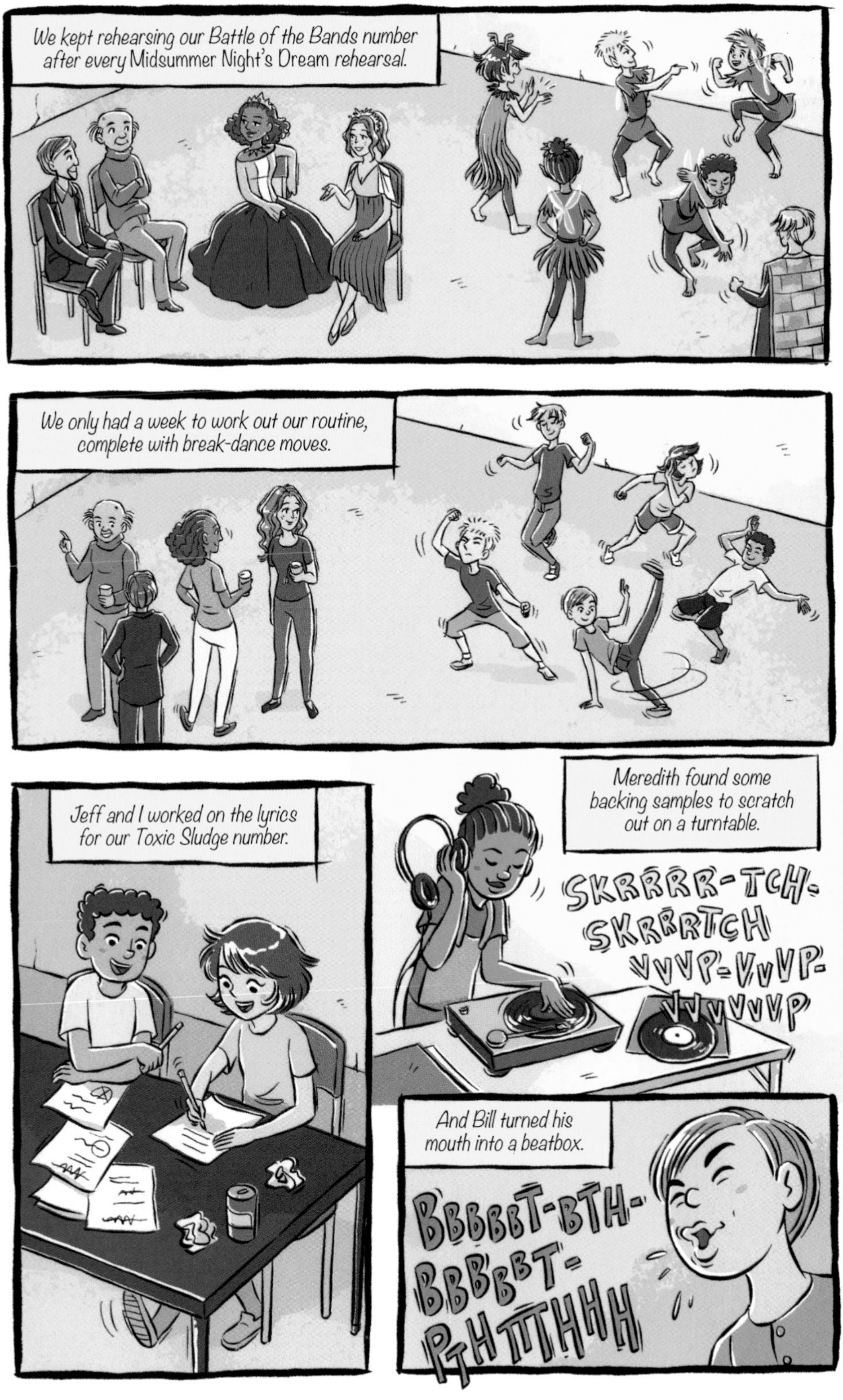
We kept rehearsing our Battle of the Bands number after every Midsummer Night's Dream rehearsal.
We only had a week to work out our routine, complete with break-dance moves.
Jeff and I worked on the lyrics for our Toxic Sludge number.
Meredith found some backing samples to scratch out on a turntable.
SKRRRR-TCH-SKRRRTCH
VVVP-VVVP-VVVVVVP
And Bill turned his mouth into a beatbox.
BBBBBT-BTH-BBBBBT-PTHTTHHH

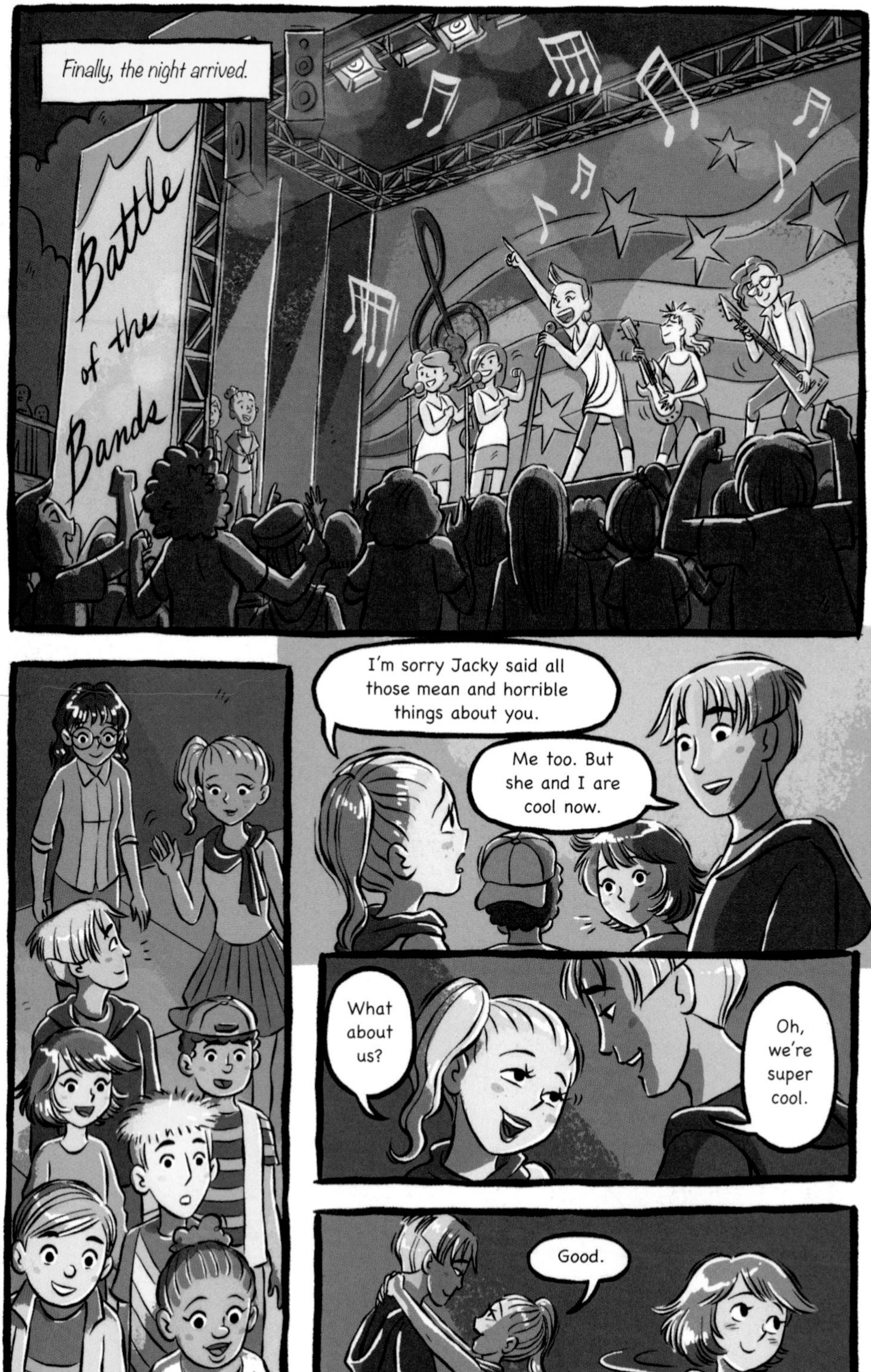
Finally, the night arrived.
Battle of the Bands
I'm sorry Jacky said all those mean and horrible things about you.
Me too. But she and I are cool now.
What about us?
Oh, we're super cool.
Good.

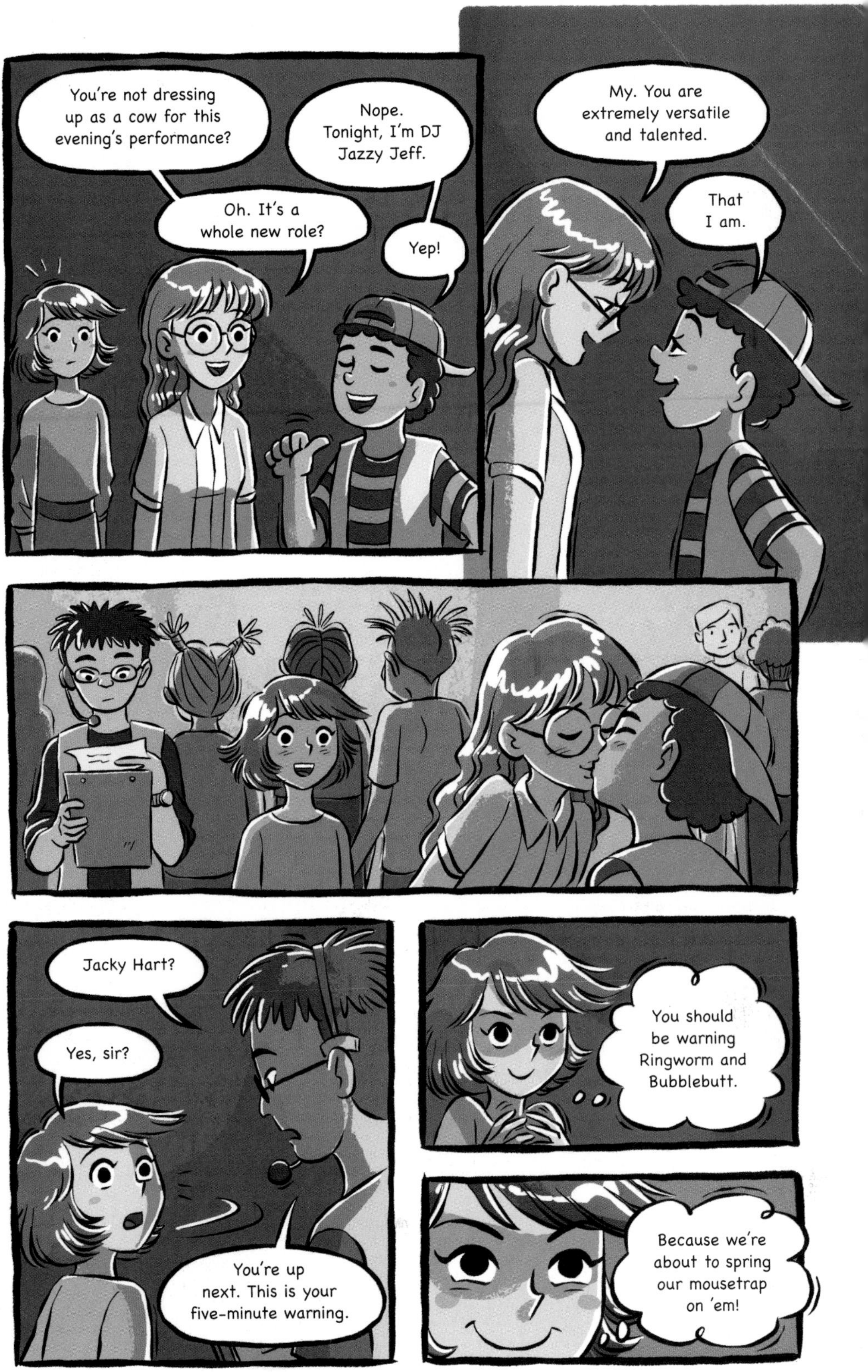
You're not dressing up as a cow for this evening's performance?
Nope. Tonight, I'm DJ Jazzy Jeff.
Oh. It's a whole new role?
Yep!
My. You are extremely versatile and talented.
That I am.
Jacky Hart?
Yes, sir?
You're up next. This is your five-minute warning.
You should be warning Ringworm and Bubblebutt.
Because we're about to spring our mousetrap on 'em!

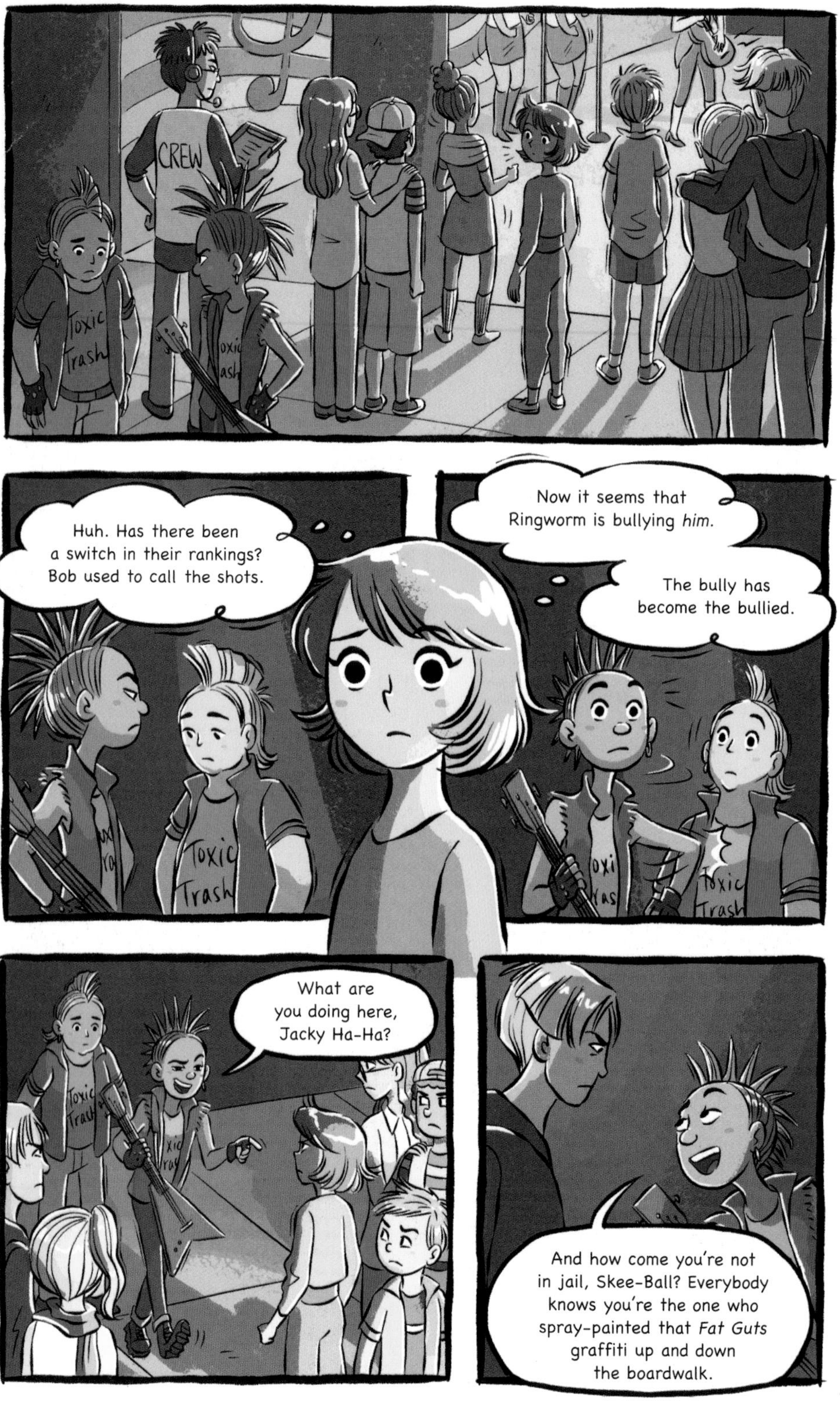
CREW
Toxic Trash
Huh. Has there been a switch in their rankings? Bob used to call the shots.
Now it seems that Ringworm is bullying *him*.
The bully has become the bullied.
What are you doing here, Jacky Ha-Ha?
And how come you're not in jail, Skee-Ball? Everybody knows you're the one who spray-painted that *Fat Guts* graffiti up and down the boardwalk.

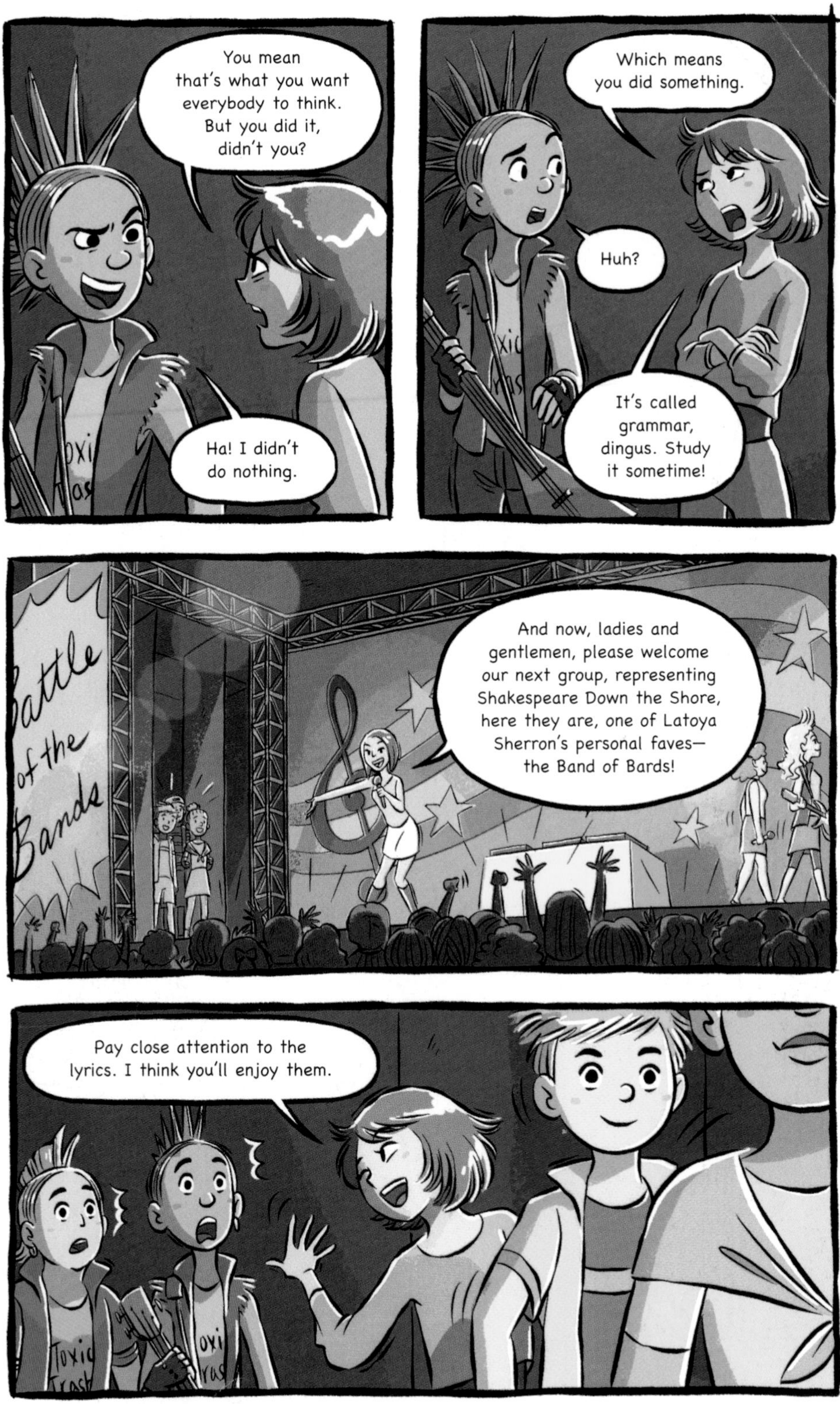
You mean that's what you want everybody to think. But you did it, didn't you?
Ha! I didn't do nothing.
Which means you did something.
Huh?
It's called grammar, dingus. Study it sometime!
And now, ladies and gentlemen, please welcome our next group, representing Shakespeare Down the Shore, here they are, one of Latoya Sherron's personal faves—the Band of Bards!
Pay close attention to the lyrics. I think you'll enjoy them.

Schuyler the liar. The thieving highflier. The sneaky, crooked smiler.

They even had a verse about Schuyler being arrested and sent to prison, which wasn't true.

But the audience didn't know that.

That's right. Toxic Trash had the same plan that we did, before we even came up with our plan.

Guess they had the same rhyming dictionary we did.

Our lyrics were better, man.

Our music was better, too.

We didn't enter the Battle of the Bands to win. We did it to clear Schuyler's name and to get Ringworm to confess.

Gee, Jacky. That sure worked out well, didn't it?

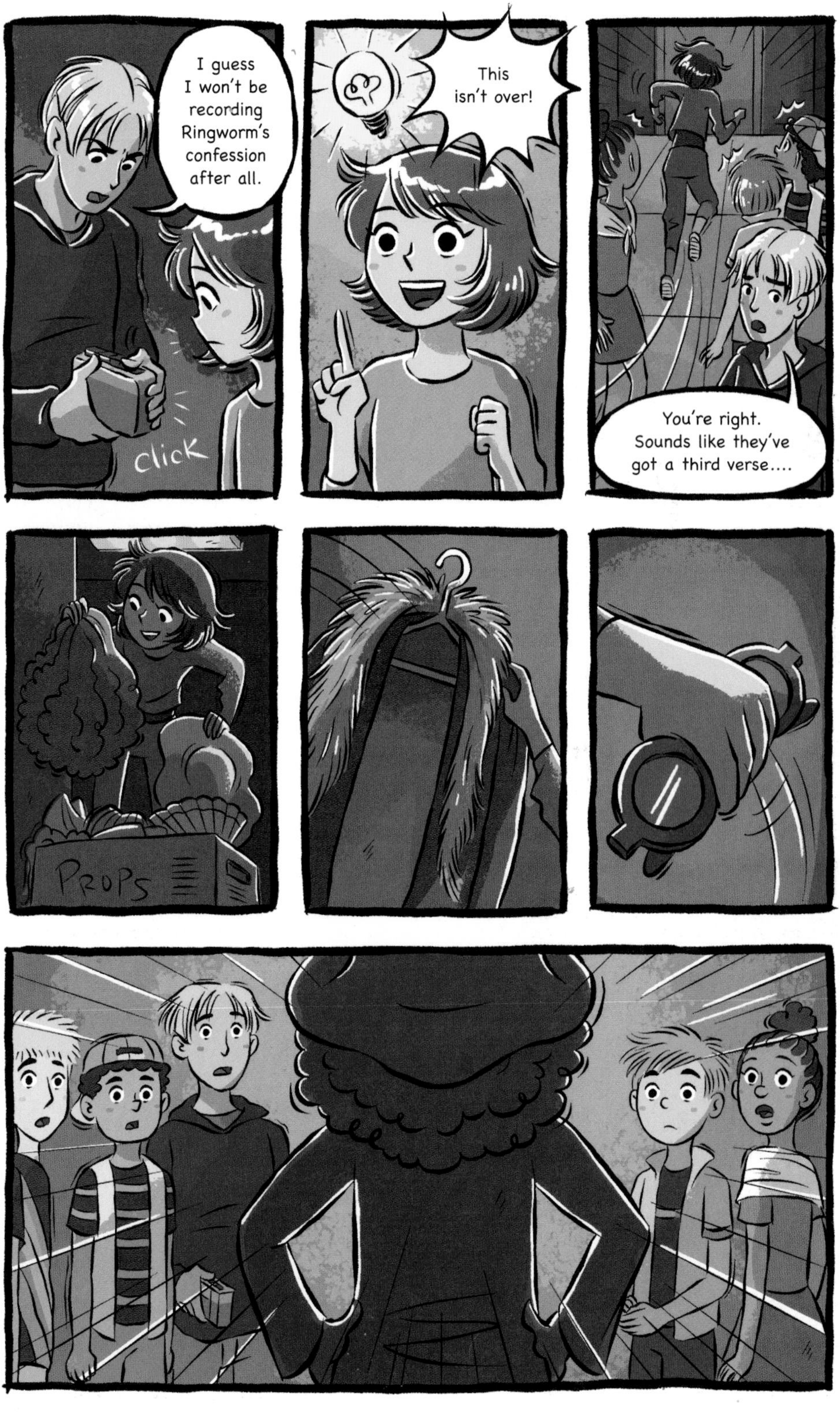
I guess I won't be recording Ringworm's confession after all.
CLICK
This isn't over!
You're right. Sounds like they've got a third verse....
PROPS

236

I'm, like, Toxic Trash's number one fan? Seriously, dudes. I am!

We're Toxic Trash!

We were totally awesome!

I'm always awesome.

Guess those middle school dweebs couldn't stand the heat.

We showed them!

It was time for the performance of my life: pretending I loved Toxic Trash and doing it without the Wormowitz brothers figuring out who I was!

Wow! That was so great!

Click

Walkman

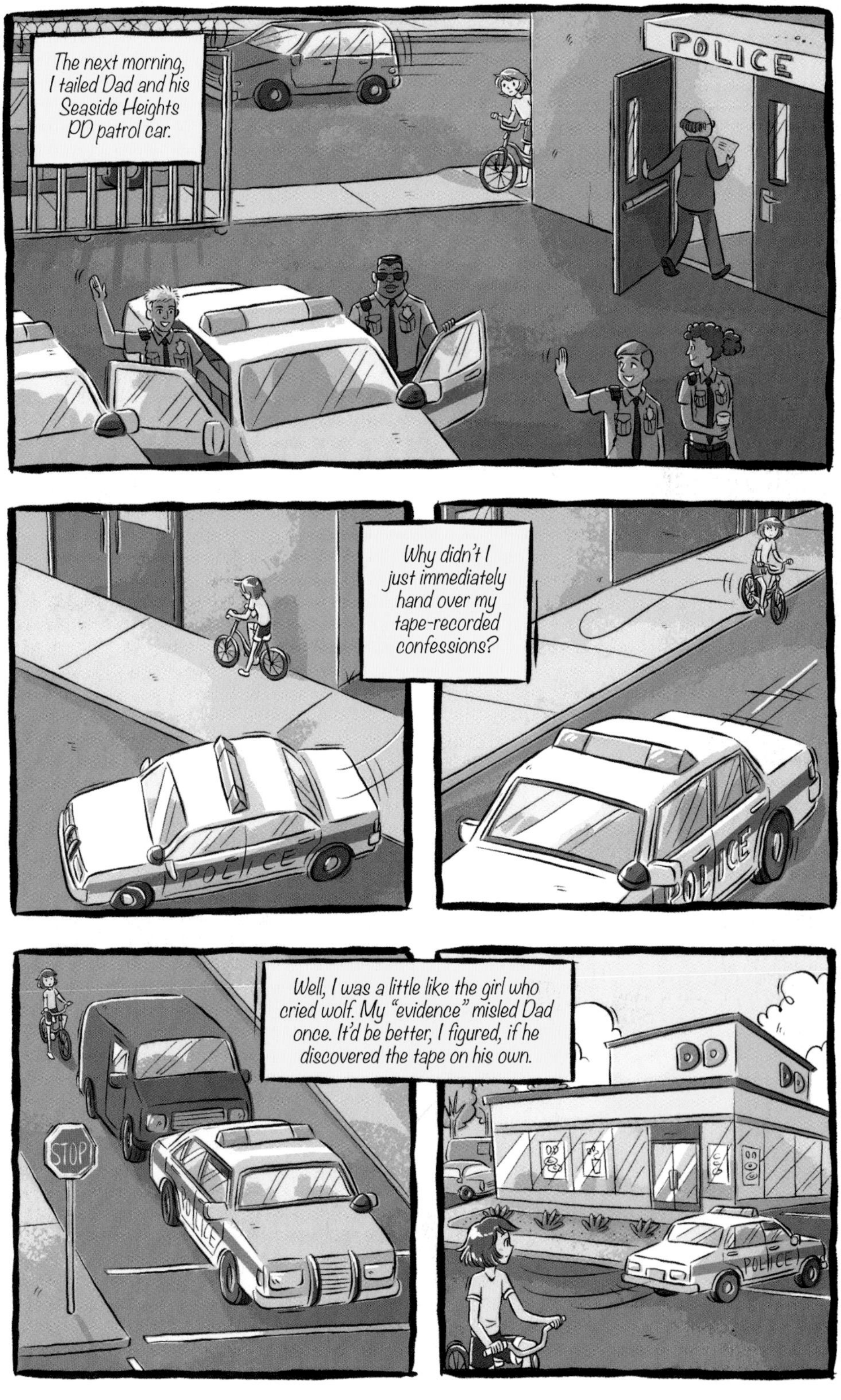
POLICE
The next morning, I tailed Dad and his Seaside Heights PD patrol car.
Why didn't I just immediately hand over my tape-recorded confessions?
POLICE
POLICE
Well, I was a little like the girl who cried wolf. My "evidence" misled Dad once. It'd be better, I figured, if he discovered the tape on his own.
STOP
POLICE
DD
DD
POLICE

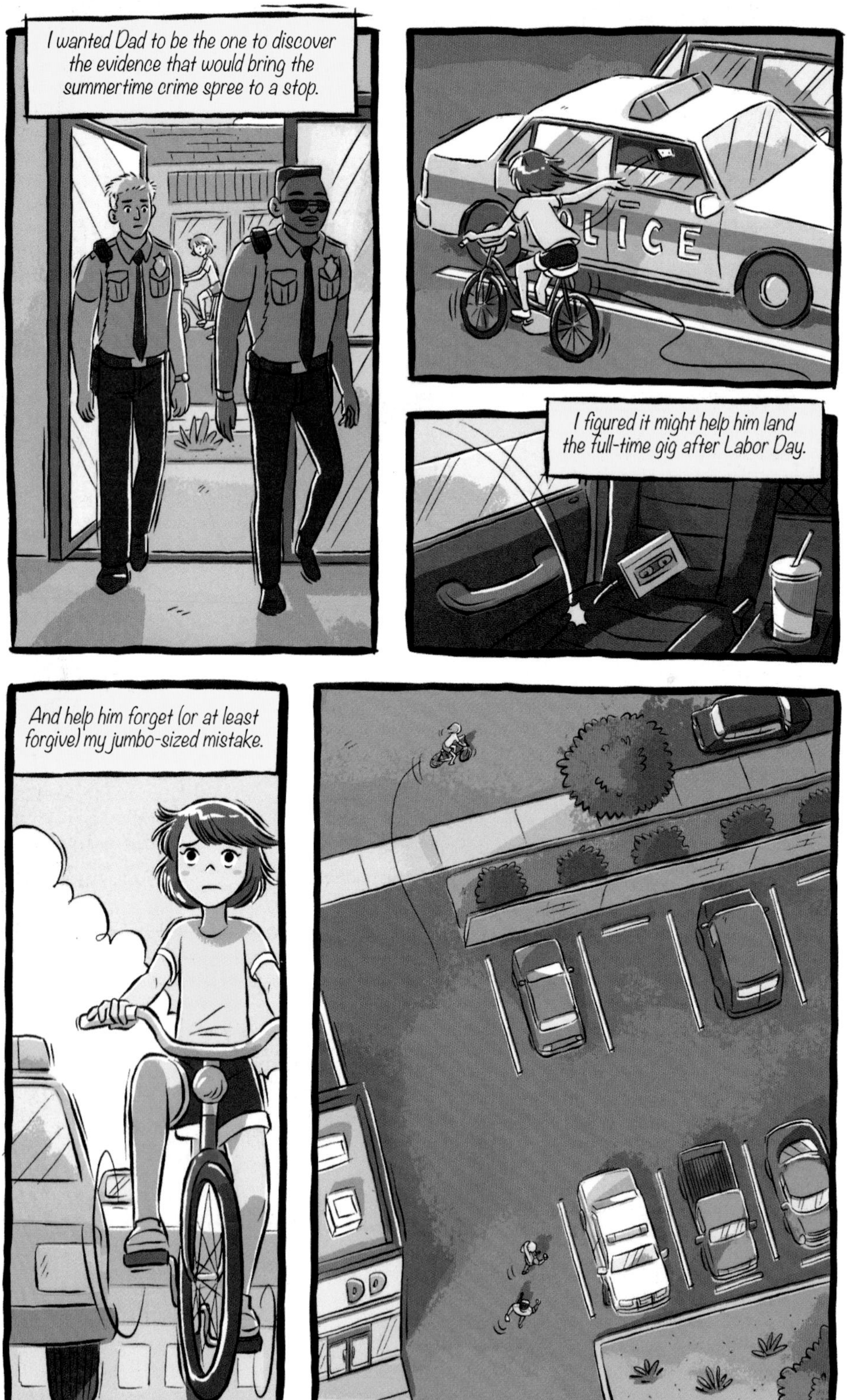
I wanted Dad to be the one to discover the evidence that would bring the summertime crime spree to a stop.
POLICE
I figured it might help him land the full-time gig after Labor Day.
And help him forget (or at least forgive) my jumbo-sized mistake.

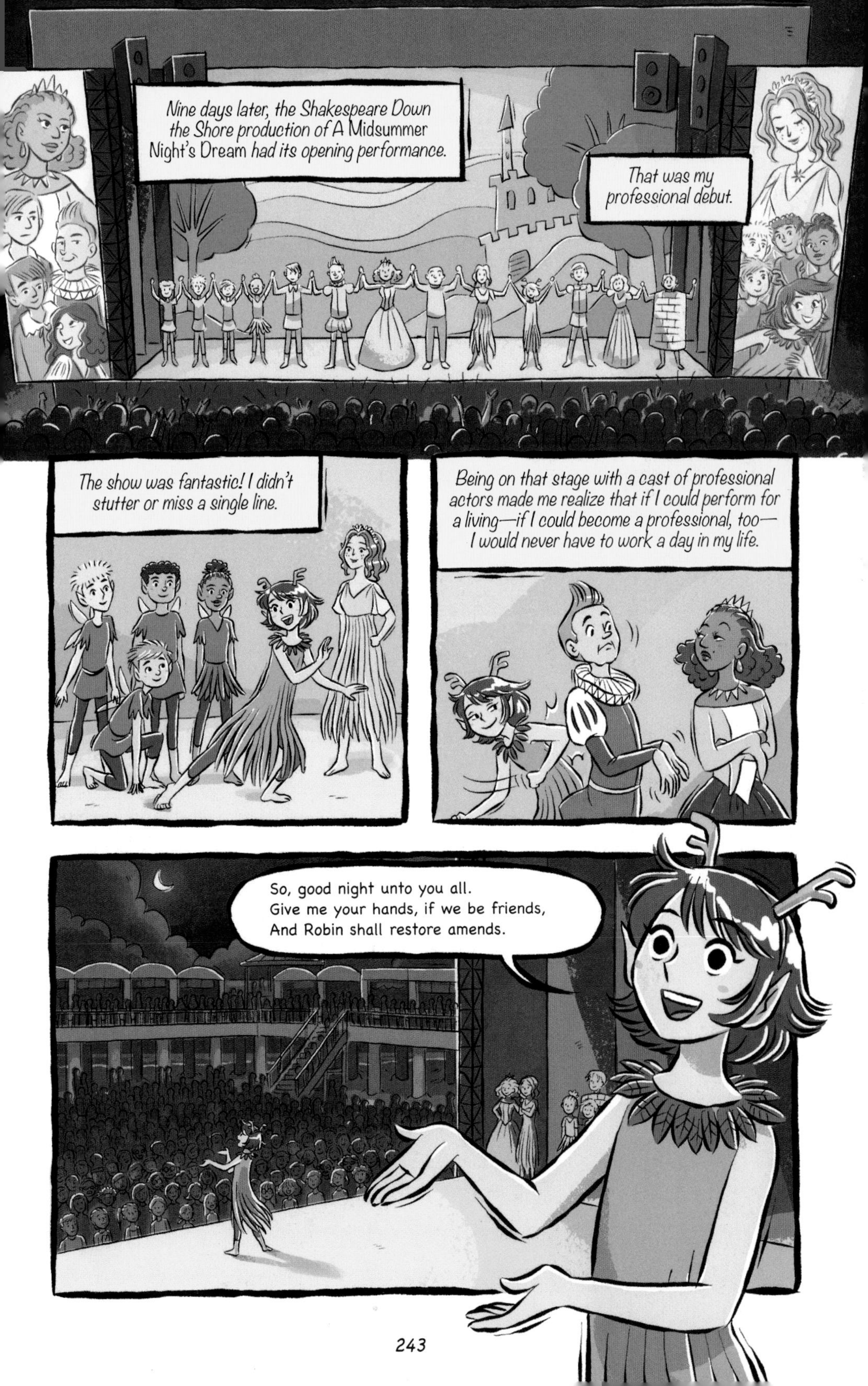
Nine days later, the Shakespeare Down the Shore production of A Midsummer Night's Dream had its opening performance.
That was my professional debut.
The show was fantastic! I didn't stutter or miss a single line.
Being on that stage with a cast of professional actors made me realize that if I could perform for a living—if I could become a professional, too—I would never have to work a day in my life.
So, good night unto you all. Give me your hands, if we be friends, And Robin shall restore amends.

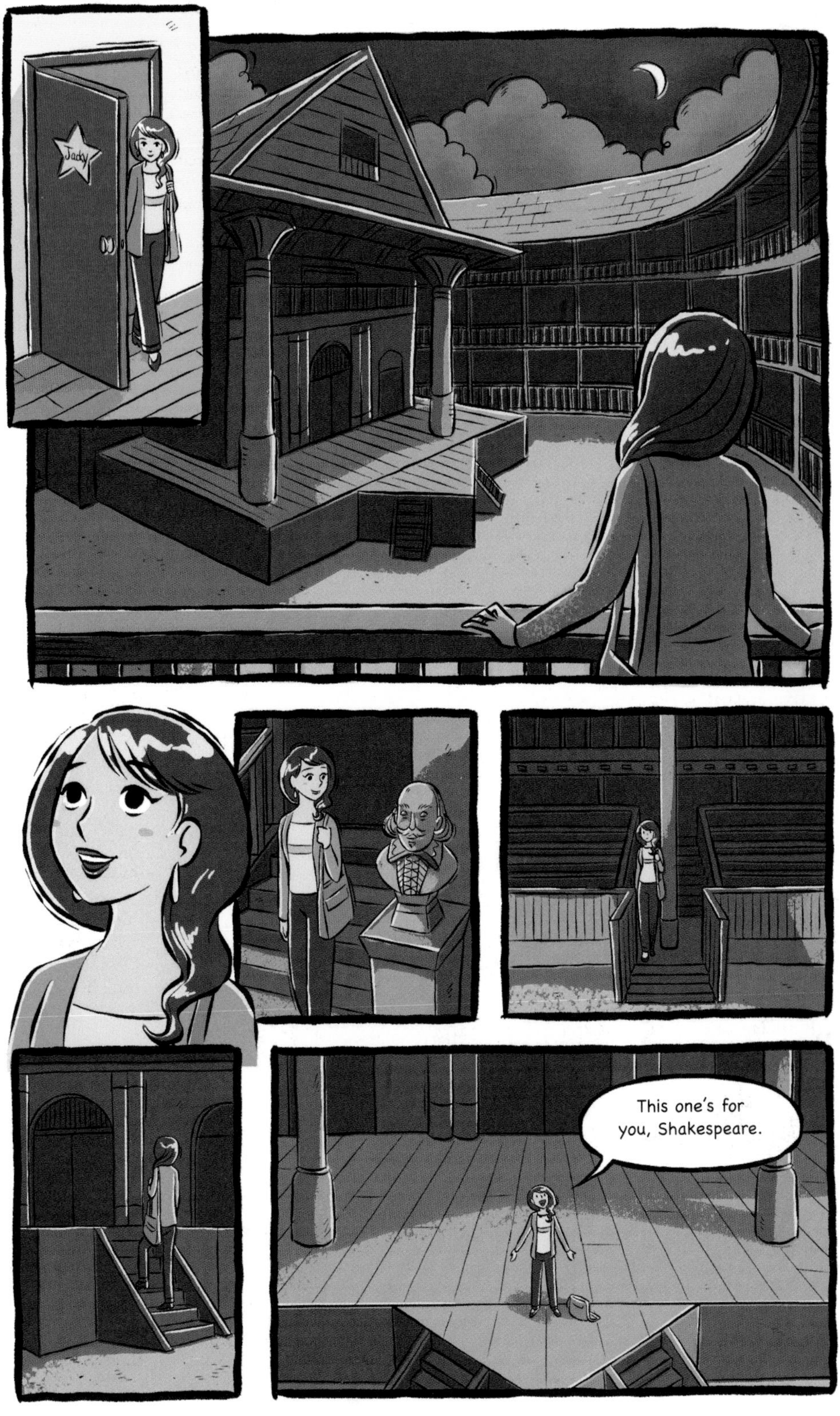
Jady
This one's for you, Shakespeare.

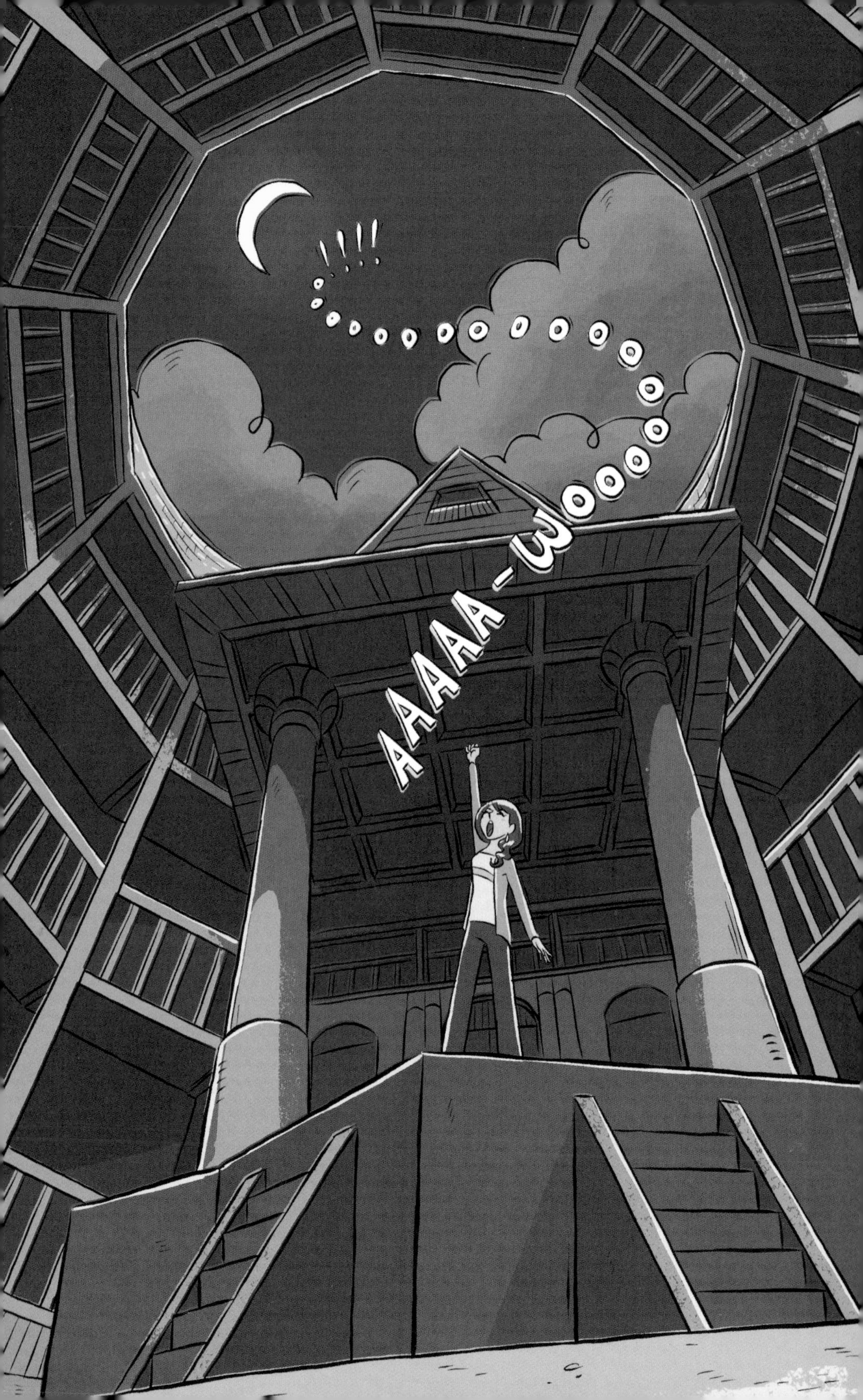
AAAA-WOOOOOOOOOOOOOOOOO!!!!

ABOUT THE AUTHORS

JAMES PATTERSON received the Literarian Award for Outstanding Service to the American Literary Community from the National Book Foundation. He holds the Guinness World Record for the most #1 *New York Times* bestsellers, including M*ax Einstein, Middle School, I Funny,* and *Jacky Ha-Ha*, and his books have sold more than 385 million copies worldwide. A tireless champion of the power of books and reading, Patterson created a children's book imprint, JIMMY Patterson, whose mission is simple: "We want every kid who finishes a JIMMY Book to say, 'PLEASE GIVE ME ANOTHER BOOK.'" He has donated more than three million books to students and soldiers and funds over four hundred Teacher and Writer Education Scholarships at twenty-one colleges and universities. He has also donated millions of dollars to independent bookstores and school libraries. Patterson invests proceeds from the sales of JIMMY Patterson Books in pro-reading initiatives.

CHRIS GRABENSTEIN is a *New York Times* bestselling author who has collaborated with James Patterson on the Max Einstein, I Funny, Jacky Ha-Ha, Treasure Hunters, and House of Robots series, as well as *Word of Mouse, Katt vs. Dogg, Pottymouth and Stoopid, Laugh Out Loud*, and *Daniel X: Armageddon*. He lives in New York City.

ADAM RAU was born in Minnesota and moved to New York to attend The School of Visual Arts. In 2004 he landed a job in children's publishing, and before long was acquiring and editing graphic novels for young readers, which he has been doing for over ten years. Adam lives in Jersey City with his wife and dog.

BETTY C. TANG has been in the animation and illustration world for more than 25 years. She has worked for acclaimed studios including DreamWorks Animation and Disney Television Animation, co-directed the Chinese animated feature film *Where's the Dragon?*, and illustrated for books and magazines. Born in Taiwan, she now lives in Los Angeles, California, and writes and illustrates for children.